A Man Most Worthy

Also by Marcus Major

4 Guys and Trouble

Good Peoples

Anthologies

Got to Be Real

Mothers & Sons

MARCUS MAJOR

A Man Most Worthy

DUTTON

DUTTON
Published by the Penguin Group
Penguin Putnam Inc., 375 Hudson Street, New York, New York 10014, U.S.A.
Penguin Books Ltd, 80 Strand, London WC2R 0RL, England
Penguin Books Australia Ltd, 250 Camberwell Road, Camberwell, Victoria 3124, Australia
Penguin Books Canada Ltd, 10 Alcorn Avenue, Toronto, Ontario, Canada M4V 3B2
Penguin Books (N.Z.) Ltd, 182–190 Wairau Road, Auckland 10, New Zealand

Penguin Books Ltd, Registered Offices: Harmondsworth, Middlesex, England

Published by Dutton, a member of Penguin Putnam Inc.

First printing, January 2003
2   4   6   8   10   9   7   5   3   1

REGISTERED TRADEMARK — MARCA REGISTRADA

LIBRARY OF CONGRESS CATALOGING-IN-PUBLICATION DATA

Major, Marcus.
    A man most worthy / Marcus Major.
        p. cm.
    ISBN 0-525-94685-3 (acid-free paper)
    1. African American businesspeople—Fiction. 2. African American men—Fiction.
3.   Married women—Fiction. 4. Millionaires—Fiction. 5. First loves—Fiction. 6. New
Jersey—Fiction. I. Title.

PS3563.A3923 M36 2003
813'.54—dc21
                                                                    2002029681

Printed in the United States of America
Set in Goudy
Designed by Leonard Telesca

PUBLISHER'S NOTE
This book is a work of fiction. Names, characters, places, and incidents are either the
product of the author's imagination or are used fictitiously, and any resemblance to actual
persons, living or dead, business establishments, events, or locales is entirely coincidental.

This book is printed on acid-free paper. ♾

In memory of my grandmother,
Wilhelmina Clark Curley
A Lady Most Worthy

A Man Most Worthy

Prologue

John anxiously gripped his steering wheel and sneaked a peek over at Mr. Duke. The old man was leaning back in his seat with his eyes closed, hands clasped at his waist. For a moment John was taken back to his childhood, when Mr. Duke would frequently fall asleep in the same position in his big leather recliner watching TV.

Also reminding John of his youth was the current of uneasiness bubbling through his stomach. As he had as a teenager—and despite all of his successes since then—John still yearned for Mr. Duke's approval more than anything else.

This, in addition to just wanting to see him, was the reason he'd brought Mr. Duke down to Charlotte this week. To see John's elaborate new estate. To see the expansion of his plant since Mr. Duke's last visit. To see John at work in hard-driving-boss mode. To meet his stunning young girlfriend. See the Hornets in his company's luxury box. Eat at the finest restaurants. Ride in this special-ordered Porsche. Yes, John had gone all out.

Yet Mr. Duke, while always humble and appreciative, had been subdued. He certainly hadn't been very forthcoming with his opinions, other than the generic "That's great, John," or "Now, would you look at that?" when John had tried to impress him with something.

Of course, Mr. Duke had told him long ago that the most impressive trait in a man is good character. Because it can't be bought or inherited. It's constantly tested and must be tended to daily.

As John turned onto I-277, Mr. Duke spoke.

"What's on your mind?"

John glanced back at him. His eyes were still shut.

John chuckled. "So, you can tell something is on my mind even without looking at me?"

Mr. Duke opened his eyes. "Sometimes a man says more when he's not talking."

"A bit of the ol' homespun wisdom, huh?" John teased. "I thought the saying was, 'Silence speaks volumes.'"

"That too," Mr. Duke said, pressing the button to elevate his seat back to the sitting position. "So, what's on your mind?"

"I was about to ask you the same thing," John rejoined.

"What do you mean?"

John tapped his fingers along the steering wheel as he searched for the words. "Well, here it is, your visit is coming to an end, and you haven't said anything about . . . about anything."

"About what?" Mr. Duke asked, puzzled.

"About anything."

"I find it hard to believe that I haven't said anything about anything over the course of the last week, John. Only a mute could accomplish that. Or a moron."

"Well, you told me when you thought it was cold outside, that it seems like there are a lot of pig farms in Carolina, that you had a touch of indigestion after eating those trotters the other day, but you haven't told me *anything*."

"Oh," Mr. Duke said. He ran his thumb along his shoulder strap. "What would you like to know?"

John squirmed. He didn't want Mr. Duke to think he was asking him to kiss his ass, because he wasn't. He just wanted to know that Mr. Duke was wowed. Impressed.

Mr. Duke spoke again. "You do know I'm proud of you and what you've accomplished, son, right?"

John looked over at him. "Yeah?"

"Shucks, yeah," Mr. Duke answered emphatically. "This past week I've felt like I've been riding shotgun with the King of Zamuda or something. That huge office at your job is as big as my condo. And that house of yours, don't even get me started on that . . . that *museum*." Mr. Duke brushed him away like he was shooing a fly.

"Is there any crime in living well?" John asked.

"You better hope not," Mr. Duke replied glibly, "because if there is, you're the first person the peasants are gonna come looking for." He continued. "And your girlfriend is so beautiful that she doesn't even seem like a real person. She's more like a painting or something. That new Porsche of yours, too, is something." Mr. Duke paused, stroked his chin, then whistled. "Yessir, she's a beaut, I would've loved to taken her for a ride."

John looked over at him. When he had shown Mr. Duke his new car, he hadn't seemed overly interested. "You could've. Why didn't you tell me?"

Mr. Duke looked back at him strangely. "You wouldn't have minded?"

"Hell, no!" John replied, slapping the steering wheel in disbelief. Didn't this man know what he meant to him? All Mr. Duke had to do is ask and he could *have* the car.

"Well, that's very kind of you, son. You're very generous," Mr. Duke said. "I'm gonna have to remember that next time I see her—since you say it's all right." Mr. Duke smacked his lips. "Those curves on that body. I can't wait to get my hands on that yella ass and *ride*."

"It's an interesting story behind the color. I chose canary yellow because—"

"Canary? They call yella different names now?" Mr. Duke

asked, surprised. "Shoot, in my day it was just yella, high yella, and redbone."

John looked over at him. "What are you talking about?"

"I know what *I'm* talking about," Mr. Duke replied. "The question is, what are *you* talking about?"

There was a pause, then they both broke out laughing.

"Congratulations," John said. "You've officially become a dirty old man."

They both laughed again.

"Well, your lady and your Porsche are similar in that both are beautiful, curvy and yella . . ."

"That they are," John agreed.

". . . expensive, high-maintenance and more for show than anything else," Mr. Duke continued.

John looked over at him.

"Well, you asked me for my opinion about anything."

"That I did," John said quietly. "Go ahead."

"John, she sure doesn't mind spending your money."

"Well, Scent is spoiled. She's used to living well. Her father is a surgeon who—"

"—who now owns his own chemical safety systems business?" Mr. Duke interrupted.

John hesitated. "Oh, I get it. I'm the daddy now, right?"

"Well, don't you think she's a bit young for you?"

"Maybe." John shrugged. And maybe it was better when Mr. Duke wasn't being so forthcoming.

"Don't get me wrong, she's sharp as a whip," Mr. Duke said, "and she's a nice-enough person."

"But?" John asked.

"Well, it's just, I tried as hard as I could to picture her being with you before you became wealthy, and I just couldn't do it," Mr. Duke said. "If a man couldn't have a woman when he was nobody, then she doesn't deserve him when he becomes somebody."

"But isn't that part of the fun of going from 'got-none to got-some'?" John asked. "You get to have things you didn't have before."

"So then, she *is* like the Porsche, the house, the big desk. . . ."

"No, I believe Scent cares for me," John said.

"Would she care for you if you were John Sebastian, schoolteacher? John Sebastian, truck driver?"

"I would like to think so."

"But is 'would like to think so' enough? Before, you had a woman where you didn't have to think about it. You *knew*."

Uh-uh. John wasn't going down that road with him. He decided to change the subject. "What about you? Or are you just a playa for life?"

"Aw, stop." Mr. Duke shooed him away again. "I'm an old man."

"That's not what I heard. Jules told me about some woman he just saw at your place a few weeks back."

"Jules is just mad because he doesn't have any women visiting him in *his* place," Mr. Duke explained. He realized that John had changed the subject, but he decided to let it go. He had said his piece on the matter. Besides, they were almost at the airport, and he wanted to talk about something else.

"John, I really do think it's wonderful, all that you've accomplished. You've become an amazing success."

"Thanks."

Mr. Duke picked a piece of lint off his pants leg. "You know, I would like to think that I played a small part in helping you to become the man you've become."

"Are you kidding me? You played a huge part in it—you know that," John said definitively. "And you didn't have to. I wasn't your responsibility, yet you still looked out for me." John turned onto the exit ramp for Charlotte/Douglas International Airport. "Jules, too, and countless others as well."

"Well, thank you, John," Mr. Duke replied. "Now, how about you do the same?"

"What do you mean?"

"Give something back to the community."

John shifted in his seat. "Well, you know, I do donate a lot of money to charity."

"I mean personally involved, John, not just writing some checks," Mr. Duke said. He studied John. "My life has been enriched by having you and Jules in it. You might find something meaningful by doing likewise. I'm sure there are many ways you can get involved in the community down here in Charlotte."

"Meaningful?" John faced him. "You don't think I'm happy, do you?"

Mr. Duke hesitated. "I think maybe you're searching for happiness. Maybe you're wondering how a man can have all that you have and still be unhappy."

John didn't say anything, so Mr. Duke continued.

"Most people think, 'If I can just make this amount of money, I'll be happy.' Or 'If I can just get this or that paid off, I'll be good to go.' I would think that it must be a kinda messed-up, lonely feeling to achieve all that, a thousand times over, and still not be content. Maybe then a person really starts to question if they can ever be truly happy."

John shrugged. "Well, I wouldn't know because I'm happy."

Mr. Duke eyed him suspiciously, but let the matter drop.

After a few moments of silence, John spoke again. "I've been saving it as a surprise, but I'm expanding the business to the Northeast."

Mr. Duke looked at him with raised eyebrows. "Yeah?"

"Yeah." John paused, letting the moment build. "Newark, specifically."

Mr. Duke studied him to make sure he was serious. After he was convinced that John was indeed serious, he slapped his knee. "Yessir! You're coming home!"

John smiled.

"How long you been planning this?" Mr. Duke asked.

"We've been exploring the feasibility of it for nearly a year."

"A year?" Mr. Duke exclaimed.

"I didn't want to tell you about it until it was a sure thing," John explained. "It just became a done deal last week."

"Oh."

"I'll be flying back and forth between Newark and Charlotte frequently," John continued.

"So you can spread your special brand of happiness in two different places?"

"What do you mean?" John asked.

"Your business is your business," Mr. Duke said evenly. "But I noticed you're kinda hard on your employees."

John had taken Mr. Duke with him to the job one day last week. When John was distracted by work, Mr. Duke had slipped away and walked around the facility. He had heard a lot of grousing about John, especially in the cafeteria. He could also tell that John was feared.

John shrugged. "Hey, I run a tight ship."

"So did the captain of the *Amistad*," Mr. Duke said. "Look what happened to him."

"I pay my employees better money than they can get anywhere else," John reasoned. "In return for that, I expect better performance."

"Okay, Steinbrenner."

"Exactly, that's my role model," John said of the New York Yankees owner. "He pays his people top dollar, but dammit, they better win or somebody *else* is gonna be paying—with their ass." John chuckled, then gave Mr. Duke a suspicious look. "Did somebody say something to you?"

"No, John," Mr. Duke said, shaking his head. "I'm just talking."

John alternated between looking at the road and at Mr. Duke, trying to see if he was withholding information.

"Not that I care, mind you," John finally said. "I don't care if I'm liked. How many people truly like their boss?"

"Not many," Mr. Duke agreed.

"Where do nice guys finish?"

"Dead last," Mr. Duke answered.

"Kick ass . . ." John asked.

". . . or get ass kicked."

"If somebody has to be in charge . . ."

". . . then it might as well be me," Mr. Duke said.

"Second sucks . . ." John said.

". . . and third is worse," Mr. Duke finished, then looked at John. "How come you only remember the cutthroat stuff I taught you?"

"Because that's all you ever taught me," John deadpanned.

They again shared a laugh.

"So, you'll definitely have a home in Newark, right?" Mr. Duke asked.

"Er, do you mean 'in Newark' specifically?"

Mr. Duke sighed loudly.

"It's just that a brotha has gotten a bit soft living the good life down here," John clarified. "I'm out of practice at making sure I have my grit on twenty-four, seven."

"I meant in northern Jersey, John." Mr. Duke said.

"Yes."

"Good," Mr. Duke repeated, still full of contentment. "So now you can do your civic good in your hometown of Newark."

Back to that subject. John knew better than to think it was over. Mr. Duke didn't forget a thing. Partly out of not wanting to disappoint Mr. Duke, but primarily because he knew Mr. Duke was right, John agreed.

They pulled into the U.S. Airways terminal.

"When are you heading up?" Mr. Duke asked.

"We'll be up and running in about two months," John replied. "Our office space is already leased in downtown Newark."

Mr. Duke smiled at that. "So, where are you thinking about living?"

"I bought a place in Bernardsville," John replied. "Scent is going up there next week to begin decorating it."

"She's moving to Jersey with you?"

"Yep."

The smile subtly eased off Mr. Duke's face. John pretended that he hadn't noticed.

"By the way," John said, "you know Zamuda isn't a real country, right? They just made it up for that movie, *Coming to America*."

Mr. Duke just stared at him.

John threw his hands up defensively. "Hey, I was just looking out for you. I didn't want you to be somewhere and embarrass yourself."

"Let me tell you something, Richie Rich," Mr. Duke said. "I don't care how much money your rags-to-riches ass accumulates, you will *never* be smarter than me."

They both chuckled. Mr. Duke looked out the window.

"Well," he said. "It's time for me to get my old ass back on a plane." He opened the truck door and climbed out.

John followed suit. "Don't even tell me you're scared of flying," he teased as he unloaded Mr. Duke's suitcase out of the back of the truck. "A big, tough guy like yourself?"

"It ain't the flying that scares me, son," Mr. Duke said. "It's the different landing scenarios."

One

As his secretary, Judith, rose to leave his office, John thought he caught an exasperated eyeroll. She was no doubt ready to get away from him—he had been challenging and driving all of his employees hard the past week. Oh well, John thought as he settled back into his chair. He needed to kick some tail. He wanted his people to work at one hundred percent. As long as they performed up to their capabilities, he didn't care what they thought. Hell, if they exceeded projections, they could call him an asshole to his face.

John had a five-year plan in Newark. Five years to make this office profitable. John didn't want his employees thinking that if this move didn't work out, they could just pack up and go home to Charlotte. He always remembered something one of his business professors in college taught him. If the boss is stressed, then his employees should be stressed. If the boss is busting his ass, then the employees should be busting theirs.

Judith and the rest of the people here probably couldn't wait for him to catch his flight that evening. He was going to Charlotte for the next couple of days. He would be doing a lot of that over the next year, flying back and forth between the two offices.

He turned around and looked out the window at downtown Newark. Broad Street was bustling. John remembered hanging out with Jules on Broad Street when they were teenagers. *Knowing* they were too sharp as they sported their two-tone jeans, Adidas, lamb's wool coats and Kangols. John smiled at the memory. Jules had been an excellent dancer, and he would take on all comers in pop-and-lock contests, and he'd almost always win.

John was brought back to the present by the buzz of the intercom.

"Yes, Judith?"

"Mr. Duke is here to see you."

John glanced at his watch. He and Mr. Duke were having lunch together.

"Send him in."

John stood up to greet Mr. Duke as Judith showed him in.

"Thank you, Judith," John said.

He waited for Judith to close the door, then smiled before he spoke again.

"Now, what dive are you taking me to?"

"Dive?" Mr. Duke sat down and crossed his legs. "Man, you oughta appreciate getting some real food in your belly."

John went behind his desk and sat back down. He started rifling through his drawer. "Now, where did I put those antacids. . . ."

"Yeah, all right," Mr. Duke said. "When you're sitting at Je's Restaurant with a heaping plate of oxtail and rice in front of you, let's see if you push it away."

As John closed his drawer, Mr. Duke's eyebrows rose. "Where did you get that tie from?"

John ran his forefinger and thumb along his blue jeweled tie. "It's a Bulgheri."

"Is that Italian for 'ugly'?"

John dismissed him. "This coming from a man who thinks Dolce & Gabbana are relief pitchers for the Mets." John looked down at his tie. "Scent picked this out for me."

"Oh," Mr. Duke said, not missing a beat, "then Bulgheri must be Italian for 'expensive.'"

John decided to change the subject before Mr. Duke asked him how much the tie cost. Or the cuff links he was wearing, which Scent had bought as well.

"Did you pick out a school yet?"

John had asked Mr. Duke to select a school in Newark that Sebastian Industries could donate some computers to.

"Yeah, I made a call to the Board of Education this morning."

"Yeah? You didn't have to," John said. "Judith could have taken care of all that."

"I didn't mind. Shoot, you forget, I'm a retired gym teacher," Mr. Duke reminded him. "It felt good to tell those bigwigs downtown about the donation. For once to be able to talk to them about what I was gonna do for *them*." He chuckled, then looked at John. "How many computers are we talking about again? You did say a *hundred*, right?"

John stood up and smoothed his tie out. "Yeah, a hundred."

Mr. Duke whistled.

"It's a tax write-off," John said. "You ready to go?" He walked over to his closet and slipped on his sports coat.

Mr. Duke stood up as well and followed John to the door. "Um, John, I know you're very busy, but I was wondering if you still planned on getting personally involved in the community."

John adjusted his collar, a touch uneasy at the idea of giving up time. "Yes."

"Good." Mr. Duke smiled. "Because I was thinking, why not do so at the school where you're donating the computers? That way you can see firsthand the impact your gifts have provided."

"Well, I had planned on keeping a low profile," John said. "I don't want to go in there like some big shot."

"You can remain anonymous if you want," Mr. Duke countered. "It'd still be good to see if they make proper use of the computers."

John agreed. And a school seemed as good a place as any. After all, he had met Mr. Duke through school. "Why not?"

John opened the door for Mr. Duke.

"Oh, by the way, you never told me the name of the school that you chose."

Mr. Duke smiled and patted John on his shoulder. "How about we drive by there after lunch?"

Two

Josephine Prescott sat at her desk holding an envelope from her husband. It contained a card that had come with a box containing six pink roses. She looked up at the two giggly fifth-grade girls who had brought the items to her.

"How did you get this?"

"He gave us a dollar to bring it in to you," Samantha said, smiling.

With his cheap ass, Josephine thought. But she wasn't through with her young charges yet. "Oh, so is that what you do now?" she asked. "Take money from strange men?"

The girls recoiled, but recovered quickly. Newark girls don't scare that easily, especially if they think they have done something right.

"But, Mrs. Prescott," Sabrina said, "we knew he was your husband."

Josephine cut her eyes at Samantha, still unconvinced.

"Yeah, Mrs. Prescott," Samantha assured her, "we've seen his picture." She pointed to the one mounted on Josephine's desk.

Josephine gave in. "Okay. Thank you both. Now you two go back to the playground. The homeroom bell is about to ring."

Sabrina and Samantha made their way toward the outer office. Josephine had started reading the card when she overheard Sabrina whisper to Samantha, "She probably had a fight with her husband last night."

"Sabrina," Josephine said sternly, "please come back in here."

Sabrina turned around and goggled wide-eyed. She and Samantha made their way back into the doorway.

"Samantha, you're excused. Go back to the playground."

Samantha briskly took off, leaving Sabrina alone with a sheepish grin.

"And I mean the playground, not the hallway, Samantha," Josephine called after her. "Don't let me catch you loitering. You hear me?"

"Yes, Mrs. Prescott."

Josephine turned her attention back to Sabrina. "Now as for you, young lady, tell me, how old are you?"

"Eleven," came the muted response. Sabrina kept her eyes on the floor.

"Excuse me?" Josephine asked.

"Eleven," Sabrina said a little louder, lifting her chin.

Josephine continued. "Is it safe for me to assume that in addition to your fifth-grade studies here at Lyons Avenue School, you aren't a marriage counselor, too?"

"No," Sabrina shook her head, "I'm not."

"Then I would strongly suggest that in the future you remember that you're eleven years old. Do you understand me?"

Sabrina nodded. "Yes."

At the child's grave seriousness, a smile threatened to form at the corner of Josephine's mouth. Sabrina was a bright child and one of her favorite students. Her mother was raising her on her own, and she was a hardworking woman who made sure Sabrina came to school clean and prepared to learn. When Josephine spoke again, her voice no longer had its edge.

"Don't be in such a hurry to be grown. It's an overrated experience. Believe me, you will have your own husband to fight with before you know it."

Sabrina had detected the change in her mood and looked up. She saw that Josephine's eyes had softened.

"Not me, Mrs. Prescott. When I get married, I'm never gonna fight with my man," Sabrina said with a swagger in her voice.

"Why not?"

Sabrina curled her lips, like a female twice her age would do. "Because he's gonna do what I tell him to do. Ain't gonna be no fighting 'bout it."

Josephine suppressed a chuckle as the girl headed off smartly to her homeroom. Then she glanced down at the card. It was one of those with long, fake, "personally" written notes. Josephine didn't like this type of card, something she was certain she had told her husband at some point. To her, it seemed insincere and insubstantial to let some person at a card company express your feelings for you. The cards always contained some generic sentiment based on some universal theme like, "In any relationship, there will be ups and downs. . . ." or "When I woke up this morning, I thought about how much you mean to me. . . ."

This one was "Sometimes when I do or say things that cause pain, it's only because I love you so much. . . ."

Josephine stuck it in her desk. Though well intentioned, she was sure, the card was impersonal and passionless. He knew better. She looked at the picture of Darren on her desk and closed her eyes.

It had been a rough summer for Darren and her. They had clashed over everything—her career choices, her burgeoning weight, having a baby, where to vacation, investments, cars—everything. Nothing was too obscure for them to bicker over. What station to listen to in the car, where to eat, the machinations of Tony Soprano—whatever, it didn't matter. Both of them had been looking forward to the beginning of the school year so they could get a break from each other.

As always, career was a major bone of contention. Darren was a superintendent in Morris County, and he wanted Josephine to work in his district or another similarly suburban one. It was beyond his realm of comprehension why Josephine chose to be a vice-principal in the inner city instead of the suburbs.

"That's where the most need is," Josephine would say.

"Yeah? Well, I *need* you to stay alive," he would counter.

The cavalier way he spoke of Newark would piss her off. The fact that his wife had been born and raised there never seemed to register.

Josephine glanced at the clock. She wanted to check on the first-period history class of the rookie eighth-grade teacher, Ms. Murphy. She had heard they had been getting rowdy already and wanted to nip that nonsense in the bud. Ultimately, of course, it would have to fall on Ms. Murphy's shoulders to bring order to her classroom.

Josephine stood up and looked inside her purse for the key necklace she always wore in school. On it were the keys to the lavatories on each floor and other rooms in the building.

While rummaging through her purse, something unfamiliar caught her eye. She pulled it out.

It was a Slim-Fast bar. A Post-It was attached.

> *For your lunch*
> *Don't forget your diet!*
> *Darren*

Like she could ever forget with him hawking her about it constantly. He always couched his concern as strictly health-related, but Josephine didn't buy it. She no longer got undressed in front of him because of the look she had once caught on his face.

Maybe he had a right to bitch a little, she admitted. She had met him as a size 10/12 and now was a 16. She looked back at the picture of Darren on her desk. In it, his chin was resting between his thumb and forefinger. Only now he looked condescending and patronizing. She could almost imagine the lips moving to say, "*Babe, it's only because I love you so much.*"

"Asshole." Josephine turned the picture down on its face and left the office.

In another hour, Josephine was sitting in Mrs. Derossa's office, waiting for her to finish her phone conversation. While she had been making her morning rounds through the school, Mrs. Derossa had summoned her to her office over the P.A. system.

"Yes, you bet!" Mrs. Derossa spoke excitedly into the receiver. "Um-hm. You bet we'll make good use of them."

Josephine could tell by the deferential tone in her voice that she was talking to a superior from the central office. Probably the assistant superintendent. This was definitely not the voice she reserved for the people who worked for her.

Josephine scolded herself. Mrs. Derossa had only started in July. She had known her for all of ten weeks and should give the woman a chance. It was hard to maintain her objectivity, though. She wasn't sold on Mrs. Derossa's ability to run an urban school. After all, Mrs. Derossa had been plucked from a high-performing, suburban district and foisted on Lyons Avenue School that summer—for what Josephine was certain was a huge bump in salary.

She was state-appointed, put in place to show the downtrodden ghetto folk how to run a school effectively. Part of Josephine's dislike toward her was that she herself had been a candidate for the principal's job. Hell, it made the most sense. She was a fixture at the school, was well known and for the most part well liked by the parents. She knew the community and its particular bright spots and drawbacks. She had intimate knowledge, in fact, for she herself was a child of the South Ward of Newark.

As such she knew there were a thousand things more productive she could be doing right now than sitting in this woman's office. In September, she liked to set the tone for the year, to be as visible as possible. Right now she could be visiting the different classrooms, making examples of unruly kids in front of their potentially unruly classmates. She needed to talk to the child-study team about a student in Mrs. Henderson's second-grade class, meet with the custodians about the conditions of the bathrooms, talk to the lunch aides—hell, there were a million things she needed to do.

As Josephine made a move to get up, Mrs. Derossa held up her index finger to indicate that she wanted Josephine to continue waiting.

In what she supposed was a subtle act of defiance, Josephine stood up anyway and walked over to the window.

She saw a group of eight men loitering on the corner across the street. Josephine sighed. Year after year, looking through the window was like watching a long-running off-off, way-off-Broadway production. The characters changed from time to time, usually whenever one of the men was incarcerated (he'd then be replaced by an eager young understudy), but there was always a cast of able-bodied young black men ready to put on another performance fraught with joylessness and stagnation. It was like the play Jules had taken Josephine to see years ago called *Waiting for Godot*. The two bums in the play entertain themselves while they wait for the arrival of someone who isn't ever going to come.

She didn't know what this collection of men was waiting on, other than the next time they were going to get high. Several of them were known drug dealers. Josephine concentrated on a tall, slim, scruffy-looking man sitting on a stoop at the back of the group. He was the father of one of her most disruptive students, Akeem. Josephine hadn't seen him in a while. She had heard that he was locked up. She shook her head in disgust. He didn't care how much ridicule he was exposing his son to by hanging out on the corner directly across from his son's school—and all the children knew what the men on this corner were about. Even worse, he came into the school from time to time, on those occasions when he remembered that he was a parent, to check on his son.

He would then berate Akeem in front of his classmates for whatever transgression he had committed. Of course, he never checked himself for his indiscretion of coming into his son's school looking and smelling like he had slept on Lyons Avenue itself.

The sound of Mrs. Derossa happily slapping her desk with her palms brought Josephine back. She turned around to see Mrs. Derossa smiling at her.

"I want to tell you that I received wonderful news from the superintendent early this morning." She nodded at the phone. "That was the assistant superintendent calling to give his congratulations."

"What is it?" Josephine asked.

"Lyons Avenue School is receiving a hundred brand-new computers," Mrs. Derossa answered excitedly. "And software for grade levels K through eight."

"What?" Josephine matched her excitement. One hundred new computers? She had a thousand questions but didn't know which to ask first. "When did this happen? When will we get them? Is this for the whole district? Or just our cluster? I didn't hear of any new—"

Mrs. Derossa laughed and motioned for her to calm down. "You didn't hear of it because central office was just notified about them earlier today. The donor dealt directly with the superintendent and wishes to remain anonymous." Mrs. Derossa began playing with her necklace, rubbing one of the pearls in between her thumb and forefinger. "What is weird is that the donor insisted that every single one of the computers go to Lyons Avenue School."

"Really?" Josephine leaned back in her chair while she absorbed that revelation. Mrs. Derossa took a pen out of her desk and began scribbling some numbers on a pad. Josephine's mind raced. Who would specifically donate computers to Lyons Avenue School? After all, all the schools in the area were in distress— Lyons was no better or worse off than any of them. A corporation getting a tax break? Josephine ruled that possibility out. Why would they want to stay anonymous—whoever heard of a business turning down free positive publicity? And why would they insist on the computers going to a specific school? Maybe it was a past alumnus? A definite possibility, but unlikely. Though Mrs. Cook, the former principal, had informed her of some of Lyons' prominent white alumni (the school had been predominantly Jewish and Italian up until the fifties) who were now well established in the business community of northern New Jersey, Josephine was certain that the school had long become an afterthought in those people's minds. They would donate computers to the schools in the suburbs where they now lived, and where their children and grandchildren attended.

Those affluent suburban districts were swimming in money. They had all the advantages, Josephine thought. They got businesses to invest in them, to donate equipment and resources to them. Districts with healthy tax bases like the one where her husband works. And Darren was very good at soliciting the businesses in his communities to get involved with the schools. Josephine remembered one time when Darren had told her about . . . Darren!

Josephine now realized who was responsible for the computers. Obviously, only someone with a vested interest in Lyons Avenue School would have insisted they go there. Who else had the ability and the motive to send a hundred computers to her school? No doubt her husband had steered them in her direction. It made perfect sense. Darren would send them anonymously so as not to give the appearance of impropriety. He couldn't have that, he was far too straitlaced. Besides, how would the members of his district react if they found out he had steered even *one* computer to a bunch of poor black and Latino children in Newark, much less a hundred. A *hundred.* Goodness!

Fine, her husband's secret was safe, Josephine decided. Her lips formed a slight smile. Her dear, sweet husband, who, though he could be a major pain in the butt sometimes, was proving how much he loved her.

Josephine was thinking of the ways that she was going to reward her Good Samaritan husband when Mrs. Derossa finally looked up from her writing.

"I was just thinking of how we're going to divide the computers."

Josephine had thought of that as soon as she heard the word "hundred." "Well, we have nine grade levels, with three classes apiece. That's twenty-seven classrooms. But in the second and fifth grades we have only have two classrooms apiece, so that gives us twenty-five. So I figure we can give each classroom four computers each."

Josephine smiled at the thought of informing the staff. The teachers and aides were definitely going to appreciate this—it's not often they got good news. Before now, the only computers available to the children were the twenty-five in the computer lab. Computers in the classroom would be a great boon for learning. A computer, utilized properly, was almost like having another teacher in the room.

"Actually, I was thinking of putting one computer in each class and putting the rest on the top floor," Mrs. Derossa said.

Josephine's smile fell. "Huh?"

"Yes, I think we should concentrate the computers on the third floor. I think they would serve their best use up there."

Josephine leaned back in her chair. She peeped this woman's game now. The fourth- and eighth-grade classes were on the third floor. Not so coincidentally, those were the two grades tested by the state to determine the worthiness of a school. In the spring, every fourth and eighth grader in the state of New Jersey was tested. The eighth-grade test was called the GEPA and the fourth-grade test was called the ESPA. You would think they were called Pestilence and Famine the way some people acted when they made their appearance.

Some administrators went all out over these tests, not wanting to bring heat from higher-ups or cost themselves a chance at promotion. Back when Josephine was still teaching, she and her colleagues had a term for them. They were known as "door closers." They were self-promoters who made themselves look good to higher-ups by concealing problems.

Evidently, Mrs. Derossa was one of those administrators. Style over substance.

"Mrs. Derossa, are we certain that's the best course of action?"

Mrs. Derossa was looking at some papers on her desk, avoiding eye contact. "Well, there are very few things in life that are a hundred percent certain, Mrs. Prescott," she said in a saccharine voice.

You forgot old, condescending white women, Josephine thought. There seemed to be a hundred-percent certainty of running into one of them since the state had taken over the school district.

"But, yes, I do believe this is the best path for us to take." Mrs. Derossa shuffled the papers into a neat pile, all edges straight. Undoubtedly, this was her signal that the discussion was over.

Undaunted, Josephine pressed on.

"I think the computers would serve the greater good if they were more dispersed throughout the school. Isn't it better to reach as many children as possible?"

Mrs. Derossa nervously adjusted a school book–shaped brooch on her jacket. Then she seemed to remember who was boss. She smoothed out her mustard-colored lapel and looked directly in Josephine's eyes. The look was as sharp as a scalpel. Yet when she spoke, her voice remained as sugary as before.

"I understand what you're saying, but I feel my way is best. So, that's what we're going to do."

The two women stared at each other unblinking for a couple of beats. The bell went off to signal the end of the period. Mrs. Derossa stood up.

"Well, I'm sure you have things that need your attention, Mrs. Prescott, as do I, so . . ." She held her palms out, giving the air in front of her a push.

"Of course." Josephine rose. "I have a million things on my to-do list." She headed out the door. And you need to get back to your "things to fuck up" list.

"Mrs. Prescott."

Startled, Josephine stopped. She knew she hadn't said that aloud. Had she? She turned around.

"Yes?"

"Close the door behind you."

Josephine gave her a wintry smile. "Of course."

Three

"Make this left," Mr. Duke said.

John's full stomach was churning as he turned the car, and he exhaled woefully. Mr. Duke laughed.

"Hey man, nobody told you to eat that second slice of sweet potato pie."

"True," John groaned. It had been good, though.

Mr. Duke checked his watch as they headed up Lyons Avenue. It was nearly three o'clock.

"Stop right here."

John pulled over and parked behind a Jetta. He looked through the windshield.

"Lyons Avenue School, huh?"

"Yeah," Mr. Duke said.

"Why this school?" John asked. "You didn't teach here."

"I have my reasons."

John was looking at the old three-story brick building when children started spilling out of the entrance. Alarmed, John checked the clock in the car. "Wow, I didn't realize it was three o'clock already. I need to get back to the office." John checked his side mirror for oncoming traffic, ready to pull out.

Mr. Duke put his hand on John's forearm. "Can you wait a few minutes, son? I want you to see something."

John heard the earnest plea in his voice, so he relented. Whenever Mr. Duke called him "son," he thought it was something important.

The scene in front of the school was becoming chaotic. Brightly dressed kids with a colorful array of backpacks were running around screaming like little banshees. John's gaze scanned this kaleidoscope. What was he supposed to be seeing?

Parents came up and greeted their children. The crossing guard's shrill whistle blared for all to hear. Big brothers and sisters gripped the hands of their younger siblings and began to guide them home.

And then it happened.

Josephine appeared. John stiffened at the sight of her.

John watched her as she appeared on the steps of the school, stopping to chat with one of the parents. She was still adorable. Adorable the way CeCe Winans is adorable: dimples, disarming smile, cute-as-a-button nose. The same glowing skin. Hers being just a shade or two darker than CeCe's, the color of milk chocolate. And from what John remembered, it was as sweet to the taste.

He watched as she talked to parents, hugged and admonished children, listened to teachers, watched her for as long as he could before his fear of being spotted made him turn away.

And more important than what John saw was what he felt.

His full, bloated stomach now felt hollow and empty, save for a fierce, unmistakable longing. A longing to be able to manipulate the hands of time.

He forgot all about Mr. Duke's presence. The clatter of the children. The beckoning duties at the office.

His world was minimized to the woman holding court on the steps of the school. The woman from his past.

Someone called Josephine, and she headed back inside the school.

After about thirty seconds of waiting—for a reappearance, for his heart to stop pounding, for Mr. Duke to speak, he wasn't sure quite what for, John numbly started the car.

Mr. Duke finally spoke.

"Now, like I asked you before," he said, clasping his hands in front of his waist with the contented look of a man who has been proven right, "are you happy?"

John didn't respond. He just gave him a vacant glance. Mr. Duke leaned in closer to him.

"Do you still have to think about it, or do you now know?"

John lay the folder down on his marble-top desk. It contained the status of the Argos bids as well as projections for the—"Fuck this," John muttered as he closed the folder and pushed it aside. Where the hell was Jules?

John had hired Jules' car service to take him to the airport. After his lunch with Mr. Duke, he had called Jules and asked if he could come himself, rather than sending an employee. John wanted to talk to him.

"Mr. Anthony here to see you, Mr. Sebastian."

"Thanks, Judith."

Judith followed Jules into the office. "Will you be needing me for anything else, Mr. Sebastian?"

"No, Judith, thank you. I'll see you Monday."

Judith left Jules and John alone in the office.

Jules looked at his watch. "It's almost seven o'clock. What kind of slave driver are you?"

John ignored him. "What's up with you? I thought I called a car service."

"You did."

John motioned at him with his hands outstretched. "What the hell is this ensemble you're wearing?"

Jules looked down at his clothes: button-down light-blue ox-ford shirt and khaki pants. "What?"

"Where's your chauffeur uniform?" John said, laughing. "That's what."

"Aww, nigga, please," Jules said.

"With the cute little hat?" John continued. He looked at the top of Jules' head. "The hat may be a necessity. What's going on up there?"

"You don't like the baby dreads?" Jules asked, touching his hair. "Don't hate just because you're follically challenged."

"True," John laughed. Though they were the same age, Jules, with his thin build, lack of facial hair, high cheekbones and smooth skin, had always looked younger than John. With the new hairstyle, their difference in appearance was even more pronounced.

"Well, we better get a move on," Jules said, "if we're gonna catch your flight."

"I just canceled it," John said. "I'll fly down tomorrow morning."

"What?" Jules said. "You had me come out here for nothing?"

"Well, no," John said. "I needed to talk to you."

"Shit," Jules said, plopping down in a chair, "you ain't heard of a phone, man?"

"I decided while you were on your way that I didn't want to fly down. Judith just rescheduled for me."

"Where's Millicent?" Jules asked.

"In a cab on her way to the airport," John said. "I told her to fly down and that I'll see her tomorrow morning." Truth be known, John didn't want to be around Scent tonight. His mind was too full of Josephine.

He looked at Jules. "Sorry, man, if you have something to do . . ."

Jules waved him off. "I'm your diaper buddy. What's up?"

John sat on the corner of his desk. He exhaled deeply. "I saw Josephine today."

Jules' expression perked up. "Yeah? How?"

"Mr. Duke drove me by Lyons Avenue School. She works there."

"Yeah, I know."

John's eyebrows lifted. "You knew?"

"Yeah, I have some clients in the South Ward: the Boys and Girls club, and the mosque. I talked to Josephine a couple of times, briefly. It's been a while, though."

"You spoke to her and didn't tell me?"

Jules looked at him disbelieving. "Didn't tell you? No, John, I didn't tell you about any 'hi and bye' conversations I had with the woman you asked me years ago to never bring up in conversation."

"You're right, my bad." John stood up and walked around to the other side of the desk. "It's no big deal." He set his briefcase on the desk and opened it. He slid the folder on his desk into it. John noticed Jules studying him over the open briefcase lid. He did his best to act nonchalant, trying to keep the emotion off his face. He busied himself riffling through the contents of his briefcase.

"Oh, shit," Jules said, shaking his head.

John finally closed the briefcase. "What?"

"Oh, shit," Jules repeated.

John shrugged his shoulders. "What?"

Jules mocked his shoulder shrug. "Save the poker face for those people you do business with, Sebastian, I know you too well."

John stood up straight and adjusted his belt. "What do you *think* you know?"

"I know enough to know why you sent Millicent home tonight by herself."

"Because I didn't want to reschedule *two* flights?" John asked sardonically. "All right, Sherlock Homey!"

"I know enough to remind you that Josephine Flowers is now Josephine Prescott. That means she is a married woman."

John hesitated momentarily, then finished tucking in his shirt and sat back down. "Don't get this twisted," John said defensively. "We're just talking here. I see a woman—a woman I used to care for very deeply—for the first time in over seven years. So excuse me if I have a thought or two, a couple of questions."

"All right, all right," Jules said.

John picked up a pen and rolled it between his thumb and forefinger. "What did you say her last name was again?"

"Prescott," Jules said. He rose out of his seat and walked to the window. "Wife of Darrell—no, Derek. No, it's . . ." He looked at the ceiling, trying to remember. "Something like that," he shrugged, giving up. "I know it starts with a 'D.' I met him once a few years back outside the Performing Arts Center."

"It doesn't sound like he made much of an impression." John said.

"Not much. Typical bullshitting, bourgeois asshole." Jules turned to John, frowning at the memory. "I was covering for an employee who had called in sick, so I was wearing my chauffeur suit. I had just dropped off a couple at the Center. That's when I saw Josephine and her husband. Anyway, when Josephine introduced us, it was like it pained him to shake my hand. He had this look on his face like 'Who is this working-class hump, and how does he know my wife?'"

"What's he do?" John asked.

"I think he's a superintendent of a school or something."

"Shit," John snarled. "You make way more than he does. Did you tell him you *owned* the company?"

Jules shook his head and chuckled. "No, John, it didn't come up. I couldn't find a way to work it into a very brief conversation."

"I would have," John said emphatically.

"I know you would have," Jules said. "That's why I'm laughing. As soon as Darius—I think that's his name—gave you the limp handshake, you would've said"—Jules puffed his chest out and imitated John's gruffer voice—"'Yo, my man, I own this muthafucka. Yeah, the whole damn company, that's right. How much you make in a year? What? Kiss my natural black ass, you milquetoast, pencil-pushing fuck!'"

"Come on, Jules, I wouldn't have said that," John said.

Jules shot him a wry look. "You wouldn't have?"

"Nah," John said, shaking his head. "I would have used 'geekass' instead of 'milquetoast.'"

They had a good laugh. Then Jules' face turned inquisitive. "Do you think Josephine married this guy because of what you did to her?"

John's skin crawled with shame. "I don't know, Jules, it's definitely a possibility," he said quietly. "Do you remember how shocked we were at how fast she married him?"

"Yeah, I also remember you telling me it wouldn't last. What's it been, over seven years?"

"Yeah," John replied in a subdued tone.

Jules looked back out the window. "Remember when we used to hang out downtown when we were teenagers?"

John was glad to change the subject. "I was just thinking about that earlier today. You had some moves then, Boogaloo Shrimp."

Jules started popping and locking as he walked back to the chair. "I still got 'em."

"Uh-oh! Uh-oh!" John said excitedly. He began doing a beatbox.

"I still got it, huh?" Jules asked.

"No, I was saying 'uh-oh' because I thought you were gonna pop something out of joint," John said. "Sit your old ass down, man!"

"Old?" Jules narrowed his eyes and looked toward the top of John's head.

"Hey, hey," John warned. "Don't do it. Don't talk about the hairline."

"You mean scalp line, don't you?" Jules asked. "Ain't no hair there anymore."

They laughed once again. John rolled his neck, easing his muscles. It was nice to be able to relax in his office.

"You know, Jules, I was BSing earlier."

"No, John." Jules put his hands to his face like the *Home Alone* kid. "Not you!"

"I remember asking you years ago not to bring up Josephine with me. But I did think you still hung out with her, at least occasionally," John said. "Especially to see those plays y'all used to always go see together. You two had a friendship."

"Yeah, I know," Jules said, sitting down. "I can't even count how many movies and plays we went to see together." He rubbed his chin. "That was my partner."

"So what happened?" John asked.

Jules shrugged. "Demetrius—or whatever the fuck his name is—happened. She got married."

"Which means what?" John asked. "Y'all never had anything going on, so why couldn't you continue to be friends with her?"

"That's the way I felt about it, too," Jules said. "If our relationship was platonic before her husband came along, why wouldn't he think it would continue to be after they got married?"

"Exactly," John answered emphatically. "Unless that nigga Danny—or whatever the fuck his name is—is just insecure, or doing something dirty himself, why would his mind even go there?"

"You *know*," Jules agreed.

"This Damian cat sounds like a real jackass," John said out loud, but more for himself.

"Damian?"

"Or whatever the fuck his name is," they said in unison.

John leaned forward and rested his elbows on the desk. "Jules, does Josephine have any children?"

"No. I don't think so."

"You're sure? You haven't spoken to her in a good while, right?"

Jules hesitated before he spoke. "I bumped into Gloria about three months ago on Lyons. She must have been on her way to see Josephine. I asked about her, and she told me that Josephine still didn't have any children yet."

John smiled broadly. "So, you saw Gloria, huh?"

"Yeah," Jules replied, "and you can take that chuckle out of your voice. The conversation didn't last long."

"Okay, man," John said. "I'm just saying that there was a time when you loved you some Gloria."

"Yeah, yeah, there was a time I was once into Play-Doh, too. So what? We move on. At least most of us do."

"What's that supposed to mean?" John asked. "You're getting this twisted again."

"And so are you."

John knew his friend was only pretending not to give a damn about Gloria. He tried a different approach. "Is she still fine?"

"Is she? Damn!" Jules affirmed exuberantly before he could catch himself.

John fell out. After fighting it for a while, Jules joined him.

"But honestly, John, that doesn't mean anything," Jules said. "Gloria was always fine. Thing was, Gloria always knew she was fine, too, and had the attitude to go along with it."

"Did she still seem that way?"

"I don't know, we didn't talk long. Nor did we do any of that phony-ass, exchanging-of-the-numbers-we-need-to-get-together bull-shit. People who want to stay in each other's lives don't lose contact with each other in the first place."

John nodded in agreement. "Did she have a man?"

"She was by herself."

"I mean in her life, fool."

"When have you ever known Gloria not to have a man? A man? Shoot, most times she had at least three: her main one, her spare, and her emergency dick. She didn't have a ring, if that's what you're asking."

John thought about Jules' and Gloria's past involvement, wondering if Jules had been her main, spare, or emergency dick. John had never been quite clear on why they hadn't worked out. What he did know was that Jules had always been into Gloria more than Gloria was into him. Which he knew was a sore spot with Jules.

"You know, John," Jules said softly, "it's been my experience that women don't talk the same game at thirty that they did at twenty. Or at forty that they did at thirty. They evolve a lot more than we do. Men in their fifties or sixties sometimes still behave like adolescents."

John realized that the contact with Gloria had had more of an impact on Jules than he had let on earlier. "Yeah, is there anything sadder than an old-ass man dressed in a young man's clothes, up in some spot he has no place being, trying to cop some pussy?"

"Only one thing, maybe," Jules replied. "And that's him doing all that and still dying alone."

"Yeah," John agreed. Then, thinking Jules might be referring to him, too, he asked, "What do you think of Scent?"

Jules shrugged. "What do you mean?"

"What do you think about her?" John repeated. "You've been in her company, gotten to know her. What do you think?"

Jules looked down at the carpet. "I don't know. I think she's beautiful, smart, classy. . . ." He looked up and caught sight of how John was studying him. "What?"

"Don't you think she's too young for me?" John asked.

"Come on, John, *you* know she's too young for you."

"Do you think she loves me?" John asked.

Jules rubbed his cheek. "I don't know. I guess. At her age, how many people have experienced enough to know what love is?"

"True," John conceded. "But I think Scent is ahead of the curve. She's smart."

"*Very* smart." Jules smiled.

"What's that mean?" John asked

Jules decided to stop pulling punches. "She's *smart* enough to know what you can do for her. She *loves* the idea of being with a wealthy man. You're a wealthy man, so you qualify. You know you would have no shot with a woman like that if you weren't rich."

John started to defend his relationship, but couldn't muster up the will to do so. "So why do you think I'm with her?"

Jules scrunched his face up and sniffed the air.

"Seriously, Jules," John said. "You know it's not just the pussy. I could have had that without making her my woman. You know me better than anybody else. Why?"

Jules leaned forward. "Personally, I think you're with her because you think that's what you're supposed to do. Be with a woman that is fine. And as you get even richer, the women will get even younger and finer."

John exhaled slowly. "You really think I'm that simple?"

"No, I think you're quite complex," Jules said, rising. "You've never been a simple person who is easily contented. And you've never been one to lie to yourself. Which is why you know things don't feel quite right in your life, and you've known it for a long time. That's why the sight of Josephine jolted you. Which is why Scent is on that plane alone tonight."

John decided to change the subject.

"How is Nakira?"

"She's doing great," Jules replied, happy to go along. "You know what she told me last night on the phone?"

"What?"

"I asked her how school was and she said, 'Fine, Daddy. I believe I'm up to the challenge of second grade.'"

John and Jules laughed. Nakira was Jules' pride and joy.

"How's her mother?"

"Yolanda's cool," Jules replied. "After we split up, all I ever asked of her was not to have a bunch of niggas around my daughter. But that's not really in her nature, anyway." Jules paused before speaking again. "She's a great mother. Things didn't work out with us, but we're still friends. Hell, we get along better now than when we lived together."

Things probably didn't work out because you've been gun-shy ever since Gloria, John thought. He didn't say it, though. Why rehash bad memories?

"Nakira's looking forward to having you back in the area. Somebody else to spoil her rotten," Jules said.

"You *know* that," John agreed.

"As if Mr. Duke isn't enough," Jules added. His voice softened. "John, you know I love having you back in the area, but I'm wondering if business was really what pulled you back here."

The statement caught John by surprise. "Yeah, I want to expand the business into the—"

"Oh, you're looking to expand something, all right," Jules said, cutting him off. "Expanding your dick inside Josephine again."

John burst out laughing. Jules was being ridiculous, of course, but he decided to play along. "I'm sure I don't know what you mean," he said in a purposely dignified voice. "You . . . ghetto folk . . . are so hard to figure out sometimes."

"Ghett—?" Jules sneered. "Nigga, your captain-of-industry ass grew up in the house right next door to mine."

"Shhh!" John whispered furtively. "What are you trying to do, ruin me? I'm a golf course–living nigga now."

"You?" Jules replied. "I got cats up here thinking I'm from Montclair."

They shared a big laugh, knowing that neither of them meant what they were saying. They had a great affection for their city. The sights, sounds and smells of Brick City were forever embedded in their souls.

Both John and Jules found it funny to be sitting in the seats of success that they now occupied, considering their humble beginnings. Jules and his mother had lived next door to John and Mr. Duke in the Vailsburg section of Newark. Jules' father had been a Newark police officer who had died in the line of duty when he was just a baby. So Mr. Duke had been like a surrogate father to him as well.

While John had made his fortune in the safety systems business (his company designed and maintained safety systems for chemical plants, specializing in hazardous materials), Jules owned a transportation and limo service. His company had a number of contracts, from taking methadone and heroin addicts to treatment centers to busing seniors to Atlantic City. Jules' company was a success, though nowhere near the level of John's. This didn't bother Jules in the least because he wasn't born with a competitive spirit. John had long ago realized that Jules wasn't cutthroat enough or driven enough to achieve monster prosperity in the world of business. As long as he made a good living, enough to comfortably provide for his mother and his daughter, Jules was content.

"So, now that you're reflecting on your life's deeds, I wanna know what you're gonna do about that baby you stole," Jules asked. "Just return her to her cradle?"

"What baby?"

"That pretty young thing who's currently residing in your house in Bernardsville."

John shot him a look. "You think it was a mistake to move her with me up North, don't you?"

"It would've been a chance for a clean break," Jules offered.

John stared at the ceiling, then back at Jules. "Who says I'm looking for a break? Scent and I have been together a year and a half—"

"A year and a half?" Jules asked with mock surprise. "Was she even legal then?"

John ignored him. "She has never cheated on me. She has never lied to me. She has—"

"—She has never turned down a chance to spend your money," Jules interrupted. "You just make sure you keep those funds coming, buddy."

John scowled. Jules was starting to irk him.

"Didn't you tell me last month that you bought her her own town house?" Jules asked.

"Yes," John said defensively. "It was her birthday, and besides it made sense. It was listed below market value, and she's also going to need her own space closer to Durham for her doctoral—"

Jules waved him off. "I'm not questioning whether the purchase was justified," he said. "Your money is your money. It's just that I was practically raised by Mr. Duke, too, so I know how you think," Jules said. "And I know when you start buying big shit for women, that usually means they're about to get the boot."

"That's bullshit." John leaned back in his chair.

"Is it?"

"Yes, it is," John insisted. "If I choose to, I'll do for a lady I'm seeing throughout the course of a relationship."

"Why?"

"Because I want to."

"Yeah. But *why?*"

John furrowed his brow. What did this cat want from him? "Because I've reached a level financially where I can afford to do so? Because I'm generous? Because I like to see a woman's face light up? What?"

"Or because you know you better," Jules said ominously.

John sighed. "What are you talking about?"

"Didn't you tell me that Scent is Creole?"

"Yeah, so?"

"So? Son, don't you know Creole women aren't to be trifled with? She might be working dem roots on you."

John laughed and loosened his tie. "You're a funny guy."

Jules continued, "I'm serious. Creole women are crazy. They got that angry blood. You remember my uncle Jimmy and aunt Hazel, right?"

"Who?"

"Remember how every summer my mom would send me down South to visit relatives? Well, it was them. I used to stay with them. They lived in Baton Rouge. My aunt Hazel is Creole."

"Oh, yeah." John rubbed his chin. He remembered that he used to be without the company of his best friend for a period every summer. "I do remember that. You never talked much about it then."

" 'Cause I was traumatized, nigga!" Jules said. He lowered his voice to a hush. "To be honest, I-I still don't feel comfortable talking about it."

John laughed. "So what happened? You're gonna tell me your aunt was eccentric, right?"

"Eccentric?" Jules repeated loudly, apparently forgetting he was supposed to be scared. "Uh-uh, I ain't gonna tell you that at all. Michael Jackson is eccentric. My aunt Hazel, on the other hand, is a fucking nut."

"Really? What did she do?" John asked.

"Well, once a visit, she was good for getting her drink on and chasing all of us out of the house in the middle of the night."

"What?"

"I'm serious, John. She would get drunk, then start rummaging around her house for a gun and tell us she was gonna blast every black-ass demon she saw."

"Who were the demons?"

"She didn't say. I had a black ass, though. That was close enough for me."

John chuckled. "Did she even own a gun?"

"My uncle said no. But I wasn't trying to be the fool who found out the hard way," Jules answered.

"What was your uncle doing while this was going on?"

"Oh, he'd do about a four-point-four, forty-yard dash from their bedroom to the front yard. He'd be standing outside in his drawers right next to me and my cousin Charles. So I guess he wasn't too sure whether or not she had one, either."

John laughed at the thought of them outside in the middle of the night, terrorized by a crazy woman looking for an imaginary gun. It was unspoken but understood that Jules was probably embellishing a little.

"Even so," John said, returning to Jules' original point, "your aunt's curious actions were a direct result of the alcohol in her blood, not the Creole in her blood."

Jules went quiet for a moment, then answered, "You might have a point there."

John raised an eyebrow. He hadn't expected his friend to give up so easily. When Jules spoke again, John knew his original assumption was right.

"When she wasn't completely drunk she would at least allow us time to get dressed before putting us out of the house."

Four

Josephine left Mrs. Derossa's sorry ass stranded somewhere along I-78. She was on her way home and was determined to have nothing but happy thoughts. She wasn't going to let that woman interfere with the enjoyment of her weekend. She and Gloria were meeting for lunch and shopping at the Short Hills Mall the next day. Gloria was always fun, with her crazy ass. And tonight Josephine was going to prepare a king's welcome for her wonderful husband. She was going to prepare his favorite meal, wait on him hand and foot, massage his body from head to toe, and then seduce him. She had a lavender chemise that she had been saving for just such an occasion.

Despite the pain-in-the-ass North Jersey traffic, she knew that she was still okay as far as time. Before she left school, she had called her husband's office. Darren had told her not to expect him home until late—around eight o'clock—since he was going to a sports bar with some of his colleagues. That gave her plenty of time to set things up for a special evening at home.

He deserved it. She remembered telling him a few months back how disappointed she was to learn that the schools in her cluster wouldn't be getting any computers for the upcoming school year. At the time he hadn't seemed too concerned about it.

Josephine frowned at the recollection. In fact, she remembered him saying something that pissed her off. *"If the Newark schools didn't have to spend so much on security guards, they would have plenty of money for computers."* Or had he said, *"New computers? After having to feed the kids free breakfast, free lunch and an after-school-program free dinner, who has money left for computers?* Or maybe it was his all-too-familiar refrain of *"That's why you need to come work in my district."*

Josephine put those unpleasant memories out of her mind. Why dwell on the negative, especially on a day when he had shown himself to be so thoughtful? Evidently, all that apathy was a front, because he had come through when the chips were down.

The traffic was starting to move a little better, so she switched her Avalon to the fast lane. She turned the radio from the all-news station to WBLS.

Her cell phone rang. She turned down the radio volume and put it on speakerphone.

"Hello?"

"Hey, girl."

"Hey, Glo. I was just thinking about you. We still on for tomorrow, right?"

"Yeah, if I can get out of here tonight," Gloria answered. "Why don't you come by and help me close up?"

"No can do, I got a heavy date with Darren planned."

There was such a prolonged silence that Josephine thought they had lost their connection. "Hello?"

"I'm still here," Gloria responded. "I'm just wondering how I got the date of your wedding mixed up. After all, I was the maid of honor. I could have sworn it was in June."

"You know good and well that it was in June. Why does it have to be my anniversary for me to do something special for my husband?"

"It doesn't. But it ain't his birthday or Christmas, either."

Josephine laughed. "Shut up, Gloria." She looked in the rear-view mirror to see if it was safe, then got off at the Route 24 exit.

"Hey, I'm glad you're rekindling the flame in your marriage."

"What makes you think it needs rekindling?"

"You're right. It doesn't. Darren is a regular Mr. Electricity."

"All right, now," Josephine warned. "Don't get your skinny be-hind whupped."

"It ain't so skinny anymore."

Josephine sucked her teeth. She glanced over her left shoulder as she came up the ramp and merged with the Route 24 traffic.

"I'm serious," Gloria said. "I'm getting older. I'm just about a size eight now."

"What I wouldn't give to be a size—You know what? You're gonna make me drive this car to Plainfield and strangle your just-about-a-size-eight ass."

"Just promise me one thing," Gloria said. "In my casket, squeeze me into a size six dress."

She and Gloria laughed.

Gloria said, "So there's no special occasion?"

"Well . . ." Josephine decided to tell Gloria about Darren's largesse, though it wasn't something that she wanted to get around. If it did, it could really piss off some folks in his home dis-trict. "My man," she said proudly, "sent a hundred brand-new computers to my school."

"Get out of here! How did he do that?"

"I'm not sure," Josephine replied. "You know how Darren is chummy with the businesses in his district. Anyway, he must have told them to send them to my school, where the need is greater."

"Wow, that was good of him," Gloria agreed. "He does deserve some coochie."

"And that's what he's gonna get."

Josephine lay in bed staring at the ceiling. Her mind was on the dinner she and Darren had eaten earlier. The red sauce she had made was brimming with lobster meat, shrimp, clams and mussels, and Darren had enjoyed it. Yet to Josephine it seemed to have been missing something. Unnh. She mentally retraced her movements around the kitchen. Basil. Ground pepper. Oregano. Could she have forgotten to add oregano? Yep, she was sure that was it.

Unnh.

She was satisfied with the way she had looked in her chemise. It did a good job of hiding her bulges. Darren had been pleased when he saw it on her. When combined with her fuzzy pink high-heeled slippers and her lavender, purple and gold kimono, it had been a sharp ensemble.

Unnh. Errh.

Maybe she could find another one like it tomorrow when she and Gloria went shopping. One with the same relaxed fit. In cream maybe.

She had liked the look of surprise on Darren's face when he came in the door that evening. The candlelight dinner, the sexy outfit, even the Chanté Moore mood music. Usually Josephine refrained from playing her. Vanessa Williams and Sade, too. Darren was a big fan of theirs, and Josephine was sure that it was in some part due to their looks: thin and light-skinned. The exact opposite of what she was.

Urrgh. Unnh.

But tonight was his night, so Ms. Moore had serenaded them over dinner. Josephine had to admit that she liked her sound. She was remiss in letting her envy get in the way of some good music.

Errh. Unnh.

The only thing that had been slightly puzzling about the evening was that Darren never mentioned the computers. Since he was playing coy, so was Josephine.

Unnh. Unnh.

The grunts were coming more frequent now. That was Josephine's cue that it was time for her to perform. She wrapped her arms tighter around Darren's back.

"Oh, yeah. Don't stop, baby."

"You like this dick! Don't ya?" Darren kissed her hard on the cheek, leaving a trail of slobber.

"Uhh, yeah, I like it," Josephine said, making sure she was speaking in the light, feathery voice that she knew turned him on. Like he was fucking the very bass out of her voice or something.

"Unnh. You *know* you need this dick!"

"I need it, Darren. I need you to fuck me. Don't stop, don't stop!"

Josephine then grew quiet so she could listen to the cadence of his breathing. Not yet . . . not yet.

Errh. Unnh. Unnh.

Almost there . . .

Unnn, ahhh.

Now. "Owuh, owuhh," Josephine moaned softly.

"Ergh! Take this dick!" Darren's back stiffened.

"Yeeesss!" Josephine cried.

"Errrrgh!" Darren cried as he collapsed on top of her. "Take that dick, Josie," he said, still panting. "Take that dick."

Darren kissed her on the cheek again and rolled over onto the other side of the bed. He exhaled loudly, clearly satisfied with himself. "Take that dick," he said again.

Take it? Josephine thought. Shit, I can take it or leave it.

Josephine walked into the kitchen to find her husband reading the Morris County *Daily Record* and sipping on a glass of orange juice. He had on the red-and-black J. Crew flannel shirt he insisted on wearing whenever there was the slightest chill in the air. She walked over to the cupboard and got herself a glass. She then sat next to him, after scooting her chair so close that she was practically on top of him.

Darren smiled when he felt his wife's breath on the nape of his neck, but continued reading the paper.

"Hi," she whispered.

"Hi," he answered.

"What you doin'?"

"Reading the paper."

"I see." She softly rubbed her cheek against his neck. "What section?"

"Sports."

"Oh." Josephine flicked her tongue along his neck. "Will you do me a favor and turn to the medical page for me?"

"Hmm?" Darren asked, distracted by the article on the Giants he was reading. "Why?"

"Because I need to find a gynecologist."

Darren instantly put the paper aside and turned to face Josephine; the best he could anyway. She was too close for him to turn around fully.

"A gynecologist?"

"Yes."

"What's wrong?"

"I have a problem," Josephine said calmly.

"What's wrong, sweetheart?"

Josephine was now satisfied by the level of concern she heard in his voice. She decided to put him at ease. "Well, it's just that I need a new pussy, 'cause you wore mine out last night, *luh-ver*."

Darren smiled and turned back to the paper, trying to conceal his mixture of blush and pride. "Josie," he admonished, "you shouldn't scare me like that."

Josephine laughed. "I'm sorry, but I just don't have my wits about me. You must have fucked me senseless last night."

Darren laughed. Josephine knew it was partly because he thought what she said was funny and partly because he always enjoyed when she talked dirty to him.

Darren folded his paper and set it down. "Speaking of last night," he said as he poured her a glass of orange juice, "I would like to thank you for it. My favorite foods, my favorite music, the candlelight, the ambience, the seduction—thank you." He handed her the orange juice.

"You're welcome." She gave him a kiss on the cheek and moved her seat closer to the table.

"So, what was the occasion? I'm pretty sure it isn't our anniversary."

He was as bad as Gloria, Josephine thought as she finished her sip. "Why does there have to be an occasion for me to show my man how much I love him?"

Darren smiled. "You're right. There doesn't."

"I mean, really. Who am I, Santa Claus?" Josephine asked. "I can only spread mirth and joy once a year?"

"You're right, babe, I apologize." Darren patted her knee and picked his paper back up.

"I mean, *really*." Josephine took another sip of juice. She looked over her glass at Darren. His eyes were busily scanning the lines of the newspaper, and his face didn't reveal anything. He had to know that last night was in large part a reward for his generosity. He was doing a good job of playing sly, even better than usual.

She decided to relent. "However, sometimes a mate does something so special that it reminds a person how lucky they are."

"Hmm?" Darren asked, again distracted. He checked his watch. "I think I'm gonna go watch the Randolph-Denville game today. The Rams have a good quarterback, you know. He's being recruited by Florida, Virginia Tech and a couple of other big-time schools."

Josephine stared at him so long that Darren looked up. When he saw the intent behind her gaze, he put his paper down for good and gave his wife his undivided attention. "What were you saying, honey?"

"That sometimes we can live with a person and not realize how wonderful they are. That it's human nature to take them for granted on a daily basis. But sometimes they do something so special that they remind you all over again what beautiful people they truly are."

She paused and studied his face. She was surprised to find him doing the same thing back to her. Darren spoke first.

"Honey, I know how wonderful you are." He slid his hand on top of hers. "I don't need a special evening to remind me—though it's greatly appreciated."

Lord. He was starting to aggravate her.

"I'm talking about you, Darren. *You* doing something special for me."

Darren sat there blankly. Josephine wondered how long he was going to try and milk this for. He just had to make her say it, didn't he? Hadn't she shown how grateful she was last night? Josephine decided to put an end to it before Darren completely ruined the happy feelings she was having.

"The computers, Darren."

He continued to stare at her. "The computers," he repeated slowly. "The one in the office or the laptop?"

Damn. Why was he doing this? "The computers you sent to my school, Darren," Josephine said tiredly. "Last night wasn't only about me loving you, but thanking you for sending the computers to my school."

Much to Josephine's chagrin, the stupefied look still maintained residence on Darren's face.

"I didn't send any computers to your school."

Now he wanted to play games with verbs. Josephine suddenly felt a hunger pang and rose from the table. She went to the sink and rinsed her glass out. "Darren, I know that technically you didn't *send* them, but you did divert them to my school and I'm just thanking you for doing so. Why are you making this so difficult?" She opened the fridge.

"It's not my intention to make—"

He stopped in midsentence. Josephine had taken turkey bacon, eggs, cheddar cheese, jelly and biscuits out of the fridge and laid them on the counter. She still had the refrigerator door open and was looking for anything else that might catch her fancy when she noticed that Darren had stopped. She glared at him over her left shoulder. He'd better not even start.

Apparently, Darren thought better of it. "Um, yeah, it's not my intention to make anything difficult. I really don't know what you're talking about."

Josephine took out a plate of strawberries and closed the door. She turned and faced Darren. He looked, for all the world, totally clueless. Josephine studied him closer. Even more so than usual, she decided.

She shouldn't have to go through this with her husband, Josephine thought. She should be able to take him at his word. But she knew too well how sly he could be. She remembered the first time she found out, about six months into their marriage, that he had been married before. Shocked, she had asked him why he hadn't told her.

Darren had simply replied that she hadn't asked.

Her mother, her sister, and Gloria had all warned her that she was getting married before she really knew Darren well enough, so she had been too embarrassed to tell them about her newfound revelation. Instead, she decided that if the subject were ever to come up, she would pretend she had known about it the whole time.

Darren spoke, snapping Josephine back to the present. "Someone sent your school computers? Anonymously?"

"Yeah." Josephine turned back around and turned on the burner. She began laying strips of bacon in the pan.

"How many?"

"A hundred. And accompanying software."

Darren gagged. He either had trouble digesting a piece of pulp or the figure he just heard.

"A hundred! I can't believe you even thought it was me,"

Darren said in disbelief. "Do you really think I would send a hundred computers to a bunch of Newark kids? What the hell would people in my district think?"

"*Newark* kids, huh? You make it sound like something contagious," Josephine snapped. "You're right, though. I shouldn't have thought it was you."

Darren rose from his seat and walked to the stove. "I didn't mean it like it sounded, Josie. I meant any kids outside of my home district." He kissed her shoulder blade. "One hundred computers? Think about it, that's like a hundred-thousand-dollar gift, right? Tax write-off or not."

"Yeah." Josephine considered that idea. If it wasn't Darren who sent them, then who?

"And it was just your school that received them?"

"Yep."

"Well, someone must love your school very much."

"Maybe an alum?" Josephine asked.

"Probably." He reached around her to grab a strawberry off the counter. "And you're right about one thing," he said as he bit into the strawberry. "If it was me, I would be hesitant to tell you. I love you to death, but there would be no need to put my career in jeopardy doing something nice for my wife, right?"

As Darren made his way back to the table, Josephine turned around and followed him with her eyes. Now, she wasn't completely sold that he hadn't had a hand in it.

He sat down and smiled one of his shit-kicking grins at her.

"Do you want some breakfast?" she asked, deciding not to ask him what was behind that smile.

"*I'll* just have two slices of turkey bacon and an egg-white omelet."

Mr. Moderation. Thin as a rail and still doesn't eat anything fattening. I hope you don't expect me to follow your lead, Josephine thought as she opened the fridge and took out the Egg Beaters and green peppers.

Darren folded his hands behind his head and leaned back. "Well, Josie. Now that you found out that I'm not the one who is responsible for the computers, I hope you don't feel that the trouble you went to last night was for nothing," he said devilishly. "But then again, you said there doesn't have to be an occasion for you to do something special for me, right?"

Right. And that's why I hope you like your bacon burnt black and your omelet jacked the fuck up.

Five

Gloria and Josephine watched their waiter walk away. They were sitting in a booth at Ruby Tuesday in the Short Hills Mall. Beside them on their seats lay bags that were like a relief map of the exhaustive journey they had taken that day. They had traipsed the entire mall. Gloria had bought two new outfits from Saks, a suede ensemble from Neiman Marcus, a pair of jeans from Guess? and the cutest little floral slip from Betsey Johnson that she had found on sale. She also had tried on clothes at DKNY, Ann Taylor and The Limited. Because of her size, Josephine was pretty much relegated to shopping at the anchor stores and had found a wool skirt at Nordstrom, rayon slacks and a blouse from Bloomingdale's and a denim dress at Macy's. They both had bought shoes at Kenneth Cole, and Josephine had picked up a purse as well. Gloria had also bought a pair of sharp-looking sunglasses at Fossil.

It was during these shopping trips that Josephine envied Gloria—the way her petite figure allowed her to shop in all the specialty stores and try on any cute little outfit that she wanted. It was also during these trips that Josephine resolved to go on a diet and start going back to the gym. Her resolve would then dissipate a day or two later and lay dormant until the next shopping trip with Gloria.

Gloria had ordered a strawberry daiquiri while Josephine stuck with an iced tea.

"I think Jarold is quite smitten with you," Josephine said.

"Ya think?" Gloria looked at the waiter's butt as he turned the corner and headed to the bar.

"We're the customers," Josephine continued, "but he's looking at you like he's the one who wants to eat something— Oh, Jesus!"

Gloria noticed the alarm crease Josephine's face. She also noticed that she was attempting to hide behind her menu and her hand.

"What is it?" Gloria asked.

Josephine answered without looking up. "That couple standing up over there, are they gone yet?"

"Where?" Gloria asked.

"Near the window."

Gloria saw a gray-haired gentleman helping his wife with her coat. "That older couple?"

"Yes."

Gloria looked closer at them. "Isn't that the lady who was your—"

"Yes," Josephine interrupted. "Are they gone yet? And stop looking at them," she whispered harshly.

"Okay, okay," Gloria said, dropping her eyes to her menu.

"Are they gone yet?" Josephine asked.

"How am I supposed to know?" Gloria asked, turning the page of her menu. "You told me to stop looking at them."

"Come on, Glo," Josephine said impatiently.

Gloria looked up just in time to see the couple leaving the restaurant. "Yeah, they're gone."

"Toward the mall or out of it?" Josephine asked.

"Lord, girl," Gloria said with exasperation, "they're going home. What, you owe them money or something?"

Josephine finally lifted her head and exhaled. She thanked God they hadn't seen her come into the restaurant.

"No, that's Dr. and Mrs. Harris," Josephine explained. "And

you're right, she helped me get my start as an administrator in the school system. She's retired now."

"So why are you now avoiding her like she's got the plague?" Gloria asked.

"Dr. Harris used to be Darren's physician. For a long time, too," Josephine said. "A while back Darren got rid of him, telling me that Harris was now a quack bordering on senility."

"What's that got to do with you and her?" Gloria asked.

Josephine twisted her mouth. "Darren kinda hinted that he thought it would be for the best if I distanced myself."

Gloria rolled her eyes.

"Well," Josephine defended, "like Darren said, I didn't want to be put in a position to explain why he stopped going to her husband. That he thought he was now senile." Josephine paused and stared at the table. "I miss her, though."

Gloria shook her head. "Severing ties with someone just because your mate wants you to? Marriage is more trouble than it's worth."

Jarold walked past them carrying drinks for another booth. He smiled wickedly at Gloria.

Josephine and Gloria laughed after he was out of earshot.

"With his young ass," Gloria said. "How old do you think he is?"

Josephine shrugged her shoulders. "I guess about twenty." She went back to perusing the menu. She was leaning toward the Tuesday's Trio platter. She liked the barbecued steak skewers that came with it.

"Though you know, now that I think about it, Jarold may be a step up from my last offer," Gloria stated.

"What do you mean?" Josephine asked without looking up.

"The other day," Gloria set her menu aside, "I went through Wendy's drive-thru for a junior bacon cheeseburger. A cute young brother working the window took my money, right?"

"Yeah?" Josephine said, closing the menu. Definitely the Tuesday's Trio, she decided.

"Well, how come when I went to wipe my mouth, I found a phone number written on the napkin?"

Josephine looked up at her. "Are you serious?"

Gloria nodded.

"Well, what did you do?"

"I turned my car around, went right back there and asked to see the manager, that's what I did," Gloria said emphatically.

"Aww, Glo, I know he was wrong, but you didn't get him fired, did you?"

"Fired?" Gloria asked incredulously. "I talked to the manager to find out what kind of worker he was. Was he dependable? What were his chances for promotion? I have standards, you know. I ain't gonna date just any old loser."

Josephine's mouth fell open.

"Did I mention he was cute?" Gloria added.

They sat there looking at each other for a second, then burst out laughing.

"Girl, you had me going there," Josephine said. She looked at the back of the menu, at the different desserts the restaurant offered.

"You know me better than that, Jo," Gloria scoffed. "Imagine me dating the drive-thru guy. A man has got to bring a little something more to the table than *that*." Gloria sucked her teeth. "Shiiit. I'm an educated, hardworking, own-business-having, grown-ass woman. And that's why I asked to see the drive-thru brotha before I left. So I could straighten his young ass out."

Gloria left off there. Josephine suppressed a grin. She know Gloria was waiting for her to look back up before saying something patently ridiculous.

Josephine teased her by refusing to make eye contact. She knew Gloria was just chomping at the bit. She drummed her nails along the table and hummed to herself. Gloria waited patiently, not saying a word. Finally, Josephine looked up.

"All right. What did you tell him?"

"I told him that he had some nerve slipping me his number—though I'm sure he mistakenly thought I was around his age."

Josephine rolled her eyes, twisted her mouth and gave Gloria the "Yeah, right," look.

Gloria acted like she didn't see it and finished her story.

"But nevertheless, I simply don't date men so far beneath my station in life."

Josephine scoffed. "Excuse me? Since when, tramp?"

Gloria suppressed a smile but again ignored her. "He seemed to take it well. I gave him some hope." She looked over at her bags and started riffling through them. "I gave him my phone number," she said in a voice barely above a whisper.

"What?" Josephine asked. She was pretty sure that Gloria was kidding, but with her outrageous ass one could never be too certain of anything.

"Did I mention how cute he was?" Gloria asked again.

"That's it, I'm leaving," Josephine made a move like she was getting her bags.

Gloria reached over and placed her hand on Josephine's forearm to stop her. "Wait a second now, I told him to only call me after he worked his way up to working the fry machine—that a sista like me needed me an upwardly mobile brotha."

They both fell back against their seats giggling like schoolgirls.

As they neared the end of their meal, Gloria took a sip of her drink and looked at Josephine.

"So how was your big night?"

Josephine instinctively dropped her eyes in embarrassment, realized she had revealed too much by doing so and quickly lifted them again to Gloria's.

Too late. Gloria had caught it.

"It didn't go as planned?"

Josephine pushed her plate aside, put her elbow on the table and rubbed the back of her neck. "No."

"What happened? He didn't make it home until late or some-thing?"

"No, he made it home in time." Though he needn't have both-ered, Josephine wanted to add, but didn't.

Momentarily, Gloria was puzzled. Then her face eased up as she found an answer that satisfied her. "He wasn't in the mood, right? I hate when men do that. You put yourself out, go through a whole bunch of trouble and preparation for a special evening and they say they ain't in the mood. Worse, they don't even seem to be aware of how much you put yourself out for them and how bad we want some. They just wanna grab something to eat, watch the game on TV and lay down on the couch or some bullshit like that. Grab something to eat? You grab some Burger King on the way home; you do not 'grab' some gourmet meal I've been slaving over a stove for hours preparing for your ass. If anything, you go grab a shower and a suit and sit at my table like you got some sense."

Gloria was on a roll and she showed no signs of abating. Josephine was happy to let her, because she was uncomfortable sharing what she was feeling anyway.

"And that 'not in the mood' shit—what is that? I'm like, 'Brah, it ain't your mood I'm interested in. As long as you can produce a stiff one, then you're in the mood. So, get to work so I can get *my* shit off. 'Cause you know what it's like when it's the other way around, Jo. Are they understanding when they want some coochie and we ain't feeling it?"

Gloria didn't wait for an answer before continuing.

"Oh, *hells* no. Then we gotta deal with all kinds of guilt trips and pouting and veiled threats and nonsense like that. Because whether we're in the mood or not, whenever *they're* in the mood, it's supposed to be of supreme importance to us. I really think that men think women get a speech about it around the same time we are told about our periods." Gloria chuckled as she picked up her glass again. "Like after our mothers finish telling us what menstru-ation is all about, they stroke our sweet faces and say, 'One more thing, baby. Now that you're on the cusp of womanhood, always remember: When you're blessed enough to have a man of your very own, your top priority at all times is to tend to your man's dick. Pleasing it should be on your mind twenty-four hours a day, three hundred and sixty-five days a year. If it's soft, make it hard. If it's dry, make it wet. If it's unhappy, tell it a joke. And whenever your man wants some, it's your duty to stand and deliver. Or lay and deliver, kneel and deliver, or bend over and deliver or whatever. Now, "whatever" depends on just what kind of sick pervert you end up with.'"

Josephine laughed.

"You're laughing, but you know I'm right," Gloria said. "Remember that guy I was dating that wanted me to pee on him?"

Josephine pushed the thought away with her palms. "Please, Gloria."

She shrugged. "I thought it was weird too, but I remembered what my mama said about always catering to my man—"

"—and how 'whatever' depended on just what kind of sick pervert you were with," Josephine added.

They both laughed again.

Gloria leaned back in the booth and tapped her nails along the table. "Well, anyway, I really do believe that men think that way."

"You're probably not too far off," Josephine agreed. "Men are just naturally selfish creatures."

Gloria nodded at her. "So, is that what happened last night?"

Josephine's jaw tightened. She thought Gloria had forgotten. She'd rather talk about Gloria's pissboy than this.

Still, she did need someone to talk to. And if not Gloria, then who?

"No, Darren was appreciative of my efforts last night. We had a candlelit dinner, listened to some mood music, then went into the bedroom and made love," Josephine said matter-of-factly.

Gloria studied her. "I want to give you a high-five and a 'you go, bitch,' but it doesn't jibe with your somber tone."

Josephine took a deep breath before she proceeded. She knew what she was about to say would unleash a floodgate of questions, suggestions and recriminations. Besides, she was more than a little embarrassed about her situation.

"Well, Glo. It's just that Darren and I aren't what we used to be."

The comment sat there in lonely silence as Gloria digested it. Then she said, "I'm hardly an authority, Jo, but I thought all married couples slowed down at some point. Maybe at the beginning, it's four or five times a week. Then after a while it slows down to two or three times a week. Then once a week, or once every couple of weeks . . . or even once a month. . . ." Gloria waited for her friend to interrupt her. "Once every couple of months?"

Josephine shook her head. "It's not the frequency that's the problem."

Gloria looked puzzled. "Well, if it's not the quantity, then it's the—" She stopped short.

Josephine closed her eyes. This was so embarrassing.

"I mean, I understand that part of it," she said when she saw Josephine's agitation. "What I mean is, you never made Darren out to be some kind of stud, but you always made it seem as if he was a hard worker. A plodder. Someone who eventually got the job done in workmanlike fashion through his own dogged effort. Like the postal service. Neither rain nor snow, nor gloom of night stops Darren from the swift completion of his appointed rounds." Gloria chuckled at the characterization, then stopped herself suddenly. "Uh-oh, have his completions been *too* swift?"

Josephine shrugged, trying not to give anything away.

"What I'm saying, Jo, is that you never said he had a problem delivering the goods."

"Well, I ain't received a special delivery in a long time," Josephine said dryly.

"I'm confused. You said you made love last night."

"Like I said, the *mailman* still comes, all right, but he doesn't give me any *special* deliveries."

"Oh . . ." Gloria said as she mulled it over. "Oh!" she repeated loudly when she realized what Josephine was saying.

Josephine and a middle-aged white lady in the booth behind Gloria made eye contact. They exchanged awkward smiles.

"Would you lower your voice, please?" Josephine asked. "Like this isn't embarrassing enough."

"Why are you embarrassed? You're not the one with the problem. He is."

Josephine shook her head. "You're right."

"Thank you."

"Not about that," Josephine corrected. "It's just that you can tell you're not an authority on marriage."

"What's that mean?"

"Gloria, if it is indeed his problem, then it's *our* problem."

"Yeah, okay."

Before she could continue, Jarold returned and asked them if there was anything else he could get them. When they declined, he set the check on the table.

"I'll take that when you're ready," Jarold said, flashing a set of pearly whites at Gloria, which she totally ignored as she was busy thinking about what Josephine had just told her.

Josephine put in, "Thank you, Jarold."

Jarold waited an extra second, then clumsily smiled and walked off, no doubt wondering what he had done to fall out of favor with Gloria so fast.

Gloria resumed the conversation.

"At least tell me he licks the stamp for you."

Josephine gave her a twisted look.

"What?" Gloria put her elbows on the table. "He ain't beating it right *or* eating it right?"

"Gloria . . ." She wished Gloria would just drop the matter. Or at least lower her voice.

But Gloria wouldn't be dissuaded. "Just when was the last time that you had a 'special delivery'?"

Josephine couldn't bring herself to answer. One, because it was embarrassing. Second, because it had been so long, she couldn't remember.

"Daaamn," Gloria said, stupefied.

Her reaction irritated Josephine, mainly because she knew Gloria's amazement was genuine. Gloria didn't put up with a man not pleasing her for too long. She often stated that she could excuse a man's lackluster effort the first time they slept together, because the first time seeing the wondrous sight that is her beautiful nude body may have overwhelmed him and hindered his performance. By the second time, however, he'd better have gotten himself together. There were no third strikes in Ms. Gloria Lawson's bed. Her motto was, "If I ain't coming, then you will be going."

"Listen, Gloria, sex ain't everything."

"But it's something," Gloria countered. "A big something. A man should be able to satisfy his woman. To what does Darren ascribe his inability to please you?"

"He doesn't . . . I don't know . . ." Josephine abruptly decided to tell the truth. She braced herself before saying it. "He doesn't know," she mumbled.

"What?" Gloria's body jerked with a start.

Her exclamation had not only gotten the attention of the people in the booth behind her, but a young couple sitting in the booth across the aisle as well.

"Come on, let's go," Josephine said.

Josephine and Gloria found an unoccupied bench in the middle of the mall near a group of potted plants. They sat down, setting their many bags alongside them.

A lot of shoppers were walking around them, but at least they were in transit and not in the next booth.

Gloria was itching to resume their conversation.

"You've been faking it?"

"Yeah."

"Girl, we made a promise that we wouldn't do that way back in college. That no man's ego is more important than our needs. That little dutiful woman nonsense is some played-out nineteen-fifties shit."

"I know, I know." Josephine adjusted her position on the bench so that she was facing Gloria. "But when you get married, the rules change. You take your husband's feelings into consideration. In fact, in a lot of ways you put your spouse ahead of you. You'll see when you get married."

Gloria scoffed. "If marriage means I can't tell a man when my needs aren't being met, then you can keep the whole sorry institution." Gloria looked toward a woman changing the display window at the Benetton store as she thought it over. "Uh-uh, I ain't faking shit. If I wanted to be an actress, I would've went to school for it."

"Do you think I planned on being in this situation? Do you think any woman does?" Josephine asked with an edge in her voice. "The first time you fake it—the first couple of times you fake it—you have no idea that you're gonna be put in a position where you have to fake it indefinitely. For example, maybe there's a night when you're just tired and not in the mood, so you fake it so he'll get done quicker. Or maybe one evening he comes home looking like the world has beaten him down, so you fake it that night to make your man feel empowered."

"That's some bullshit, Jo." Gloria raised her hands. "I ain't buying it. No matter what, we're supposed to be in the mood? Even if it's to our own detriment, we have to make sure he feels good about himself?"

"Marriage is a partnership, Gloria."

"Fine, so where does the quid pro quo come in? When does the man sacrifice himself for his lady?"

"Glo—"

"And how can he, anyway?" Gloria snarled. "He doesn't even know that there is a problem. You don't tell him because you don't think his little ego can take it. So, you'd rather have his non–pussy-eating, limp-dick ass thinking he's *working* something."

Josephine scowled. "Listen, Gloria, I know Darren isn't your favorite of the men I've been with in my life—"

"This is true."

"—but he is the one I chose to marry. I am not comfortable with you disrespecting him."

"And I'm not comfortable with my best friend in the world voluntarily forfeiting her sexuality. Forgetting she has a right to be pleased in bed."

"I'm not forgetting it," Josephine said, louder than she intended. She sighed and repositioned herself on the bench.

"Gloria, you know how badly I want a child. You know how long Darren and I have been trying to do so, right?"

Gloria nodded.

"Well, my willingness to go without orgasms isn't all about Darren's ego. I'm doing it for me as well. My primary passion right now is to become a mother. And to accomplish that, I need Darren reaching completion, not me. So yes, I fake it. I don't want to do anything that lessens that possibility of me becoming a mother. If I get inside Darren's head now, about what he is or isn't doing for me—"

"Mostly *isn't*," Gloria clarified.

"—then it may inhibit his ability to perform."

Gloria was incredulous. "So you don't say anything to him?"

"Right now, getting pregnant is more important to me than getting off."

"A woman forfeiting her sexuality at the altar of motherhood is no better than doing it for the sake of marriage," Gloria chided. "When are men asked to be so selfless? Hell, with them it's just the opposite. A man will risk his family, his marriage, his position—everything for some new pussy."

"Well, that's them, not me and—" Josephine rotated her head in agitation. "Why are you giving me such a hard time, Glo?"

Gloria looked her squarely in the eye. "Because I don't believe you."

"You don't believe what?"

"I don't believe that your reluctance to tell Darren that he ain't working the middle stems solely from your desire to have a baby."

"I know, you think it's because of his ego, too. Right, I got that." Josephine looked at her watch. She was about ready to go home.

"No," Gloria said quietly. "More like your ego. Or lack thereof."

Josephine's head snapped toward her. "What's that supposed to mean?"

"It means that I heard what you said back in that restaurant whether you meant to say it or not."

"What?"

"What did you mean when you said *if* he has a problem?" Gloria asked. "It sounds pretty obvious that he does have a problem."

"I meant that . . ." Josephine tried to think of something that wouldn't incriminate her. "Maybe it's something physiological with me."

"Like what? You haven't had your clitoris removed. You haven't lost the ability to be pleasured. How is it your fault?" Gloria's voice teemed with rising anger.

Josephine's eyes fell to the floor. She decided to be honest. "I was thinking that maybe I don't excite him anymore. That maybe Darren is just going through the motions because I've put on weight."

Gloria loudly stamped her boot on the floor. "And that's why I think Darren is an asshole."

"He's never said that's the reason, Gloria," Josephine said, still keeping her eyes on the floor.

"No, but he lets you go right on thinking it is, though, doesn't he?" Gloria asked. "As pretty as you are? He ought to be dropping to his bony knees nightly to thank God that you're with him. Shiiit."

Josephine saw the deep scowl on her face. Knowing that Gloria had *meant* that, that her girl would defend her like that, made Josephine feel warm.

"You ready to go?" Josephine asked, her voice softened considerably. She stood up.

"You know I just want you to be happy, right?"

"I know you love me," Josephine said, chuckling as she began gathering her bags.

"That's right," Gloria said, getting up. "And I ain't gonna let any man make my girl feel bad about herself. Husband or not."

After making sure they had their purses and all their bags, they began walking toward the exit near Lord & Taylor, where they had parked.

"Have you considered the other possibility?"

"What's that?"

"Maybe Darren just doesn't do it for *you* anymore."

Josephine looked over at Gloria. "You're a trip. You know that?"

"Why?" Gloria asked, full of innocence.

"Because you want me to consider that possibility, but then act like it's a sin against God, nature and country to think of Darren not wanting me anymore, though, right?"

Gloria shrugged. "Hey, *you're* my friend."

They reached the exit. A man entering the mall held the door open for them. Gloria had to turn sideways to get through the door with all her bags. Josephine then waited for Gloria to set all her bags down, search for her new sunglasses (located in the last bag that she looked in, of course) and put them on. They then headed toward the crowded parking lot in the direction of Josephine's car.

"Well the answer to your question is no, anyway," Josephine said. "I'm still very much attracted to my husband."

"Just how long has it been since you've had an orgasm, anyway?" Gloria asked.

"Last week."

Gloria looked at her over her sunglasses. "Not counting the self-induced ones that came when you were taking a bubble bath."

"Oh, in that case," Josephine said, "no comment."

They reached her car. Josephine unlocked the trunk so they could put their bags in.

"What is he doing wrong?" Gloria asked.

"I feel like he's just going through the motions," Josephine said. "Not only that. Sometimes he makes me feel like it's a chore for him to do it. And don't let me ask for any extra attention." They finished putting their bags in, and Josephine shut the trunk. "He gets this look of exasperation on his face . . ." She stopped short as she thought of it. She wondered if Darren knew how much that look hurt her feelings.

Gloria waited for her to finish.

". . . that makes it seem like I'm being such a pain in his ass. Like he just can't be bothered."

"You okay, Jo?"

Josephine realized that her hurt must be registering on her face. She did her best to remove it. "Yeah, come on." She pressed the button to unlock the car doors and headed for the driver's side.

Once she and Gloria were inside, the topic was again broached. This time Josephine didn't mind. It felt cathartic to share her feelings with someone.

"Did you guys ever think of counseling?"

Josephine gave Gloria the you-know-better look again.

"Yeah," Gloria agreed, flipping down the visor mirror to see how she looked in her sunglasses. "Darren is far too uptight and proud to consider that."

Josephine started the car. "You know, Glo, what you said in the mall made me think. You're right. Darren has never been a fantastic, take-the-skin-off-your-bones-and-leave-you-giddy-and-twitching kind of lover, but he was earnest in his effort. His strength was in his attentiveness and his desire to please."

"And now that he ain't even doing that . . . oh, girl!" Gloria said, horrified.

"Shut up," Josephine said, laughing. She looked in the rearview mirror and started backing out. "It ain't *that* bad. I can show you a school full of single moms who would kill to be married to a bread-winner like Darren."

"Probably," Gloria acceded. "But you make good money by yourself anyway." Satisfied that she was gorgeous, Gloria closed the visor and adjusted the seat so that she was in full recline.

"Besides," she continued, "a woman can't live on bread alone. She also needs to be buttered and jammed."

Six

"So, who's your favorite player, Nakira?" John asked.

"I like Jason Kidd, Uncle John."

John, Scent, Nakira, and Mr. Duke were sitting in a luxury box at the Continental Airlines Arena watching a preseason game between the Nets and the Heat. Sebastian Industries had purchased the luxury box for the upcoming season.

"Are these luxury boxes good investments, John?" Mr. Duke asked.

John nodded. "It definitely helps with schmoozing clients. With the Hornets leaving Charlotte we thought it would be good to invest in a box up here." He looked at Mr. Duke. "The box is also good for all events hosted at the arena. Concerts, the circus—"

"Are you gonna bring me to see the WWE when it comes here, Uncle John?" Nakira asked.

"What's that?" Scent asked.

"WWE stands for World Wrestling Entertainment," John replied.

"Oh." Scent leaned back in her chair, flipping her hand. "That stupid nonsense."

Nakira frowned at this comment. "You'll have to ask your

father," John said gently. "But I definitely want to bring you here to see the circus."

Nakira smiled.

"That would be more appropriate," Scent sniffed.

Nakira frowned again.

John, who was sitting between the two, then turned to Scent and shook his head. She returned his look with one of her own, one of blissful innocence.

John knew she was disappointed. She had wanted to go into New York tonight for some dinner and a play, or maybe to a club. The way she was dressed, John could tell that she was still hoping they would go out after the game.

She was going to be disappointed again, John feared. By the time they dropped off Nakira and Mr. Duke, it would be past eleven o'clock. After the long day he had put in at the office, John's ass wouldn't be ready to do anything except go home.

Not only that, but Jules had had one of his employees, Marquis, drive them to the game in a company limo. John didn't think it fair to ask him to drive them into New York and hang around until three or four in the morning.

It was at these moments that he felt their difference in age—when Scent wanted to be on the move and he wanted to be in front of a fireplace.

Marquis rejoined them in the box and took the seat next to Mr. Duke. He was holding a plate of pasta and chicken the suite server had prepared for him.

They settled in. For the next ten minutes the only sound was of Mr. Duke munching on his nachos and Nakira's clapping and hooting.

Scent again spoke. "You know, this arena isn't very aesthetically pleasing," she said, looking around. "It's very cookie cutter. It certainly doesn't have the charm of Madison Square Garden."

"No place can compare to the Garden, Millicent," Mr. Duke said. "It's the most famous arena in the world."

"Still," she said, "they could have done better than this. They should bury this place in a hole next to Jimmy Hoffa and start again. Whose bright idea was it to build a sports complex in the swamp anyway?" she snarled.

Nakira let out a groan. John had to agree. Scent was being a downer.

They watched the game for a while. With the shot clock running down, Kenyon Martin got loose on the baseline for a thunderous dunk. The crowd roared its approval.

"Yeah, K-mart!" Nakira yelled.

Scent looked at her with bemusement. "What did she call him?"

"K-mart," John said. "That's Kenyon's nickname."

Scent pursed her lips. "What kind of fool would want his nickname to be a cheap store?"

Nakira had had enough. She stood up, placed her hands on her hips and faced Scent. "I betcha if his name was Saks Fifth Avenue, you'd like that, wouldn't you?" Nakira rolled her shoulders. "You conceited yella thing. I'm tired of you!"

The four adults gasped.

Mr. Duke recovered first. He snatched Nakira by her arm and plopped her back into her seat. "You sit down and close your mouth!" he admonished her. "Have you lost your mind talking to an adult like that?"

Scent got up and stormed out of the luxury box.

"But, Poppy," Nakira said, "she's ruining everything. Why is she here if she don't want to be?"

"I said, close your mouth!" Mr. Duke growled. "Your mother and father didn't raise you to disrespect adults. Did they?"

Nakira was not used to being reprimanded by Mr. Duke. She started tearing up. "No."

"When she gets back in here, you're gonna apologize. I don't want to hear nothing else about it."

Nakira began to protest but thought better of it.

John got up to go get Scent. Mr. Duke got up with him. They walked to the door.

Making sure he was out of Nakira's earshot, Mr. Duke whispered, "Out of the mouths of babes, huh?"

John suppressed a laugh. He straightened up, then went out the door to find Scent.

She was standing in the concourse about fifty feet away with her arms folded. Before John approached her, he had to gather himself. How does an eight-year-old know about Saks?

John sidled up next to her. "Don't worry, I straightened her out, babe. I told her your store is Bergdorf's, not Saks."

Scent rolled her eyes. "That's not funny, John. That little heifer is a disrespectful mess!"

"Take it easy, Scent," John said. "You're talking about my best friend's child. I'm sure Jules will take care of it when he finds out what she said." Well, after he laughs his ass off, John thought.

"Regardless, Jules is doing a bad job," Scent said, stressing her statement with a head thrust.

John decided to let it go. She was being ridiculous.

"Why are we even here?" she asked. "I don't like basketball. But I know if I want to go out with you at all, I better take what I can get. I thought moving up here to the metropolitan New York area meant excitement."

"Scent, I didn't twist your arm to come."

She gave John a stunned look, which quickly morphed into a nasty one. "Do you mean come to New Jersey with you, or to the basketball game tonight?" she asked.

Honestly, John wasn't sure which he meant. Scent was taking a semester off, maybe two, from completing her graduate studies. John hadn't liked the sound of that when she first told him. He had hinted to her that he was going to be flying home to North Carolina frequently and maybe it would be best if she stayed behind.

But she wouldn't hear of it. And truthfully, how could John

point-blank tell his woman that she wasn't welcome to move with him?

"Look, Scent," he said, "going to clubs and stuff ain't really my thing anymore. I'm pretty much done with all that."

"Well, I'm not," Scent said. "What am I supposed to do, go by myself? I know you don't want that."

John knew the thought of his beautiful young girlfriend being out by herself was supposed to fill him with morbid fear, so he went along with it. He stepped close to her and took her in his arms. At first she resisted, then she allowed John to hold her.

"Look, I'll try to do better," he offered as he rubbed her back. "I know I've been preoccupied with work. It's just since this move up North, more of my time and vigilance is required. I gotta make this expansion work. I don't plan on failing."

"I understand that, John," Scent replied. "I know that time is limited right now. That you wanna gain a foothold in the region, establish your presence—all that." She exhaled and put her hands on his waist. "Which is why when you do get some time to yourself, it should be just about you and me. You have to think about your needs. About taking care of your happiness, too."

John knew that Scent didn't understand. His choice this evening hadn't been made out of a sense of obligation. He had wanted to spend the time with Nakira and Mr. Duke.

Scent wrapped her arms around John and flicked her tongue along his lips. She leaned toward his ear and whispered, "I know of another region that needs your attention."

"Yeah?" John asked. He kissed her fully. "Well, I'm definitely gonna grab me a foothold."

"Mmm, hmm," Scent whispered. "But I also need you to . . ." Her left hand made its way down. John looked around to see if anybody was watching them. She lightly massaged his member through his pants.

". . . establish your presence," she murmured.

Seven

Josephine stood up as she saw a blur along the far side of the room.

"Boy, have you lost your mind, running in this school?" she boomed at a child whose name she didn't know. "Come here!"

The child sheepishly walked back to where Josephine stood.

"What's your name?"

"Charles," he answered meekly.

"Charles, what school did you attend last year?"

"Peshine Avenue."

Josephine noticed Mrs. Derossa walking through the entrance on the other side of the cafeteria. "Did they let you run in the cafeteria at Peshine Avenue School?"

"No," he replied, voice growing softer still.

"Well, we don't let you run in the cafeteria here at Lyons Avenue School, either. The next time I catch you running in this cafeteria, you won't be going out on the playground at all. You'll be sitting at this table right here next to me for your entire lunch and recess period. Understand?"

"Yes."

"All right, then." Josephine eyed the boy. He seemed to be sufficiently cowed to be getting a warning from the vice-principal. Charles still wasn't looking her in the eye, but that was a product of intimidation, not disrespect. He didn't act like a problem kid. Josephine knew right away which kids were going to be a headache—the ones who were so used to dealing with administration that a scolding by the vice-principal meant nothing to them. The ones who would roll their eyes at you like you were just another pain-in-the-ass adult whom they had to deal with during the course of their day.

"You're in Mrs. Walker's class, right?"

"Yes."

"Have you made any friends yet, Charles?"

Charles looked up at her for the first time. "Yes, Mrs. Prescott. And my cousin Jeffrey is in my class."

Jeffrey Patterson. Good kid, from a good family. Josephine caught sight of Jeffrey loitering by the exit to the playground, waiting for his cousin.

"Jeffrey, come over here, please."

He came over to where she and Charles were standing.

"This young man says he knows you."

"He's my cousin, Mrs. Prescott. He lives with me now."

"So you can vouch for him, then?"

Jeffrey gave her a look of puzzlement.

"Is he okay? I don't have to worry about this young man, do I?" Josephine asked. "Because you know I trust your opinion."

"Naw, Mrs. Prescott, you don't have to worry about him," Jeffrey said, beaming with importance. "He's an all right cat."

Josephine laughed.

"Okay." Josephine turned back to Charles. "Well, Charles, I think you should know that Jeffrey is one of my favorite and most trusted students in the whole school. He speaks highly of you, so I have to believe you are a quality young man."

Charles looked at his cousin and smiled.

"Now, I suppose you two would rather be out in the playground than standing in here talking to an old lady, right?"

The boys hesitated, then nodded their heads. "Yes."

"What was that?" Josephine asked in a playful tone. "Are you two calling me old?"

The boys realized she was teasing them and laughed. "No, Mrs. Prescott."

"You better not be," Josephine said, her hands authoritatively placed on her hips. "Now, you two *walk* out onto the playground before I get upset in here."

After Charles and Jeffrey left, Mrs. Derossa approached her.

"Mrs. Prescott, I'll take over down here." Mrs. Derossa smiled grandly. "You're needed in your office."

Mrs. Derossa volunteering for cafeteria duty? What in the world . . .

"Is everything okay?"

"Yes," Mrs. Derossa replied. "I just had a lovely chat with a very distinguished and charming gentleman. He has requested your presence and is waiting to talk to you in your office."

"Who is he?"

Mrs. Derossa was beaming away. "He wants to surprise you. But I can tell you that he is our formerly anonymous computer bene-factor."

Josephine studied Mrs. Derossa's grinning face. She looked like the Cheshire cat. Whoever it was must have really turned on the charm.

"I assume I know this person?" Josephine asked.

Mrs. Derossa nodded.

As Josephine headed toward the exit, her thoughts went to her original suspect, her husband. She remembered the look of bewilderment he had given her when she had asked him if he was the one responsible for the computers. His denials had been utterly convincing. Then again, he could be so deceptive sometimes.

She reached the perimeter of the outer office and quickly checked her appearance. No chalk dust or smudges on her dress. Good. It wasn't easy staying clean in a school with little children hugging you all day.

Josephine stepped in the outer office, where the two secretaries were sitting at their desks. When they saw Josephine, they both started cheesing with grins as wicked as Mrs. Derossa's. Their faces were positively aglow.

Well, it was definitely a man, that's for sure. Josephine had to chuckle at the sight. "What is it, Tia?" she asked her secretary.

"Nothing, Mrs. Prescott." Tia went back to pretending she was typing.

Josephine eyed the other secretary, Deloris. She started busily rummaging through a file cabinet before Josephine could say anything to her.

"I believe I have a visitor waiting in my office, correct?" Josephine asked.

They both nodded profusely. They reminded Josephine of those bobbing head dolls.

Josephine walked to the door of her office, put her hand on the knob and gave one last quick look over her shoulder. She busted them looking at her. The secretaries quickly went back to pretending they were busy again.

Josephine grandly swung her door open and walked into her office. "Hello. Sorry to keep you—"

"Hi, Josephine."

Josephine gasped and recoiled.

"No," she whispered. She backed up until her palms were flat along the wall. Her heart thrashed furiously in her chest.

John took a few steps toward her and stopped. He saw the horrified reaction that his surprise visit had invoked. It didn't seem like such a good idea now.

He didn't know what to say. He tried levity. "I was just in the neighborhood. . . ."

Josephine remained pressed along the far wall, looking like she wished she could claw her way through it.

John leaned against the front of her desk. A smile tugged at the corner of his mouth. He could only play it so cool, because he was genuinely happy to see her.

He exhaled deeply. It was deathly quiet, save for the cars traveling up and down Lyons Avenue.

They stood there in silence for what he figured must have been at least thirty seconds. He tried to wait for her to speak, but when she remained silent, he spoke tentatively.

"Look, Josephine, I—"

He stopped short as Josephine took a step toward him. Followed by another. He quickly straightened himself.

Now it was *his* heart's turn to pound.

Josephine methodically advanced, her eyes focused on his, until she stood within a foot of him.

Neither said a word. The only sound was their breathing.

Then Josephine balled her hand into a fist and punched John in his mouth.

John careened against the desk. After he balanced himself, he looked up at her. She looked like she was ready to deliver another blow if need be.

Josephine took a step back and pointed to the door.

"Now get your ass out of my office."

Eight

Jules eyed the Italian-style hot dog that John had brought back from Frank's Grill for him. He was a study in measured contemplation. Completely motionless. Jules seemed lost in the pile of green peppers, fried onions and French fries and ketchup that spilled from his roll; all of which sat on top of the two hidden Best beef franks slathered in mustard tucked snugly inside the bread.

They were sitting in Jules' office in Livingston, Jules behind his desk and John on the cloth couch along the wall.

Jules was transfixed by the swirl of colors, shapes and textures that his mountainous hot dog contained. Like it was a subject that he planned on commissioning an artist to paint.

Or maybe he was intoxicated by the aroma that tickled his nose. After all, there were few culinary pleasures more enticing to the nose of a native Newarker than an authentic, Italian-style hot dog.

Or maybe he was simply blessing his food. Giving prolonged thanks to the Most High for the nourishment that his body was about to receive.

But John knew better.

"It's okay, man. You can laugh," he said.

Jules exhaled loudly, quickly pushed his food aside and dropped his head onto his desk. He laughed long and hard. John watched his shoulder blades bounce up and down as he wheezed and chortled. The man looked like he was having a fit.

John let him have his laugh uninterrupted. After some time had passed, Jules' laughter began to subside. Maybe they would be able to have a conversation after all, John thought.

But not yet they weren't. Because unfortunately for John, Jules happened to look up at the same time that John was putting the bag of ice back on his swollen lip. That sight set him off again. Jules popped out of his chair and leaned against the wall behind his desk, burying his head in his forearm.

After more time spent enduring Jules' seemingly endless chortling, John had finally had enough.

"All right man, ha-ha, I get it," John said.

"I know you get it," Jules said, lifting his head. "That fat-ass lip on your face is proof that you 'got it' all right . . . right in the mouth."

John sighed. This fool was gonna have a seizure.

"Okay, okay," Jules said at last. He took a deep breath and summoned up the courage to look at John.

"So Josephine, she just, um, clocked you, huh?" Jules picked up his food and walked to the microwave in the corner.

Before he turned his back to him, John could see that Jules was suppressing a smile. But at least he wasn't still laughing.

"Yeah," John said as Jules programmed the microwave. "I guess that wasn't one of my better ideas."

"More like one of the worst," Jules said. "Who told you that you could just step into that sista's world like that? I don't know what kind of deluded fairy tale shit you were tripping on."

John put the ice back up to his lip. "Still, do I gotta get punched in the mouth?"

"Nigga, you lucky that's all you got," Jules said, removing his food and walking back over to his desk. "I'm surprised Josephine didn't follow up with the classic knee to the groin."

"I got the hell out of there before she could."

Both men laughed. Only one did so pain-free. John told himself that it was because of the ache in his mouth, but he knew better. Josephine's rejection of him had caused him far more hurt than was possible from just a puffy lip.

John put his bag of ice aside and lay down on the couch. He felt a spring poke him in his back. "You need to replace this ratty thing."

"Why? I don't entertain bigwigs like you do in your office."

"You still have to look at it. How about exhibiting a little class, Jules?" John sighed loudly. "Must you constantly reveal your humble Newarkan origins?"

Jules laughed. "Me? Where you from again, John? I forgot. Or a better question than that is, which one of us was the one who just got his ass kicked in Newark?"

"That's all right. But which one of us is kicking his heart's ass right now by eating that cholesterol-laden, artery-clogging catastrophe?"

Jules gasped. "I know you lost your mind now, putting down a Newark Dog. You've been down South too long, in the land of hog maws, okra and hot water bread. I don't know why you didn't get yourself one. You know you want one."

"We can't eat that stuff anymore, Jules. We're not teenagers."

"As my daughter would say, *whatever*," Jules said, popping a French fry into his mouth.

Damn, if it didn't look good.

"Save me some."

"No can do," Jules said, taking another bite. "You should've gotten one for yourself."

He smiled as he wiped his mouth. "You know, of all the schools for Mr. Duke to pick to donate those computers to."

"Don't think that I haven't thought about that," John said. "Or about his suggestion that I volunteer at the school—"

"—knowing that Josephine works there," Jules finished the thought. "What was he trying to prove?"

John propped himself up and stared at the bag of ice. He thought about Mr. Duke's last trip to Charlotte and the conversation they'd had on the way to the airport.

"You know how Mr. Duke is with his life lessons," John said. "Maybe he wants me to face some truths about myself. Question my past, the road not taken."

"Or maybe he just wanted to see you get your ass kicked."

"That, too," John said, lying back down.

"So what are you gonna do now about volunteering at the school?"

"I'm gonna volunteer at the school," John answered emphatically.

Jules stared at him. "You wanna go another round with Josephine Frazier?"

"It's a big school. I'll stay out of her way."

"Why not just volunteer at another school?" Jules asked.

"Because I already had a conversation with the principal at Lyons about volunteering there," John said. "What am I supposed to do now? Back out of it? Tuck my tail between my legs and scoot?"

Jules nodded that he agreed with that sentiment.

"And in the meantime, if I can have a positive effect on some young black males, then that's what it's about, right? Where would we be without Mr. Duke?"

John took Jules' silence as an invitation to continue. "Think about it, I have been *blessed*. I grew up with nothing, and now I have more money than . . ." John exhaled. "And other than taking care of Mr. Duke and writing an occasional check for some charity—half the time for tax purposes—I haven't done a bit of good with my life so far."

Jules walked over to his little office refrigerator and pulled out a can of Mountain Dew. "And is part of your need to give back to the same school as Josephine out of any desire to prove something to her?"

Jules knew him too well. "Probably," he admitted. "Why is Josephine working at Lyons Avenue instead of at some cushy, stress-free job in the suburbs?"

Jules took a sip as he thought about it. "That's the type of person she is."

"Exactly. And it's more the type of person that I need to be," John said strongly. "When we were together, Josephine was always a better person than I was. She was always willing to give of her time, and any resources she had at that time, to do for others. I was all about making money. My comfort level. What I wanted to have." John vaguely eyed the baseboard that ran along the wall of Jules' office. When he spoke again, it was in a decidedly more subdued voice. "Hell, let's be honest, it was my selfishness and single-mindedness that cost me Josephine in the first place."

Jules' phone rang. While he tended to business, John stood up and stretched. He then picked up his bag of ice, walked into Jules' bathroom and put it in the sink. He looked at his lip in the mirror. The swelling seemed to have subsided. He took out his handkerchief and checked his mouth to make sure there was no more bleeding. John heard Jules hang up and went back out into the office.

"So what was it like for you seeing Josephine for the first time in all these years?" Jules asked.

John smiled. He felt himself getting aroused at the thought. "She looked good."

"She's put on weight, right?"

John shrugged. "That girl could be three hundred and fifty pounds, one-legged, in a wheelchair with an eye patch and she would still do it for me. She's just sexy like that."

Jules laughed at John's imagery. "So what are you gonna be doing at the school?"

John answered. "I want to help with the basketball team, if possible. They also have a program that meets on Friday afternoons called Boys to Men, where positive men from the community meet with the eighth-grade boys. I definitely want to be a part of that. Other than that, we'll see. I don't know right now. I still have my business to tend to."

Jules nodded approvingly. "Sounds like a plan."

John checked his watch. He needed to call his plant manager in North Carolina. He grabbed his blazer off the back of a chair.

"I'm heading out."

"All right, man." Jules finished his hot dog and threw the wrapper in his wastebasket. "I gotta go soon, too. I gotta make a run."

"What are you doing this weekend?" John asked, jingling his keys.

"I have my daughter. We're going to that Northlandz Museum to see the toy trains and dollhouses."

"Yeah? Maybe Scent and I will stop by so she and Nakira can renew their acquaintance."

They both laughed.

"You know," Jules said, "I was about to wear her little ass out when you told me what she said at the Nets game."

"I know you were," John rejoined. "That's why I had to tell you that Scent damn near had it coming. She was being a pain all night."

"Well, you gotta expect her and Nakira to clash," Jules said matter-of-factly. "They're about the same age, right?"

John laughed. "You're an asshole." He stood up and began making his way to the door.

"I hope you're right, John."

"About you being an asshole? Without question."

"No," Jules said ominously. "About that school being big enough for the both of you."

"*When?*"

"Today, girl. Today. At my school. In my office."

"Uhn-uhn. Get the hell out of here."

"That's just what I told him."

Gloria was still shaking her head in disbelief. She and Josephine were standing outside Saleem's Collectibles, the ethnic fine art, clothes, book and greeting card shop in Plainfield that Gloria owned. Her father, Saleem, had opened one back in the 1960s in Paterson that over the years had practically become an institution. Gloria had kept her father's name and opened this one seven years ago.

"What did he want?"

"I don't know—or care," Josephine added. "He didn't have long enough to tell me before I popped him in his mouth."

"You didn't!"

"The hell if I didn't," Josephine said. "It felt good, too. That bastard. Who is he to be surprising me? Like he doesn't know the deal."

"Maybe he thinks time heals all wounds."

"I don't know what he was thinking, but now he's knowing," Josephine said. "And I haven't told you the rest of it yet."

"There's more?"

"He was the one who donated the computers to my school."

Gloria's mouth fell open. Josephine gave her the I-ain't-lying nod while she waited for her to say something.

"What is he up to?"

Josephine looked up like she was searching the heavens for an answer. "Who knows, girl?"

Josephine watched Gloria kick at a pebble. She appeared to be attempting to process and make some sense out of the bombshell that her friend had dropped on her. It wasn't often that Gloria was speechless.

"Don't know what to make of it either, huh?"

"No, I honestly don't," Gloria said, looking up. "He has to know that you're married."

"Married?" Josephine repeated, snapping her head back. "You

say that like it's the only impediment to me and him being to-gether. I could be single and dateless for twenty years, and I still wouldn't look at John Sebastian." She took a deep breath and folded her arms. "You know what that asshole did to me. I'm still paying for that to this day."

"Josephine," Gloria warned in a cautionary voice.

Josephine had no desire to debate it. "Whether or not I truly am, I feel like I am," she said, "and that's all that matters. Because all I know is that I'm not at peace, and haven't been at peace since it happened."

They stood there in silence as a stirring wind gently touched their faces. The setting sun had brought a drop in temperature with it. Though not quite there yet, winter was definitely afoot and preparing to make an entrance.

Gloria peeked through the glass door. Shanna, a student from Rutgers who worked part-time in the shop with her, was ringing up a lady at the register. A teenager was browsing through the greet-ing cards. A lady was looking at some kente cloth, and her hus-band was looking at a sculpture.

"Let's go inside," she said.

Josephine placed a hand on her forearm to stop her. Gloria's eyes widened.

"There's more?"

Josephine nodded. "I told you that Mrs. Derossa came and got me out of the cafeteria, right? Well, anyway, apparently they had a nice long conversation before she came, because this fool has be-come a volunteer at the school."

Gloria looked like she was going to fall over. "Girl, that man is trying to win you back!"

On the drive over, Josephine had thought the same thing, but then decided that she was probably mistaken. "Even he ain't that idiotic. I think he's looking for atonement. He wants to clear his conscience by making things right by me." Josephine snarled wickedly, "Like *that's* possible."

The customer walked out.

"Good night, Mrs. Leary, enjoy the piece."

"Good night, Gloria. I will."

Mrs. Leary and Josephine exchanged tight smiles, the kind people who don't know each other exchange.

Josephine and Gloria watched her walk back to her Lincoln, the gravel of the small parking lot shifting under her feet.

"What are you gonna do?" Gloria asked. "With him there every day?"

"It's not every day," Josephine answered. "Only on Fridays. I assume the man still has a business to run."

"To say the least," Gloria agreed. "From the articles I've read on him, he's been handling his business quite well." She paused to look Josephine squarely in the eye so she could properly gauge her friend's reaction to her next question.

"How did he look? Like a million bucks?"

More like thirty or forty million bucks. Josephine felt her insides churn. Like her, John had put on weight, too, only his looked to be in all the right places. Under his olive green sports coat and beige mock neck, Josephine could tell that John's shoulders were broader. His arms more muscular. His back wider. Josephine knew that part of her being upset by his unexpected reentry in her life lay in her being self-conscious about her own appearance.

"He looked all right," she said coolly, looking out toward the parking lot.

If Gloria detected any disingenuousness in Josephine's casual response, she let it go. Instead, she moved on to another weighty topic.

"Are you gonna tell Darren that you saw John today?"

Josephine turned back to Gloria. She was moving a couple of stray wisps back into place. Josephine liked that hairstyle on her. It was a retro, 1960s style, blunt cut. She looked like a chocolate Jacqueline Kennedy. Josephine thought of cutting her long hair, but she knew her husband would have a fit if she did.

"Of course I'm going to tell him," Josephine answered as if that issue wasn't ever in doubt. "Why wouldn't I? He's my *husband*, isn't he?"

Gloria nodded, but didn't say a word.

"As a matter of fact, I should head home now," Josephine said, looking at her watch. "It's getting late."

Gloria and Josephine started to walk over to her car. "It's just that you once told me that Darren seemed a little threatened by John."

"Well, he wouldn't even know about John if it wasn't for somebody's big mouth."

About a year and a half ago, Gloria had brought a copy of *Black Enterprise* over to Josephine's house, the issue that featured an article on John's company. For some reason, Gloria had felt the need to tell Darren that John was an ex-boyfriend of his wife. Josephine could have killed Gloria. She was up the entire night dealing with Darren, trying to calm his fears, soothe his ego, nurse his wounded pride. For while Darren had accomplished a lot in his life, he wasn't comfortable with Josephine having someone as wildly successful as John Sebastian as a part of her past. Josephine knew that would be the case, which is why she'd never told him about John.

"Girl, I've done told you I'm sorry a thousand times. I just assumed he knew."

Josephine flipped her wrist to tell Gloria it was cool. Truth was, she didn't feel like rehashing it. "I have to tell him," she said. "From what Mrs. Derossa told me, John now has some business interests up here."

Gloria's eyebrows lifted quizzically.

"Exactly," Josephine said, answering her unspoken question. "Apparently, he's living up here, full-time, running some business. I can't take the chance of Darren finding that out and then asking me if John has come to see me."

"Yeah, then you'd be forced to lie. . . ."

"Or explain why I didn't tell him." Josephine unlocked her car door and slid in behind the wheel. She started the car and rolled down the window so that she and Gloria could continue their conversation.

"So, you're gonna tell him about John volunteering at your school, too, then. Right?" Gloria asked.

Josephine had already thought about that. "Nope."

"Why wouldn't you? He's your *husband*, ain't he?" Gloria said, mimicking Josephine's tone from earlier.

Josephine playfully rolled her eyes to let Gloria know that she had gotten her, making Gloria laugh.

"It's not that I want to be secretive, Glo," Josephine explained. "It's just that I know Darren. He will cut the fool if he finds that out. I'll have to hear about what a mistake it is for me to be working at that school in the first place, how I should tender my resignation immediately, how can they let uncertified people in our building. He'll start calling people downtown, telling people that they've created a hostile work environment for me—he may even try to get me to file a restraining order on John." Josephine shook her head. "I need those headaches?"

"Hell, no," Gloria agreed. "But if he finds out—"

"He won't," Josephine interrupted. "One, because Darren never steps foot in my school. And second, once John realizes how futile his . . . his—whatever he's hoping to accomplish is, he'll give up. Trust me."

A brand-new Ford Explorer pulled into the parking lot. Josephine and Gloria watched as a handsome, well-groomed man and three kids got out.

The man smiled broadly at Gloria and waved. "Good evening."

She waved back. "Evening."

The four of them walked into the shop. As the man opened the door for his children, he took the opportunity to sneak a long look back at Gloria. He flashed his toothy grin again before stepping inside the shop.

"Uhnnnn," Josephine said. "You and him got something going on?"

Gloria laughed. "Hell, no. He'd like to, though. I told him I don't break up families."

"He said that he wanted to leave his wife for you?"

"No, he didn't say that," Gloria replied. "He claimed that all he wanted to do was 'spend some time with me.' Which, as you very well know, is malespeak for 'I'm offering the services of my dick.'"

"Yeah." Adultery was such a slimy business. And one that Josephine knew Gloria didn't do. Well, not knowingly anyway. "You'd better stop playing with that man."

"I ain't thinking about that fool," Gloria said, uncaring. "I only play with his simple ass because he spends ridiculous amounts of money in here thinking that it's going to impress me."

"You're taking food out of his kids' mouths," Josephine teased.

"More like away from his mistress in East Orange. But he doesn't think I know about that."

Josephine laughed. She looked back at the store, thinking about it. She made sure her voice sounded as casual as possible when she asked her next question. She didn't want Gloria to think she had any reason other than natural curiosity for asking it.

"If all he's offering is sex, then what makes you think he'd leave his wife for you?"

"I'll tell you the same thing I told him. Once I put some of this"—Gloria pointed both of her index fingers downward to the area of her crotch—"good stuff on him, he *will* leave his wife."

Josephine cackled. She was somewhat relieved that Gloria had made a joke out of her question. "And on that note, I'm gonna leave."

"I don't know whether you're dismissing the power of good pussy, or underestimating how simple men are," Gloria said, "but you'd be wrong to do either." She looked at another car pulling into the parking lot.

"I'd better get back in before those kids tear up my store." Gloria took a step in that direction. "I'll give you a call later this week. Okay, tramp?"

"You do that, hookah," Josephine said, putting the car in reverse.

"By the way," Gloria said, "maybe it's the power of *your* coochie that brought John back up here."

Josephine instinctively lifted her foot off the gas pedal. An acidic uneasiness took root in the pit of her stomach, even stronger than the earlier churning.

"What makes you think he's gonna give up so easily?" Gloria asked. "You seem awfully sure of yourself."

"Because I know him. He's far too self-centered to subjugate himself for too long. Once he gets tired of me ignoring him, and the eighth graders getting on his nerves, he'll take his ass back down South. Trust me."

They said their final good-byes. On her drive home, Josephine began formulating her approach to telling Darren of John's visit to the school. Not that she had to sugarcoat it or anything. She just didn't want him to get worked up, because there wasn't anything to get worked up over.

She knew that she despised John Sebastian. Hated him for what he had put her through. What he had stolen from her.

And as far as that churning in her stomach, the hell with it. She was intelligent enough to recognize its cause and it wasn't from any fairy-tale my-Prince-Charming-has-returned delusions. That was some silly schoolgirl nonsense that too many sistas fell victim to because they so desperately wanted to believe it. Mistaking earthly lust for heaven-sent opportunity.

The things some women would put themselves through for a stiff one. Uh-uh, I'm not the one, Josephine thought.

She'd always held herself above that. She remembered her mother's advice to her when she was fifteen years old. "A wet vagina is not a good substitute for dry logic."

She talked to her mother every Sunday on the phone. Her mama despised John for what he had put Josephine through back when they were together.

Josephine quickly decided that her mother didn't need to know anything about John Sebastian's reappearance. She was thankful that her parents had moved from the area several years back, because her mom's nosy ass definitely would've sniffed something afoot.

Or she might have heard her daughter's insides churning. And yearning. But that didn't matter, Josephine decided, because she was discerning. "Learn to discern," was a motto she often used in school when talking to the children about making proper choices.

Besides, she knew exactly where her uneasiness stemmed from. It was in remembering the quality of the sex that she and John shared. No man in her life had ever worked her body like John did. She remembered how he made her body tingle and sizzle. The frenzied state of exhilaration. The ecstasy an optimal orgasm brought.

And how unsatisfying Darren and her sex life had become in comparison. Not that she and Darren had ever been like she and John were.

Josephine scolded herself. How unhealthy a notion was that? Stop giving that man's dick some kind of mystical power. No, what you're gonna do is focus on your husband. That's the man who loves you. Who decided you were worthy of marriage and proposed to you. Who sacrifices for you. Who worries about you. Who wants to have a family with you. Your husband, your partner, your life.

And since Darren wanted her to lose weight, she resolved to do it. She wanted to please her man. And maybe their prayers would soon be answered and God would bless them with a baby.

She would turn John's reentry into her life into a positive thing. It would help her to remember what a blessing a selfless, supportive man like Darren was. Maybe to fully appreciate the good she had to see the bad. Then, after a while of seeing the amount of loathing that she truly had for him, John would crawl back to whatever rock he'd come out from under, leaving Darren and her to enjoy their lives in peace. A peace that she hadn't known since she had the misfortune of loving John all those years ago. How delicious would the irony be if the bastard who once devastated her could now be the catalyst for her focusing on rediscovering happiness with her husband.

Yes. She would focus on what was truly important. And that was all the things that Darren represented.

And if there was anything that she was perfectly clear on, it was this. Everything that Darren was, John wasn't.

Nine

John was sitting at the baby grand in his sunroom, pretending he knew what he was doing, when Scent came up behind him and wrapped her arms around him. She began kissing him softly along his neck. John reached over his shoulder and stroked her cheek.

"Good morning," he said.

"Mm," was the muffled response as she continued her kissing.

John went back to playing. Scent stopped her nuzzling.

"I'm gonna call the police."

"Why?"

"Because you're assaulting my ears." Scent said playfully. "What do you call yourself doing?"

"Just tickling the ivories," John said, grandly wiggling his fingers.

"More like torturing them." Scent sat on the bench next to him. She was wearing one of John's white button-down oxfords with the sleeves rolled up. The crisp, starched, gleaming white shirt was a perfect contrast to Scent's supple butterscotch skin.

"I plan on taking lessons," John said. He looked at her sideways. "You talk like you can do better."

Scent brushed John's hands away and began playing "Ribbon in the Sky." Her rendition was so expertly done that John half expected Stevie Wonder to come through the door to sing along with it.

After she was done, Scent looked at John expectantly. His face remained impassive and thoughtful. "I just have one question. What did you do with the money?"

"What money?"

"The money your parents gave you for piano lessons."

Scent pinched his ear. "Shut up, man, you're just jealous because I can actually play, while your 'playing' sounds like the call of the alley cats."

John laughed. "Maybe I am. A little." John rubbed his throbbing ear. "I didn't know you could play."

Scent shrugged. "There are a lot of things you don't know about me, John Sebastian."

"What's that supposed to mean?"

Scent gestured as if to say, "You figure it out."

John let it go. "Where did you learn how to play?"

"Eight years of lessons." Scent started playing Michael Jackson's "She's Out of My Life."

John watched her. Scent was amazing. To be that young, pretty, talented and sharp as a tack. John had no doubt in his mind that whatever happened between them, Scent would not only land on her feet but thrive.

And that thought gave him some comfort. Because while he didn't exactly know what the future held, he knew that last night he still couldn't get the image of Josephine's face out his mind. The combination of hurt, betrayal and anger that had been in her eyes when they had met in the office.

"So what's going on with you?"

John came back to the present. "Huh?"

"Last night," Scent said. "You've never had trouble performing before."

John's skin flushed. "I was just a little tired, that's all," he said nonchalantly.

Scent eyed him. John didn't reveal anything, so she continued. "And yesterday I stopped by your office."

"You did?" John asked, surprised. "I asked you not to do that without calling first. What if I'm not in?"

"I know, I know," Scent said. "I took a chance. Sure enough, you were out."

"See?"

"Your secretary told me you were at a school. That you were gonna be doing some volunteer work there on Fridays."

"Nothing wrong with giving back to the community, is there?" John interrupted, flexing his fingers.

"No," Scent said. "But if you had some free time, I would've thought you'd want to spend it with me."

"I don't really consider the volunteer work that I want to do 'free time,' Scent."

"You told me that I had to take a backseat while you get the business off the ground. I understood and accepted that." Scent stood up. "Now you're telling me that I have to take a backseat to something else, too?"

John turned on the piano bench to face her. "Are you asking me to choose between you and some at-risk children?"

"I didn't say that." Scent scowled. "It's just that I don't know anybody up here. I thought it was going to be me and you in New York doing things. Wining and dining, meeting the beautiful people, soaking in all the city has to offer. That ain't happening." She exhaled in frustration. "Why did you bring me up here?"

John wasn't letting that one go. "Scent, *I* brought you up here? I'm the one who wanted you to finish your last year of grad school."

"So what are you saying?" Scent folded her arms. "You don't want me here?"

John exhaled. "Not if you're gonna be unhappy."

Scent looked down and dug her big toe into the carpet.

John had an idea. He wasn't sure whether it was a good one or not, but he said it anyway. "How about you volunteer at the school with me?"

Scent looked at him blankly.

"You're an educated young lady, working toward her master's," John persisted. "You'd make an excellent mentor to the girls at the school."

Scent continued to stare. John could almost look inside her pretty little head and read her thoughts. Mentoring a bunch of kids in Newark was not her idea of "meeting the beautiful people and soaking it all in."

"What's going on with you?" she asked again.

"I'm simply evolving," John said coolly.

"Yeah?" Scent asked. "Evolving from what, into what?"

John shifted on the bench. "Scent, I've come to the realization that there are larger things in this world than my own personal gratification. And that there are other things in this world besides making money. Closing a deal. Winning a bid. What's the point in accumulating wealth if you don't do a bit of good with it? Other than buying a bigger house, or a fancier car. Not only that, but at some point you realize that it's a trap. It's never ending. Unlike a poker game, there's never a point where you can say, 'I'm out.' Instead the stakes just keep getting raised higher and higher. If you have ten million, you want twenty million. If you have twenty million, you want fifty million. The constant dissatisfaction, constant restlessness, constant need for expansion, constant need to win and drive your competition into the ground, the stress . . ."

John paused, and then laughed so harshly that it startled Scent.

"You know, I almost forgot what stress really is. Stress is not knowing where your next meal is gonna come from. Stress is being a ten-year-old child and believing that no one in the world gives a damn whether you're alive or dead. Stress is not worrying about how you can turn forty million into a hundred million."

John closed the piano and stood up. Scent's eyes followed him inquisitively. He walked over to the wall window and looked out onto the backyard.

"The way I see it, is this. If you're in the constant pursuit of money, you can never truly win. It isn't like the U.S. Mint is ever gonna stop printing it and the game is gonna one day be called for lack of funds. You will never be able to stop and be satisfied." John shook his head. "There's always gonna be a more exclusive neighborhood to move into. A newer model car. It's never over, you can never win."

He folded his arms across the front of his Rutgers T-shirt and turned back to Scent.

"So, I've decided that I'm not gonna end up like one of those old men with nothing to show for his life. I'm ashamed to say it, but I've been one selfish bastard."

"What do you mean, John?" Scent said. She walked over to where he stood. "You're very generous. You give to charity."

John said nothing. He knew Scent wasn't understanding him.

"You pay your employees better than your competitors do."

"Yeah, but that's only because I believe they will be more beholden to me if I do. That they will value their jobs more and work harder for me. Be more productive for me—and make me more money." John shook his head as he thought about it. "It seems like even the supposed good that I do is still for *my* benefit."

Scent shrugged. "That's our society, that's capitalism. Everybody has an agenda, everybody uses somebody."

John looked at her suspiciously, thinking about what Jules had said.

Scent continued. "You can go live in China under communist rule, but it will still be the same thing, except there it's just fewer people exploiting more people. You should feel proud of what you accomplished. I never thought I'd meet a man more driven to success than my father, but you surpass even him."

She motioned back toward the piano. "A great pianist is impelled by the call of the piano. A master artist is bound by his desire to create art." Scent playfully tugged at the drawstrings of his sweatpants. "You might have to accept that your tremendous impulse to succeed—and your knack for achieving greater and greater success—might be what you're *supposed* to do."

John looked down at her. He knew she was trying to be complimentary, but what she had just said sounded pretty damn depressing to him. Pianists and artists create beauty. Things that touch people's souls and move their spirits. But according to Scent, his sole reason for being was to work like a rat in a rat race to acquire more and more superfluous wealth? To die rich, but mourned by few, missed by fewer and loved by even fewer? Some legacy.

"I want my life to mean something, Scent."

She looked at him like the statement was preposterous. "It does. Ask the hundreds of families who depend on you for a paycheck."

John allowed a tight smile. He didn't feel like debating it further.

"Now . . ." Scent began walking over to the couch, unbuttoning her shirt along the way. Once there she lay down and spread her legs provocatively. "How about you close the deal you started last night?"

"Babe?" Josephine asked tentatively. More tentatively than she intended, for the last thing she wanted to project was any kind of guilt or culpability.

Darren was sitting on the edge of the bed with his back to her. A minute ago he had been lying under the covers with his arms wrapped around her.

In between, she had told him about John's visit to the school.

"When did this blessed event occur?" Darren asked nastily.

"Friday," Josephine answered, lying. She knew if she told him the truth, Tuesday, that she would never hear the end of it. She had planned on telling him earlier in the week—the night after she told Gloria—but kept putting it off. She couldn't muster the energy to deal with it during the week.

Darren must have realized how harsh his tone was, because his voice softened. "What did he want?"

Josephine rested on her elbows. "I don't know. I suppose just to say hi. Like I was telling you, he said he had some new business in the area, so he just stopped by."

"How does he know where you work?"

"Well, Mr. Duke knew. He was in the system until he retired a few years ago. And Jules knew."

"Jules." Darren snarled with maximum derision.

"I haven't seen John in over seven years," Josephine continued. "He probably didn't even know I was now a happily married woman."

Second lie. Damn. Jules had no doubt told John that she was married.

"So why would Jules tell him where you worked but not tell him you were a married woman?"

Josephine didn't have an answer. Dammit. See, that's why she hated lying. She wasn't very good at it—certainly not Darren's equal. She had gotten snagged by volunteering more information than she had needed to.

She shrugged her shoulders. "Maybe he did know, Darren, I don't know. The conversation lasted all of five minutes. He said hi, I said hi, he asked how my family was, I asked him how Mr. Duke was, and then I went back to work and he left. It was one of those awkward we-don't-know-each-other-anymore conversations. Nothing substantial whatsoever."

Lie number three. But she couldn't very well tell Darren that she had hit the man, could she? That John could still stir that kind of passion in her after all this time. That would lead to too many other questions. Questions that she didn't want to have to answer.

Josephine hated that John had already made enough of an impact in her life to have her lying to her husband.

Darren tried to give the appearance of someone unperturbed. "Did he ask about your husband?"

"No."

Darren stopped. Josephine could see his mind racing as he tried to decide whether that was a good thing or not.

"But I caught him looking at my ring, so I know he knows the deal."

Darren relaxed and smiled.

Josephine did, too. She was happy that the inquisition was coming to a close. Darren knew how successful John was, and she supposed that any man would be a little intimidated by that. Hell, men were intimidated by previous boyfriends, period, no matter what their station in life—much less multimillionaires. But the insecurity Darren had toward other men was a bit much. And the coddling required to reassure him wasn't a task that Josephine enjoyed.

Darren rolled back onto the bed. She lay back down, and he laid his head across her chest so she could stroke his hair.

"So, it was just a one-time thing?" he asked. "There will be no other meetings? Right?"

"Right, babe," Josephine said, lying yet again.

As John heard the car peel out the driveway, he looked down at his limp-as-a-dishrag dick.

It had just betrayed him for the second time within a span of twelve hours. And apparently that was one more slight than Scent could stand.

She had tried stroking, rubbing, licking, sucking, cajoling, talking and damn near even threatening it, but when it still wouldn't respond, she was highly pissed off. She threw on some jeans and left, ignoring all of John's entreaties, and going God knew where.

He had tried to diminish the significance of his nonperformance by saying it was something temporary, but Scent wouldn't be placated. John couldn't blame her. He had never had trouble getting aroused by Scent before. Usually all she had to do was wink at him and he was stiff. So John knew it had to be a blow to her ego. He didn't know how extensive Scent's past was, but he doubted that this had ever happened to her before.

And they hadn't had sex all week. That might not seem like a long time, but that was like a month for other couples. John simply hadn't been interested. Scent had to have noticed that John wasn't trying to jump her bones all the time anymore. Honestly, John was at a loss himself to pinpoint the cause of his sudden erectile dysfunction.

Well, that wasn't completely truthful.

John had noticed over the past week that his penis was working just fine as far as getting aroused.

It was whenever he thought of Josephine.

Ten

Josephine sat in the kitchen sipping a cup of coffee out of her *Boondocks* mug. It was Sunday morning and Darren was at the gym. He had made a big production out of going ("Honey, you seen my weight belt?"), trying in his not-quite-subtle way to motivate her.

The gym was second on the list of places she needed to be today, Josephine thought as she took another sip. Her ass really needed to be sitting in someone's church. If her mother in Alabama knew just how sporadic her daughter's appearances in the Lord's house was, she would have a fit.

Josephine stood up, went to the sink and rinsed her mug out. She walked up the back stairs, stopping in the closet for a set of bed linens before going into the master bedroom.

On a chair in the bedroom were some suits of Darren's that needed to go to the cleaners. Why he couldn't take them there himself was beyond her. Josephine knew they were dirty because on the top of the pile was the blue suit Darren had on yesterday. Every Friday without fail, Darren wore a navy blue suit with a red tie. He would vary between his plain navy blue or navy blue–pinstriped suit, and his red paisley or red-and-blue–striped tie, but he always insisted on wearing the same color combination.

Josephine had once asked him why, and Darren had told her that they were his lucky colors. He wanted to end the work week on a good note. Josephine didn't have the heart to tell him that most black men shunned navy blue suits. Besides, she figured Darren having a little luck might be worth his being a little corny.

She'd run them by the cleaners tomorrow morning. Setting the clean sheets down, she removed the comforter and yanked the soiled sheets off the bed and tossed them on the floor.

She'd had sex twice the previous night. Darren three times. The discrepancy being caused by the four a.m. occurrence when Josephine awoke to find Darren masturbating while rubbing her ass.

Not only that, but in a stunning turn of events, Darren had even taken some interest in her satisfaction. There had been an attempt at foreplay, though it didn't last as long as Josephine had hoped. She enjoyed the nibbling, kissing, nuzzling aspects of lovemaking as much as she did the actual penetration, maybe more so. And while last night hadn't been completely satisfying on that front, Josephine appreciated Darren making the effort.

Still, she knew what it was all about: their discussion that morning about John. Men are so simple. It takes them thinking another man wants their woman for them to remember that they had one that needs to be thought of.

Darren had also been very messy last night. Maybe it was just her imagination, but the sheets felt even heavier from his sweat and semen. She had never seen or felt that much semen in her, on her, on the bed. Josephine checked the ceiling—no, that was okay.

So maybe last night was the night, Josephine thought as she dropped the sheets onto the floor. Maybe last night was the night her baby was conceived, the baby she wanted so badly. On the day she had told her husband about John's resurfacing. Now, that would be some more irony, if John was the impetus by which she finally became a mother.

Josephine finished making the bed, picked up the dirty sheets and carried them to the laundry room, where she put them into the machine. As she went into the closet for detergent, she paused, knelt down, moved some cleaning items and old rags aside and spied her stash of home pregnancy kits. She had four left. She hid them because she didn't want to spook Darren. He always complained how she was "baby crazy," conveniently seeming to forget how she had told him of her ardent desire to be a mother during their brief courtship.

So Josephine had taken pains lately not to press Darren so much on the topic. She attributed his annoyance at her constant harping on it to their inability to conceive. Hell, maybe it even in some ways inhibited it, jinxing it in some fashion. Lord knows, there were women every day who got pregnant unintentionally.

Six months ago, they had a talk about it. Darren compared Josephine's constant baby preoccupation to watching a pot of water on the stove, and suggested that Josephine needed to stop worrying so much about her cycle, the moon's cycle, the tides, etc. If it was meant to happen . . .

If? Josephine had asked, alarmed at his choice of conjunction.

When it was meant to happen, it would happen, he had corrected himself. Then he took her in his arms and held her, stroking her hair. However, this comforting, warm feeling was short-lived because Darren then had said . . .

We could always adopt.

Josephine had pulled back. Darren, I want my own child. I want to be pregnant. I want him or her to come from me.

Oh, I know, babe. I'm just saying there's a lot of children in need of a good home. You know that better than most, working in Newark. You see it every day.

I know that, she had replied, feeling a pang of guilt for her selfishness. Nevertheless, I want my own.

I know, babe. I know. I'm just saying if you were to hit forty and still not be pregnant, then adoption is an option available to us.

There was that "if" word again. Why would you even suggest that as a possibility? I'm five whole years away from turning forty.

Talk to me about being pragmatic once I'm too old to be having a baby, not now. There's no reason why I can't get pregnant and have my own child. I know that—

Josephine remembered that she had had to catch herself. She had almost told her husband more than he needed to know. Not that she liked keeping secrets from him. She just knew there were some things men preferred not to know about their women.

Josephine came back to the task at hand. Doing the wash. She took the detergent to the washer, measured a scoop, and poured it in the machine. She tossed a fabric softener packet in, replaced the circular lint filter, closed the lid and started the washer.

Josephine went back into the bedroom and took off her robe, revealing her nude, still-smelling-of-sex body, and hung it up. She quickly strode past the full-length mirror like she always did when she was naked, lest she discover a new bulge of fat on her body.

She walked into the bathroom and began to run a bath. She grabbed her cucumber melon bath formula—shucks, she was running low—and sat on the rim of the expansive tub. The huge marble and granite tub was her favorite feature of the house, in probably her favorite room of the house. The bathroom and sitting area were vast. The double-sided fireplace for the bathroom and master bedroom had been a clincher for her. Hanging in the corner near the door, Darren had installed a TV. Hell, all she needed was a refrigerator in there and she would never leave this room. Back when they were shopping for homes, this one had won her over because of the bathroom and its pièce de résistance, the garden-style tub. She enjoyed nothing more than a nice, long, hot soak.

Josephine chuckled to herself when she remembered what Gloria had said about the true purpose for her long baths. The hell with her. She was just jealous she didn't have a tub like this in her place.

After fiddling with the faucet and wondering why she couldn't get the water temperature right, she remembered that she was running the washer. She adjusted the faucets to allow for more hot water to compensate.

She began pouring what was left of her cucumber melon formula into the tub. As the last of the thick, pale green fluid exited the tube, it began to spurt erratically. It reminded her of Darren's penis from the night before.

At least there wasn't anything physically inhibiting her from getting pregnant, though that was an assumption that had once plagued Josephine.

She had given up that thought after she'd gone to see the fourth specialist—that there was something physically wrong with her. That something had gone horribly wrong when she had had that procedure eight years ago.

There had been a lot of bleeding.

Revisiting this unpleasant experience brought her mind to John. Josephine had been thinking about what happened during their abrupt meeting in her office. She regretted her actions. Not that hitting John hadn't felt good, or wasn't warranted, Josephine thought, flexing her fingers. It's just that she wished she had played it differently. That she had acted cool and disaffected. That she had simply shook his hand and said, "Pleasure to see you again, John. Thank you for stopping by. Can you believe this weather? Hm? What's that you say? You're the one responsible for the computers? Thank you for your generous gift, we'll put them to good use."

By flying off the handle the way she had, she let John know that he could still affect her. Anger is still a show of emotion. How much better would it have been if she had been reserved and dispassionate? Damn. Josephine thought about all the different consequences of her action.

John might now be encouraged to pursue this folly of his at the school. He was probably sitting somewhere right now telling Jules,

"I can still get a rise out of her," "The opposite of love is not hate, it's apathy," or some other tired-ass saying.

Not only that, but he would have the opportunity to do greater harm to the children. Josephine felt that John was involving himself in the Boys to Men program at the school only as a means of getting closer to her. Once he realized that he had no chance of getting close, his selfish, egocentric, callous ass would abandon those boys, leaving them feeling worthless and unwanted. John was never one to see how his actions affected the world, only how things affected him.

And make no mistake, Josephine knew Gloria was right. John's intentions were hardly honorable. He wasn't there to right any wrongs from his past. He was going through all this rigmarole because he wanted Josephine back in his bed.

She was hardly flattered.

Because she knew what drove John, and it wasn't love, or even the desire to do some good. It was ego. He didn't really want Josephine as much as he wanted her to want him. And since Josephine didn't want him, he was going to make her want him. Regardless of any consequences.

What a bastard, Josephine thought as she turned off the water. How can a person be so self-centered that they don't see how their carelessness hurts people around them?

Josephine made a tactical decision right there. She didn't want to be in a position of waiting for each of John's schemes to unfold.

Rather, she would be proactive.

She would invite John out to lunch that Friday. They would catch up about Jules, Mr. Duke, Gloria and old times, like any two people who were once close would do. John will see that she didn't have to avoid him, that he had no power over her anymore. She gave a thought about inviting Darren, too. Maybe having Darren show up at the restaurant ("Oh, you didn't think we were gonna be alone, did you?") just so she could see the stupefied expression on John's face that his appearance would cause. Showing John that she and Darren were a united front.

Josephine walked over to the wastebasket and threw away the empty container. She grabbed her loofah and climbed the three steps up into her tub. She flipped the switch to turn on the jets. As usual, as she sat she positioned herself so that one of the streams was pulsating against her sweet spot. She quickly moved away from it, though, her mind being too preoccupied to enjoy it.

Knowing John, she believed that he would simply interpret Darren being there as meaning she was scared to be alone with him. He wouldn't see the gesture as a husband and wife being united, just as a wife being scared.

And he would feel more powerful. And determined. No, Josephine decided, this would have to be something she did alone.

She knew Darren wouldn't understand that, so she made a decision right then not to tell him about the lunch. It was just lunch, and besides, Darren wasn't driving from Morris County to Newark in the middle of a workday anyway.

John folded his cell phone and numbly stared at it. Had Josephine just called him and in the most pleasant way in the world ("I got your phone number from Mrs. Derossa, I hope you don't mind") invited him to lunch on Friday? Was this Jules pulling a prank on him? Getting somebody that sounded like Josephine, so that he would be sitting at Seabra's portuguese restaurant in Ironbound looking stupid? Would Jules be somewhere watching him from behind a potted plant, laughing his ass off?

He was sitting in his Jaguar in the parking lot of Kings supermarket. He had just picked up some cold cuts and was looking forward to watching the Knicks-Nets game on TV later that night.

John was certain that it was Josephine he had spoken to, but decided to call Jules anyway, just to be sure. The Nets game was at the Garden, so he knew Jules would be at home getting ready to watch.

"Hello?" a child's voice answered.

John smiled at the sound of his goddaughter's voice. "Hello, Nakira, this is Uncle John. How are you doing?"

"Hi, Uncle John. I'm doing fine."

"You're staying with your daddy tonight?"

"Yes. Mommy dropped me off today after school."

"How was school today? Did you learn a lot?"

"Yes."

Nakira didn't seem in a mood to elaborate, so John decided to cut their conversation short. "Is your big-headed daddy there?"

That made her giggle. "Yes. Do you want to talk to him?"

"Yes, I do. Put him on."

John heard Nakira telling her father that he had been called big-headed, and Jules feigning indignation ("You mean to tell me that big ol' rock-headed Uncle John is calling *me* big-headed? He's got a bigger head than Ferocious Beast") which made Nakira laugh even more.

"What's up?" Jules asked.

"First of all, who is Ferocious Beast?"

Jules laughed. "You can tell you're not a parent. He's a cartoon character."

"How is Nakira?" John asked. "She wasn't as talkative as she usually is."

"Shoot, you're lucky you got what you did. You interrupted *SpongeBob SquarePants*. That's must-see TV around here. Speaking of which, I know you know that my Nets are about to come on."

Sponge what? John thought. Never mind. He decided to get to the point.

"Josephine just called and invited me out to lunch."

"Really?" Jules replied. "Janet Jackson just invited me, too. Maybe we can double-date."

"I'm serious, man."

"Get the—" Jules remembered that his daughter was in the next room. "You've got to be kidding me. She clobbers you, then a couple of days later she asks you out to break bread? That doesn't sound right."

John decided that Jules wasn't scamming him. His confusion seemed genuine.

"You're right. It doesn't," John agreed. "Maybe she's just had a change of heart. It happens, right?"

"Or maybe it's a setup."

"Setup?" John asked, alarmed. "What do you mean by that? She's not gonna show up or something?"

"Maybe worse."

"What do you mean?"

"Just don't let her excuse herself to go to the bathroom. She might come out blasting like young Corleone in *The Godfather*. One minute you're sitting there feeling good about yourself, next thing you know, your head is buried in your pasta."

John laughed dryly. "That is so stupid, in so many ways, that I'm gonna just leave it alone."

"You're right," Jules agreed. "Josephine wouldn't do the shooting herself—though I'm sure it would give her a feeling of bliss to do so. But why should she go to the bing-bing over your ass?"

"Oh, I'm sorry, I didn't realize I'd called Dial-a-Joke," John said derisively.

"Yo, but seriously, it could still be a setup."

"How do you mean?"

"I don't know," Jules said. "What I do know is that we're no match for women when it comes to diabolicalness. And only the most foolish man thinks he is."

"I'm not arguing with you; I *know* that's true," John said. "I'm just saying, what could be involved with her 'setup'? Other than your preposterous gangland slaying scenario?"

"Maybe she'll have her mother, grandmother, Gloria, her pastor, psychiatrist and everybody else in her life waiting for you there to curse you out."

"Well, if that's the case," John answered, "Gloria best not open her mouth, with her scandalous ass."

They both laughed.

"Or maybe she wants you to meet her husband. That 'Dennis' nigga."

Now, that was possible, John agreed. It'd be a way of showing John how strong she and her husband's relationship was. How they kept no secrets from each other. How John was just wasting his time if he thought he had a chance:

"John, this is my husband. Honey, this is John. The man I was telling you about. You know, the one who wants to fuck me."

"You could bring Scent," Jules offered.

"No, I can't, she's in Carolina," John said.

"Really, since when?"

"Since Sunday." John decided he didn't want to get into the reasons Scent was mad at him. "She has some things she needs to tend to. I'm flying down to Charlotte later today. I'll see her then."

But even if she was available, John wouldn't want to bring her. He'd be embarrassed for Josephine to see how young Scent was.

The Nets game was starting, so he and Jules said their good-byes, with John promising to keep him abreast of the events later that week.

That evening Scent and John strolled arm in arm down Graham Street toward John's car. They had just finished a meal of fried catfish, macaroni and cheese, greens and sweet potato pie at Simmons restaurant.

Scent slowed down, clutched John's hand and gave him a kiss on the cheek. "Thanks for dinner. That was a serious throw-down."

"You can afford to do that more than me, Scent—you're young. I can't eat like that too often."

Scent abruptly released his hand, rolled her eyes and resumed walking. John noticed her exasperation but decided to keep pursuing the subject anyway.

"As a person gets older, their body has a harder time dealing with rich foods."

Scent sighed. "John, you're thirty-six, not sixty-three."

"I know. But this is the age when men start to go downhill."

"You take good care of yourself," Scent said, still looking straight ahead. "You don't smoke, drink—you work out."

"Yeah, which just means my slope won't be as steep as some others," John replied. "I'm still going downhill all the same."

As they neared John's canary yellow Porsche Carrera, he disarmed the alarm.

"Maybe I should turn this in for something more age-appropriate. Like a burgundy Lincoln or a big ol' white Caddy."

"That does it." Scent stopped dead in her tracks and held up her palms to indicate that she had had enough.

John shrugged his shoulders innocently. "What?"

"What, nothing," Scent said, folding her arms across her chest. "I want to know what's up with all the references to age lately. Specifically, my youth and your premature entry into your twilight years. Lately, you've been talking like you're ready for the old folks' home."

"Have I been doing that?"

Scent narrowed her eyes at him until they were slits.

"Okay, maybe I have been preoccupied with age and mortality and things of that nature lately." John looked at the setting sun over Scent's shoulder. "I've been thinking about a lot of things."

Scent's face turned sober. She looked down and dug the toe of her suede ankle boot into the ground. "Me, too."

After a moment or two of stillness, John stepped close to her and moved two stray braids off the shoulder of her tweed sweater. She lifted her chin.

"I'm not going back to New Jersey." She awaited John's reaction.

"No?"

"I just picked up an independent study," she said. "If I pick up an extra class during the spring semester, I can still receive my master's in May." She exhaled. "Then it's on to my Ph.D."

John didn't say anything. He was surprised, but not shocked.

"Our understanding still stands, right?" he asked. "I'm paying for your education. However many degrees you want."

Scent exaggeratedly sighed, pretending as though the decision was difficult to make. "Umm, okay."

"When did you decide this?" he asked. He wondered if it was a direct result of his non-performance last weekend.

"I've been thinking about it for a while," she replied. "But I just decided for certain about a minute, a minute and a half ago."

"What?"

"When I first told you that I was staying down here and you didn't try to talk me out of it."

John hemmed and hawed. "Scent, that's not—"

She put her index finger to John's lips. "John, please. It's cool, trust me," she said. "I'm a twenty-three-year-old, sexy-ass bitch. I'll be fine—and for a long time."

John allowed a tight smile. His hands slid to her waist. She gripped his forearms.

"There's so many years between us . . ." John began.

"Ahh, shut up with that melodramatic nonsense. It's the same amount of years between us as when we first met a year and a half ago."

"I know." John moved his head slightly. "It's just that sometimes I feel like I'm stealing your youth."

"No, actually you've enriched it, rather nicely," Scent insisted. She smiled. "Hey, how many women my age have the portfolio I do? Or a car like I drive. Own their own town house. And I'm not going to even mention my wardrobe. Though I may be giving you a call when the spring lines come out."

John smiled and took his hands off her waist, causing Scent to release his forearms. John had noticed how well Scent's portfolio was doing. By the time she got that Ph.D., she was going to be a wealthy woman.

"I'm twenty-three years old. I haven't had a chance to experience life yet. To know what might make me truly happy."

"Aw, now you shut up with the melodrama. You just wanna go shake your ass a little."

"Maybe a little," Scent agreed.

They both chuckled. She looked up at him.

"I want to experience what a man can do for me"—she motioned with her hands, trying to explain—"beyond what a man does for me. Understand?"

John knew exactly what she was saying. But the cynic in him also couldn't help but notice that Scent hadn't come to the realization that she needed more until she was well set up for the future. Or that it coincided with his declining interest in sustaining their relationship.

But that was fine by John. He wanted Scent to be financially secure. And if she wanted to save face by breaking up with him before he could do so, John felt he owed her that much.

"So, you're saying that what you feel for me is tied up in what I'm able to do for you?" he asked.

"As if you don't like spoiling me, Negro," Scent replied. "It appeases your guilt about robbing me of my innocence."

"Innocence?" John asked. "Methinks the lady was robbed long before I made thoust acquaintance."

"Shut up." She punched him in the shoulder. She brushed her braids out of her face. "You do know what I mean, don't you? About me wanting more."

John nodded. "I do." You want to be able to run around unencumbered by an old man. You want to be able to party. You want some twenty-three-year-old dick.

Stop being such an asshole, John told himself. Maybe Scent

was sincere in her quest to find someone who truly loved her. After all, that's what he wanted. Maybe she just wanted the same.

And if so, it was only right that Scent have the opportunity to be with someone who did truly love her. In fact, John wondered if she had already met someone else; if all those nights spent studying with girlfriends were just a cover. But he wasn't curious enough to ask.

They embraced. He rubbed her back. He noticed an elderly couple across the street staring at them.

"Come on, let's get into the car."

John opened the passenger side car door for her. He walked around to the other side and slid in.

Before he turned on the ignition, he looked at Scent. "I just want you to be clear about something. If there were any failings or shortcomings, they were mine."

Scent turned her head to face him. "Agreed."

Eleven

Josephine sat at one of the small square tables in a far corner of the back room of Seabra's. Each table was covered with a royal blue tablecloth and a gleaming white table topper. The same colors as the tiled walls. The restaurant had an Old World charm to it and was one of the favorite haunts for Josephine and her colleagues. In fact, she was having second thoughts about inviting John to lunch at such a popular place. She wanted to be on familiar turf, but she didn't exactly relish the thought of co-workers seeing her having an intimate lunch with a man who wasn't her husband.

She dismissed the notion. There was nothing intimate about it, not in the middle of the day. Besides, all of her colleagues were still at work, which is where Josephine would be returning to as soon as this lunch was over.

A car passed by outside, its radio loudly thumping. Josephine recognized the voice as Lauryn Hill's but couldn't quite place which song it was before the sound receded.

She looked around the room. No one she knew was here. But then again, that was also the reason she had invited John here. She wanted to be where she could be seen. Because she wasn't hiding anything. Well, except from Darren, and Gloria, and her mother . . .

A better way of putting it was that nothing was going on with the man she was about to eat lunch with. It was completely inno-cent. Josephine and her waiter made eye contact across the room and exchanged smiles. His cute, bushy-haired, olive-skinned ass had a better shot of getting some from her than John.

So as she sat there noshing bread, she ascribed that concern as the reason for the butterflies in her stomach—not being alone with John for the second time in over seven years.

She saw John walk in. The hostess pointed him in the right di-rection, and he made his way over to the table.

He looked like a million bucks. Or thirty or forty million. He was wearing a brown three-button suede sports coat over a ribbed tan cotton stretch turtleneck, flecked tweed slacks and soft brown leather boots. Sharp. The man could always dress, even back when he didn't have a lot of money to work with.

John was never good looking in a traditional way. On first glance, he would never turn heads like Boris Kodjoe or Morris Chestnut. Rather, what John had working for him was a com-manding presence. A regal bearing and cool, confident demeanor. Like Laurence Fishburne, Josephine decided. It just sucked you in.

She self-consciously tugged at the lapels of her black jacket. Underneath she had on a slate-colored rayon blouse. She was wearing a long matching skirt and black leather boots. It was one of her favorite outfits, and she thought she looked good in it. Ap-parently, Darren agreed because it warranted Josephine some extra groping from him before he left for work that morning.

"Hi," John said, arriving at the table.

"Hi. Please have a seat."

John sat down across from Josephine. "I'm not late, am I?"

"No, I'm early."

The waiter came by, said hello, filled John's glass with water and handed him a menu. He again smiled at Josephine. "May I get you something else to drink?"

"I'll have another iced tea."

"I'll have the same."

"Thank you, Jorge." He walked away to get their beverages.

"Still don't drink?" John asked.

"Rarely. If I have my husband with me and I don't have to drive home, then I might have a glass of wine." Josephine was happy that she worked her husband into the conversation so early. She tried to gauge John's reaction, but there was none. "You?"

John shook his head. "No. I still don't drink. I don't like to lose my inhibitions."

I bet your repressive, controlling ass doesn't, Josephine thought. She remembered how John always liked to be in control. He couldn't stand to be in a position of having to deal with things he couldn't direct.

"You come here a lot?" John asked, still studying his menu.

Josephine decided to seize the opening, to keep him on the defensive. "Why did you ask that, John? Is it because I look like I've been eating a lot of rich restaurant food?"

He looked up, clearly startled. "Huh?"

"You heard me. Or haven't you noticed I've put on weight?"

John furrowed his brow. He seemed honestly distressed. "Josephine, you're beautiful. You know that, don't you?"

His words made her cheeks flush. She was grateful that Jorge came back to the table at that moment with their teas.

"Would you like to hear the lunch specials?" Jorge asked.

"Yes, we would."

As Josephine watched Jorge run down the different house specials, she could feel John's eyes running amok along her hair, her face, her neck, her breasts. . . .

After Jorge finished, Josephine spoke. "I'll have the garlic shrimp appetizer, Jorge."

"No oysters today?"

She looked over at John and saw him trying to hide a sly smile.

"No, the garlic shrimp will be fine. Can you do me a favor, Jorge, and tell the chef I want extra garlic?"

"Sure."

After she added beef short ribs as her entree, she handed the menu back to Jorge. That's right, extra garlic. After all, she had no reason to be concerned about bad breath. No one here that she would be kissing later.

"You, sir?"

"I'll have the oysters." He stole a furtive glance at Josephine. She was busy putting Equal into her tea. "And the rock lobster tail, filet mignon special. Well done, please."

Jorge thanked them and left the table.

"You never answered my question from earlier."

"Huh?" Josephine raised her eyebrows over her glass while she drank her tea. Surely he wasn't expecting her to answer his corny-ass do-you-know-how-beautiful-you-are bullshit.

"Do you come here often?"

"Oh, yeah," Josephine said, flushing. "It's a popular spot among Newark public school employees."

"Well, thank you for inviting me to lunch."

"I figure it's the least I can do," Josephine said. "We definitely got off on the wrong foot back in my office last week."

"Actually, no, you didn't. *You* went off the proper foot."

Josephine shot him a puzzled glance.

"What I mean is that you threw a textbook left hook. Perfect balance. Perfect form. Textbook technique." He was smiling in that old way she remembered. "The way you planted your right foot, evenly distributed your hips, drove your legs and delivered that blow with maximum effect—shoot, I was impressed," John said, nodding. "Great technique."

Josephine laughed.

"Who taught you how to throw a punch like that?" John asked.

"Mr. Duke."

John gave her a look of mock irritation.

"Well, don't be trying to fish for any compliments, then," Josephine said. "Besides, wasn't he the one who taught you how to box? So, in effect he was my teacher, too—by proxy."

"True."

"In any case, I would like to apologize for hitting you," Josephine stated. "As much as I get on the children for resorting to violence."

John waved it off. "It was my fault, Josephine. I knew better than to surprise you like that."

You got that right, Josephine thought as she squeezed her lemon into her tea.

"And thank you for the computers, John. Mrs. Derossa told me you were responsible for the gift."

"That was a pleasure, Josephine." John rubbed his goatee. "Lord knows, I have been blessed. I could stand to give back more."

Josephine was impressed both by the selfless sentiments John was voicing and by the goatee. It looked nice on him. Neither the philanthropic sentiments nor the goatee had been evident seven years ago.

"And speaking of that, are you looking forward to your first Boys to Men mentor program this afternoon?"

Her question caught John in mid-sip, but he signaled by nodding that he was. John finally swallowed. "I sure am."

"Out of my office window last week, I saw you leave the school driving a Ford Taurus?"

John waited before speaking. "I'm sorry, was that a question?"

Josephine gave a mock smile. "You know what I mean."

"Maybe you were expecting a Lamborghini?"

"No, just not a Taurus."

John shrugged. "It's a rental. I figure I don't need to be driving anything too flashy in the hood. As a matter of fact, I told Mrs. Derossa that I'm trying to keep a low profile."

"What's the matter?" Josephine teased. "You don't want all the available teachers and single moms of pupils at Lyons Avenue School to know that you're Sebastian, John Sebastian, international playboy, founder of Sebastian Industries?"

"With a license to thrill, baby."

"Um-hm, I bet. Well, don't worry, your secret is safe with me," Josephine said as she unconsciously fiddled with her wedding ring. "I won't tell everybody we have a fabulously wealthy man walking around the school."

"Thank you. Though I'm not as 'fabulously wealthy' as people think."

"That's a sure sign that you are," Josephine said. "Rich people always try to downplay their wealth. It's those bourgeois suburban black folk that are two paychecks from being back in the hood who are always fronting."

They shared a laugh.

"Well, congratulations on all your success," Josephine said. She added, her voice dropping an octave, "I never had a doubt."

"Thank you."

"How is Mr. Duke?" Josephine inquired, changing the subject.

"He's fine," John answered. "He has a condo out in Maplewood."

"Wha-at?" Josephine asked raising her eyebrows. "Mr. Duke moved out of his beloved Newark?"

"Believe me, it wasn't easy for me to convince him. He's a stubborn old man," John said with a chuckle. "You should give him a call. He still asks about you."

Josephine smiled. "Really?"

"Why are you acting surprised?" John asked. "You know that old man loved him some Josephine."

"Yeah, I know. I think the world of Mr. Duke, too," Josephine said. "It's just that . . . you know."

Jorge brought their appetizers to the table. The pungent aroma of garlic filled the immediate vicinity.

"No, I don't know," John said after Jorge had left.

"I'm surprised that he still remembers me," Josephine said, stabbing a fork at her shrimp. "I just figured there were probably a lot of women that you've introduced to him in the last seven years."

"Even if that were the case—"

"You mean, it's not?" Josephine interrupted. "A young, single, enormously successful brother. I wouldn't think you want for company."

John rolled his tongue around his mouth before answering. "I do okay."

Josephine gave him a slight nod, complete with an I-bet-you-do smirk.

"However, Mr. Duke is a wise man. And as such, he never confuses quality with quantity."

Josephine smiled. John assumed it was because of the compliment that he had just paid her, by proxy, from Mr. Duke. But it wasn't.

"Quality versus quantity. That's one of my husband's favorite catchphrases."

"Your husband. Derone, right?"

"Darren." Josephine cracked him off a sharp look, trying to discern whether the error was one of commission or truly accidental.

"Of course," John replied. "How's that working for you?"

Josephine set down her fork. She didn't appreciate him speaking of it with such casualness. Like it was an art project or something. "What, my marriage?"

"Yeah." John slurped an oyster.

"My *marriage* is going well, thank you for asking. We are two people in love. A love that is growing stronger by the day. My husband adores his Josie," she said, smiling.

"Josie?" John asked, incredulous.

"Yep," Josephine replied with satisfaction.

John set his napkin on the table, got up and walked around behind her.

"What are you doing?" she asked.

"Just looking for your tail," he replied neatly, "and for the rest of the pussycats—*Josie*."

The way he said it made it sound so inane. Josephine picked up her fork, then put it right back down again, she was so aggravated. "Why are you asking how my marriage is going anyway?" she snarled.

John seemed taken aback. Josephine couldn't tell whether his surprise was genuine or not.

"You brought up what I was doing since we'd been together," John said. "Why is it so unfair that I ask you the same?"

"Don't compare my marriage to your sordid little escapades."

John dabbed at the corners of his mouth with his napkin. "That's not fair, Josephine."

She reactively pushed her plate aside, set her elbows on the table and began rubbing her knuckles. She realized she was overreacting, probably playing right into his hands. A doth-protest-too-much–type thing. Besides, she had brought up other mates first.

"You're right, I apologize," Josephine said sweetly. "Fire away. Ask me anything about my husband, my life, my career, my credit rating, anything."

She thought that her blunt openness would discourage John from pursuing the topic further. Unfortunately for her, John knew that was what she was banking on.

"Okay." He pushed his plate aside as well. "How long have you and Darrell been married?"

Josephine flashed a toothy smile. *Darren*, motherfucker.

"It's Darren, John."

"Oh, my bad. Darren."

"No problem, I'm sure it was an honest mistake."

"Indeed it was," John said emphatically. No doubt purposely being vague as to what he was alluding to as being the mistake—the marriage or his misstating of the name.

"Darren and I have been married for seven wonderful years," she said, peering down at her ring.

John whistled.

"What was that for?" she asked.

"Seven years?" John repeated. "We broke up seven and a half years ago."

Josephine shrugged her shoulders as a busboy cleared their plates away and refilled their glasses. "What's your point?"

"How long did you two date before, um"—John hesitated as he seemed to search clumsily for his next word—"*Darren* proposed to you."

"Around three months."

John whistled a second time.

Again with the whistling. What is he, a fucking choo-choo? Josephine kept her irritation in check.

Jorge brought their entrees out, set them on the table, and told them to enjoy their meal. Josephine wasn't of a mind to just yet.

"Is there something about the phrase 'around three months' that distresses you?"

"No, it just doesn't seem like a lot of time."

"It is when a man knows what he wants," Josephine said, "when he's mature enough to see a good thing when it's staring him in the face."

"I knew what a good thing you were," John protested. "In my eyes, our getting married was never a question of if, but when."

Now it was Josephine's turn to whistle. "You must have had some keen eyesight, because that's not the way I remember it at all." She started in on her rice.

John wasn't going to let her sit here and rewrite history. "How could you get any other impression, Josephine? Who else was there? Did I ever cheat on you?"

"Not with a woman—work was your mistress. An especially needy one."

"Well, excuse the hell out of me, Josephine. Most women would appreciate a man willing to work his ass off to build a future for himself and his lady."

Josephine raised her glass. "Cheers to you industrious brothers, and the women who appreciate you."

John leaned back in his chair and shook his head.

"What do you want from me, John? I hope it's not to take you seriously. Your desire to damn near kill your fool self working one-hundred-plus-hour work weeks had nothing to do with me."

"It had everything to do with you—"

"That's bullshit!" Josephine's whole body tensed up. She didn't notice or care if people had heard her curse. In her anger, all she could focus on was John, and more specifically, their past. "While you were out working, then working some more, researching, exploring and investigating, meeting with backers, then organizing, re-organizing—"

"Yeah, I get it. What?"

"You had a woman at home, that's what. A woman who needed you."

"So punish me for wanting to make a success of myself, then?"

"Who's punishing you?"

"And for doing a pretty damn good job of becoming one as well, I might add."

"So, Mr. Successful, what are you doing in my face? Mr. Pull Yourself Up By Your Own Bootstraps, last time I checked, we're in Jersey. You don't see my ass looking for you down in Charlotte."

There. She had put it out there. The notion that John was back home for more than just business purposes.

"You don't, do you?" John asked. "Then again, it's already been established how long it takes you to forget a man. Around three months. Hell, how long after we broke up were you in his bed? 'Around' three days?"

Josephine tore a piece of bread and stared at the ceiling like she was honestly trying to recall. "No, it was more like three *hours*. I met him at the airport. We shared a cab. Next thing I know, I'm at his place on all fours with his dick on my ass."

John felt a surge of rage swell inside of him. He picked up his knife and fork and began cutting his steak.

For the next few minutes not a word was exchanged between them as they ate in silence. No doubt much to the relief of the other patrons and restaurant staff, who couldn't help but notice their animated conversation.

"How are your parents?" John asked without looking up.

"They're fine. They relocated to Alabama." Josephine decided to have a stab at being civil. "You still talk to Jules, right? How is he doing?"

John nodded approvingly.

"And his daughter, Nakira? How old is she now?"

"Seven."

"Wow. I think the last time I saw her she was two." She smiled. "I remember when she was born."

"Yeah, I believe that was right around the time you left me."

Josephine sighed. "Physically, yes, I did the leaving. But you had left me a long time before that." She wavered momentarily, then went on. "Don't even try and tell me that you didn't know how much it pained me to do so."

"Yeah, right," John snarled, not trying to hear that. "A woman who loved me so much that 'around three months' after we break up, she's engaged to another man? Sure didn't take long for you to forget me."

"Longer than it took you," Josephine snapped right back. "You forgot me when we were still together."

John was about to come back at her, then stopped. When he again spoke, the edge was removed from his voice.

"Josephine, how can you honestly say that you even know a man that you've only dated for three months, let alone love him?" He shook his head, disbelieving. "Much less be sure that you want to spend the rest of your life with him?"

"Hey," Josephine said casually as she dipped her bread into olive oil, "when it's right, you know."

"More like when it's *flight*, you know."

"Excuse me?"

"You heard me, Josephine," John said. "You married this man on the rebound and you know it."

Josephine drew back and gave John a sideways look. "On the rebound from what?"

John stared at her, not believing she'd try to pull this.

Josephine laughed nastily. "That is the most preposterous thing I've ever heard. You act as though I left Camelot or something."

"Maybe not, but I can provide that, you know."

Unbelievable. This fool still thinks it's all about money. "Where is your white steed, Lancelot? Are you ready to whisk me back to Camelot?"

John was tired of her mocking him. "Yeah, and with me not only would you live in Camelot, but you'd 'come-a-lot' too, which is a lot more than what you're doing now, ain't it?"

"W-what?" Josephine sputtered for air.

John leaned in and spoke in a harsh whisper. "Oh, yeah. I bet it wouldn't take long for you to forget your husband completely. I'd give it *around three months*."

Josephine fumed. "Why do you keep saying that?" she asked. "Oh, I know why." She got up and walked around to his side of the table, put one hand on the back of his chair and leaned toward him. Her breath was hot on his cheek. "That was the age of our child," she whispered into his ear, "when you made me kill him—*around three months*."

Josephine gave him a long, slow kiss on the cheek before she pulled back and righted herself. She opened her purse.

"I got it, Josephine," John mumbled. He was looking straight ahead at her vacated seat and had his hands clasped like he was in prayer.

She eyed him contemptuously. "No, John. I got *this*."

She laid a hundred-dollar bill on the table, readjusted her purse strap, and strode out of the restaurant, all the while humming the bars to Lauryn Hill's "Lost Ones" in her head.

Yeah, that was the song she had heard earlier.

Twelve

Gloria came out of her kitchen holding a large plastic pitcher of water. Josephine watched her as she silently walked around the living room of her apartment, going from plant to plant and watering them. First the big palms near her terrace, then the fern she had hanging in the corner and finally the African violets she had sitting on a small bookshelf.

After Josephine finished her school day, she wasn't ready to go home yet. She had tried to call Darren to tell him that she was heading to Gloria's place. He hadn't picked up, so she left a message.

Josephine had found Gloria sitting at home alone, eating a bowl of soup and watching TV. Josephine thanked God that her friend was available on a Friday night to lend her an ear. Though, truth be told, Gloria didn't go out or entertain company nearly as much as she used to.

"Well?" Josephine said.

"Well, what?" Gloria replied in a disinterested tone as she planted a food pellet in the soil of one of her violets.

"Aren't you gonna say anything?"

"You don't want to hear me say anything," Gloria said as she walked back into the kitchen. "If you did, you would have said something to me about this *before* you had lunch with John."

Josephine sighed but remained silent because she knew Gloria was right. Sometimes, it was a pain in the butt how well Gloria knew her.

Gloria returned from the kitchen and sat in the forest green leather recliner facing Josephine. She leaned back so that the chair was fully extended, crossed her ankles on the footrest and shut her eyes.

She looked like she was preparing for oral surgery, like having a root canal was as bad as what Josephine was about to tell her.

"Well, let's have it. What happened?"

Josephine was relieved that Gloria wanted to hear about it. She desperately needed someone to talk to.

"I called him earlier this week to invite him to lunch—"

"Stop. How'd you get his number?" Gloria asked.

"From Mrs. Derossa. John had left it with her in case she needed to get in touch with him."

"Mrs. Derossa? So now your principal knows that her married vice-principal is calling another man?"

Oops. Josephine dropped her gaze to the carpet. She hadn't thought of that.

"You didn't think of that, right?"

A real pain in the butt, Josephine thought.

"So, let's assess. So far since John has been back, you are lying to your husband, lying to your best friend and compromising your standing with your superior at your job. Am I missing anything else?"

"Yeah, some perspective," Josephine replied smartly. "Get real. How have I lied to Darren?"

"Oh, so you told him about John volunteering in your school?" Gloria innocently asked. "Or not?"

A real, *real* pain in the butt.

"Not," Josephine admitted, unzipping her boots and taking them off. She didn't even have to look up to feel Gloria's scolding look. "You know how Darren would've reacted."

"With good reason," Gloria said. "What business does his wife's ex-boyfriend have in that school?"

"That's what this lunch was about," Josephine explained, "so I could ask John point-blank what he was doing up here."

"That's all fine and good, Josephine, but don't you think it should have been you *and* Darren asking John that question?"

Josephine tucked her legs underneath her on the couch. "Maybe, Gloria, I'll concede that point."

"Which is what I would have told you beforehand, if you had told me about your lunch date. Your husband should have been there."

"Maybe. But you know that Darren doesn't know everything about me, and I knew there was a chance that I would want to bring up some things with John that Darren doesn't know," Josephine said. "Like the abortion."

Gloria bolted upright and nodded. "That's true," she said, "you would have had to censor your comments around Darren."

"Not only that, I'd have to sit there and hope that John did the same," Josephine said. "Who wants to be in that position?"

"Understood," Gloria said. She sat quietly but grew impatient when she saw Josephine focus her attention on the movie playing on the TV.

"Well?" she asked. "Did you bring up the abortion?"

"Yeah."

"What did he say?"

"Nothing, he just sat there looking stupid."

Gloria shook her head. "You know, I'll bet he has no idea how much it has affected you all these years."

"Wouldn't surprise me," Josephine answered. "He didn't realize how much it affected me when we were still together." She paused before speaking again. "You know, Gloria, whether I die tomorrow or live to be a hundred and ten, I'm always gonna be a woman who killed her own child."

"Josephine, a lot of women have made that decision. And many of them didn't have the father of the child breathing down their neck to get them to do it. So stop beating yourself up, okay?"

The conversation with John had revived the haunting events of all those years ago, which left Josephine feeling raw and exposed. "Still, I had sovereignty over my body. I could've told John to go to hell."

"And risk alienating the man you thought you were gonna spend the rest of your life with?" Gloria asked. She gazed intently at the bare wall over Josephine's shoulder, as if she was replaying the scenes from eight years ago on it. "Uh-uh, I'm not gonna let you do that to yourself. I remember too well. I remember how much you loved John. And I remember how much you were hurt when he told you he didn't want to be a father. So what were your choices? To either terminate the pregnancy or to have the child against John's wishes—which would have most surely broken up you two—and to then bring a child into a world where only one of her parents wanted her, and to raise her alone, without the man you loved?"

Gloria pinned Josephine in her gaze. "You were in a difficult position, and you made a tough choice. Given the circumstances, it's the choice I would've made, too. It doesn't make you a bad, soulless person, Josephine. In fact, you're the most thoughtful, loving person I know. You have a good heart, and you're gonna make a fantastic mother one day. Okay?"

Gloria wasn't sure how much her words resonated, but she took Josephine's slight nod as acknowledgment that it was okay to move on to another subject. In fact, moving on seemed like the best thing to do.

"Did he brag about his success? Try to throw it up in your face as proof that you should have stayed with him?"

"No, he didn't do too much bragging about that," Josephine said. "But then again, how could he?"

Gloria's eyes widened. "What do you mean, 'how could he?' The man is a multimillionaire."

"I know—I don't mean 'how could he,' but why would he?" Josephine explained. "John knows that money has never been a driving force with me. I was with him when he didn't have a dime, because I wanted to be with him. Hell, I always knew he was gonna be rich. He was too smart and too determined not to make that happen. I didn't leave him because I didn't believe in his ability to make a great pile of money. I left him because I didn't believe in *him* anymore, period." Josephine waved her hand, dismissing the thought of him. "What good is all the money in the world if you feel bankrupt inside?" she asked. "I felt that John stole something precious from me, and money couldn't replace it."

"Understood," Gloria said. "Besides, you're no chickenhead just out for a man's dollars. You make a good living. If you want something, you can go to the bank, withdraw some money and buy it your damn self."

Josephine raised her glass. "You know."

"How-everrr, you could buy a lot more if you were withdrawing from John's bank account."

"Cluck, cluck," Josephine said dryly.

"What else did you guys talk about?"

Josephine leaned back on the couch. "He took swipes at my relationship with Darren."

Gloria's eyebrows furrowed. "How? He doesn't even know him."

Josephine gestured with irritation. "You know, saying that I married Darren on the rebound from him, that I didn't love him."

Josephine took another sip. Over her glass, she could see Gloria's expression had changed considerably.

"Don't tell me you believe that, Glo."

"No, I know you love your husband," Gloria said cautiously. "It's just that . . ."

"Just what?" Josephine asked, slightly annoyed. "The last seven years of my life is part of an elaborate ruse?"

"Jo, like I said, I know you love your husband. But don't sit there and tell me people didn't have misgivings about you getting married so soon after the relationship with John ended. Me, your mother—"

"That's because you're not using the right timeline. My relationship with John ended way before y'all were thinking it did. I hadn't been happy for some time. Darren made me happy. God blessed me with a good man who treated me right who asked me to marry him. So why wait?"

"Why not?" Gloria asked. "A better question is what I asked you seven years ago. What was Darren's hurry?"

Josephine curled her upper lip, Elvis Presley–style. "'Cause he didn't want to lose this good stuff I was putting on him."

Gloria rolled her eyes and tried to stifle a laugh. "Yeah, okay, Ms. Goodpussy." She picked up the TV remote.

"Thank you—thank you very much," Josephine said, imitating the King.

"However, you weren't so confident on your wedding day, though," Gloria pointed the remote at Josephine like she was zapping her. "Were you?"

Low blow. Josephine decided to use that moment to go into the kitchen and rinse her glass out.

"That's not fair, Glo," she called out from the kitchen. "A lot of people are nervous on their wedding day."

Gloria joined her in the kitchen. "True. But there is a difference between having butterflies and looking like you wanted to Marion Jones your ass out of there when I asked you if you were sure about what you were doing."

Josephine didn't respond. She leaned over, opened the dishwasher and put her glass in it.

Gloria leaned against the sink and folded her arms. "I remember it like it was yesterday. We were alone in that room in the back of the church, when I asked you if you were sure you wanted to go through with this. I told you that I could send every one of those people home if you weren't a hundred percent sure this is what you wanted to do. You didn't have to be buffaloed into doing anything you didn't want to do. It wasn't too late."

Josephine closed the dishwasher and faced Gloria as she finished.

"I'll be damned if for a second there, I didn't honestly think you were gonna say cancel the whole damn thing."

"Glo, I don't see how you can take a moment of vulnerability like that and derive any kind of reasonable conclusion from it," Josephine said. "A woman is going through a whirlwind of emotions pulling and tugging her every which way on her wedding day."

"Really?" Gloria asked, frowning. "I thought that was supposed to be the day you were surer than any other day in your life."

Oh, did you now? Josephine thought. I'm surprised you ever thought of wedding days or any notions of permanency at all when it came to men, Ms. Interchangeable Boyfriends. It was time to turn the tables. She had something to make Gloria's ass pipe down.

"John and I also spoke about Jules."

Gloria's body stiffened, then relaxed again to give the appearance of nonchalance.

Too late. Josephine had caught the first reaction. She sauntered over to the breakfast nook, hiding her smirk, and took a seat on one of the stools.

"Yeah?" Gloria opened the dishwasher and busily started rummaging through it. Rearranging dishes that didn't need rearranging. "So how is Jules doing?"

"Oh, fine, he's doing fine. Do you know his daughter is seven now?"

Gloria shut the dishwasher door and gazed out the window.

"Yeah, I guess it has been seven years," she said softly. She started the dishwasher.

Josephine picked up Gloria's intricately cut crystal saltshaker and closely inspected it. "You know, I find that actually using detergent gets my dishes cleaner than just water alone, Glo."

Gloria cut her eyes at her. Josephine was still concentrating on the swirls and patterns of the crystal.

"Smartass." She stopped the dishwasher, reached under the sink and grabbed the Cascade.

Josephine chuckled. "John says that Jules asked about you," she said, blatantly lying.

"Yeah?" Gloria asked as she poured the liquid in. "Now why would Jules ask John about me? I haven't spoken to John since you stopped speaking to him."

Uh-oh. Josephine had to think quickly. "Jules knew John was gonna see me today. Guess he wanted to relay the thought."

"See there?" Gloria said, starting the dishwasher again. "John *tells* his friend about monumental happenings in his life."

"It was just lunch," Josephine reminded her, putting down the saltshaker.

Gloria joined her on the other stool. "A meal shared between you and John after all these years qualifies as monumental."

"Well, anyway," Josephine continued, "John told me Jules is still at a loss as to just why you broke up with him."

Gloria frowned as she moved the saltshaker back to its rightful place. She paused introspectively, then looked at Josephine and chuckled.

"Stop lyin', girl."

"Shoot, I almost had you."

"No you didn't," Gloria said. "Not hardly." She got up and walked back over to the sink. Josephine spun around on her stool to follow her.

"Well, I want to know," Josephine said.

"You already know," Gloria said as she wet and wrung out a dishrag.

"No, I know what you told me."

"It's not complicated—why are we rehashing this?"

Josephine dropped her chin and stared at her like she was touched. "Uh-uh, no you didn't. You can bring up every painful facet of my past, but we can't talk about your shit?"

Gloria reached into her cupboard and took down a bag of microwave popcorn. "What do you mean? I tell you everything."

"Except when it comes to Jules."

"I told you that, too." With her back to Josephine, she put the bag in the oven and set the timer.

"Tell me again, I forget," Josephine said, placing her hands in her lap in anticipation.

Gloria winced with annoyance. When she turned around and saw Josephine's expectant posture, she couldn't help but laugh. "I know how much you liked Jules, Jo—"

"That's right, especially for my friend. Jules is a great guy."

"I know Jules is a great guy." Gloria hopped up on the counter next to the microwave. "I've known Jules since I was seventeen years old. You can't tell me anything about Jules that I don't already know."

Oh, yeah. Josephine sometimes forgot that Gloria and Jules predated her and John. In fact, she had met John through Gloria's relationship with Jules.

The smell of popcorn filled the kitchen as the noise from the microwave competed with the racket emanating from the dishwasher.

She got up and walked over to where Gloria sat.

Gloria said, "You either feel that spark for someone or you don't. Jules was always a great friend to me. When he wanted more, I was game—I tried. But it just wasn't there. That spark."

The timer went off and Gloria hopped down to get the popcorn. Josephine eyed her suspiciously as she carefully opened the bag to let the steam escape. The steam rose and formed a hazy cloud above Gloria's head. Appropriate, Josephine thought, because Gloria's memory was certainly foggy.

For Josephine distinctly remembered how happy Gloria was with Jules. She could never get an answer from Jules or Gloria when she asked why they had broken up. Nor had she seen Gloria as close to a man since.

One thing for sure, that "spark" excuse didn't carry a flicker of truth.

"Well, look at the bright side. At least you didn't get hit this time."

Not physically, John thought. But Josephine's words had inflicted far more damage than any punch could have.

"Yeah, I guess you're right."

"By the way, how's Scent? Did you patch things up?"

John switched the receiver to the other ear. "Scent is gonna do her own thing."

"What?" Jules asked. "That was quick."

"Not as quick as you think," John said. "It's been brewing for a while."

"You dumped her?"

"More like the other way around," John said.

"Uh-uh," Jules said, not buying it. "She wouldn't give up the gravy train."

"Well, she did," John said. "Though maybe she thought I was gonna drop her, or she met someone else, I don't know. She's young. She still wants to party."

"That makes sense. Besides, she probably figures she's done okay for herself," Jules reasoned. "A town house, a Benz, a closet full of clothes . . ."

"Exactly," John said. Jules didn't know about the portfolio. "She's getting her master's in May. What's she need with some old man slowing her down?"

"Nothing anymore." Jules laughed. "She cashed out."

"Shut your ass."

"So, that clears up the muddled picture a little now, doesn't it?"

"What do you mean?"

Jules paused. "I gotta ask you something. What do you honestly expect from Josephine?"

"I don't know," John said uneasily. "But I do know I still feel something for her, Jules. I knew the first time I saw her outside that school."

"No, *really?*" Jules smirked.

John ignored his sarcasm.

Jules continued. "And you're no doubt wondering if she still feels something for you, too. Right?"

"Maybe so," John agreed. "Josephine and I had a connection, that special chemistry. And frankly, no matter how much time has passed, I'm still the man that could whip her into a delirium in bed. Women don't forget those men."

"How do you know Donald isn't a chemist, too?" Jules asked.

John laughed. "First of all, it's Darren. You got me calling that nigga by the wrong name."

Jules chuckled as well. "Aw, man, like you care."

"True," John agreed. "I don't. Second, I can tell Josephine isn't getting fucked right."

"What do you mean?"

"I think the reason Josephine is overeating is because she's not happy."

"John, a lot of sisters gain weight as they get older. So, I guess they're all miserable?"

"I'm not talking about 'a lot of sisters,' I'm talking about Josephine," John said emphatically. "Besides, it's not just her putting on some pounds. I can look at Josephine and see she's not happy."

"And you've come to rescue her?"

"I don't know. Maybe save myself as well." John rubbed his

scalp. "I'm not gonna lie and say I have all the answers. I just know I don't feel complete."

Jules digested that before speaking again. "You have more money than a sheik, pretty women falling all over you, a thriving business, a friggin' mansion, hell, sounds like a pretty complete existence to me."

"A doughnut is complete, Jules, but is it whole?"

There was silence on the other end. Then the sound of uproarious laughter.

"Oh, John, you're so deep!" Jules said in a woman's voice when he was finally able to catch his breath. "Does that stupid shit work with those young girls you're with?"

John grinned as he stood up and walked toward his kitchen. "Again, shut your ass."

"*A doughnut is complete . . . but is it whole?*" Jules repeated in a professorial, earnest tone, then broke up again.

John joined in, too. "Damn, Jules, it was just for analogy's sake."

"So you use a doughnut to make your point?" Jules said. "I believe Mr. T would call that jibber-jabber."

"Yo, man, I can see you're no good tonight, I'm gonna hang up."

"Wait-wait, I got one for you," Jules said. He cleared his throat. "An éclair is filled . . . but is it *fulfilled?*"

John hung up laughing.

Thirteen

The three eighth-grade girls filed into Josephine's office. Their transgression had been leaving school grounds and cutting class. During lunch, they had walked down the street to the pizza shop and hadn't gotten back until after their sixth-period class had started. Josephine was guessing they figured they wouldn't be missed because they had a substitute teacher that period. Fortunately, a security guard caught them sneaking back into the building and ferried them to Josephine.

Two of the girls looked repentant, the other one, defiant. Jabriah Jackson.

Josephine sighed underneath her breath. Jabriah was a royal pain in the ass, primarily because her mother and father had the child believing that she peed liquid gold. Teachers hated dealing with her because her parents would come in blaming everyone and everything except their daughter. If Jabriah got a bad grade, it was because the teacher didn't know how to teach. If Jabriah refused to dress for gym class, then the gymnasium must have been too cold. If Jabriah was in a part of the building she had no business being in, she was simply getting a drink of water. If Jabriah got into a fight, which was fairly often because of her big mouth, then the other child always started it.

Mr. and Mrs. Jackson couldn't stand Josephine, primarily because she didn't respond to their attempts at intimidation. The Jacksons were quick to call downtown and complain to the main office. And everybody, especially the Jacksons, knew how much the higher-ups downtown hated getting calls from irate parents. The Jacksons were masters at the art of subtle intimidation. They always talked about starting petitions. Of attending school board meetings to expose the school's shortcomings. They were the ghettoized versions of Connie Chung and Geraldo Rivera, threatening to expose every ill that afflicted their local school to the world.

If they had been sincere in their objectives, Josephine would have greatly admired their activism. However, she had long ago peeped the true intent of their mission. They weren't crusaders for anything other than getting their child accorded preferential treatment.

Which Josephine wasn't going to kowtow to. She and the Jacksons had butted heads before, but Josephine had remained strong. They had tried to circulate a petition among the parents seeking her dismissal, but the overwhelming majority of the parents respected and trusted Josephine, so they abandoned that tactic. They had tried to call downtown on Josephine, but each time she had stood her ground with her superiors, because she had merely followed procedure. That was critical when dealing with this family. She had to be sure to dot her i's and cross her t's because the Jacksons were waiting for the slightest slip-up so they could blow it out of proportion.

Part of Josephine's fearlessness she knew was attributable to her husband. Darren was the superintendent of one of the most prestigious districts in the state and had friends in the state educational office. The people downtown knew who Josephine's husband was and probably treated her more carefully than other vice-principals in the district.

Even still, Josephine simply didn't believe in backing down to the parents. The importance of being strong with parents was one of the first lessons taught Josephine by her mentor, Mrs. Harris, when she was a rookie administrator. Some of the more ignorant parents would run roughshod over you if they could. Then their kids wouldn't respect you. Once the other students saw that, you would lose the class. Then it was impossible to teach and you might as well find a new line of work. To lose your job because of some loudmouthed, know-it-all parent, who couldn't do half as good a job as you if they tried?

Uh-uh. Josephine couldn't see going out like that.

"Ladies, you know you're not allowed to leave the grounds during school hours," she said, looking at each of the girls in turn. "Frankly, I'm disappointed. As eighth graders—the senior students in this building—I would expect you to set a better example."

Josephine paused. While two of the girls, Maria and Veronica, had their eyes on the floor, Jabriah was pointedly looking at the ceiling as if Josephine was wasting her time.

"Not only that, something could have happened to you. Your parents think that you are secure in this building between eight and three, getting an education. You betrayed their trust and put yourselves in jeopardy by doing so. You could have been the victims of an attack or a robbery, or hit by a car out on the street. All because you wanted a slice of pizza. When you should have been in this building where your parents think you are. Is that how you justify your parents' faith in you, by putting yourselves in danger? By violating their trust? By breaking the school's rules and cutting class?"

"But, Mrs. Prescott, we had a sub."

"Jabriah, I don't care if you had a sub, pizza or chicken wings, it was still wrong."

There was a pause in the room, then the three girls looked at each other and laughed. Josephine allowed a slight chuckle as well. Truth be told, Josephine kind of liked Jabriah, and she could tell Jabriah kind of liked her as well. If anything, Josephine felt sorry for Jabriah. Her parents were doing her a grave disservice by deluding her into thinking that the world owed her something.

"I meant, Mrs. Ford is absent," Jabriah explained unnecessarily. "We have a substitute teacher in science."

"I know what you meant," Josephine said. She opened her desk drawer and took out a stack of her discipline forms.

"Subs don't teach anything."

"That's not for you to decide, Jabriah. Your job is to go to your assigned class."

Josephine took three of the slips out and put the rest back in her drawer. Cutting class was an automatic day of in-school suspension for each class cut. However, leaving campus was an automatic out-of-school suspension. Even if Josephine wanted to give the girls a break by giving them in-school suspension, she couldn't. Not with Jabriah involved. Whenever she committed a transgression, Josephine made sure she followed the book to the letter.

She knew the family too well not to. They were lawsuit happy, always angling for a case. If in the future Jabriah cut lunch to go get pizza again, and was robbed or assaulted while doing so, her parents would sue Josephine and the school for not punishing her more severely the first time she cut.

Josephine noticed Maria's eyes begin to water at the sight of the pink suspension slips. Veronica looked unnerved, too. Jabriah, on the other hand, was as composed as a Kennedy in court.

"You don't have to do mine, Mrs. Prescott."

Josephine looked at her like something bulbous was growing out of her ear. "Thank you, Jabriah, but I don't mind."

"My mom said Mrs. Derossa is to handle all my issues herself."

"Did she now?" Josephine asked. She got up and went over to the file cabinet where she kept her parental contact forms.

"Um-hmm." Jabriah continued, "She and my mother had a meeting about it."

Josephine felt her fingertips go icy as a chill swept over her body. Surely, the child was mistaken. Surely, Mrs. Derossa wasn't crazy enough to do that. Was she? But then, where did the child get the word "issues" from? That sounded too much like one of

Mrs. Derossa's antiseptic terms. "Issues" instead of drama, "issues" instead of nonsense. "Issues" instead of "silly, alcoholic father and lazy, triflin' ass mama."

Too much.

Josephine, with her back to the children, quickly pondered what to do. She realized she needed the full low-down.

"Girls, my secretary is out to lunch and I need some information from her. You three go back to class, I'll deal with you later."

As soon as the girls were out the door, Josephine made a beeline for Mrs. Derossa's office. Inside, Josephine found her sitting at her desk munching on a chef's salad.

"Mrs. Derossa, is there some special arrangement between you and Jabriah Jackson's mother that I need to be aware of?"

Mrs. Derossa put a forkful of ham into her mouth. She eyed Josephine while she chewed. Josephine could tell she was using the opportunity to decide how she was going to respond.

"Arrangement?" Mrs. Derossa asked after swallowing. She busily began gathering another forkful together.

"Yes. Jabriah was just in my office for cutting class. She left school grounds at lunchtime."

Mrs. Derossa's fork did a midair pause and twirl, then continued into her mouth. Again she chewed. She then set her fork down and wiped the corners of her mouth with a napkin.

"I was made aware of some issues that had occurred in the past between you and the Jackson family. So, to alleviate any feelings of persecution, I volunteered to deal directly with any concerns regarding Jabriah, or their second grader, Jamillah."

Josephine couldn't believe this shit. She unfolded and refolded her arms and shifted her weight from foot to foot. "Who made you aware? Central office or the Jackson family?"

Mrs. Derossa rubbed her thumb and her middle finger together. "Both."

"I would have liked to have had the opportunity to present my side of the story to you."

Mrs. Derossa quickly waved her off. "Oh no, Mrs. Prescott. There was no assignation of blame whatsoever—no one is holding you at fault."

"Then, why—"

"Rather, this is an attempt to make your job easier. We know how difficult parents can be once they feel a teacher or an administrator has it in for their child. I don't have any history with the Jacksons, so it was an opportunity to wipe the slate clean."

Please, Josephine thought, give me a break.

"I appreciate the sentiment, Mrs. Derossa, but Jabriah is under the misguided impression that I am not allowed to discipline her."

Mrs. Derossa took a sip of Pepsi One. Josephine noticed the wrinkles form around her mouth as she sucked on the straw.

"Her impression is misguided, isn't it?"

"Mrs. Prescott, it's only one child."

Josephine's arms fell limply by her side. Was this woman so dense that she couldn't see what kind of position she was putting her in? A vice-principal powerless to deal with a student?

Mrs. Derossa noticed Josephine's body language and tried to put her at ease. "I'm not saying that I don't want you to discipline her, Mrs. Prescott. If she's cursing I want you to tell her to watch her language; if she's chewing gum, I want you to tell her to spit it out—"

"And if she leaves the school to go get pizza?" Josephine asked.

"Then I want you to send her to me," Mrs. Derossa replied curtly. "For that and all other serious transgressions. As a matter of fact, I'm going to call her down to the office as soon as I've finished with my lunch."

Josephine was too stunned to do anything, except stand there and be stunned.

"Anything else, Mrs. Prescott?"

"Do you want to handle the disciplining of the other two girls who were with Jabriah today?"

"Other two?"

"Yes. Maria Soriano and Veronica Pratt. I'm sure you want to make sure the girls receive the same uniform treatment."

Josephine thought she caught Mrs. Derossa cutting her eyes at her as she leaned back in her chair. "No, you handle those two."

Josephine waited for her to continue. When she didn't, Josephine spoke again.

"What should their punishment be?"

"What would it normally be?"

"Out-of-school suspension. The parents have to come in to re-admit them."

"Then that's what their punishment should be," Mrs. Derossa said, standing up to signal that the conversation was over. "I'll deal with Jabriah directly."

Josephine turned and headed for the door.

"Mrs. Prescott," Mrs. Derossa said as Josephine opened the door.

"Yes?"

"Speaking of the Jackson family has reminded me of something else," Mrs. Derossa said, coming around to the front of her desk. "I want to inform you that I've chosen Mrs. Jackson to help me with the disbursement of the discretionary fund."

Josephine knew she hadn't heard that right.

The discretionary fund was 10,000 dollars allocated to each school for the principals to use as they saw fit. The money was used for a variety of purposes: to reward classes with pizza parties, to buy Christmas presents for children who wouldn't otherwise receive anything, to purchase clothes and shoes for children whose parents are too destitute or strung out (or locked up) to provide for them, magazine subscriptions, athletic equipment, guest speakers, school supplies, etc. The principal of each school was given a great deal of latitude in using the money the best way they saw fit.

But Mrs. Jackson? Josephine smelled a rat.

Mrs. Derossa leaned against her desk. "Mrs. Jackson is going to help me decide where the money will do the most good in the community. She knows the neighborhood and the families in it quite well. She's sort of an unofficial liaison to the community already, so . . ."

Mrs. Derossa's voice trailed off. She studied Josephine to measure her response.

Who did she think she was kidding? Out of that ten thousand, Josephine could guess a good five of it was going to end up in the "Jackson family fund." Mrs. Derossa was buying the Jackson family's complicity at the expense of the other, more needy, children.

But it was Mrs. Derossa's call, so there was nothing Josephine could do about it. At least she couldn't think of anything right then that she could do about it, so she simply smiled.

"Yes, Mrs. Jackson is very proactive. I'm sure she will be an asset."

Josephine walked back to her office and closed the door behind her. She saw the stack of suspension forms on her desk and remembered that she had to deal with Maria and Veronica. She guessed all that slush money Jabriah's parents were receiving would make her coming suspension easier to take. She heard a racket outside her window.

Josephine turned around and saw that the usual group of men who loitered across the street were having an argument over a loud game of dominoes. All she needed was for one of those fools to pull out a gun and start shooting. That would really cap off her day nicely. Between Mrs. Derossa, the Jacksons, bums across the street, embezzlement . . .

Honestly, Josephine thought, can it get more depressing than this?

She glanced at her desk calendar. Tomorrow was Friday.

She would have to deal with John.

Josephine dropped her head on her desk.

Fourteen

At least Friday didn't start out so badly. Josephine was smiling as she left Ms. Murphy's room. She had completed an observation of the young teacher and was pleased with the way Ms. Murphy had presented her lesson and run her classroom.

Ms. Murphy had had a rocky September, but she seemed to have found her stride now. The children really seemed to take to her and her teaching style. Josephine knew from experience how helpful it was to have the kids like you. If they didn't, they could make your life miserable. Without that rapport, the teacher had to resort to bullying and intimidation to keep order. Personally, Josephine never had the stomach for that.

Josephine was simultaneously walking and jotting down a few notes she wanted to discuss with Ms. Murphy later when she nearly bumped into a child coming out of the rest room.

"Good morning, Mrs. Prescott," the smiling face said.

"Good morning, Jabriah."

Jabriah?

Josephine watched Jabriah leisurely make her way to the water fountain like she didn't have a care in the world. Which might not be too far from the truth if the suspicions Josephine was having were true.

She cut short her walk and went back downstairs to the main office area on the first floor. She knew she'd find Mrs. Derossa in her favorite spot: in her office, with the door closed, perched behind her big desk, chilling.

"Is she in?" Josephine asked Deloris, her secretary.

Deloris's exasperated response had "When *ain't* she in?" written all over it.

Many in the school didn't realize how much time Mrs. Derossa spent hiding in her office. Other than a little paperwork, Josephine had no idea what Mrs. Derossa did all day in there. Was she knitting? Playing video games? Downloading porn off the Internet? Who the hell knew?

One thing the faculty and staff did know is that a good administrator is visible. There were grumblings among many that Mrs. Derossa was "stealing money."

Josephine knocked on the door.

"Yes?"

"It's Mrs. Prescott."

"Come in."

Josephine entered and found Mrs. Derossa at her desk reviewing some paperwork. She decided to get right to the point.

"Mrs. Derossa, do you know that Jabriah is in school today?"

Mrs. Derossa looked like she hadn't a clue where Josephine was going with this. "Why wouldn't she be, Mrs. Prescott?"

"I thought she was to be suspended yesterday."

"Oh," Mrs. Derossa went back to her papers. "I decided to handle the incident another way."

How? Josephine thought. By doing nothing?

"I thought we had agreed to suspend the girls."

Mrs. Derossa continued riffling through her papers, not even giving Josephine the courtesy of eye contact. "Mrs. Prescott, I don't recall any such agreement. Perhaps you misunderstood me."

"I've already suspended the other two girls," Josephine protested.

"How's it gonna look that Jabriah gets off scot-free for committing the same infraction?"

Mrs. Derossa finally looked up. Her face had a sternness to it. When she spoke again, her voice reinforced it.

"I didn't say Jabriah got off scot-free. I said, I handled the incident another way."

There was a tense silence as the two women stared each other down. During which time, Mrs. Derossa must have come to the realization that a confrontation with her invaluable, dedicated vice-principal wasn't such a good idea. During the course of the day, Josephine did her job and most of Mrs. Derossa's job. She also knew that the only thing keeping Josephine at Lyons Avenue School was Josephine. Mrs. Derossa could ill afford to lose her to some school in Morris County.

"Mrs. Prescott, when I reviewed Jabriah's record, I saw that she was suspended three times last year."

"Yes, she was," Josephine said. She recalled each of the incidents clearly. "Twice for fighting, and once for cursing out Mr. Watkins."

"I'm not disputing the validity of the reasons, Mrs. Prescott. Rather, what I'm suggesting is that it would be wise for us to hold on to the suspension card—until we really need it."

Josephine literally swayed, as if that volley of stupidity had really hit her.

"Mrs. Derossa, isn't this a time when 'we really need it'? The child walked off campus in the middle of the day."

Mrs. Derossa gave Josephine a smug I-understand-your-concern head nod. "Yes, that is quite serious, and I gave her a stern talking-to, believe me. She's been dealt with."

Talking-to? Josephine thought. Is this woman mad? Words rolled off Jabriah's back like pee down a drunk's leg. And what, she didn't even bother telling her business partner, Mrs. Jackson, about it?

Josephine shifted her approach. "And what of the other two girls? The ones I suspended for the same offense that Jabriah committed?"

"What of them?" Mrs. Derossa asked. "It's not like they didn't do something wrong."

Unbelievable. Josephine shut her eyes for a few seconds and made a wish. When she opened them, she was still there. No such luck.

Mrs. Derossa saw Josephine just standing there blinking, and must have decided that she needed to add something else to justify her actions.

"Mrs. Prescott," she said, standing up, "you're aware that Downtown frowns upon too many suspensions. This is why I think it's best to keep some in our hip pocket."

Oh, so that was what this was about. She wanted to show Central Office how effective an administrator she was by reducing suspensions—particularly of problem students like Jabriah. So therefore, the baddest of the kids were going to have impunity to cut the fool this year so that Mrs. Derossa could look good to a bunch of suits in some office downtown. Never mind the teachers and staff that had to deal with these headaches. There was no quicker way to lower morale among the faculty than to let them know that there was no support from administration for disciplinary problems.

"Is there anything more, Mrs. Prescott?" she asked. "I have something that needs my attention."

"No," Josephine said. At least she hoped not, she thought as she headed for the door. She couldn't take too much more. Then again, how could it get worse?

She had to ask.

Outside her office door, in the outer lobby area, she saw John. He stood up and approached her.

"Mr. Sebastian is here to see you, Mrs. Prescott," Tia said.

"Thank you, Tia."

Josephine caught a whiff of John's cologne. Whatever it was, it smelled terrific.

"Hi."

"Hello, Mr. Sebastian," Josephine said in a tone devoid of any cordiality.

"Do you have a minute?"

"Actually, I don't," Josephine said, brusquely brushing past him.

"Mrs. Prescott."

Josephine turned back around and saw Mrs. Derossa standing in her office doorway. Her face was contorted like she had just swallowed a piece of chalk.

"I'm certain you can find some time to talk to Mr. Sebastian." She smiled genially. "Perhaps he wants to discuss some aspect of the Boys to Men mentoring program with you. Good afternoon, Mr. Sebastian."

"Good afternoon, Mrs. Derossa."

"Those computers are working out great."

"I'm glad that the kids are putting them to good use."

Josephine grimaced. She gave a thought to bringing up how they were concentrated for just the eighth- and fourth-grade use.

"Actually, Mrs. Derossa, I have a seventh-grade department meeting to attend." Josephine looked at John and gritted her teeth. "Perhaps, if Mr. Sebastian would make an appointment next time . . ."

"Oh, Mrs. Prescott," Mrs. Derossa said, flipping her hand and walking toward John. "Friends of the school like Mr. Sebastian needn't bother with appointments. Particularly if it's something that pertains to the well-being of our children."

Oh, so now you're all about the children, huh? Please. You just don't want to miss out on another possible donation to the school.

"I'll take your meeting for you," Mrs. Derossa added.

Josephine sighed and, knowing it was pointless to argue, began to trudge toward her office.

"My, that's an arresting cologne you're wearing, Mr. Sebastian," Mrs. Derossa said, sniffing the air. "May I ask what it is?"

"Sure, it's Acqua Di Gio."

"Well, it's quite charming."

"Thank you," John said, "And may I say that's a sharp ensemble that you're wearing today."

Mrs. Derossa blushed and giggled. "Oh, thank you."

Geesh, Josephine thought as she stood in her office and waited for them to finish. Were they going to fuck or what?

Mrs. Derossa and John exchanged toothy smiles and then both turned and faced Josephine.

She honestly couldn't decide which one of them she disliked more.

Josephine closed her door behind her. John took a seat at one of the two hardback chairs facing the desk and draped his coat over the other one.

"She seems like a great boss to work for."

"She's just peachy keen," Josephine said, still standing by the door. "What do you want?"

Her nasty tone caught his attention. John knew she might hold some simmering animus toward him about their conversation at the restaurant, but this anger etched on her face seemed too fresh for that.

"Are you okay?"

"I will be as soon as you tell me what you want." Josephine still was gripping the doorknob.

"I wanna talk to you, about last Friday."

His eyes followed Josephine as she went behind her desk and took a seat. She seemed defeated and deflated.

"Are you sure everything is okay, Josephine?"

"Like you care."

"Try me."

Josephine looked at John's face. His concern seemed genuine, and she had to admit it was tempting to unload all her concerns on him. She remembered how protected she used to feel when she was his lady. How warm and comforting it was knowing John had her back, no matter what the circumstances.

John had never failed her. Up until she got pregnant, of course.

Josephine reminded herself that he was the enemy.

"What you said, at the end of lunch last week—"

"Look, John—"

He raised his hand. "Please Josephine, I've been waiting many years to say this to you."

Josephine wasn't sure whether it was the urgency in his voice, or the look she saw in his eyes or what. But she all of a sudden very much wanted to hear what he had to say.

John nervously stood up, thought again and sat back down. He exhaled deeply and leaned forward in the chair.

"I want to tell you that the single greatest regret, the greatest failing in my life is . . ." Josephine watched John struggle for the words. He emitted a nervous cough and continued, ". . . is browbeating you into having that abortion."

She closed her eyes tightly.

"I'm sorry, Josephine," he continued. "I know that there's nothing I can do to make up for it." He rested his elbows on his knees and rubbed his eyes. "I'm ashamed of what I did. I live with my shame every day."

Josephine opened her eyes and stared at her desk. On it lay a piece of construction paper. It was unfamiliar to Josephine. Tia must have put it there when she was out of the office. Josephine gave it a closer look. It was from a second grader, a little boy named Eli. It looked like one of those assignments given to children before Thanksgiving where they were asked what they're thankful for. Eli had written down that he was thankful for Mrs. Prescott, because "she's pretty and nice and she helps me. I love her." Josephine smiled. He had even drawn a crude picture of her, with pink hearts surrounding it. Josephine was touched, but it was a bittersweet feeling, particularly in the context of what John had just said to her. This was somebody else's child saying that he loved her.

"I do too, John," she said quietly. "My shame is that I let you talk me into it. I hate myself for letting that happen."

John bowed his head. "You were just going along, Josephine. You wanted the child, I talked you out of it. It's my deficiency of character, not yours."

Josephine saw a tear fall from John's eye onto the carpet. It both moved and startled her. During all the time that they were in a relationship together, she had never once seen him cry. She remembered asking him why, and he had told her that he had done enough crying during his fractured childhood. As an adult, he was all cried out.

Josephine felt a numbing grief swell against her bosom. So many different emotions were clawing, pulling, tugging at her. A part of her wanted to comfort John. A part of her wanted to strangle him. A part of her wanted answers. That's the part she listened to.

"John, why were you so dead-set against the child?"

John clasped his hands near the bridge of his nose. Then he wiped his eyes. Josephine was again surprised that he had no pretense about being so emotional in front of her. It was so out of character from the John that she remembered that she didn't know what to make of it. While his pain truly looked genuine, Josephine couldn't help but wonder if it was an attempt to con her.

"Josephine," he said in a quiet voice, "the reasons that seemed so valid at the time seem so foolish now." He gestured futilely with his hands, as if trying to stop the scenes of the past from playing in his mind. "I wanted you to be able to stay home with our baby, and I didn't think I was making enough money to support us."

"John, you were making fifty thousand a year," Josephine interceded. "I think we could've managed for a while."

John continued, "And I had plans to start my company. I knew I was going to be devoting a huge amount of time and resources to starting and building my business. And I didn't want to be an absentee father—"

"So you chose your business over your child?" Josephine asked, though it was more of a statement than a question, for she already knew the answer.

"Yes, I did," John admitted. "I was so obsessed with success and money that I couldn't be waylaid." He laughed harshly. "I even convinced myself that I was doing the right thing for our children—when we eventually had some. See, I wanted everything to be in place and ready when we finally had children. I didn't want any child of mine to know what it was like to want for *anything*, like I did growing up."

He saw that Josephine was staring off into space, no doubt replaying scenes from their past just as he was.

"I guess aborting a child in order to provide a better life for your children is some pretty twisted logic, huh?"

Josephine continued to be silent, so John spoke again.

"I wanted us to be married before we had children. And I didn't want any shotgun wedding, either. I wanted to give you a huge wedding. The kind you used to always talk about. Family, friends, tents, band. Remember?"

Josephine nodded. She still wasn't looking at him.

"I had my eye on so many long-term goals, long-range plans that I couldn't see the present, what was right in front of me." John grimaced. "So I apologize to you, Josephine, for being so selfish about what I wanted to do—my plans, my agenda, my expectations—that I couldn't see how another person was also affected."

Josephine said quietly, "*Two* other people were affected. Except one isn't here for you—or me—to apologize to."

John gave a slight motion of acknowledgment.

They sat in silence for a minute, each coming to terms with their collective past. Each wondering, "What if?"

John spoke first:

"Josephine, why haven't you had any children?"

Nothing like that subject to bring her mind back to the present. She stiffly righted herself in her chair. "Well, Darren and I plan on having them soon, probably next year, as a matter of fact. We decided to wait, you know, until now."

Josephine made up a reason to go into her desk drawer. As she did, she felt John's eyes on her. She wondered if he could tell that she was lying. She closed the drawer and stood up.

"Well, I have something that needs my attention," Josephine said, using the same line that Mrs. Derossa had used on her.

"Right," John said as he rose from his chair, "you are at work."

"Yes, I am."

John smiled at her. The same smile that used to melt her.

"Do you have any idea how proud I am of you?"

Josephine looked at him strangely. "Huh? What?"

"'Huh?'" John mimicked. "I'm proud of you, that's what, Ms. Vice-Principal."

"First of all, it's *Mrs.* Vice-Principal."

John yawned and rolled his eyes.

"Second, you're the one who is the multimillionaire entrepreneur, rags-to-riches success story." Josephine hesitated as she thought about how far John had come. "I should be proud of you." And she was, though she couldn't bring herself to say it.

"Uhhn-uuhn," John said. "Any fool can get lucky and make money. You, on the other hand, are a rich *person*. You could have any job you wanted, and yet you chose to come back here and try to make a difference."

Josephine needed to hear that. It had been a frustrating week. The kind of week that made her question whether she'd made the right decision.

"I'm trying to be more like you." John looked at his watch. "I have another hour until I meet with the fellas." He put his leather jacket back on. "I'm gonna go grab me a bite to eat."

"You know," Josephine said, "I'm just allowing you to get your feet wet a little longer before I ask you how the Boys to Men program is going."

"More likely you're expecting me to quit anyway, so you figured, why bother?"

Josephine smiled.

"Right?" John needled.

"Maybe," she replied.

"Well, you can forget that, Josephine. As P. Diddy and the Family have been known to say, *'I ain't go-ing nowhere.'*" John rapped the lyrics and completed his performance with a rendition of the Harlem Shake.

Josephine chuckled despite her attempts not to.

Buoyed by the sound of Josephine's laughter, John went into full-fledged shit-talking mode. "I ain't going nowhere because *(a)* I'm a changed man with different priorities. One of which is to be of some benefit to someone other than myself. To give back to the community."

"Yeah, yeah, we'll see," Josephine said. "Just get to *(b)* so you can hurry up and leave my office."

John slowly strolled to the door. When he got there he turned back to face her. "And *(b)* is"—John zipped his coat up and grinned at her—"well, you know what else I'm here for."

Josephine smirked. "You should've stuck with *(a)*."

Fifteen

Darren was busily cutting up onions and green peppers when Josephine walked into the kitchen. She came over to him and gave him a kiss. "Hey, babe."

"Hey, honey."

"What'cha doing?"

"Making my world-famous beef kabobs."

"Umm, good." Josephine wrapped her arms around him and rested her head on his back. She began rubbing his chest. "How was your day?"

"Same as usual," he replied. "Excuse me."

Josephine was hoping he would inquire about hers, but she released him so he could check on the beef in the refrigerator.

"I've been marinating these babies since yesterday morning." Darren held them under her nose so that she could see his handiwork.

"Very nice, babe."

Darren set the bowl down and went back to his chopping board of vegetables. Josephine again sidled alongside him and rested her head on his shoulder. She whimpered softly.

"Josie, can you get the rice down for me?" Darren asked without looking up.

Josephine went over to the cupboard and grabbed a box of Uncle Ben's and placed it next to the stove. She was on her way back to her husband when he asked her to get the skewers out of the drawer. After that it was the grill out of the closet. When Darren asked her to get the pot out of the cabinet for the rice, Josephine had had enough of his busy work.

"Aren't you gonna ask me how my day went?" she asked.

"No," Darren said, again without looking up from his food. "I tend not to ask questions I already know the answer to."

"What do you mean?"

Darren finally did her the courtesy of facing her. "You had a lousy day. An awful day—you can't believe the nonsense you have to put up with." He showily waved the knife in the air. "You're surrounded by incompetents. The people downtown, your principal, staff members, the parents. You can't take it!" He took the knife and pretended he was cutting his throat.

Asshole. "Don't let me stop you," Josephine said.

"Josie," Darren said, setting down the knife, "it's just that it's the same thing every day."

Josephine folded her arms. "It is not every day."

"All right. Every other day."

"Or every other day," Josephine said. She bit her bottom lip, trying to keep from crying. Darren had hurt her feelings, or maybe she was just emotional from her day, or maybe she still had a cry in her from what she and John had spoken about earlier, but whatever the reason, tears started streaming down her face. "I barely come to you at all with anything, for fear of the reaction that I'll get. Don't worry, though, I won't anymore."

Josephine brushed past him and out of the kitchen. She went into the living room and sat on the sofa. Ten seconds later, Darren appeared in front of her holding a box of tissues. "Here, babe, blow your nose."

Josephine snatched a couple of tissues out of the box.

"May I sit down?"

"Isn't George Foreman awaiting you?" Josephine asked coldly.

"The cooking can wait." Darren sat down and began rubbing Josephine's shoulder. She shrugged him off.

"I deserve that," he said. "Josie, I apologize if I seem callous. It's just that I don't know what you want me to do."

Try being a husband.

"You tell me these problems every day. . . ."

Josephine turned and glared at him.

"Not every day," John said, smartly rephrasing. "But when you do, I feel powerless. I can't help you if you won't let me."

"Darren, it's not always about you helping me. Sometimes I just want you to listen to me."

"Josie, do you think it's easy to hear the woman I love complain constantly—"

Oh, so, now we're back to *constantly* again, Josephine thought.

"—about her job? It's not. Sometimes I dread bringing up my job to you for fear that you will bring up yours, and tell me about a thousand indignities you had to suffer through while attempting to do your Mother Teresa act in the hood."

"How come it's always about you?" Josephine asked. "About what you have to put up with, how things affect you?"

Darren sighed. "That's not what I meant, Josie, and you know it."

"No, that's exactly what it sounds like you meant to me."

"Josie, I see that my wife has a problem," Darren chopped his hands to emphasize his point, "so I want to fix the problem. Luckily, I'm in a position to fix the problem. It frustrates me that my wife won't let me."

"I don't want you to fix my problems, Darren," Josephine explained. "Like I said, I just want you to listen to me."

Darren spread his arms out in exasperation. "Why would you tell me about problems that you don't want to find a solution for? That makes no sense."

Josephine wiped her nose. "Not everything has to have your imprint on it for you to be of help to me. Sometimes I just need an encouraging word. Sometimes I just need your ear, to know that I'm not in this alone."

Darren looked at her like she was babbling Swahili. "An encouraging word? No problem. How about I give you a bunch of encouraging words? I have a vice-principal at one of my schools going out on maternity leave in February. We're starting the process of interviewing for her replacement next week. I can guarantee you that position. Once you're in the district there are two more full-time administration jobs opening up in September. I can guarantee you one of those positions as well." Darren held out his hands like he was holding a platter. "Are you interested?"

"You know the answer to that," Josephine sniffled.

"Of course not," Darren exclaimed showily. "That would make too much sense. That would actually *address* your problem." He shook his head repeatedly. "No, no, no, we can't have that. What would we have to complain about every day?"

There was nothing Josephine hated more than when Darren started making with the dramatics. The man overacted worse than Sidney Poitier. Even more troubling to her, however, was what he had just said.

"You think I work in Newark just so I can have something to complain about?" She looked at him, amazed. "That I need to be pitied?"

"If the Timberland boot fits, sport it, my sista."

No, there was one thing she hated more than Darren's drama, and that was his attempts to talk urban. The only hood Darren had ever been in was made by J. Crew.

"I cannot believe you think that low of me."

"I don't believe it's something you do consciously, Josie," Darren said. "But think about it. Why would someone want to go someplace miserable every day when there is a better alternative awaiting them?"

"If you have to ask, then it's obvious you wouldn't understand, so why should I even bother?" Josephine muttered.

"Oh, here it comes, the blacker-than-thou speech." Darren raised a fist in the air. "Each one, teach one; power to the people; no justice, no peace; without struggle there can be no progress—did I forget any?"

"Yeah, this one." Josephine stuck her middle finger up at him.

"Ah," Darren said, laughing, "you can take the girl out of Newark—"

"Fuck you," Josephine said, getting up and away from him.

"Oh, further proof. But you can't take the Newark out of the girl." Darren's voice followed her out of the room.

When Darren came into the bedroom a while later, Josephine was under the covers in bed facing the wall.

"You want something to eat?"

"No."

Darren sat on the edge of the bed. "You want some company?"

"No. I know how tired you are of my constant whining."

Darren exhaled deeply. "I deserve that, I suppose. But I'm not going to apologize for loving my wife."

"Humph, is that what you call it?"

"Yes, it is, Josie," Darren said, taking off his shoes. "I want to see you happier, less stressed. The administrators in my district don't have to deal with one-tenth the nonsense that you have to deal with on a daily basis." He grimaced. "When I'm in one of the schools, I take special note of the female administrators. I see them walking around there. Their biggest concern is what to wear to work. Then I think about my wife, having to deal with ignorant parents, kids who know no boundaries because of said ignorant-ass parents, incompetent, poorly trained staff, an incomprehensible bureaucracy, violence—"

"Violence? Darren, the place where some kid is more likely to shoot up the place is in one of your affluent schools."

"You know what I mean."

Josephine turned over to face him. "Yes, I do. The problem is, you don't even try to understand me."

Darren shook his head. "Josie, I was just thinking when I was downstairs eating. When we first got married, I had no idea that you were going to want to stay in Newark."

"I guess there were a lot of things we didn't discuss before we were married." Josephine thought about how Darren hadn't told her about his first marriage. "We didn't date very long beforehand."

"I know," Darren said, "but I never envisioned that being an issue."

"You never asked me."

"Again, I didn't think there would be a need to. How could I? Who could foresee someone wanting to stay in Newark instead of Morris County?" Darren asked, incredulous. "I thought once I rose to a position where I could secure you a job in my district, you would leap at the chance to make the move."

"Again," Josephine came right back at him, "I don't know why you think you've got some utopia over where you work, but I don't want to work in a school ninety-percent Caucasian. I'm sorry if you can't see why I would want to work where I can help at-risk black and Latino children."

"What's the difference?" Darren asked. "You're lucky if you reach ten percent of them. You might as well be dealing with the ten percent black and Latino children in my district."

"Your kids are hardly at-risk, Darren," Josephine said dryly.

"Oh, okay." Darren stood up. "I see. The only way one can really 'represent' and all that jazz is to do so in the hood. Perhaps we should move to Newark so we can 'keep it real' all the time."

Josephine laughed. "Is that supposed to be some sort of threat? I grew up in Newark. You're the one who would die without a Starbucks on every corner."

"'Grew up in Newark,'" John grumbled. "You say it like you're proud."

"'*Grew up in Newark,*'" Josephine mimicked. "You say it like I should be ashamed."

"No, but I see it for what it is: a circumstance, not a badge of honor. My parents could afford to raise me in Connecticut, so they did. If your parents could have afforded to raise you in another environment, don't you think they would have? I see they moved out once they had the opportunity to do so."

Josephine rolled her hands. "Your point?"

"That maybe it's time for you to follow their lead and do the same."

"If and when that time comes, you will be the first to know. Until then, leave me the hell alone about any and all things Newark."

"Oh, really?" Darren sniffed haughtily.

Josephine turned her ass back to him. "Yeah, really."

"Well," he snarled, "let me make it abundantly *clear* so there is no confusion about the matter in the future."

The nasty edge to his voice made her take notice. Josephine turned back over to see his face. The anger in his eyes matched his tone.

"I constantly offer you a way out of your predicament, and you never take it. Fine. If you don't want to hear me speaking ill of your beloved city or school, then I don't want to talk about it anymore, period. I'm not going to censor myself for you. You hear me, Josie?"

It wasn't often that Darren got this loud and animated. Josephine was taken aback. She also noticed he had his fists clenched by his sides.

Darren leaned over the bed. "I don't wanna hear a good goddamn about Derossa, your problems with staff, red tape"—John pounded his fist into the mattress with each problem, causing the bed to shake—"Downtown—nothing about your wretched fucking job! You want pity, look for it elsewhere! You want a solution, you come to me. Got it?"

Darren glared at her to see if she had anything to say. Josephine turned back toward the wall and listened for the sound of Darren's footsteps leaving the room.

Only after she heard them was she able to release her tears.

Sixteen

"My boys," Mr. Duke said warmly. He greeted John and Jules with hugs as they stepped into his condominium.

"It's okay if we stop by unannounced, right?" Jules asked. "You ain't got no pretty young thing up in here, do ya?"

"What?" Mr. Duke said, feigning confusion. "Y'all didn't pass her on the way up?"

They all laughed and sat down in the small living room, Jules and John on the sofa, Mr. Duke in his favorite recliner.

"Speaking of pretty girls, where's Nakira?" Mr. Duke asked, turning down the volume of the Clint Eastwood western he was watching so they could talk.

"I don't have her this weekend. She's with her mother."

Mr. Duke frowned.

"What, I can't come up here without my daughter?" Jules asked.

"Not when you with this cat," Mr. Duke said, jabbing his thumb toward John. "That's just too much concentrated ugly in one place. Y'all need Nakira to help balance y'all out."

John waved his hand at Mr. Duke. "Aww, go somewhere, old man."

Mr. Duke slapped his knees with his palms. "That's the whole point—I'm not going anywhere. I gotta live here. Last time y'all came by here, they raised my association fees, 'cause you two ugly jokers killed every blade of grass y'all passed on the way up here with y'all's concentrated ugliness. It's bad enough when one of you funny-lookin' cats is alone, but when y'all together—geesh." Mr. Duke said, shaking his head, "A double whammy of ug-ly."

John turned to Jules. "Mr. Anthony, does this Redd Foxx–looking, Don Rickles wannabe, old-timer got jokes?"

"I believe so, Mr. Sebastian. But what should one expect from a man wearing janitor pants?"

"Wh-what?" Mr. Duke exclaimed.

"True, true, true," John said, nodding his head in agreement. "Which he owns in a wide array of colors from blue to green to . . . well, to blue-green. . . ."

"Ahh," Jules said, "and I believe he is sporting a pair of the permanently creased blue-green ones right now."

"Now I know you fools done lost your collective minds," Mr. Duke said, standing up. He pointed to his pants. "Y'all don't know anything about style." He stuffed his hands into the pockets. "Look at these deep pockets, you like that, don'cha?" Next, he turned sideways and pulled on the back of a leg. "Lookit all that leg room, boy!" Next came the creases. "Sharp, ain't they? What you two know about that?" He then pointed toward the floor. "Check out those cuffs, they tight, ain't they? Stitched the whole way around . . ."

As Mr. Duke went over each feature, Jules and John broke up a little more each time.

"And check out the room in this crotch. . . ." Mr. Duke reached for his zipper.

"Hey, hey, hey!" they both said simultaneously. "We don't need to see that."

Mr. Duke smirked. "Worried about not measuring up, huh?"

With that they all laughed.

"Yo, man, we just came by to treat you to dinner," John said, "and this is the thanks we get? Insults?"

"Dinner?" Mr. Duke perked up. "Now you boys are talking my language."

Jules looked at Mr. Duke's belly protruding underneath his undershirt. "Looks like some of the languages you've been speaking lately are Italian, Chinese, Mexican. . . ."

"What are you talking about, son?" Mr. Duke said, patting his stomach. "That's all solid."

"By solid you mean 'thick,' 'substantial'?" Jules asked.

"Naw, we're talking about my stomach, not your noggin." Mr. Duke looked at it and ruefully shook his head. "I always told your mama that she should've sued the doctor over the size and shape of your cranium. It just doesn't make any kind of sense."

John chuckled. "Where you wanna eat, Slappy?"

Mr. Duke stroked his chin. "Mrs. D's. I got a hankering for some smothered pork chops, oxtail, rice. . . ."

John groaned. "I just left the city. You can't think of anyplace out here?"

"Son, if you want quality, you gotta be prepared to travel."

"John already knows that, Mr. Duke," Jules said. "He's already traveled six hundred miles back to Jersey seeking a quality woman."

John shot Jules a look that screamed the word "asshole."

Mr. Duke gave John a sly look and sat down. "I thought you came up here for business reasons."

"I did," John said, catching the look as he also took a seat. "But somebody set it up so that I was going to be in close proximity to an old flame of mine."

"You don't say?" Mr. Duke said innocently. "What happened next?"

John just stared. He was doing a great job of looking clueless, knowing he had been the one to put these wheels in motion. "Well, I've begun to reassess some things about my life, that's all."

"Yeah? Imagine that," Mr. Duke said. "And the young chippy?"

"Gone," Jules chimed in.

Mr. Duke faked startlement and looked at John with widened eyes. "Imagine that!"

"All right, you two," John said, "knock it off. If a by-product of me being up here is that I can get reacquainted with Josephine, then . . ." His voice trailed off.

"How you ever let that good girl get away is beyond me," Mr. Duke said, shaking his head.

John shrugged his shoulders. He had never told Mr. Duke the true cause of the breakup. He had been too ashamed. He also knew that Jules hadn't, either.

Mr. Duke looked at the two of them. "Is Josephine still married?"

"Yeah."

Mr. Duke grunted, leaned back in his chair and closed his eyes, the way he did whenever he was in deep thought. John had once asked him why he closed his eyes. His response was that sometimes a man could see things more clearly in the dark.

Mr. Duke opened his eyes and stood up. "Be careful." He then briskly rubbed his hands together. "Now let's go eat."

John and Jules looked at each other, surprised.

"Is that it?" John asked.

Mr. Duke, who was already on his way to the closet to get his coat, stopped and turned back to him. "You're right, I wanted you to see Josephine again. I was hoping her reentry into your life would allow you to do a little introspection—since you're hardheaded and don't listen to anybody else." Mr. Duke gestured slightly. "Maybe deep down, on some level, I was hoping that you two would get back together again. You know how fond of her I am. Of course, that was wishful thinking on my part. I was also hoping that she was available.

"You know what? The last time I trusted a woman with you was

Josephine. I always felt my boy was safe when you were with her—like there was no way in hell that she would let harm befall you, if she could help it. Now, I don't know why y'all broke up," Mr. Duke stretched his palms out, "and I'm not sure I wanna know. But what I do know is how much that girl loved you, and how rare a love like that is. A person should consider himself lucky if he finds it once in his lives. Now, if Josephine has been blessed to find it twice, then okay, but if she hasn't, then. . . ." Mr. Duke left it at that as he rubbed the back of his graying head.

"So like I said, be careful. Okay?"

John nodded. He stood up.

"I mean it, John," Mr. Duke emphasized. "There's many a man lying in a plot buried somewhere because of a woman."

"I know, Mr. Duke. I will."

"Don't worry, Mr. Duke," Jules said, also rising out of his seat. "Josephine's husband is a softie." He remembered how Dorian (or whatever the hell his name was) had ended his and Josephine's friendship. "A jealous, insecure softie."

"Those are the main ones you gotta watch out for," Mr. Duke said, "the ones that feel their entire manhood is measured by the woman they got. They feel they got the most to lose, because they don't think they can get another woman. At least, not another good one like Josephine. You gotta ask yourself, where does that insecurity come from? It's a short walk from insecurity to instability to plain ol' nutty."

John and Jules looked at each other, both thinking the same thing. Some background information on Darren would be helpful.

"All right, let's go eat." Mr. Duke opened his closet door. "If everything works out for you, John, then we can work on finding this joker here a woman." He shook his head mournfully at Jules. "Talk about the deck being stacked against you. . . ."

Jules sneered. "Yeah, okay. By the way, why don't you wear the jacket that matches your pants?"

"What are you talking about?"

"You know, the one with the patch that says Custodian next to the lapel."

John and Jules laughed, and even Mr. Duke had to admit it was funny.

"Oh, so now Chris Rockhead got jokes. . . ."

Josephine lay in bed looking at the ceiling.

She and Darren had just had make-up sex, but she hadn't been into it at all. Hadn't even put forth the effort of faking an orgasm.

Darren had apologized for raising his voice. But Josephine's problem wasn't just how he had said it, but what he had said, period.

Josephine had played her dutiful role, though. She had played it so many times by now that it had become second nature. She would accept Darren's apology, whatever gift he had in hand (this time a little "I'm sorry" teddy bear from the Hallmark store down the street), act like his words hadn't hurt her as much as they had and then eventually end up just as she was now: with his arm draped over her, his nose snoring into her ear and his still wet (or, by now, dry) penis rubbing against her backside. She knew Darren loved her, but damn, he could be so extra at times.

She was also thinking about that conversation she'd had with John earlier in her office. Now was as good a time as any, she figured. She took a deep breath and nudged her husband.

"Darren . . . Darren, wake up."

"Umph."

"Darren, wake up."

"Wh-what is it, babe?"

"We need to talk." Josephine reached over and turned on the lamp.

Darren squinted, then shielded his eyes from the light with his forearm. "About what?"

Josephine took a deep breath. She wasn't of a mind to be dismissed tonight. "About having a baby."

"Good Lord." Darren buried his face beneath his pillow.

"Darren, I think we should both go to that fertility clinic in Morristown."

Even under the pillow, Josephine could hear Darren sigh.

She sat up. "You know what? I don't get you. When I married you, I was twenty-eight and you were thirty-six. We both said we were ready for children back then. Here it is seven years later, and you have no sense of urgency."

Darren removed the pillow. "Hey, men can father babies well into their eighties."

"You should've kept the pillow over your head if you were gonna say something that stupid."

"Josie, those fertility clinics are just a waste of money—a lot of money, I might add—designed to prey upon vulnerable couples." He touched her shoulder. "We'll have children when God sees fit for us to be parents."

Josephine hated how Darren did that, used God to his advantage whenever it was to his benefit. Never mind the fact that he hadn't seen the inside of a church since he was christened.

"Maybe God wants us to go to the fertility clinic," she retorted.

Darren lifted himself up onto his elbows. He put that fake sincere look on his face that Josephine immediately recognized. It usually was the harbinger of some bullshit.

"Josie," he said softly.

Uh-oh. Josephine now *knew* she was in trouble. He had the phony heartfelt tone in his voice, too.

"Before we worry about spending thousands of dollars at some fertility clinic," Darren said soothingly, "why don't you knock off those extra pounds and see if we can get pregnant naturally?"

Josephine felt her whole body flush with anger and embarrassment. Mostly anger. Every extra pound of her wanted to smack Darren.

"What in the blue hell does that have to do with me getting pregnant?" she asked.

"Well, first of all, I'm not the unfeeling jerk you're trying to make me out to be—"

"You could've fooled me," Josephine said, "with your insensitive ass. What are you trying to say? That you're not as attracted to me as when I was thinner?"

"Josie—"

"Because I hope that's not it," Josephine said. "Otherwise, we have a problem. Some man's semen is constantly making messy appearances around my body. Doesn't look like you have a problem getting your rocks off to me."

Now, me, on the other hand, Josephine was going to say, but she decided not to play that card just yet. She knew once she told her husband that she hadn't had an orgasm since God knows when it could have a devastating impact on her marriage. A man's ego was too fragile for that.

"That's because you got some good pussy," Darren said, making an attempt at levity.

Josephine narrowed her eyes at him.

Darren hesitated, but then decided that since he had already broached the sensitive subject, he might as well see it the whole way through.

"Josie, it has nothing to do with aesthetic reasons. Of course I'm still attracted to you. I'm talking strictly physiological." Darren shrugged his shoulders and tilted his head to the side, as if it pained him to have to say what he was about to say. "Dr. Kolb told me that obesity in a woman can hinder pregnancy."

"Obesity?" Josephine kicked off the covers and clambered out of the bed. "Who the fuck are you calling obese?"

"Babe—babe, it's just a word. That means thirty percent above your recommended weight," Darren quickly explained.

Josephine glowered at him. "And what in your highly valued opinion is my recommended weight?"

"Well, according to all the governmental and insurance charts, a woman your height should be about one hundred and twenty-five pounds."

"One hundred twenty-five pounds!" Josephine said, shocked. "I haven't weighed that since I was in high school. If that's what you want, then I suggest you go get you a skinny white woman, which is whom those charts were designed for. Shiiit, a black woman's hips, thighs and ass alone weighs *one twenty-five*."

"Whatever, Josephine," Darren said as he sat on the edge of the bed. "You can get cute all you want, but let me hit you with some facts. You've gained a lot of weight since we've been married. If you get pregnant, you're gonna gain even more weight, which puts you at risk for hypertension, diabetes and a host of other ailments. In addition, with the weight added from the pregnancy on top of the weight you've already gained, that doesn't bode well after the delivery. You'll then have a ton of weight to lose."

Did this Negro just say "a ton"? Josephine looked around the room for something to hit him with.

"Not to mention that Dr. Kolb showed me a study where couples who had trouble conceiving went for fertility treatment. In the samples where the woman was significantly overweight, the cost for them to have a baby was 250,000 dollars. The cost where the woman was of normal weight was 4,500 dollars. That's a helluva difference, Josie. One is life savings–second mortgage money. The other is the cost of a vacation." Darren took a deep breath. "Now, I'm not saying you're significantly overweight—"

"Naw, you're just saying I'm *obese*."

"But doesn't it stand to reason that before we even *think* about going to a fertility clinic and spending, let's say half that amount—125,000 dollars—that we get your weight down first? For all the health reasons and for the financial reasons."

Josephine leaned against the dresser. She couldn't argue with that, because it was the truth. But her feelings were badly bruised. For a long time she had thought something had gone terribly wrong during her abortion that prevented her from having a baby. When all the tests proved otherwise, she thought her inability to get pregnant was God's punishment for the abortion. To now have to deal with the notion that she was inhibiting pregnancy because she was too fat? And even more, that if by some miracle she was able to conceive, she would place undue stress on the child because of her being overweight? That was too much for her to take.

She lashed back at her husband. "Why are we so sure it's me? Maybe it's you."

Darren sighed. "Josie, every sperm test I've ever taken indicated that everything is normal for me. Part of the reason I left Dr. Harris was because you wanted me to get a second opinion."

Josephine glowered at him. "Why are you putting that on me? I never told you to leave Dr. Harris. I liked Dr. Harris."

Josephine had never really understood why Darren had dropped Dr. Harris as his primary doctor. He had been his doctor since Darren got out of college.

Darren ignored her. "So I switched physicians. My current doctor, Dr. Kolb, tells me the same thing. I have an average sperm count for a forty-three-year-old man. If you want me to switch doctors again so they can run the same battery of tests, I will do so, but I am not going to some clinic and wasting untold tens of thousands of dollars. That's what I'm *not* gonna do."

"Not even to make your wife happy?"

"No, not even to make my wife happy. I'm making an executive decision. How happy will you be when that money is sucked out of our savings needlessly?"

Josephine knew he was right. If she was sincere in her desire to have a baby, she should put herself in the best position possible to do so. If that meant losing weight, she should buckle down and do so.

Darren joined her by the dresser. He kissed her shoulder.

"Babe, for all you know, you may be pregnant right now, so relax." He began stroking Josephine's thick hair. "I know one thing. When it happens, you will make a fantastic mother. You ready to go back to bed?"

Josephine nodded.

She lay back down with her husband, but she was hardly able to relax. In fact, the thoughts taking residence in her head only caused her more turmoil.

Seventeen

Jules shut the heavy door behind him. It was a frigid December day, and it felt good to get indoors. His cheeks felt like he had just traversed the Arctic tundra walking the short distance from his car to the building. Fuck what the weatherman said about it being average temperature for this time of year. The wind chill made it feel like it was ten degrees below a witch's tit, he groused silently.

He took off his gloves and stuck them into his coat pocket. Straight ahead of him lay the auditorium.

"May I help you?"

Jules noticed the school security guard sitting at a desk to his left—a slight, balding, older gentleman reading the *Star-Ledger*.

"Yes, can you tell me where the main office is?"

"Third door on your left."

"Thank you. By the way, do you know where the Boys to Men club meets?"

"They'll be able to tell you all that in the main office."

Jules walked into the office.

"Hi, may I help you?" Tia perked up, as she did every time an attractive man walked into the office.

"Hello, I'm looking for Mrs. Flowers, er, I mean, Prescott," Jules said, remembering Josephine's married name.

"Do you have an appointment?"

"No."

"And who may I say is asking to see her?" Tia asked, playing with her earring.

"Jules Anthony."

"Does she know the nature of your business?" Tia asked. She was trying to find out more information about Jules, to find out whether it was safe to go into full-fledged flirtation mode.

"No. But I'm an old friend."

"Okay," she said. She left Jules with a lingering smile. Jules checked out her butt as she walked to Josephine's office. Not bad, but she seemed a little young.

"Mrs. Prescott will see you now."

"Thank you."

Jules walked into the office and was greeted by a warm hug from Josephine. "Hey, stranger."

"Hey girl, how you been?"

"I've been great. How's Nakira?"

"Grown."

Josephine laughed and motioned to a chair. "Sit, sit."

Jules couldn't help but contrast his greeting from Josephine with the one John had received in this very office. He'd take a hug over a slug any day.

"You've been to Broadway lately?" she asked as she settled into her chair.

Jules had to think about it as he took off his coat. "It's been a while. The last play I saw was *The Producers*. You seen it?"

"No, I haven't," Josephine said. "Was it good?"

"Very," Jules said. "I wouldn't mind seeing it again. Maybe we can catch it together."

"Maybe." Josephine smiled wistfully. She'd bet Darren would just *love* that. Seeing Jules reminded Josephine of how much fun they used to have.

"So what do I owe the pleasure of this visit, Jules?"

"I'm here to meet with my partner in crime, and to see about signing up for that mentor program thing he's doing."

"That's great, Jules," Josephine said, then frowned. "Oh, shoot. I forgot there's a game today. An away game. The Boys to Men meeting was cut short because of it. John is with the team at West Kinney School."

"With the team?"

"He's an assistant coach with the girls basketball team."

"Oh, yeah?" Jules checked his watch. "That's just my luck," he added, leaning back in his chair. He sat up again with a start. "Wait a minute, the *girls* team?"

Josephine smiled mischievously. "Hey, that's where the need was."

Jules laughed.

"He wasn't expecting you?"

"Naw," Jules said, "I thought I'd surprise him."

"Well, you'll just have to settle for surprising me," Josephine said, smiling.

"No problem," Jules said, returning her smile. "How's the school year coming for you so far?"

Josephine waggled her hand to signify that it's been up and down. "How about you? How's the transportation business?"

Jules nodded. "I can't complain."

"Yeah, Jules," Josephine said, "John has been a nice addition around here."

"Has he now?"

"Yes. Did he tell you that he donated a hundred computers to the school?"

"Yeah," Jules said, crossing his legs casually, "I believe he did mention something about that."

"But even more impressive has been how giving he has been with his time. The boys in the program really like him—he's had a positive impact on a couple of them already. Their behavior, their performance in school."

"Yeah?"

"Mm-hm." Josephine nodded. "And you know the girls on the team just adore him. Half of them have crushes on him."

Jules eyed Josephine carefully. "Sounds like John is really making an effort."

"Yeah," Josephine vacillated, then relaxed and smiled. "I've got to hand it to him, he really is. Meets with the boys on Fridays, girls basketball practice a couple of days a week after school. Sometimes he'll even pop in on a Monday to check on one of his mentees. I don't know how he's running a business."

Good point, Jules thought. Whereas before he and John could scarcely have a conversation without work coming up, now John rarely brought up his business. Jules wondered how truly motivated John still was to expand his company.

"You know, he rented office space right in the National Bank Building on Broad Street."

"Really?" Josephine said, tapping a pencil on her desk. "I didn't know his base was in Newark. What exactly is his business?"

Jules threw his arms out. "You gotta ask him 'cause I still don't know. He's like Tommy off *Martin*. Nobody knows what he does for a living."

Josephine chuckled. "You really don't know?"

"Something about chemical systems . . . safety . . . filtration-designing—I don't know," Jules admitted. "It's a lot more complicated than driving people around in limos, that's all I know."

Josephine had been thinking about something Jules said earlier. In the past, she would have felt more than comfortable asking Jules to explain something, whether it pertained to John or not. But now they were practically strangers. She decided to ask him anyway. At least then she would know where she stood with Jules. Whether to keep him at arm's length or not.

She leaned forward and rested her forearms on her desk. "Jules, what did you mean earlier when you said, 'John is really making an effort'?"

Jules shifted in his chair. "What do you mean, Jo?"

"That's what I'm asking."

Jules hoped he sounded convincing. "The things you were talking about earlier. The girls basketball, the Boys to Men thing. It sounds like he's really making an effort to do some positive things around here."

"Oh, okay." Josephine set her pencil down and reached in her drawer for a mint. "Have one?" she said, holding the tin of Altoids out to Jules.

"No, thank you," Jules said. "What did you think I meant?"

"Oh, nothing—just what you said. I just wanted to be clear, though."

An uncomfortable silence followed as she and Jules sat quietly, each waiting for the other to speak.

"Well," they both said at the same time, which made them both laugh.

"You first," Josephine said.

Jules decided to go for it. "Look, Jo, how long have we known each other?"

"Forever."

"Then even though a lot of time has passed since we've last spoken, can we be honest with each other, like the old friends we are?"

"I would really like that, Jules."

"Well, then," Jules said, grinning. "You know exactly what I meant when I said he was making an effort. Don't you?"

"Yes, I believe I do," Josephine said, matching his grin.

Jules stood up with his arms outstretched. "Well, tell a brotha what's up!"

Josephine laughed but cut it short when she heard a knock at the door.

"Come in."

Tia walked into the office, purposely passing close by Jules so he could get a whiff of her perfume. "It's three-thirty, Mrs. Prescott. If you don't need anything else, I'm going home."

"Sure, Tia. Have a nice holiday. Be safe, now."

"Thank you, I will." She turned to Jules and stuck out her hand. "It was nice meeting you, Mr. Anthony."

Jules took it. "A pleasure, Tia."

She hesitated for a moment before she left. It looked like she was debating how much flirting she could get away with in front of her boss. It also served the purpose of giving Jules the opportunity to say something to her if he wanted to.

"Ummm," Josephine said after Tia was safely out of range, "It looks like Ms. Tia is sweet on you. Lemme see your hand. I know she slipped you her phone number."

Jules held open his empty palm. "Please, she's a zygote."

"She's twenty-three."

"Twenty-three," Jules repeated. "That's—" Jules caught himself. Damn, if he didn't almost say, *right up John's alley.*" John would've wanted to kill him behind telling Josephine something like that.

"That's a little too young for me, Jo," he said. "What did you mean by 'nice holiday'? Is it Christmas break?"

"For her it is. Only one secretary works over the break. Administrators have to be here every weekday except Christmas and Christmas Eve."

"That sucks."

Josephine laughed. "It's not that bad. You get used to it."

"Well anyway, back to what we were talking about before. What do you think of John's efforts?"

Josephine slowly swiveled back and forth in her chair. "Well, I have to admit that at first I hated seeing the sight of him in this school. It was almost tantamount to optical assault. Ya know?"

"I can imagine." Jules chuckled. "And now?"

"Now I've gotten used to it. We're civil to each other. I can even hold a conversation with him without belting him." She pointed at Jules. "And don't even try to tell me you don't know about that."

"What? Your Larry Holmes impersonation? Naah," Jules said unconvincingly, "I don't know nothing about it."

Josephine smirked. "To be honest, for someone that has been coming here for only three months, he's done a lot of good here. He's really revitalized the Boys to Men program, brought two new members on board—I think they're employees of his. We can always use more positive role models, though, hint, hint."

"That's why I'm here, boss lady."

Josephine was very pleased. "That's great, Jules. I think you're gonna enjoy spending time with the boys."

"We're allowed to smack them up if they act a fool, right?"

Josephine rolled her eyes.

"Hey, I'm just kidding," Jules said, then he paused before adding, "So, um, just to be clear, the answer is no, right?"

"On second thought," Josephine said, "maybe you don't need to be a mentor."

"Okay, so he has been a wonderful addition to the school," Jules said, going back to the subject at hand. "How do you personally feel about him?"

"You mean in *that* sense?" Josephine asked. She shifted in her chair. "I don't."

"Oh." Jules nodded that he understood.

"Coming back to Newark as Mr. Big," Josephine said softly. "To be serious, though, when I see John, I don't see the money, I just see him. I guess it's because I knew him back when he didn't have enough money to eat at White Castle."

"I know that, Jo," Jules said. "To be honest, I think that's part of your mystique to him."

Josephine looked down toward the desk where her hand rested. She fingered her wedding ring with the thumb and middle finger of her other hand.

"Jules, I hope your buddy doesn't quit on the kids when he comes to this realization, but he truly is wasting his time. I'm a married woman. Even if I could get past the mess that John put me through, the situation remains what it is. I'm spoken for."

Jules nodded in acknowledgment. He didn't feel it was his place to try to convince her otherwise. "So how is Davron?"

Josephine gave him a bent smile. "I don't know how Davron is, because I don't know who Davron is, but I can tell you how Darren, my husband, is. And he is doing just fine, thank you."

Jules snapped his fingers. "That's right, Darren. I don't know why I have such trouble with that cat's name."

"Funny, John seems to have the same trouble."

There was a knock at the door.

"Come in."

Gloria entered. When she and Jules saw each other, they both froze.

"Hey, girl, look who surprised me with a visit," Josephine said.

"I see," Gloria said, determined to keep her composure.

Jules stood up to greet her. "Hi, Gloria." There was an awkward exchange as they couldn't decide whether to kiss or shake hands. Gloria finally offered her cheek, which Jules bussed.

"You're looking good, Jules," Gloria said as she sat in the chair next to him. "I like that shirt."

"Thanks," Jules said.

"So what brings you by here?"

"I was looking for John. I need to talk to him." He looked at Josephine. "In fact, I think I'm gonna head over to West Kinney." He stood up.

"Do you know how to get there?" Josephine asked.

"Yeah." Jules started putting on his coat.

"I hope you aren't leaving on my account," Gloria said, trying to make eye contact.

Jules shook his head. "No, not at all."

Josephine came around the desk to hug him again. "It was so good to see you. Now, I hope you were serious about participating in the Boys to Men program," Josephine said as they separated.

"Oh, I am, Jo. I'll be here next Friday."

"Well, they don't meet again until school starts back up. The next Friday they'll meet is"—she looked at her wall calendar, then turned back to Jules—"on the fifth."

"No problem, the fifth. I'll be here."

Over Jules' shoulder, Josephine could've sworn she'd seen Gloria make a mental note of that information. She could practically see the pencil transcribing it onto her brain.

Gloria stood up and hugged Jules as well. At first, Jules was a little taken aback, but then he seemed suddenly to realize Gloria was in his arms and took full advantage, squeezing her tightly before letting go.

" 'Bye now," she said.

" 'Bye."

Josephine walked him to the door and shut it behind him. She turned back and faced Gloria. "Now, that was weird."

"What?" Gloria asked. "Seeing Jules?"

"Yeah, that, and seeing Jules see you." Josephine walked to the chair Jules had been using and sat down.

Gloria frowned at her. "What's that supposed to mean?"

"I don't know, you tell me." Josephine crossed her legs and studied her friend. "I want to know why the man goes from glib and cracking jokes to barely being able to put a sentence together once you enter the room."

Gloria massaged her chilly fingers. "I don't know," she said. "Other than maybe he feels awkward because me and him used to have a relationship."

"John and I used to have a relationship, and I can hardly shut him up."

"Now, come on, Jo," Gloria admonished, "you know John and Jules are two completely different animals."

"Maybe so," Josephine said, rising from the chair and heading back behind her desk, "but that doesn't explain why Jules goes from lion to lamb once you enter the room." She opened her desk drawer to put some items away but paused to look up at Gloria. "And you have no explanation for it?"

Gloria shook her head. Josephine went back to what she was doing.

Actually, Gloria could explain Jules' reaction to her, but she didn't want to. She was invoking her Fifth Amendment right to not incriminate herself.

"Speaking of alpha dogs," Gloria said, "the blast from the past I was expecting to run into was John. Is he in the building? I wanna say hi."

"No, he's away at a basketball game." Josephine felt weird saying that. It felt strange being able to account for John's whereabouts again.

"How's it been going here working around him?" Gloria asked. "You don't tell me anything anymore."

"Look who's talking," Josephine said, shutting her drawer. "You don't think I'm buying your Ms. I-Haven't-a-Clue act about Jules, do you?"

Gloria laughed. "I don't."

"Yeah, right," Josephine said, putting on her brown leather gloves. "Well, if you have any interest, you better buy a clue fast. I know you noticed how good Jules was looking."

Gloria had noticed. Jules had looked good enough to eat. Chomp, slurp and burp. That man knew he could wear some jeans.

"He looked a'ight, I guess," Gloria said. "What do you mean by 'I'd better buy a clue fast'?"

Josephine smiled. "Because when Ms. Tia saw him, she was batting her eyelashes like it was a dust storm in here. You know men don't often say no to the Tias of the world." Josephine headed to her closet to get her coat. She also reached on the top shelf and pulled down a leather knapsack.

Damn that hoey-ass young girl, Gloria thought. She didn't

know what irked her more: that Tia was after Jules or that her hot ass reminded her so much of herself ten years ago.

Josephine opened her knapsack and peeked at the books inside. "*Sugar*, check. *Warmest December*, check. *This Bitter Earth*, check. I'm excited that I'm gonna get my books signed. My mother and sister are gonna be so jealous. McFadden is one of their favorites."

"Mine too, girl," Gloria agreed. "I just hope she reads from her work. I hate when an author sits there like some prima donna and just signs books. This one asshole author halfway didn't even want to give me the courtesy of eye contact. I'm plopping down my twenty-three ninety-five and he acted like he was doing me a favor. I wanted to shove a book up his ass. Sideways. Hardcover. Large print edition."

Josephine laughed. "It's at the Newark Public Library. I'm sure she's reading."

"Yeah." Gloria stood up. "After the signing, are you in a rush to get home? I need to stop by the shop."

"Nope," Josephine said, finding her keys in her coat pocket. "Darren goes to some sports bar with a bunch of his colleagues on Fridays. He won't be home until late."

"So you saw Gloria, huh?"

"Yeah," Jules said, stopping for a red light on MLK Boulevard. "In Jo's office."

"So how did she look?"

Spectacular. Black leather pants that accentuated every luscious, bedeviling curve. Tight, powder-blue turtleneck sweater that shaped her already well-formed breasts even better, and was the perfect contrast to her smooth cinnamon skin. Her hair was immaculate-looking as always, like she had just come back from the shop. She had it parted in the middle and flipped at her shoulders with honey-blond highlights.

For John, he yawned nonchalantly. "She looked good as always.

You know Gloria. She has the ass that launched a thousand erections."

"So what's up, man? Are you gonna try to talk to her, or what?" John asked.

The light changed, and Jules pulled off.

"No."

"Why not?" John asked.

"Why not, *not*? Just 'cause she's fine?"

John decided to let it go, though he knew it was bullshit. Gloria was the one area Jules clammed up on.

Besides, there were other concerns occupying his mind.

Lyons Avenue had just split a doubleheader against West Kinney in basketball. The boys team had narrowly lost, while the girls team had won a hard-fought game. John had noticed some tendencies that he wanted to talk to the girls about. Lola, the team's star guard, wasn't looking inside enough. Dana, the team's center, still was bringing the ball down to her waist on rebounds rather than keeping it aloft.

John was really enjoying his time with the kids. It made him feel warm inside.

Maybe he was on his way to finding out whatever Mr. Duke wanted him to find out about himself. He wasn't sure.

But what John was certain of, was that he was changing.

And for the first time in a long time, he was sure it was a change for the better.

Eighteen

"Were your mom and Jazlyn jealous about the book signing?" Gloria asked from the kitchen.

"Yeah," Josephine said, laughing. "I talked to them last night. Not too many authors make their way down to Huntsville, Alabama."

"I guess that's the disadvantage of living just south of North Bumblefuck."

"Gloria, Huntsville is hardly the boonies. It's a city of a hundred-eighty thousand people."

"Do they got a professional football team within fifty miles?" Gloria asked.

"No."

"Baseball, or basketball?"

Josephine sighed loud enough for Gloria to hear. "No, Gloria."

"Hockey? Tell me they at least got hockey."

Josephine laughed. "Now you're just being silly. Like you've ever been to see the Devils play."

"But I have the option to, don't I?"

"Okay, so they don't have professional sports," Josephine admitted. "In fact the whole state doesn't have any professional teams."

"Good Lord," Gloria exclaimed. "Does the government even know those people are out there?"

"What Huntsville does offer, however, is culture."

"Really?" Gloria said. "You mean, besides the annual frog hopping and butter-churning contests?"

"There are some parts of New Jersey that make you think that civilization hasn't reached them yet. Some of them little backwater villages in the Pine Barrens."

"I ain't trying to go there, either."

"The next time I go to visit my family, I'm taking you with me," Josephine said. "Your ass is gonna be eating okra and whistling Dixie."

"Girl, you gonna have to knock me out to get me to go to 'Bama. Like they used to have to do with Mr. T on *The A-Team* whenever he had to fly somewhere."

Josephine chuckled at the memory of *The A-Team*. How was such a ridiculous show popular for so long?

"Have they gotten that bus situation resolved yet?" Gloria asked.

Josephine looked in the direction of the kitchen. "What bus situation?"

"You know, when they made that sista give up her seat on the bus. Are we still boycotting and marching down there?"

"First of all, that was Montgomery, Ms. Gotjokes. Second of all—why am I even answering your silly self?"

Gloria cracked up. She was wondering the same thing.

"You're going with me, next time I go, and that's all there is to it," Josephine said. "I'll give you plenty of notice so you can juggle the schedule at the shop."

"Well," Gloria said, "at least I can meet one of those slow-talking country brothas. You know, like Bubba from *Forrest Gump*. I like the way they take their time when they talk. Uhnn," she said, considering. "I wonder if they take their time like that with everything. By the way, where did you say Darren was again?" Gloria asked, walking back into the den with a cup of cocoa in hand.

Josephine rolled her eyes. "Nice segue, heifer."

"You like that, huh?" Gloria said, taking a sip.

"Oh yeah, Ms. Gotjokes, you're in rare form today. To answer your question, he's at some holiday basketball tournament in Toms River."

She threw Gloria the bag of mini marshmallows. They were spending their Saturday evening lounging in the den of Josephine's house, watching movies. They had just returned from doing some Christmas shopping at the mall and had picked up some DVDs at Blockbuster on the way home. They were about to start *Two Can Play That Game.*

Gloria looked at the case cover. "Now you can see where I got this hairstyle from," she said. "I stole it from Tamala Jones."

"I'll try to squeeze in noticing that, while I'm not looking at Morris Chestnut," Josephine said. She looked over at Gloria. "Though I could tell that Jules loved the style on you."

"Could you, now?" Gloria said, still looking at the case.

"Umm, hmm. The way he reacted when you walked into the office yesterday, I thought the brotha was gonna get down on one knee and start singing 'Enchantment' in there. *"Glorrrriaaaaa, my Gloria . . ."*

"Yeah, yeah," Gloria said, flipping her hand. She was about to take a sip of cocoa when another thought came to her. "By the way, thank you for setting me up like that, trick."

"You can't blame me for that, Glo," Josephine said. "Jules surprised me. What could I do?"

"You could have excused yourself and called me on my cell phone."

"Shoot, and miss that priceless look on your face when you walked in? I don't think so."

Gloria threw a pillow at her.

"Besides, I didn't get any warning when John just showed up out of the blue in my office. What, are you better than me?" Josephine asked as she got more comfortable on the couch.

"Yes."

"Whateva, skank."

"All right, bitch."

"Yeah, ho."

"Regardless, slattern."

Josephine lifted her head up to view Gloria more clearly. "'Slattern'? I'm impressed."

Gloria winked. "I've been saving it. Speaking of which." She reached toward the coffee table for a sugar cookie as she continued. "I notice you don't talk about Sebastian too much anymore."

Those cookies looked good, but Josephine was trying to stick to her diet. Darren's words the other night were still fresh in her mind.

"How is that 'speaking of which'?"

Gloria bit into her cookie. "Maybe you're being hush-hush because you and John got something going on, slattern."

"Yeah, okay," Josephine said, dismissing the notion. "Anyway, I don't talk about him because there isn't anything to tell."

"No?"

"No. He's been doing a great job in the Boys to Men program and with the girls basketball team." Josephine fingered the remote. "Other than that, what's there to tell?"

"Well, do you speak to him—acknowledge his existence?"

"Oh yeah, it's not contentious or anything," Josephine answered. "I even treated him to lunch last week."

"Oh, *really?*" Gloria got comfortable by bringing both of her legs onto the couch. "Interesting."

"'*Interesting.*'" Josephine imitated Gloria. "Don't get it twisted, Glo. I treated him to lunch in the school cafeteria. He had a pizza pocket and peaches in syrup."

"Still, you have to converse with him. What do y'all talk about?"

"I don't know, nothing major," Josephine said. "Let's watch the movie."

"Hold up, hold—hold, the movie can wait," Gloria said, giving Josephine the stop sign. She then repositioned herself so that she could see Josephine's face better. "Am I out of the loop?"

Josephine took the pillow Gloria had thrown earlier and laid her head on it. "What are you babbling about?"

"You heard me. I wanna know if I'm out of the loop." Gloria cut her eyes at Josephine. "Are you keeping things from me?"

Josephine looked at her dully. "I wish my life was half as interesting as you're making it sound."

"So what do you two talk about?"

Josephine grimaced, as if to say that Gloria was making much ado about nothing. "The program he's in, the girls basketball team, Mr. Duke. Maybe he'll ask me how my family is doing. Like I said, nothing."

"Have you guys talked about the abortion?"

Oh, so that's what she wanted to know. Josephine prepared herself for the onslaught that she knew was coming after she uttered her next sentence.

"Yes, a while back."

"A while back!" Gloria repeated, except much louder. "I knew it! I am out of the loop!"

"It's not exactly my favorite subject, Glo."

"I know that, but I've been the one going through it with you more than anyone else the last seven or eight years, right? I've seen firsthand how it has affected you. I've been the one who has tried to help you get past it. You would think I would get the courtesy of hearing what John had to say about it."

That's true, Josephine conceded. As a matter of fact, she wasn't quite sure why she had kept Gloria in the dark. Maybe because it had been so deeply personal.

Or maybe because she was starting to feel closer to John than she wanted to let on. She was getting used to the idea of seeing him regularly, and maybe those feelings were scaring her a little bit.

If she didn't mention John, she was better able to deny his relevance.

"I thought I told you," Josephine said, lying.

"What?" Gloria looked around for something else to throw at her.

"Okay," Josephine said. "Specifically, he apologized for browbeating me into getting the abortion, and in general, for not being there for me when we were together."

Gloria's mouth fell open. "Wow."

Josephine wanted to try to downplay its significance, even more than she already had.

"What do you expect him to say, Gloria?" she asked. "The man wants some butt."

Gloria shook her head. "I don't care. An admission of wrongdoing from John Sebastian is still momentous. From what I remember of him, you had a better chance of seeing Haley's Comet than seeing John apologize, and they happened with about the same frequency. Right?"

"Maybe. So?"

"So, maybe . . ." Gloria looked at the TV screen. A show called *Conexion Latina* was coming on. Josephine still hadn't started the DVD player. "Maybe the man has really changed. As much as I would've previously thought it impossible."

"And maybe it's irrelevant whether he has or hasn't," Josephine said. "In case you've forgotten, we're watching TV in a room of a house that I share with my *husband*."

"I haven't forgotten, dearie," Gloria said casually. "We're *just* talking."

"Yeah, right." Josephine started the movie.

"So," Gloria took another sip of cocoa, "is Darren ambushing the bush any better, or are you still waiting to detonate?"

"Very good, Gloria. You think of that one yourself?"

"I got a million of 'em."

Josephine sat up and reached for a cookie. She took a bite as she decided what she was going to say.

Her hesitation was enough of an answer for Gloria. She drew back.

"Still that bad, huh?"

"It's gotten a little better," Josephine reasoned, mostly for her own benefit.

"But you still haven't popped the cork?"

"No." Josephine grabbed two more cookies.

"Interesting contrast," Gloria said as she repositioned herself on the love seat.

"What is?"

"Well, I was just thinking, back in the day when you were with John, I know it wasn't utopia or anything. . . ."

"Well, thank you for remembering that," Josephine said. "He was controlling, stubborn, jealous—"

"Yeah, like I said, y'all had your problems," Gloria continued. "It's just that I remember them all occurring when you were vertical."

Josephine wrinkled her brow.

"Because when he got your ass horizontal, the only problem you had was bumping into furniture and shit when you were done. All disoriented and shit."

"Oh, shut up," Josephine said as she rose to her feet. She wanted to get something to drink.

"Don't front, girl," Gloria called out after her. "I remember getting a call at three a.m. with your frantic ass on the other line saying, 'Come get this nigga off me, Glo! Or else he's gonna fuck me inside-*out*. Come get 'im, Glo! Ohhhhhh.' "

Josephine nearly spit up her soda.

" 'Glo, I-I think this fool done pierced my small intestine. . . .' "

"All right, all right, that's enough," Josephine called out from the kitchen. "I called you once. And it was a joke."

"Maybe, but your ass sure sounded happy on the other end." Gloria lapsed back into imitating Josephine, " 'Ooh, oh, not my ass, John, no, no, ohh! Yes! Yes! Yes, my ass, John!'" Gloria tipped over on the couch and tittered.

Josephine came back in the room and waited for her silly friend to calm down.

"Unfortunately, we couldn't spend all our time horizontal," Josephine said. "John on two feet wasn't nearly as much fun. In fact, he could be a real egocentric jerk."

"True," Gloria said as she stretched out on the love seat, "but from what you're saying, it sounds like he's addressed those issues, and has enough money to make you forget the ones he hasn't."

Josephine didn't say anything. There was silence in the room except for the movie playing on the TV. Josephine picked up the remote and pressed the mute button. As she did, she noticed her wedding ring.

"Glo, what are you trying to do to me?"

Gloria could tell by her friend's voice that she was serious. "What do you mean?"

"You know what I mean," Josephine said. "Speaking about John like he's an option or something."

"I'm just playing devil's advocate, Jo."

"I believe you. Only the devil would advocate adultery. It's a sin."

"True," Gloria agreed. "But it's also a sin for a person to be miserable when there's a chance to be happy. And if that ain't a sin, then it damn well needs to be."

"*Miserable?*" Josephine repeated. "Gloria, I'm hardly miserable."

"You ain't happy, and haven't been in a long time," Gloria said. "And rather than demanding happiness, you've relinquished the expectation that you're ever gonna be happy, and that ain't right."

Josephine was stunned by Gloria's characterization. More hurt than angry.

Gloria correctly read her friend's face. "Look, Jo, I just want you to be happy."

"Yeah, but you don't think I want to be?" Josephine asked curtly.

"No, that's not it. I just believe you've tricked yourself into thinking it's not important. Or that it's achievable by other things. Like if they would just promote you to principal you'll be all right. Or if Darren and you could just have a baby, y'all would be all right." Gloria leaned forward. "None of that has anything to do with it. You're unhappy because your marriage isn't working, and hasn't been working for a while now—if it ever worked at all."

Now Josephine *was* angry. "You're an authority on marriage, now, huh? If you know so much about husbands, why don't you have one?'"

"Because I ain't met the right man yet," Gloria said. "Or maybe I did and was too stupid to recognize it. However, the better question is, how can you *have* a husband and still be lonely?"

"Go to hell, Gloria."

"Jo, get mad at me if you want," Gloria remarked, "but you know it's not normal for a man to show so little interest in his wife's happiness. Your problems at work, your sexual dissatisfaction, your desire to be a mother—Darren couldn't give a flying fuck. So what do you need a husband for? Just to say you have one? No, thanks."

Josephine was steamed. Mainly because Gloria was so on point.

"How come my life is always the one being scrutinized?"

Gloria shrugged. "What do you mean?"

"You know what I mean," Josephine pursued, "you aren't nearly as forthcoming when it concerns you."

"I tell you everything," Gloria defended, "or at least I did, when I was out there like that."

"I ain't talking about that inconsequential *Sex in the City* shit," Josephine said. "You don't share anything important with me. What are *your* hopes, *your* dreams, *your* fears?"

Gloria looked like she hadn't a clue as to what Josephine was saying. "Motherhood. Not something I particularly aspire for. Marriage. If it happens, it happens. Career. I like owning my own store. If I can expand at some point, I'll—"

"What about Jules?"

Gloria looked like she swallowed a bug. "What about him?"

"I want to know why you never gave him a proper chance."

"What do you mean?" Gloria asked. "We went out. It didn't work out, so we went back to being friends. He really couldn't handle that, so we drifted apart."

"Yeah, yeah, that's the official version," Josephine said. "Now I want to know the truth. And both of y'all have been mum about it long enough. You're up in my business, and I'm sure Jules is in John's. Now it's time for one of y'all to spill the beans."

"Th-there are no beans to spill," Gloria stammered. "We just didn't connect on the level of boyfriend and girlfriend."

"Try that bullshit on someone else, Glo," Josephine said. "That's the excuse you used to use with any guy you tired of. Jules wasn't like those other nondescript brothas." Josephine turned the TV off and leaned forward with her elbows on her knees. "I want to know what really happened."

Gloria twisted her face up and looked toward the window. "We just didn't—"

"Gloria, the *truth.*"

Gloria fell back onto the couch and closed her eyes. She sat like that for a good fifteen seconds.

Josephine was prepared to wait fifteen hours, if need be. She loved Gloria and cared for Jules as well. She had always wanted to know what happened.

When Gloria finally opened her eyes they were misty.

"Why am I such a fuck-up, Jo?"

"What do you mean?"

Gloria shut her eyes again and slowly rolled her neck from shoulder to shoulder, like she was trying to exorcise some demon. When she spoke again her eyes were still closed, and her voice was shaky.

"Who else do you know has slept with as many men as I have?"

"What?"

"You heard me. Who else?"

"No one," Josephine said as casually as she could. "But that was a long time ago."

"Yeah." Gloria stood up and walked to the end table for a box of tissues. "Well, Jules has known me for a long time, too."

She sat back down on the love seat, dabbed her eyes, then stared at the carpet. She half smiled and emitted a muffled chuckle. "Do you know Jules has been after me since we were teenagers?"

"I knew it had been a long time," Josephine said.

"And I always kept him at arm's length," Gloria said, shaking her head at her own stupidity, "while I slept with damn near everybody else around him. It seemed the sorrier the nigga, the more willing I was to spread my legs."

The tears began streaming down Gloria's face. Josephine, not knowing what to say, said nothing.

"But the problem is, the men we want at twenty, twenty-two, are not the men we want when we're thirty, thirty-two. And the men we run from when we're young, hot and gullible, are the ones we want when we've wised up."

"Gloria," Josephine said soothingly, "but that's true with most of us. Most women have bedded men that, in retrospect, we wondered what the hell we were thinking. You're supposed to make better choices as you get older."

"Yeah." Gloria looked over at her. "But when you make your better choice, are you supposed to choose a man that has watched you make an utter fool out of yourself? A man that knows your every misstep, a man that has heard your name bandied about so disrespectfully by other men? A man . . . who loved you the most from the start, yet you were too busy running from him to notice?"

Josephine moved over to the love seat and held Gloria as she sobbed. She rubbed her shoulder and consoled her the best that she could. Truth is, the roles were usually reversed. Generally, it was Gloria who was comforting Josephine. Helping her get through a rough patch.

Gloria rested her head on Josephine's shoulder and exhaled deeply. She began to speak again.

"So, when I was what, twenty-six, no, twenty-seven, you and John started pressuring me about Jules, remember? 'He's a nice guy, he's crazy about you, y'all been friends forever.'"

"I remember," Josephine said, rubbing her shoulder.

"It made sense to me," Gloria said. "I thought, why not? I see how he looks at me. Like I'm some tiara he just wants to place on a velvet pillow somewhere and admire." A sad smile formed on Gloria's face. "You know, I used to love that look. I've gotten a lot of attention from men in my life, but nobody ever looked at me the way Jules did. Other men looked at me like I was something they wanted to deface, use. To conquer. Jules looked at me like I was something worthy of protecting, you know, something dazzling."

Josephine smiled and hugged her tightly. "Well, that's a good thing, isn't it?"

"Yeah, if I believed it myself," Gloria said in a subdued, almost automated tone. "Which I didn't. So, I set out to kill it."

"What did you do?" Josephine asked. "Cheat on him?"

"No," Gloria said. "Even worse. Cheating on him would've been honorable compared to what I did. Rather than having him think there was something wrong with me, I made it seem like there was something wrong with him."

"What did you do?" Josephine asked bluntly.

"I lied. I told him that no matter how much I tried, I just didn't feel anything for him. That there was no spark there."

"Oh, Gloria."

"I told him that the sex was only barely adequate, that he just wasn't my idea of . . . that I didn't . . . and never could love him. Oh, Jo!" Gloria said, completely disgusted with herself.

Josephine held her tightly and stroked her hair. She knew her friend was truly remorseful. Lord knows, she'd suffered by not having a good man like Jules in her life. She'd had a parade of losers instead.

She couldn't help thinking about Jules and what he must have suffered. How he kept it all in. She highly doubted he had ever told John, or anybody else. A man just doesn't go around admitting that the woman he loves got rid of him because she didn't think he measured up.

Gloria must've been thinking the same thing.

"I'm such a horrible person. I let Jules think that he was less of a man than all those sorry bastards he had seen me with. I let him go around thinking that something was wrong with him, all because I was too much of a punk to be with him."

"But why?"

"Jo, I just couldn't imagine it was possible to be happy with a man that knew everything about me. Like you always say, it's not good for a man to know everything about a woman's past. That's why you never told Darren about your abortion, right?"

Josephine nodded.

"So I guess I figured it was better to get rid of Jules before he could change his opinion of me. Before he could see that I was never of the high quality he thought I was. Before he could see that I didn't measure up, that I wasn't deserving of that look he used to give me. Before he could bring up my past and call me a whore. I just didn't think I was good enough for him, Jo."

"That's not your decision, though," Josephine admonished. "You should've let Jules decide who is or isn't good enough for him. Who is worthy of his love. Hell, whether you know it or not, you were always a catch. Smart, business savvy, great personality, and goo-orgeous."

Gloria gave a half-hearted smile.

"Jules always saw it. The brotha deserves credit for having good taste."

Gloria tried to smile again. After a couple more moments, they separated. Josephine didn't want to pursue the matter any further right now, but she couldn't help but wonder if it wasn't too late for Gloria and Jules.

"You know," Gloria said when she was ready to speak again, "I always suspected that was why Jules fell into that relationship with Yolanda so fast afterward. What better way for a man to prove that he is indeed worthwhile and significant than to produce a child? He was shattered and he had to get his confidence back."

Or, what better way for a woman to get her confidence back when the man she loved made her feel worthless and that she wasn't worthy of being the mother to his child? Josephine realized that Gloria might as well have been talking about her. She and Jules' situations were reverse. Her "rebound" relationship had produced a wedding ring, but had yet to produce a child.

But it wasn't too late for any of them, Josephine figured, for Jules and Gloria to find their way to each other, or for her to have a baby.

It certainly behooved her and Gloria to put themselves into the best position, should these blessed events occur.

For Josephine, it meant dropping some pounds. For Gloria, it meant dropping her guard.

Nineteen

Josephine walked into the janitorial office in the basement of the school. Mr. Davis, the head custodian, practically jumped from behind his desk when he saw her.

"Good morning, Mr. Davis."

"Good morning, Mrs. Prescott. Is there anything I can help you with?"

"I just came down to see the gifts for the children. They're in the supply storage room, right?"

"Um, yes, they are." Mr. Davis pulled the chain on his huge set of keys and went through them until he found the right one. They walked around to the storage room.

Mr. Davis opened the door and turned on the dim light—appropriate for the dim sight that was in front of them.

There were four bikes, two pink and two blue. On one of the metallic set of shelves were some board games, basketballs, footballs and dolls. On the other shelves were stacked what looked to be about a dozen pairs of sneakers and the same number of shirts and jeans. Packages of socks, underwear and panties were on the shelf beneath it. Josephine walked over to the coat closet and opened it. There were three children's winter coats and three light jackets. She turned back to Mr. Davis.

"Is this everything?" Josephine was hoping against hope that the rest of it had already been given out, but she knew better.

"Yes," Mr. Davis mumbled as he scratched his head. He looked over at Josephine, trying to decide whether it was safe to continue. "There sure was a lot more last year, huh, Mrs. Prescott?"

"There sure was. Last year this room was filled with toys." Josephine started calculating in her head. She was certain the clothes had come from Valley Fair on Chancellor Avenue. She inspected the toys a little more closely. Hell, everything had come from Valley Fair. There was maybe a thousand dollars' worth of merchandise in the room. Maybe. And Josephine had a feeling she was probably being way too generous in her assessment.

Josephine left the basement and trudged back upstairs. She thought about the number of children who would go without anything this year because of Mrs. Derossa's and Mrs. Jackson's unholy alliance. Last year they had been able to reach out to probably fifty, maybe sixty of the school's neediest families at Christmas. This year they'd reach out to ten. Well, eleven, because Josephine was certain the Jacksons were having an especially joyous Christmas.

John was sitting in the conference room of the eighth floor of the National Bank Building. He was surrounded at the big table by his employees, the team he had brought to New Jersey with him—his engineers, Claire and Lawrence, and accountant, Gerald; his sales team, Donald, Jeff and Michelle; and his secretary, Judith.

"So we're still in the running for the Dorn account," Michelle said. "We have a bid that I'm pretty confident that none of our competitors are going to be able to match. They've assured me that they will make a final decision sometime next week."

"And the numbers are still what we discussed?" Gerald asked.

"Yes," Michelle replied. "I told them for the quality of the service we provide, that's the lowest we could go."

"Heck, they're still getting a bargain," Jeff added. "We're due to win a couple of these things."

John looked at each of his employees. They had relocated without much of an argument. He had given them financial incentive to do so, and he had tried to ask people that didn't have roots in the Charlotte area, but if you live anywhere for some time you're going to start to take root.

John turned his chair and looked out the window. It was one of those frigid December days when the sky seemed especially blue. He could see the Brick City denizens bundled against the cold as they walked up and down Broad Street. Two mounted policemen were chatting as their horses trotted along in step with each other.

John turned back to the people seated around the table. He wondered how they were doing on a personal level. How many of them were sitting there with their minds preoccupied like he was?

John knew things weren't going as well for the company in New Jersey as they had envisioned. They had recently lost out on two big accounts that they'd thought they had locked up. John could see the stress etched on his employees' faces, along with a little confusion. They were probably wondering why the boss wasn't as concerned as they were.

"Jeff, how are you doing?" John asked.

"You mean, with the Pumont proposal?" he asked. "Well, I touched base with their senior—"

"No, no." John waved his hand. "How are you doing? You've lived in the South your whole life, right? What do you think of New Jersey?"

Everybody at the table looked at each other in bafflement, then at Jeff.

"Well, Mr. Sebastian," Jeff said tentatively, "it's definitely colder."

John nodded. "Have you been muscled by Paulie Walnuts or Furio yet?"

Everybody laughed, except Gerald, who didn't get the joke because he didn't watch *The Sopranos*.

"Michelle and I were thinking that when we first found out we were coming to New Jersey."

"Me, too," Judith chimed in. "I halfway expect to bump into Tony Soprano every time I go to the bakery."

John laughed. "I know you guys think my place of birth is a hotbed of mob activity."

"You mean, it isn't?" Lawrence asked.

"Well, yeah," John replied.

Everybody laughed.

"It sure is a lot more expensive than down South, that's for sure," Gerald said.

"How are your living arrangements, Don?" John had put them all up in corporate apartments in Montclair.

"Er, fine, Mr. Sebastian. They're very nice."

"By the way," John said, "I want to thank you and Jeff again for volunteering at the school with me. I really appreciate that."

"Sure, no problem, Mr. Sebastian."

John swiveled his chair back toward the window. Puzzlement washed across his employees' faces as they looked at each other for answers.

"Judith, what's the date?" John asked, still looking out the window.

"The twenty-second."

John turned back around. "I want to thank everybody for working so hard up here in New Jersey. We've had a tough stretch thus far, but it'll turn around."

Everybody nodded their heads, but their tight faces couldn't belie their anxiousness.

"And if it doesn't, we gave it our best shot, right?" John said. "We'll go back home—bloodied but unbowed."

There was stifled, nervous laughter at the table.

"You guys need not worry about coming in tomorrow. Fly home early if you can. I'll see everybody back here on Monday, the twenty-ninth. In the meantime, I'm gonna see if I can schmooze those good ol' boys from Dorn, maybe throw some steaks and liquor down their throats at a Nets game. Maybe I'll even take them to see another thing that North Jersey is known for—gentlemen's clubs."

"You gonna take them to the Bada Bing?" Claire asked.

Everybody in the room chuckled, except for Gerald, who made a mental note to start watching *The Sopranos*.

"No, I can't disrespect the Bing," John replied glibly. He stood up. "Happy holidays, everybody. Now, if you'll excuse me, I have a basketball practice to attend."

"Happy holidays, Mr. Sebastian."

John left the room.

After a minute of stunned silence, Gerald pointed at the door. "Who was that?"

"Hey, you busy?" John knocked on Josephine's open office door.

"No, come in," she said. She was going to ask him what he was doing there, but she could tell by the way he was dressed that there had been basketball practice.

"What are you doing?" he asked, motioning toward the stack of books on her desk.

"I'm just checking over the teachers' lesson plans," Josephine answered. "Making sure they're following core curriculum standards."

"Core curriculum standards?"

"It's a way to ensure that all the children of New Jersey receive a 'thorough and efficient' education."

"That's a good thing, right?" John said as he settled into a chair.

"Well, it does stop teachers from teaching just anything they want. They have guidelines and benchmarks that are supposed to be met," Josephine explained. "It also is designed to prepare the children to be competitive in the 'international marketplace of the future.'"

"Lofty goals," John said.

"Not so lofty," Josephine said. "They're also designed in conjunction with the state assessment tests of fourth, eighth and eleventh grades. Gotta get those test scores up, now." Josephine pumped her fist derisively.

John laughed. "Those test scores must be important. The eighth-grade boys tell me that that is all their teachers talk about."

"Important?" Josephine deadpanned. "Man, careers are made or destroyed based on them. Ask your buddy Derossa if you don't believe me."

John gave her an affected smile. "So, that's my buddy, huh?"

"Hey," Josephine gestured with her shoulders, "y'all seem like buddies to me. By the way, your buddy took off another Monday. Just letting you know in case you were thinking of stopping by her office."

John nodded his head at her. "Are you and I buddies?"

Josephine felt the back of her neck get warm. She went back to checking her lesson plans. "No, you and I are definitely not buddies," she replied coolly.

"Are we friends?" John asked.

She looked up at him. "*Maybe* we're friends."

"I'll take what I can get," he said.

"I'll bet you would," she retorted quickly, making John grin.

"So why don't you view the statewide tests with the same sense of urgency as everybody else?" John asked.

"Because it's silly to consider it a barometer," Josephine said, "until you even the playing field. We know the average child in Morris County or Haddonfield isn't dealing with the same realities and stresses as the average child in Newark, Passaic, Camden or Jersey City. A child in Randolph might be upset because his computer doesn't have enough memory. One of our kids might be upset because he saw his mom shooting up that morning, and might not know what he's going to see that evening when he gets home. That child is supposed to perform as well as the other?"

"So what do you suggest?" John asked. "We can't excuse the kids from assessments, and just accept and expect their failure. These same kids are gonna have to compete with those kids from Morris County in the workplace one day."

"Understood and agreed," Josephine said, "but we should be implementing programs, plans and studies built around these children's realities. Our children have to be reached and motivated by different strategies than their suburban counterparts. Take you, for instance."

"Me?"

"Yeah, you went through the Newark school system, and you were a poor student for most of your years in school, correct?"

"True."

"Look at what you were dealing with outside of school," Josephine continued. "Being bounced around from foster home to foster home like you were an afterthought. Being mistreated in most of them. What turned it around for you?"

"Mr. Duke," John replied, remembering it like it was yesterday. "He provided me with stability. And he really was the first adult in my life who I cared about, or who I thought cared about me, who really stressed education."

"Exactly," Josephine said. "Now, would the implementation of core curriculum standards have had any effect on you if you were still bouncing around from foster home to foster home?"

John shook his head. "I was too angry to care about being taught much of anything."

"And the tests would have simply shown you to be a slow learner. Not a person capable of building a multimillion-dollar business from scratch."

"Shh," John said, looking around furtively. "You trying to get me jacked?"

Josephine chuckled, then finished her thought. "A lot of these children here are the same way, John. Angry. They can't understand why they have to put up with so much BS. Why so many adults in their lives have failed them." Josephine thought about what she had seen in the basement that morning. "Hell, even we at the school fail them. And we're supposed to be their greatest advocates."

John noticed the downturn in Josephine's mood. "What's wrong?"

"Nothing." Josephine went back to her lesson plans, thinking perhaps John would take it as a hint to leave.

No such luck.

"Josephine, tell me what's wrong."

Josephine looked up at him. He seemed sincerely concerned. Anyway, why not? she figured. Instinctively, she got up and shut her office door.

"Every year each of the principals in the district gets what is called a discretionary fund. The amount varies from year to year. This year it was ten thousand dollars," she said as she returned to her chair. "This money is just what it says, to be used at the discretion of the principal. The only understanding is that the money is to be spent in a manner beneficial to the children at the school."

"Yeah?" John asked. "Like for trips, skating parties, and things like that?"

"Or books, magazines, VCRs, guest speakers, a part-time aide, whatever," Josephine answered. "It's become commonplace among the principals in the district to spend the brunt of the money at Christmastime to buy their less fortunate students gifts so they don't feel completely left out."

"That sounds like a good idea." John remembered how much he despised Christmas as a child because of that very reason.

"It is, as long as the money is used and not pocketed."

"What?"

Josephine proceeded to tell him the whole sordid tale. By the time she was done, John was fit to be tied.

"You know," he said, shaking his head in disgust, "she struck me as a door closer and a phony, but this is beyond the pale. Bribing some pot stirrer just so she can make her own life easier. And to hell with the children. That's pretty damn pathetic."

Josephine took some satisfaction in John's being on her side. He had even used the same description for Mrs. Derossa as she had.

His first inclination was to call the superintendent. "Do you want me to call the Board and report it?"

Josephine shook her head. "No, it wouldn't do any good. Mrs. Derossa would just cover her tracks—put some money in the bank and say that was it. Even though it's customary to use the fund for Christmas, she has until June to spend the money. Or, she could say that Mrs. Jackson is an 'aide' and make up a phony list of her duties."

"And in the meantime, she would make your life miserable thinking you were the one who dropped a dime on her."

Josephine hadn't thought about that, but she realized John was right. They sat there for a moment in silence.

"Well, we'll worry about serving justice to Mrs. Derossa later," John said, standing up and leaning on her desk. "What do you want for Christmas, little girl?" He flashed a toothy grin, which was damn near a leer.

Josephine teasingly smiled and buttoned the top button of her blouse. John took a step back and sighed wistfully.

"Don't bother getting me anything," Josephine said, "because I can't say I remembered you while I was doing my shopping."

"So?" John said, sitting back in his chair. "I'm not the type of person who has to receive in order to give."

"Still."

"Well, you treated me to lunch last time we ate out. How about you letting me treat you to lunch?" John asked.

"Oh, yeah, that lunch went real well for us, didn't it?" Josephine asked. "Maybe lunch isn't such a good idea."

"Josephine, it's just lunch. You can't break bread with a brotha?" John asked, spreading his arms out.

Josephine thought it over. Again, what harm could it do?

"You know what? Let's make it breakfast instead," John said.

"All right, breakfast," she said, not knowing where this was going.

"Great, I'll see you Thursday at seven a.m." John hurriedly got up and made to leave.

"Wait!" Josephine said, looking at her desk calendar.

John had gone halfway out the door.

"Thursday is Christmas."

"So?"

Josephine stared at him like he was a fool. "Well, I planned on spending Christmas with my husband, that's what."

"The whole day?" John asked. "Can't you wait until a little later to open those bedroom slippers and that ironing board he's gonna give you?"

"Ha ha."

"Come on, it's important that it happens on Christmas."

"Why?" Josephine was intrigued.

"It just is."

Josephine shook her head.

John realized that Josephine was going to need more. "I want you to play Santa Claus with me. I want to give some gifts out to some of the less fortunate children in the neighborhood, but I don't know where anybody lives."

Josephine noticed the warmth in his face. She smiled. "So you want me to help you play Santa, huh?" she asked.

"Yes," John said.

Well, it was something worthwhile. Maybe she could spare a little time in the morning.

"All right, John. I'll do it."

Twenty

As Josephine pulled up in front of the school, she felt a pang of guilt. She had told Darren that she was going to the school to give presents to some of the less fortunate children, but she hadn't told him who with. The way she had couched it, Darren probably thought it was a school-related activity.

He hadn't asked to come along. If he had, Josephine would've had to tell him that John was the one supplying the gifts. He undoubtedly would've declined. What man wants to play second fiddle to his wife's ex-boyfriend?

But first he would've cut a damn fool about John still being in contact with her. And that had been the reason she hadn't said anything to Darren about John volunteering at the school, she reminded herself. In the beginning, Josephine hadn't told him because she didn't think John would abide by his commitment to the students for long anyway, so there was no need to bring it up and have Darren throw a hissy fit for nothing. Plus, Josephine bitterly remembered John's nastiness that night he told her that he didn't want to hear anything more about her "wretched, fucking job."

Therefore, since John only associated with Josephine through work, obviously Darren didn't want to know about it. She was just following his wishes.

Josephine knew that was a bit of a stretch, but it would serve to teach Darren a lesson once John's presence at the school came to light.

She checked her watch: 6:55. No sign of John's Taurus, though Josephine realized he might be driving his own car. She looked around. No luxury cars in sight. Just the normal neighborhood cars, some operative, some not. The only thing that looked out of the ordinary was a big blue passenger van at the end of the block.

Josephine's cell phone rang. She reached into her purse to retrieve it.

On the next ring, the LCD flashed, "Sebastian, John." Oh, he'd better not even be trying to tell her that he couldn't make it.

"Hello?"

"Merry Christmas, pretty lady."

"Merry Christmas. Where are you?"

"Where are you?" John asked.

"I'm in front of the school."

"Why?" John asked. "Y'all have school on Christmas?"

"Don't play with me, John."

"All right, all right." John yawned drowsily. "Let me get dressed. . . ."

"John!"

He laughed. "I'm just kidding. We're in the van at the end of the block. We'll come to you."

"We?" Josephine asked, but John had hung up.

She saw the van's lights come on. As the hulking vehicle slowly lumbered to her, its headlights cut a swath through the swirling snow flurries. It looked like a scene out of a Stephen King movie. The van came to a stop across the street from her. She smiled when she saw Jules get out of the driver's side.

Josephine opened her door. "Hey, you. Merry Christmas."

"Merry Christmas, Jo," he replied.

"What are you doing out here this time of morning?"

Jules rolled his eyes and jabbed over his shoulder in the direction of John, who was making his way around the front of the van.

"Jules is helping us out."

"Helping us do what?"

John smiled. He motioned for Josephine to follow him to the side of the van. He slid open the door.

"Oh, my goodness!" Josephine exclaimed.

It looked like a mobile toy store. Twelve of the thirteen rear seats had been removed, and the cavernous space was filled with toys. Josephine scanned it the best she could. PlayStations. Walkmans, Discmans and portable radios. CDs and cassettes galore. Gameboys. A huge assortment of dolls and stuffed animals. Barbie dolls and different accompanying sets. Footballs, basketballs, boxes of Legos, tins of Play-Doh, books, drawing pads, paint sets, comic books, remote-controlled cars and trucks, army men, Easy Bake Ovens, Lite Brites, Tonka trucks and packed along both walls were bicycles.

"Wow," Josephine said.

"Sorry, they're not gift-wrapped," John said.

Josephine looked at him as if he had just made the most inconsequential statement in the history of the universe.

John smiled. "I know I should've probably got some practical gifts like clothes, but I didn't have the heart to."

"Yeah," Jules agreed, joining them around back. "The last thing a kid wants for Christmas is a pair of long johns."

Josephine stared at John in amazement. "I can't believe you did all this."

He shrugged effortlessly. "I'm able to, so I did. Besides, I saw how upset you were, thinking about so many of the kids going without this Christmas," he added. "I simply can't have that."

Jules rolled his eyes and walked back around to the front of the truck.

"Well, they're definitely not gonna miss out now," Josephine said, looking back at the heaps of toys.

"I meant that I can't have you upset," John said with a twinkle in his eye.

Josephine caught sight of the twinkle. She didn't know whether it was caused by a stray snowflake or what, but it looked beautiful on him. She wrapped her arms around John and hugged him as tightly as she could.

"Thank you."

"You're welcome."

"How does that flatulent white man do it?" Jules asked. He placed an Easy Bake Oven, a PlayStation and two boxes of Matchbox cars on a bookcase, then staggered over and collapsed in a chair.

"I do not know, because I'm exhausted." Josephine put the footballs and boxes of Barbie dolls she was carrying on her desk and fell into her chair.

John wheeled the last bike into the office and parked it along a far wall.

"Santa must be on that stuff, 'cause I'm beat, too."

Underneath his arm he held a Discman and a Lil Bow Wow CD. He placed them on the bookcase, then sat down in the chair next to Jules.

"I agree," Jules said. "And we just did one neighborhood. Think about having to do the whole world. No doubt about it, Santa is definitely on something." Jules took off his Santa hat—one of the ones that John had brought along for each of them to wear. They had given away almost all of the gifts. Some of the families on Josephine's list weren't home, so they decided to store those children's gifts in Josephine's office.

Before they had gone on their gift-giving expedition, they had come inside Josephine's office, where she had matched students' names with the toys on the itemized printout John had brought along. Josephine was also able to look up the addresses of all the families she wanted to give the toys to. And she was able to match age-appropriate toys with particular children.

Josephine also realized that some parents might be too proud to accept the gifts. She made sure that they believed that the gifts came from the school district and that they were just delivering them. It sounded more believable to some of the more rigid parents and guardians.

"So, is Devon gonna forgive you for abandoning him on Christmas?" Jules asked Josephine.

Josephine rolled her eyes playfully. "If you mean my husband, Darren—Mr. Darren Prescott—then no, he won't construe this as abandoning him."

John noticed that a weird look appeared on Jules's face at the mention of Josephine's husband's name.

Jules looked at his watch. "I have to get back so I can get to my own child's Christmas."

Josephine came around the desk and gave Jules a hug and a kiss on the cheek. "Thank you, Jules, you just made a lot of people happy today."

He smiled. "Then I guess my aching back is worth it."

John reached up and extended his fist. "Thanks, broh."

Jules gave him a pound. "Don't mention it." He kiddingly glowered at John. "I mean it. Don't ever mention no shit like this to me again. Next year, you better hire some elves to help you."

They laughed as Jules said his final good-byes and parted.

Josephine took off her hat and stroked her hair. She was certain it looked a mess.

But she didn't care. She felt heavenly. And all because of John's generosity.

Twenty-one

The day after Christmas, John and Mr. Duke were in the Barringer High School gymnasium. They had just watched Shabazz defeat the home team in a Friday afternoon basketball game. As they were preparing to leave, Jules strolled into the gym. He had called John on his cell phone about an hour ago saying that he needed to talk to him.

"You missed a great game, Jules," Mr. Duke said. "My Blue Bears nearly pulled it out."

"Yeah?" Jules asked.

"Yeah. That Shabazz point guard was too much, though."

"Oh, he's a player," Jules agreed. "A bunch of Division One schools are after him."

John was more interested in the look on Jules' face. "What's up with you? You look like you stole something."

"Au contraire," Jules said as they headed out to the lobby area. "I'm in possession of some very interesting and incriminating information."

"About what?" John asked.

"Josephine's husband. One Darren Prescott."

The three of them stopped near the Barringer High School trophy case.

"What?" Mr. Duke asked.

Jules grinned again. He looked at John. "Remember when I told you that his name sounded familiar?"

John thought he did. "Yeah."

"Well, the reason it did is because it shows up on my route sheet every Friday. He uses a car service every Friday. My car service," Jules said, laughing.

"You've got to be kidding me," John said. "Why would he use your car service?"

"He doesn't know that I'm the owner of Fleetway Limousine and Transportaion Company," Jules said.

"I don't get it," Mr. Duke said. "So what? He uses one of your cars every Friday."

"And driver," Jules said. "He insists on Marquis driving him. That's how I came across the information I have." Jules checked his watch. "Marquis told me."

"Told you what?" John asked.

Jules looked back and forth at both John and Mr. Duke's eager faces before he blurted out, "That nigga's dirty!"

"How about that," Mr. Duke said, shaking his head.

John did the same. "So tell us. What's he doing?"

Jules checked his watch again. "How 'bout I *show* y'all what he's doing?"

John's stomach was twisted in knots during the car ride with Jules. Mr. Duke had declined to come. He told the guys to give him the gory details later.

When Jules finally reached their destination, John looked out the window, then back at him. Back out the window, then back at Jules again.

"You have *got* to be kidding me," he said, amazed.

They had pulled into the parking lot of Adele's Trailblazer Pub, a go-go joint on Frelinghuysen Avenue.

Jules busily scanned the parking lot. Parked in the rear, he saw the black Lincoln Town Car he was looking for. Marquis was sitting inside reading a paper.

"Come on, man," Jules said as he got out of the car.

After a burly, bald, mountain of a brother patted them down and ran a wand over them, Jules and John entered the main room.

John took a quick survey of the scene. Lil' Kim's "How Many Licks?" was blaring, and the lights were a frenzied array of colors as they whirled, sparkled and flashed around the room. Directly in front of Jules and John was an L-shaped bar. Behind the bartender, three scantily clad women were dancing on a stage that was outfitted with two poles. To the right of the men were two rows of small tables separated by an aisle. To their left was an expansive lounge area, and behind that were a couple of pool tables, then the rest rooms.

"Check your coats?" a voice came from behind them.

A middle-aged woman behind a counter was speaking to them through an opening in the wall.

"Yes." John and Jules first took their wallets out of their coats, then handed them to the woman. She gave them both tickets.

"Let's sit at the bar," Jules said.

John followed Jules to the bar area, passing a pretty light-skinned dancer wearing a white mesh outfit, who gave John a wink and a smile. Once they got to the bar and ordered their drinks, John finished taking his inventory of the place. It was early, so the place was about half full—maybe twenty guys—but there were plenty of dancers already there working the room. It was Friday night, after all.

He also noticed three doors in the back. One was open and had a red curtain covering the entrance. The other two were shut. Stationed outside one of the shut doors was another bouncer.

Next to them at the bar was a brother chatting with a cute dancer in a tiny black dress. While he was doing so, he was palming her round ass like it was an NBA-certified basketball. John figured that the "no touching" edict didn't fly in clubs like this.

In the lounge area were a couple of dancers giving two corn-rowed brothers private dances. The platinum jewelry on the men's wrists and necks sparkled as the dancers slowly gyrated against their bodies.

On the stage, a short black woman and two Latinas were dancing. All of them were thick with asses and breasts spilling out of their lingerie.

This was also the kind of place a woman had to be thick to work, John opined. No skinny model types need apply.

The bartender placed their drinks in front of them. John paid him with a twenty and took a sip of his Long Island iced tea.

"Care for a dance?"

John turned around and saw the light-skinned sister with the white mesh standing there. Underneath her mesh top, she was wearing white panties, stockings and white pumps.

Before John could say anything, Jules spoke. "No, but I'd like to talk." He slipped the woman a fifty-dollar bill and scooted down to the next stool, so the dancer could sit in between them.

"I'm Jules, this is John. What's your name?"

"Trini."

"What are you drinking, Trini?"

"Rum and Coke."

Jules motioned for the bartender to give her a rum and Coke.

"Trini, I was wondering if you could help us," Jules said as the bartender placed the drink in front of her.

"Both of you?" Trini asked, smiling at John.

John smiled back, but he really found the scene pretty depressing. This girl was no older than Scent—maybe even younger—and she was relying on firm breasts and a soft ass to make a living. Getting pawed, groped and God knows what else to pay her bills.

"Maybe," Jules said. "I was wondering where we can go to get some real action."

"Well, we could go over there for a private dance," she said, motioning to the lounge area.

"Yeahhh," Jules sighed wistfully, "but what if a brotha really wanted to spend some quality time alone with a pretty-ass woman like yourself?"

"Well, then there's the champagne room." She motioned toward the doorway with the red curtain.

"That sounds nice," Jules said. "Could you check to see if anybody is in there already?"

"Sure." Trini smiled, then hopped off the stool and walked away.

"Do you see him?" John asked, looking around.

"No, not yet."

Trini came back. "It's empty, Jules. Care to join me in there?" She tilted her head seductively.

"Completely empty?" Jules asked.

"Yes," she said softly as she rubbed a nipple with her fingertip.

"You know what? That sounds great, Trini," Jules said. "Let me finish my drink and—" He stopped suddenly. "Trini, the red door with the big brotha standing in front of it. Is that what I think it is?"

"That depends. What do you think it is?" Trini asked.

"Is behind that door a spot where a brotha is *assured* of privacy? A place where he can *really* get to know you better?"

"Maybe."

Jules cocked his head at her. "Maybe? Maybe that's a place where a brotha is assured of privacy, or maybe a brotha can really get to know you better in there?"

"Umm, yes, to the first question and, for your cute self"—Trini lightly scratched his chin—"yes to the second question. Behind that door are the AG rooms."

"AG?"

"Anything goes, baby."

"Thank you, Trini." Jules pulled out another fifty and handed it to her. "I'm gonna have to take a rain check this time."

Trini took the money and pouted. "You sure?"

"Yeah, I'm sure, baby. I'll get ya next time."

"Okay, Jules."

Trini picked up her drink and walked away. The easiest hundred she'd ever make.

"Damn," John said. "This cat is in the 'anything goes' room?"

"I figured that," Jules said, taking a sip. "Marquis said he's always bragging to him about some dancer he's fucking here."

John wanted to hate Josephine's husband, but he wanted his hatred to be valid and not just because the guy was smart enough to marry Josephine when he wasn't. Him disrespecting Josephine by fucking some stripper in a club every Friday was plenty enough reason for him.

"Another thing," Jules continued, "what are we, a good mile and a half from the school where she works?"

Damn, John hadn't even thought of that. "If that, broh, maybe less." John was really hating Darren now.

"I'm guessing that sneaky nigga is right in there getting his dick sucked and more," Jules said, pointing to the "anything goes" room as he took a sip.

Suddenly, John felt a whole lot better about his feelings for Josephine. During the time he was with her, he had never cheated on Josephine. Not once. And they hadn't been married.

Jules and John nursed their drinks as they waited for the door to open. As they did, they occasionally slipped five spots to the dancers on the stage.

The door opened and out stepped a thin man in blue slacks, an open white oxford shirt and suspenders.

"Look at that muthafucka," Jules said. "What I tell you?"

"I'll be damned," John muttered.

The man gave a head nod to the bouncer and headed for one of the tiny tables. Trailing behind him was a skinny white woman with dirty blond hair, wearing only a g-string and a red paisley tie around her neck.

"Ohhh, shit!" Jules and John said in unison.

"Come on," Jules said, "let's go to the other side of the bar. I don't want him to see me."

After they were again seated, Jules started laughing heartily. "Are you fucking kidding me? All these fine, thick, juicy-ass women of color up in this place and he chooses Gwyneth Paltrow?"

John laughed too, but it was tempered with resolve.

"That's the only one he ever asks for."

Jules and John looked to see where the voice had come from. Two stools down was a mahogany sista sitting there in pink lace.

Jules and John looked at each other and quickly rearranged themselves on either side of her. John ordered her a drink and pulled out some cash. This time he would pay for the info. He handed her four twenties. "I don't believe I caught your name."

"Mahogany," she said, putting the money into her brassiere.

That makes sense, John thought.

"What do you know about this cat?" Jules asked.

"He comes here every Friday, and the only one he ever asks for is Amanda."

"The chick he's with right now?"

"Yeah, that's her ass," she said, sipping her strawberry daiquiri. "He treats the rest of us like we have bad breath."

John looked back at Darren. Through the swirling lights, the dancing strippers' legs, and the smoke, he could barely discern Darren and Amanda getting cozy at one of the tables.

"What's wrong with him?" Jules said, shaking his head.

"I don't know, but I can't stand him. Amanda loves telling us what a big spender he is, ya know. So one time, she was out sick when he came in." Mahogany shifted and crossed her legs the other way. "So I ask him if he would like a dance, ya know? Now, why I ask that?" Mahogany said ruefully.

"Why? What happened?" John asked.

"The muthafucka frowned his face up and looked at me like I was something he forgot to wipe, turned around and left."

Jules quickly traversed Mahogany's body with his eyes. "What is *wrong* with that nigga?"

"I know one thing, he must want to get caught," John said. "Letting that girl rub all up on him and wear his clothes and shit. Her scent must be all over him."

Mahogany blew a puff of smoke and laughed. "Nah, he has that all figured out. Amanda told me that on Fridays he always wears a blue suit with a red tie. He has duplicates of them. The clean one is hanging in the coatroom right now. The boss lets him keep them there. He'll leave this one here for Amanda to drop off at the cleaners for him. Next week, when he comes, he'll switch them again."

"Daamn," John said.

Jules looked at him. "What I tell you? Ain't he a slimy piece of shit?"

"What are y'all?" Mahogany asked suspiciously. "Investigators?"

"Naw, baby, we ain't investigators."

She looked concerned. "Y'all ain't going to try to drag me to court to be no material witness or no shit like that?"

John handed her a hundred-dollar bill to ease her concerns.

Just then there was a loud commotion near the entrance. Five men entered the establishment. Four of them were younger looking and had shaved heads, while the other one was older and in a long brown fur coat.

When they checked in their coats, the four young ones revealed sweatshirts with Greek letters on them. They started doing their frat's call.

"Looks like somebody just went over," Jules said.

A group of strippers quickly approached the group. They gathered around the brother in the fur.

"Who is that?" Jules asked.

Mahogany took a drag on her cigarette. "Oh, that's Ibn."

John didn't have the guts to wear a coat like that, but he had to admit that this Ibn character pulled it off quite nicely.

The DJ's voice came over the loudspeaker. *"Adele's Trailblazer Pub would like to welcome an old friend. Ibn is up in this pieeeece!"*

All the dancers in the club raised their arms in the air and wiggled their fingers.

Ibn gave the DJ booth a closed-fist salute, and a head nod to the two brothas sporting the cornrows in the lounge area.

Slowly the entire entourage of Ibn, the four young guys and the bevy of women started making their way across the room. They got to the entrance to the Champagne Room when Ibn held up both of his hands to stop them, then pointed both his index fingers to the "anything goes" door. The throng detoured and made their way toward the red door. Ibn gave the bouncer a pound as he opened the door for the group.

Everybody disappeared into the back area as Ibn pulled out a thick wad of cash. He tipped the bouncer, yelled something, then disappeared as well, closing the door behind him. John couldn't be quite sure what Ibn had said, because the music was still playing, but he thought he had heard something along the lines of:

"Ladies, if any of my boys leave this place with a hard dick, you bitches ain't done your job!"

Jules looked at Mahogany. "We aren't keeping you, are we?"

Mahogany shook her head, "I ain't fucking with Ibn. I've been here all day, I ain't got the energy for his wild ass."

John had seen enough. "You ready to bounce?"

"Yeah." Jules stuck a napkin in his pocket. After making sure Darren was still sufficiently preoccupied, they left.

Later, John and Jules sat in the parking lot of Lyons Avenue School. They had come to pick up John's rental car and were bouncing ideas around about the best way to deal with their information about Josephine's wayward husband.

John shook his head. "I don't understand why he would frequent a joint so close to her job. He works in Morris County. He must pass two dozen strip joints to get to this one."

" 'Cause he's an asshole, that's why," Jules said. "He probably gets off on the close proximity, of rubbing Josephine's nose in it." He wrinkled his nose in disgust. "Sick, demented *fuck*."

"Maybe," John said. "More likely, he wants to make sure he's someplace where no one *he* works with will see him."

"And using my car service assures him of his car not being spotted in the area."

They sat silently for a beat or two, then Jules again returned to the topic at hand.

"Well, one thing I know is that we have to be proactive," he said. "This jackass is putting Josephine at risk of catching an STD."

John felt the anger bubble inside him. Jules continued talking.

"What are our options?" Jules strummed the dashboard. "We can go to him directly and tell him we're on to him and that if he doesn't tell his wife, we will."

They both shook their heads. That was a bad idea.

It would give him the opportunity to form a tactical defense. Lie. Start covering his tracks or, at the very least, diminish the seriousness of his maneuverings. He certainly wouldn't tell Josephine all he was up to.

Besides, Darren didn't know John from Adam. John wasn't sure how much Josephine had told Darren about their shared past, or whether or not she now saw John regularly at the school. If she hadn't, and John approached Darren, he'd be alerted to John's presence in his wife's life. Why give him that knowledge? So he could go on alert and try to put Josephine on a short leash? Not only that, why put Josephine in the awkward position of explaining herself?

"We could tell Josephine ourselves?" Jules said.

Better, but still problematic. Josephine might question their motives, since it was pretty well understood by this point that John was interested in her. Also, Darren might scream entrapment. Spin it in such a way that John would seem to be in their business because he was trying to drive a wedge in their marriage. John knew that Josephine used to find him too manipulative and controlling. She might see this as another attempt to do the same.

They sighed. Then, like a thunderbolt, the answer hit both of them at the same time. The solution to their dilemma was obvious. They smiled and faced each other.

"Gloria!"

Twenty-two

Saturday afternoon, Gloria was out on the sales floor of her store cleaning, trying to expend some nervous energy. She knelt down and opened the rectangular glass case and began busily dusting the figurines inside. She was awaiting a visit from Jules, of all people. He had called her and said that he urgently needed to talk to her. While Jules had been a frequent customer in her family's store in Paterson, he had never been to Gloria's store here in Plainfield, so she had to give him directions over the phone. She took a deep breath to calm her nerves.

"Everything okay, Ms. Gloria?"

Gloria looked up. It was her employee, Shanna, standing in the cash wrap area.

Gloria was trying to get used to Shanna putting the "Ms." in front of her name. She knew Shanna was only being respectful, but she didn't care for it. It made her feel ancient.

"Why do you insist on calling me 'Ms. Gloria' instead of just 'Gloria,' Shanna? I'm not old, nor are you a child."

Shanna shrugged. "I'm just being respectful. I'll try to remember."

"Well, I'm fine," Gloria said. "Why do you ask?"

"Because you're about to take the paint off that little boy's baseball cap if you keep rubbing it like that."

Gloria stood up and laughed. "Oh, a weisenheimer, huh?" She then noticed Jules outside the store window. "I tell you what," she said, "I'd be interested in seeing your cleaning techniques."

As Gloria began walking toward Shanna, Jules walked in. He looked great, wearing tweed slacks, a white turtleneck sweater and an open black leather coat. Gloria's eyes gravitated from the package in his trousers to the package under his arm. It was a thick binder.

"Hi, Gloria," he said.

"Hi, Jules," she answered.

A lady followed Jules into the store, and he stepped aside so that she could get by. She made her way to the poster section.

Jules stood there looking around. Gloria noticed he seemed impressed.

"Jules, why don't we go into my office so we can talk?" She pointed to the door in the rear of the store.

She first went to the counter to hand the cleaning supplies to Shanna. Shanna's eyes were on Jules as he made his way to the rear of the store.

"Umm. I see why you were distracted now," Shanna whispered.

"Respect your elders, girl. Stay in a child's place," Gloria said as she headed to the back.

Jules waited at the door for her to catch up. "Your store looks great, Gloria."

"Thank you," she said as she went in. "When we're done with our talk, I'll show you around." She motioned for Jules to take a seat. "We'll pick out a book for your daughter."

Jules smiled. Gloria returned it as she settled behind her desk.

"So to what do I owe the pleasure of this visit?" Gloria said.

Jules' face turned serious. "I'm afraid that it isn't very pleasurable." He set the binder on her desk and opened it.

"What's this?" Gloria asked.

"Route sheets from my company," Jules said. He began handing sheets to Gloria. "These are four months' worth of Fridays."

"Mm-hm." Gloria began scanning them, not yet knowing their relevance.

Jules looked at the one in his hand. He handed it to her. "See the name right here?" he said, pointing.

"Darren Prescott . . . Newark . . . Gentlemen's Club—*Gentlemen's Club?*" she repeated. She quickly began flipping through the papers, finding Darren's name on each one. "Every Friday . . ." she said thinking out loud. She then looked up at Jules. "He's been telling Josephine that he's been going to a sports bar with people from work!"

Jules shook his head. "No, he's been going solo. To Adele's."

"Adele's?" Gloria asked, looking quizzically at him. "Where's that?"

Jules reached back in his binder and handed Gloria the cocktail napkin. She read it.

Adele's Trailblazer Pub
3822 Frelinghuysen Avenue
"Helping you Get Ur Freak
On for over twenty years"

"Frelinghuysen?" Gloria looked up. "That's in the South Ward, near Jo's job!"

"And ain't nothing gentlemanly about it," Jules said. "Trust me."

Gloria looked back down at the papers and shook her head. "I don't believe this sh— Can I keep these?" she asked Jules.

"Sure, they're photocopies."

"I'm going to have to let Jo know about this," Gloria said. "I can't believe this joker would do this. Actually, I shouldn't say that. I can believe it. He's slimy like that. Yeah, I will definitely let Jo know, trust me."

Jules nodded but didn't budge.

As concerned as Gloria was about her friend's plight, the sight of Jules sitting there did inspire a selfish thought. She wondered what he was doing later that evening.

While Gloria was working up her nerve and deciding on her approach (she was thinking she might ask if he was free while they were picking out a book for Nakira), she noticed the ominous expression on Jules' face.

"There's more?" Gloria asked.

He nodded.

Josephine was trembling with rage. She let the papers Gloria had given her fall limply by her side. She was trying to absorb everything she had just been told.

The duplicate blue suits. The car service. The visits to a strip club in Newark. Every Friday. To fuck a dancer. A white girl.

"Jules said you should check his credit card bills if you need further proof."

"No," Josephine whispered. "I know it's the truth."

Anger wasn't the only emotion she was feeling. She felt stupid for believing Darren had really been going to a sports bar. She felt exposed, knowing that John and Jules had seen her husband's infidelity firsthand. Insecure and embarrassed that the girl he was screwing was white. Fearful that she might have caught something from her husband's trifling dick.

She and Gloria were sitting in her car outside the YWCA, where Josephine had recently begun exercising three days a week. Gloria had called her on her cell phone to locate her.

"What are you going to do?" Gloria asked.

Josephine decided it was time to toughen up. No point in crying. The deed was done. A proper response was now in order. She tucked the cocktail napkin in her purse.

"I'm gonna handle my business," Josephine said resolutely.

"You want me to come?" Gloria asked.

Josephine shook her head. "He's not home anyway. He's at a

science fair." She quickly added, "At least that's where he said he was going."

"What about later?" Gloria asked.

She was looking forward to her plans with Jules that evening, but if her girl needed her, she would reschedule.

"No, thank you," Josephine said quietly.

"Well, if you need me, call me on my cell phone," Gloria said. She studied Josephine's face. "You're not gonna do anything crazy, are you?"

"Define 'crazy,'" Josephine said.

"Stabbing him up."

Josephine shook her head. "He isn't worth it."

"You got that right," Gloria said. "Though he does need his ass kicked—and I know a couple of guys who wouldn't mind doing it."

"Who are you talking about?" Josephine asked.

Gloria hesitated. "Hakeem and Rashahn. They owe me a favor."

"Lord." Josephine's eyes widened. "Those crazy young brothas? You trying to get us life as accomplices?"

"They're very discreet," Gloria countered.

Josephine shook her head.

"Well, I feel like I need to do something," Gloria said. "I mean he physically needs to feel pain." She gritted her teeth. "Really get his ass . . . beat . . . the fuck *down*."

Josephine was lying in wait for Darren when he came in the door. She was determined to play it smart. She didn't want to leave any openings for him to weasel his way through.

She was on the computer surfing the Net when she saw the headlights from his car. Josephine felt a yank in her stomach and a knot in her throat. Twenty seconds later he was in the house.

"Hi, babe," she said from the office, set off the foyer, where Darren was currently hanging up his coat.

"Hey, hon." He peeked into the office. "What are you doing?"

"Just fooling around on the computer," Josephine said, turning around. Darren was standing in the doorway loosening his tie. "I'm gonna grill some chops for dinner if that's okay by you."

"Okay by me," he said nonchalantly.

"Good. I'll get started on them in a minute." Josephine wasn't happy with him standing in the doorway. It offered him too easy a route of escape. She wanted to make sure she could see his face when she questioned him.

"What, I don't get a kiss?" she asked.

Darren came into the office to give her a kiss. Josephine got out of her chair and clutched his forearms as he did. She led him over to the leather couch and sat on his lap.

Josephine gave him another kiss and nuzzled his neck.

"What's gotten into you?" Darren asked.

Josephine drew back, interlocking her fingers around his neck. "I can't just miss you? I was thinking about you all day."

Darren smiled, and Josephine matched it with one of her own.

She started lightly scratching the back of his neck with a fingernail while Darren fondled her breast through her blouse. "The reason you were on my mind is because somebody brought you up."

"Yeah?" Darren began unbuttoning her blouse.

"Yeah, they said they thought they saw you yesterday—"

Josephine noticed the breast fondling abated.

"—on Frelinghuysen Avenue in Newark."

After a moment's hesitation Darren resumed unbuttoning the blouse. "It wasn't me."

"That's what I told them," Josephine said.

"Who said that?" Darren asked, while he worked his way inside her bra.

Josephine couldn't believe the audacity of this bastard. The liar still was calm enough to continue feeling her up.

"One of the parents," Josephine said casually. "She told me she works on Frelinghuysen Avenue."

Again there was a pause in the petting. This time Josephine

saw some concern on Darren's face. It was short-lived, though. Darren shook his head.

"I don't even know where Freling—Fryling . . ."

"Frelinghuysen."

". . . Freleen-housing is," Darren said.

Josephine had had enough of him groping her breasts. In fact, it was making her sick to her stomach. She reached into the pocket of her jeans and pulled out the cocktail napkin and laid it on her lap.

Darren spied it and stopped fondling her. Josephine saw his jawbone quiver and tighten. Other than that, nothing.

"What's that?" he asked.

"I was hoping you could tell me."

"How would I know?"

Josephine got off his lap and stood over him. "You lying ass-hole." She imitated his voice: " 'Fryling—Freeleen-housing,' you know *exactly* where it is!"

Darren was quickly deciding the best way to go about this. He snapped his fingers.

"Oh, *Friday*," he said, as if he suddenly recalled some bit of pertinent information. "Yes, Friday I *was* in Newark. Some of the guys from the office dragged me there to some gentleman's club."

"I'll accept strip club, or titty bar, but don't even try to legitimize it," Josephine said.

"Whatever," Darren said. "Now you can see why I didn't tell you about it. It wasn't my idea to go, and I didn't enjoy myself."

Josephine took a step back, folded her arms, and studied him. Darren was always a little sneaky and unctuous, but this shit really took the cake.

"Wow. Bravo," she said, clapping her hands.

"What?" he asked, showing maximum agitation by pointedly jabbing his arms out.

That made Josephine laugh.

"Look, before you even try the next step, which is to throw

your hands up in a huff and say, '*I don't need this shit,*' and storm out the front door, let me save you the trouble. Don't. If you do, I will be packed and gone before you get back, and that's a promise, motherfucker." Josephine leaned toward him, resting both hands on her knees. "If you don't believe it, then go ahead and try me."

Darren slowly leaned back on the couch.

"That make-the-woman-think-she-crazy shit ain't gonna work on me, jackass," Josephine said, straightening up. "I know there is nothing in the world you would rather do than leave this house so you can start concocting some bullshit alibi, start lining up people to lie for you and shit. You must think I'm stupid. Nigga, don't you know you married a Newark girl? That suburban high drama shit don't work on us."

Darren looked down at the carpet.

"And speaking of suburban, why couldn't you do this shit where you work? Oh, I know why," Josephine said, answering her own question, "because in your fucked-up way of thinking, while Newark is not an acceptable place for me to be making a living, it is a good enough place to get your dick wet? Right?"

Josephine let out a snort of disgust. "And when I think about all the time you spent ragging on Newark, yet there your ass is sitting in one of Newark's titty bars. Those strippers aren't good enough for you to live next door to or good enough for you to educate their children, but they are good enough to get your mack on, right, Darren? You're such an asshole. Your way of thinking reminds me of Ol' Massa sneaking to the slave quarters to fuck women he claimed weren't even human. You're no better. You hypocritical, self-righteous sonofabitch!"

Darren exhaled loudly as if he thought Josephine was overstating it a bit. She ignored him and kept right on going because she knew she was on point.

"How would you like it if I was a mile and a half from where you worked doing some foul shit? Huh? Let me tell you what the real deal is," Josephine continued. "You haven't been going to any sports bars. You've been going to this fucking place every Friday, haven't you?"

Darren cleared his throat. "Well, if that's what you want to believe—"

"Lord," Josephine threw up her hands, "I give you one last chance to tell a tiny bit of truth and you can't even do that."

"Why do you assume I'm lying?"

Josephine glared at him. He of course had no idea about the mountain of evidence incriminating him. "Because you're a li-*ar*. That's what y'all do. But I'll tell you what I'll do for you. I'll drive down to that place right now. Hell, I probably know half the people that work there and I'll ask the people in there if they know you. I'm willing to bet you that everybody in there knows your name like you're Norm off *Cheers*. I betcha that white girl you're fucking—*Amanda*—knows who the fuck you are!"

Darren's eyes widened.

She knew that Darren knew he was caught dead to rights now. He was probably trying to figure out how Josephine knew Amanda's name.

He shook his head. "I'm not going to play into your—"

"Shut up, Darren, please." Josephine walked back over to the desk. She crumpled the napkin in her hand and tossed it in the wastebasket. "You're still bullshittin' instead of dealing with the reality that your marriage could very well be on the line."

Darren shot her a worried look, then tried to replace it with one of derision. "You're talking about breaking up a marriage because I went to a gentleman's—a strip club?"

Enraged, Josephine grabbed the stapler off the desk and hurled it at his head. He ducked just in time, and the stapler clanged against the wall behind him. "I know that you're *fucking* some skinny white bitch!" Josephine said. "You've exposed me to all types of diseases—I set up an appointment for Monday morning." She jabbed the air with her finger. "You'd better *pray* I come back with a clean bill of health."

Darren had a tight-lipped grimace on his face. He then made a tactical decision. He took a deep breath and stood up.

"Josephine, it's *just* sex. And I always made sure I used protection," he quickly added.

That was the final card he could play. Josephine knew that one, too. The good-men-are-so-hard-to-find-that-you-would-be-a-fool-to-leave-yours-over-"just-sex"-with-a-white-woman card.

"Go to hell, Darren." She headed out of the office.

"She isn't from Newark," he said in a quiet voice. "Her people are from Glen Ridge."

Josephine froze in the doorway. A horrible feeling came over her. The horrifying, nauseous feeling a woman gets when she first realizes that she has married a truly stupid man.

"What an idiot you are. What's sad is that you think that means something." She shook her head. "Furthermore, you can't even fuck what you have at home correctly," she continued. "Why would you feel the need to share your shortcomings with your white trash hooker?"

"Yeah, right, Josephine," Darren said, disbelieving her.

Josephine's eyes grew big and she laughed harshly. "Ooo-kay."

Darren followed her out of the office. "You're just saying that out of hurt," he said as Josephine made her way up the steps. "You know you can't get enough of this dick."

Josephine turned back and saw Darren grabbing his stuff. She had to suppress an urge to laugh. "You're right. I *can't* get enough," she said. "You ain't got enough for me to get enough!"

Now Darren was truly pissed. "Fuck your fat self, Josie!" he yelled as she reached the top landing.

Josephine stopped and looked down at him. "That's the whole problem in a nutshell, no pun intended." She wiggled her pinkie. "If I want an orgasm, I do have to fuck myself because I sure as hell know I can't expect to get one from your so-called fucking me. Now, if you'll excuse me, peanut dick . . ."

Darren was incensed. "You know what, Josie, I *know* you've

been faking. Yep, and you know what? I don't care," he said, pulling at the waist of his pants, "'cause I'm getting mine, *and* some."

That was so pathetic, Josephine thought. But she didn't have the desire to argue with him further. She had to go pack.

Twenty-three

John stuck his head into Josephine's office doorway.

"Come in, John," she said.

John took her up on the offer. "Do you want me to close the door?" he asked.

"Yes." Definitely, Josephine thought. If John was here to talk about what she thought he was here to talk about.

John took a seat. He looked especially dapper in his black suit, gleaming white shirt and silver tie.

Dressed to kill. How appropriate. Josephine figured that John smelled blood. He had to have heard by know that she was staying with Gloria.

"What are you doing here on a Tuesday morning?" she asked.

"To see you," John replied. "I came by yesterday, but you weren't in."

"Oh?" Josephine had taken off work yesterday to go to the doctor.

John measured his next words: "I just want to tell you that I'm sorry about what happened."

"Are you really, now?" Josephine asked, her voice slightly mocking.

John knew she was trying to bait him, but he wasn't biting.

"Yes, I am. I always feel bad when people I care about are hurt." He paused. "And I never stopped caring about you."

Josephine looked away from him. He wasn't trying to bully her, but there was no doubt he meant what he said. She opened her desk drawer, casting about for some other subject. A bent old key set off an idea.

"I'm sure glad that I had a key to Glo's apartment Saturday, because she was nowhere to be found."

John smiled. "Yeah, I was looking for Jules myself this weekend. Who would've thought they'd be together?"

"Not I," Josephine assured him.

John looked at her strangely. "Come on now, you had no idea?"

"I'm serious," Josephine said. "Glo didn't tell me anything. I was shocked as hell when *Jules* dropped her off at her apartment."

"And I'm sure they were just as shocked to see you sitting there waiting," John said.

"You should have seen the look on their faces."

They both laughed. They were happy to see their friends hook up again.

"So late Saturday night was when she told me everything," she said after she and Gloria had talked about Josephine's situation.

"Everything, huh?" John asked. "So what's up? Is she gonna give my boy a fair shake this time around or what?"

Josephine smiled. "I can't divulge the contents of girltalk. What about you?" she asked. "Jules didn't tell you anything?"

John shook his head. "I didn't even find out until Sunday night that Gloria had asked him out."

"Hold up," Josephine said. "Glo did the asking?"

"Yeah, that's what I was told."

"I take it back," she said. "She didn't tell me everything."

They laughed again. John's face turned serious.

"Is there anything you need?" he asked.

"Besides someone to strangle Mrs. Derossa?" Josephine asked, removing some paper clips. "No, I'm fine."

John leaned back in his chair. "She probably wants to do that to me."

"Why?"

"Friday I called Downtown and asked why the computers I donated were so heavily concentrated in the eighth- and fourth-grade classrooms. That my intention had been to service all the children equally. That I wanted them better dispersed."

Josephine's eyes widened. She had never mentioned to John her anger at the inequity of the computer distribution. She was impressed that he had noticed it on his own and taken the initiative to do something about it.

"Really? What happened?"

John laughed. "Derossa must have gotten a call, because yesterday when I came by here to see you, I saw maintenance relocating the computers. The superintendent and other bigshots don't want to risk alienating me. They love my company's luxury box too much. They gotta have their Nets."

Josephine laughed harshly. "No wonder she's in such a foul mood today."

John straightened up. "Is she giving you a hard time? Because I can call Downtown again."

"No," Josephine said. She didn't need John handling her business for her like she was helpless. "It's nothing I can't manage."

John checked his watch. "I have to catch a flight to Charlotte this afternoon."

"Yeah?" Josephine realized she was disappointed that he was leaving. She tried not to reveal it.

"I still have a business to run." John stood up. He began putting on his coat. "Keep your chin up," he said. "You're too phenomenal a woman to be dragged down by any man's defects."

Josephine smiled. "Thank you."

"You're welcome. I'll see you later." He headed to the door.

"When will you be back?" Josephine blurted out, asking the question in not nearly as casual a manner as she would have liked.

John stopped at the door, turned and looked back at her. "Thursday."

"Oh, okay," Josephine quickly busied herself with some work on her desk. After a few seconds she noticed that John still hadn't left. She looked back up at him.

"So, I'll see you then, right?" John asked.

"I'll be here," Josephine replied nonchalantly.

Satisfied with that, John left the office.

That afternoon Darren walked into Lyons Avenue School. It was as dreadful as he remembered. The security guard manning the front entrance asked him whom he was there for, but didn't bother looking up from his Newark *Star-Ledger* when he did so.

"Mrs. Prescott. I'm her husband."

"Hello, Mr. Prescott," he said, rising from her chair. "Mrs. Prescott's office is right—"

"I know where it is," Darren replied curtly.

Go back to reading your fucking horoscope. Darren took off his gloves and headed for the main office. *These inner-city schools get plenty of funding,* he thought. *It's just wasted on incompetents like him. It's ridiculous that elementary schools need security guards as it is, but if you're going to take people's money, at least have some pride in your job.*

Darren arrived at the main office doors. He was forestalled from entering by Mrs. Derossa exiting.

"Mr. Prescott?" she asked.

"Yes."

"Hello, I'm Marie Derossa." She extended her hand. "I recognized you from the picture on your wife's desk."

"Hello, Marie." He shook her hand. "Darren."

"I think we may have met years ago at an administrators' conference," Mrs. Derossa continued. "Of course, that's before you became a superintendent."

Darren gave her a thin smile. "Is Josephine in her office?"

"Yes, she is, and you must be so proud of her," Mrs. Derossa said, patting his arm. "She's a wonderful administrator. Very caring."

"Yes, I am very proud of her, Marie. If you'll excuse me," Darren made the move for the doorknob.

"Her dedication is amazing," Mrs. Derossa went on. "Who else would spend thousands of dollars buying toys for the neighborhood children at Christmas?"

"Excuse me?" Darren asked.

"Well, the toys may have been purchased by Mr. Sebastian—you know him, right? I believe he's an old friend of your wife. But Josephine was still very sweet to get here at seven a.m. on Christmas morning to help pass them out. She's a real sweetheart, as is Mr. Sebastian. He has been an absolute godsend for us at Lyons Avenue School, ever since he donated a hundred computers to us back in September. And he's not the type to just write a check and that's it, no sirree. Do you know Mr. Sebastian has been volunteering here at the school with the Boys to Men program for months now?" Mrs. Derossa flipped her wrist. "Silly me. Listen to me prattling on. I'm sure your wife has already told you how *hands-on* Mr. Sebastian is."

His jaw tight, Darren again excused himself and entered the main office.

Mrs. Derossa watched him go in and smiled contentedly. Underneath her breath she muttered, "That one is for showing me up on Christmas, bitch. And for your boyfriend going over my head Downtown."

Darren detoured to the chair outside Josephine's office door. He was full of rage, but trying to formulate the best way to go about this. Something told him not to tell Josephine he knew about John's presence at the school. To keep that bit of information to himself.

"May I help you, Mr. Prescott?" Deloris asked him.

Darren shook his head. He then stood up, took a deep breath and knocked on Josephine's door.

"Come in," she said. Her eyes turned cold as she saw who it was. "What do you want?"

"I want to talk to my wife," Darren said calmly as he shut the door behind him.

"Just in the neighborhood, huh?" Josephine asked. "Or are you on your way to Adele's Grind and Grope?"

"Josie." Darren stood with his hands clasped behind him, holding his gloves. "When are you coming home?"

She let out a snort of disgust. "I'm not."

"I made a mistake," Darren said, exhaling deeply. "A mistake that I'm very sorry about."

"Don't worry about it—we all make mistakes," Josephine said. "For instance, the past couple of days I've been thinking that my *biggest* mistake occurred on a day over seven years ago, at a church, when a whole bunch of friends and family were present."

Darren tried not to let the sting of Josephine's words show on his face, but he wasn't completely successful in hiding it. His wife calling their marriage a mistake weren't words that just rolled off his back.

He noticed that there was no picture of him on her desk, but that she was still wearing his ring. Josephine caught him looking at it.

"Don't make too much of that. I just don't feel like answering a thousand questions as to why I'm not wearing it."

Darren took a step forward. "You're right, Josephine, it doesn't matter. Because if I had been a better man, you'd be home with me. I fucked up and I'm deeply sorry, Josie." He gripped and wound his gloves tightly. "I hate that I was weak enough to do something so stupid—I despise that weakness in me." He looked at her sadly, as if he was trying to will some tears to form in his eyes. "And then I compounded it by saying some things that I didn't mean."

Josephine stared flatly at him.

"Look, Josie, I miss you—" Darren noticed that Josephine was about to say something and quickly put his hand up. "I know you don't care and it's my fault, but the fact remains that I miss you a great deal. I love you."

Josephine continued to look impassively at him.

"If I call you sometime, will you talk to me, Josie?"

Josephine sighed, then nodded, out of a desire to be rid of him more than anything else.

Darren took that small gesture as a victory and decided to quit while he was still ahead.

"Well, I'm here if you ever want to talk, or if you need anything," he said as he backtracked. He paused at the door and turned around.

"I just want to tell you something. I'm yours for the rest of my life." He put his hand on the doorknob. "I'll either spend it with you, or in pursuit of you."

That evening around eight, Josephine walked into Gloria's apartment. She looked up from her bowl of chicken noodle soup and her episode of *Trading Spaces*.

"Hey, roomie."

"Hey, girl." Josephine hung her coat up in the hall closet. She then joined Gloria in the living room.

"So did you hear from Jules today?" Josephine asked, sitting on the couch.

Gloria gave her a crazy look. "Boy, you don't waste any time, do you?" Josephine laughed.

"Yes, I've spoken to Jules, as a matter of fact. Your name came up."

"Oh?"

"Yeah, Jules told me how he was joining the Boys to Men program at John's school this Friday. It sounds like a good idea. Do you have an equivalent program for girls?"

Josephine gave her a dumb look. "You know we do. It's called

Best Friends. I've been trying to get you to join it since last year," Josephine said. "You blew me off, saying you didn't have the time."

"Really?" Gloria said innocently, "I don't recall it ever coming up."

"Yeah, right," Josephine continued. "But now that a man you want has decided to become involved, your ass has all of a sudden decided to do so too, huh?"

Gloria shook her head and sighed. "Jo, Jo, Jo. Must you take my selfless act and turn it into something calculating? Don't you think better of me than that?"

"No."

They shared a laugh.

Josephine unzipped her boots. "So did you guys talk about anything else?"

"Just more of the same things we talked about on Saturday night at dinner," Gloria said. "Nothing heavy yet. We're still just getting to know each other again."

"Take your time," Josephine said, setting her boots off to the side, "but don't take too long. Tia is still out there waiting to pounce."

"She better not," Gloria said, "unless she wants to get her hot young ass kicked."

They laughed again. But privately, Gloria had already decided that it would be better to tell Jules how she truly felt sooner rather than later. She wasn't going to make the same mistakes as before.

"So where you been?" Gloria asked. "It's after eight o'clock."

"I've just been driving around, trying to clear my head." She leaned back on the couch and clutched a throw pillow to her chest. "Darren came by the school to see me today."

Gloria's eyebrows lifted at that bit of news. She turned off the TV and turned her chair to face Josephine.

"You didn't have to turn off your show."

"That's okay, I wasn't into it. So what did Darren want?" Gloria asked. "He made a wrong turn off Elizabeth Avenue and ended up at your school instead of at Adele's Fuckem and Suckem Emporium?"

"To tell me he was sorry and that he wanted me back."

"Well, I definitely agree with the first part of that statement," Gloria said. "He's sorry. As for the second, I hope you told his ass where to go."

"I didn't say much of anything," Josephine said quietly. "I just let him say his piece so he could leave."

"You should've called security." Gloria rose from her chair and headed for the kitchen. Halfway there, she stopped and turned around. "So, let me see if I got this right. You're supposed to go back to a man who cheats on you, constantly harps on you about your weight, is unsupportive of your career, is inattentive to your needs and who *can't* fuck? Shiiiit!" She stood in the doorway of the kitchen and extended her arms, spoon in one hand, bowl in the other. "For who? For what?"

Twenty-four

"It's right this way, ladies," Jules said. "They just had the opening tap." It was Thursday night and the trio had come to the Continental Airlines Arena to watch the Nets play the Lakers. Josephine had tried to beg off, saying it was a school night, but Gloria had persisted, saying that Josephine needed to get out of the apartment.

Jules opened a mahogany door with a sign that read SEBASTIAN INDUSTRIES. Inside the suite was a bar area where a bartender was chatting up a couple sitting on two of the stools. To the left were two warming tables filled with a variety of foods. A server stood over it preparing a plate of linguini. Directly opposite the warming table, along the other wall of the suite, was a computer terminal with Internet access. In front, hanging at the corners, were TV monitors. One showed the live feed of the game, the other showed the broadcast. Beneath them were two rows of comfortable leather chairs that afforded a view of the action on the court. John was sitting in one of them.

"Sebastian, you made it," Jules said happily.

John turned around. When he saw Josephine, his face lit up.

"Yeah, I just got back an hour ago. I came straight here from the airport." He smiled at Gloria and Josephine. "Hey, ladies. Glad you could make it."

"Shoot, you know I wasn't gonna miss Shaq," Gloria said. "I had to convince Jo to come, though."

John looked at Josephine. "Oh?"

"School night," Josephine explained. She didn't want John thinking she was trying to avoid him. In fact, she was happy he was here. On the car ride over, Jules had told them he wasn't sure if John would make it.

As Jules and Gloria grabbed something to eat, John introduced Josephine to the other people in the suite. Three of them, Lawrence, Claire and Gerald, were employees of his. The other lady at the bar, Mona, was a friend of Lawrence's.

They settled in to watch the game, the ladies in the middle with Jules and John on either side.

After a Rick Fox three-pointer, the Nets called a timeout.

"Man," John said, leaning back disgustedly, "the Nets are getting their behinds kicked already."

"Shaq is just too much to contend with," Gloria said, practically conceding defeat in the first quarter. "Look how big he is."

"And athletic," Jules chimed in. "That's what makes him so dominant."

Josephine, who had been quiet, suddenly burst out laughing.

"What's so funny?" John asked.

"I just was thinking about the last time the four of us were at a 'basketball game' together."

Jules, Gloria and John had no clue what she was referring to.

"When was that, Jo?" Jules asked.

"During your and John's epic one-on-one battles."

Gloria immediately began laughing. She leaned into Josephine and the two of them cackled together.

Jules and John didn't get it.

"What was so funny about that?" John asked.

"You two would want to annihilate each other," Josephine said. "Glo and I would be on the side watching and saying, 'Would you look at these idiots?'"

"Oh-oh, Jo," Gloria interrupted, "remember how one would try to dunk on the other and damn near kill his fool self?"

Josephine's side began to hurt.

Jules interrupted their giggle fest. "I'd get mad because this guy would try and cheat."

"What are you talking about?" John said. "You're the one who used to always travel. Always picking up your pivot foot."

"Me?" Jules poked both of his index fingers into his chest. "John, you used to travel so much, you earned frequent flyer miles."

"The problem was," Josephine said, "you both were cheating, and hated being told so by another cheater."

"Exactly," Gloria added.

John and Jules looked at each other. Each had the same thought.

"I know you two aren't talking," John said. "Jules, remember us trying to play against them in Spades?"

"How can I forget?" Jules asked. "Playing against Kansas City Gloria and Amarillo Josephine was a shady proposition."

"What's that supposed to mean?"

"It means y'all cheated every chance y'all got, Glo," John said.

"What are you talking about?" Josephine asked.

"The way you would scratch your ring finger if you wanted Gloria to play a diamond," John said.

"Or rub your chest if you wanted her to play a heart," Jules added.

Josephine and Gloria looked at each other in shock.

"Y'all knew?" Gloria asked.

"Of course," Jules replied.

"Then why didn't you guys say something?"

"Because we were cheating, too," John answered.

They all fell out.

While she was tittering, Josephine leaned her head on John's shoulder for support. She left it there long after her laughter had subsided.

The next day, Jules and Gloria arrived at Lyons Avenue School to join the Boys to Men and Best Friends programs. They both went to Josephine's office, where Josephine explained the goals of the mentoring program to Jules.

Jules sneaked a peek over at Gloria, sitting there in her black leather coat and oversized sunglasses that hid half her face. Damn, if she wasn't movie-star sexy.

Josephine handed Gloria a packet across the desk. "Here you go, Glo. Info about the Best Friends program. I think you're gonna enjoy interacting with the girls here."

Gloria thumbed through it. "I just hope they aren't too much like I was."

"I'm gonna go make copies of your paperwork, Jules," Josephine said as she made her way to the door. "I'll be right back. Then I'll take you downstairs to where the group meets."

Josephine closed the door behind her.

"That was fun last night, like old times," Jules said.

"Yeah, I had a great time."

And she had. It made sense, because Jules was a great guy. Gloria had decided while lying in her bed last night that the time had come to up the ante with Jules. During the couple of times they had been out together, nothing had happened beyond a warm kiss on the cheek. It had been on the friendship level. She wanted more.

Gloria closed her eyes and prayed for courage to let him know. She knew one thing, this being vulnerable shit was for the birds. She took a deep breath, removed her glasses and faced him.

"Jules."

"Yes?"

"Do you hate me?"

"Excuse me?" Jules asked, thinking he must've heard wrong.

"I know you're being friendly toward me because you're a sweet person. But I wanna know if you resent me, even hate me," Gloria repeated. "Please be honest. Lord knows, you have every right to."

Jules turned to meet her gaze fully. He could see that she was serious.

Gloria waited for an answer. She needed it before she knew how best to proceed.

"No, Gloria," he said softly, "I don't hate you."

She exhaled. "Do you know why I'm here?"

Jules thought that question was strange, too. He thought she was there to join Best Friends. "Is that like a meaning-of-life question?"

Gloria smiled and brushed a piece of lint off her knee as she crossed her legs. "Possibly, at least my life anyway. But what I meant was, why I am in this office today."

"To join Best Friends?" Jules asked.

"And, because I knew you would be here."

Jules' face flushed. "Yeah?"

"Yes." Here goes, girl, Gloria thought and took another deep breath. "I have made a lot of mistakes in my life, far too many to recount here. I try not to be a person who constantly dwells on them, because I don't want to be consumed with regrets. Besides, I've never been a person to do a lot of introspection—which has probably been to my detriment. You know what I mean?"

Jules nodded politely. But in reality he didn't have a clue as to what the sista was saying.

Keep going, girl. You've already made an ass out of yourself, Gloria thought.

"However, in the course of trying to live my life, the one regret that I can't get past, my most glaring and costly mistake, was not recognizing what a good man you are, Jules. The reason I can't suppress that knowledge is because of the reality that I face every day. I don't have a good man. And I've never known a man as kind and loving as you, Jules. And if I live to be a hundred, I doubt if I'll ever find another one with your heart. Or who cared for me the way you once did."

Jules was looking blankly down at the carpet, so Gloria couldn't gauge his reaction. She noticed that her hand was beginning to tremble, so she stuck it and her sunglasses in her pocket. She couldn't do anything about the quaver in her voice.

"You once loved me, and I blew it. I was too immature and too stupid to recognize what a gift you were. So afraid of you telling me something that was for my own good, of having to do right, of having somebody love me. . . ." Gloria's voice cracked. A solitary tear streaked from the corner of her eye and over her cheek. "So I ran from you. I made something up to push you away from me. And went about the business of convincing myself that I didn't love you, or need you."

The tears were coming quickly now. Gloria knew she was powerless to stem them so she decided to ignore them.

"The thing is, I could only lie to myself for so long. All I accomplished was hurting myself and hurting the only man that ever loved me. I'm so sorry, Jules," Gloria said. "I'm such a rotten person."

Jules shut his eyes.

"I know I don't deserve to have you love me again," Gloria shakily continued. "I know that. But I want it. And this time I'm ready for it, Jules. I'm ready to treat you the way you deserve to be treated. The way you *always* deserved to be treated."

Jules opened his eyes and looked at her.

"I don't know if you're seeing anybody, or how serious it is if you are. I just want a little bit of your time." Gloria half wheezed, half exhaled. "I'll go as slow or as fast as you'd like—I already know what I want. I know you may need time, if you haven't already decided against me, which I pray you haven't. . . ." Gloria realized she was rambling again. "May I please have a little of your time?"

Jules waited for a moment to make sure she was done speaking. He then slowly lifted himself from his seat and stood directly in front of Gloria's chair. He looked her squarely in the eye.

Gloria looked up, the pleading still evident in her eyes despite their bleariness.

Jules glanced at the door, making Gloria's heart race. If this man tried to walk out, she was gonna throw herself around his leg.

Jules looked back at her, his expression still revealing nothing.

"I had no idea when I walked through that door this afternoon that—"

You were going to see me make a fool out of myself? Gloria thought he was going to say.

"—my life was finally gonna begin." Jules held out his arms and smiled.

Gloria leaped from her chair into his arms, knocking them both onto Josephine's desk. She pinned him down and began kissing him passionately.

"I'm gonna treat you so good that you won't want anybody else," Gloria said, resting on her elbows. "I promise that I'll try to be worth the wait." She lay back down on him and began crying again. "Thank you for a chance."

Jules rubbed her back and kissed her cheek. He wondered if this woman truly knew how much he cared for her.

"And I should thank Josephine for taking so long getting those copies."

Twenty-five

At school earlier that day, Josephine had asked John out, as a way of "repaying" him for the Nets game the night before. They had been out for dinner, had seen the new *Matrix* movie, and were now in Bernardsville so Josephine could see John's house.

"This place certainly doesn't have much in common with the place in New Brunswick we used to live in," Josephine said as she admired the granite countertops in John's kitchen. John had just finished giving her a tour of his house and was grateful that all remnants of Scent had long been removed.

He shuddered. "Don't remind me of that hovel."

"One of your walk-in closets is the size of our old living room," Josephine continued.

John opened his stainless-steel refrigerator and grabbed himself a bottled water. "I'm sorry I had you living like that," he said.

Josephine leaned on the counter. "Are you serious?"

John finished his swig. "Yeah, that place was a dump."

She shook her head in disbelief. "John, we could've been living in a box and I would've been okay. I was happy that we were together." Josephine straightened up and ran her palms along the island countertop. She was surprised at her candor.

"Me, too, of course," John said, "it's just that I couldn't be so happy knowing I had you living in a place like that. I was preoccupied with getting us out of there."

"Well," Josephine said, looking up at the ornate ceiling, "it looks like you made it, and then some."

"I gotta take you down to see my spot in Charlotte," John said. "I had that one built. That baby is my palace."

John was beaming so much that Josephine chuckled. John was chagrined.

"I didn't mean to sound so—"

Josephine waved him off. "You're proud, John, and you have every right to be. You blew u-uup! Got more dough than Pillsbury!"

John laughed at her vernacular and relaxed.

"I would love to see the house in Charlotte someday," Josephine said.

"Cool," John said, taking another sip. "We can helicopter down there whenever you like. My heliport is being put in this week."

Josephine's jaw dropped.

"I'm kidding, I'm kidding."

They had such a good time reminiscing, listening to music and just conversing, that they lost track of the time, until they noticed it was well past two.

So instead of having John drive her all the way back to Gloria's apartment in Edison, Josephine had accepted his invitation to spend the night there. In one of the guest rooms, of course. As Josephine turned down the bedspread, John came back into the room.

He handed her a T-shirt and a pair of sweats. "This certainly beats driving back to Gloria's at near three in the morning, playing dodge the drunk drivers on I-287." John rubbed the back of his neck. "It's not like there's any lack of space."

"Isn't that the truth?" Josephine said.

"Do you need anything else?" John asked.

Josephine sat on the edge of the bed. "No, I'm fine."

John yawned. "I'm beat."

"Yeah, me too."

"Well, I'm turning in. Good night."

"What do you need all this for?" Josephine asked.

John stopped in the doorway and turned around. He thought about it for a second. "I don't know. I guess I plan on having a family."

"Oh." Josephine stood up with the T-shirt in her hand. "Good night."

John hesitated, like he wanted to say something else but thought better of it. "Good night." He closed the door behind him.

Josephine lay in bed, unable to sleep. She rolled over and looked at the clock on the nightstand: 3:33.

She felt a beat through the floor. Josephine lay perfectly still and listened. When she heard the sound of footsteps coming down the hall, she scooted over to the far end of the bed, faced the wall and pretended to be asleep.

Her heart raced.

With her eyes closed, she listened to John enter the room. There was a pause, as if he was trying to discern if she was asleep, then the sound of him approaching.

"Josephine?" he whispered.

"Hm?" she answered without moving.

"May I sleep in here next to you?"

"Mm-hm."

Josephine felt the bed move. Then the covers were lifted and she could feel John's body in bed beside her.

His breath was warm on her neck, so she knew he was close and facing her. She felt a tentative hand on her hip, then his mouth softly kissing her shoulder blades through her T-shirt. Then her neck.

John's hand moved underneath her shirt, and he started tenderly stroking her breasts. His mouth moved to her ear, and he began softly kissing the lobe. She could tell that he was naked by the jabbing against her ass every time he shifted.

Josephine's body tingled. When she felt his hands slide under the drawstring of her sweats, she turned onto her stomach. Teasing him a little.

John responded by cupping her behind, kneading the flesh tenderly with his fingertips. Josephine felt the mattress deepen and then felt John's tongue lolling across the small of her back. She moaned with pleasure.

John moved again, gripped both her sweats and her panties and slid them down to her knees. He began licking the area where Josephine's thighs and butt met. His thumbs massaged the small of her back as he dragged his tongue across her behind. It felt so good that Josephine buried her face in her pillow.

John parted her thighs and rubbed down inside. He then replaced his hand with his mouth and began lapping her wetness from behind. Josephine purred with contentment.

John tugged her pants and panties the rest of the way off her legs, leaving just her T-shirt on. Then he grabbed her by the hips, lifted her onto her knees, and climbed on the bed behind her.

Josephine moaned when she felt John's thickness inside her. He was slowly rolling his hips with sweeping long strokes while buffing her ass with the palm of his hand. The way she used to like it. As Josephine slowly rode on his shaft, she realized she had long forgotten what it felt like to have a man make love to her properly.

She spread her fingers and wiggled them. Flexed her wrists. Rolled her neck. It felt like John's dick was working out every kink in her body.

John started pumping faster, and Josephine concentrated on the feeling of his manhood working her.

"Whose is this?"

Other than one gratified "Ooohhh," Josephine ignored him.

John wrapped his hands around her hips and plunged deeper and faster.

"Whose pussy has this always been, baby?" he again asked.

Josephine didn't answer his question. Instead she lifted herself onto her palms and began driving back, shedding John's hands in the process.

He watched her ass undulate in the air and then come down fully on his member. Again and again she lifted up so that his tip nearly exited her, then came down on the shaft. Flexing her hips rhythmically and rapidly. Pushing off her knees, moving her ass expertly.

John groaned with satisfaction.

"Whose dick is this?" Josephine panted. "Huh?"

"Uhnnn!" John swayed drunkenly, balancing himself on his balled fists.

Josephine bit her bottom lip. "I said, 'Whose dick has this always been?'"

John caught himself and decided to make one last stand. He willed his dick out of her, crawled off the bed, grabbed her ankles and slid her to the edge.

Standing on the floor, he lifted her back on her knees and re-entered her. Thrusting with all he had.

"Whose pussy is this?" he grunted.

"Umm—umm," Josephine hummed like she was in church. John felt so deep inside her that it made her mouth water.

John put his hand on her back and urged her down onto the mattress. Josephine's face met the mattress along with every other part of her body, except her backside. Facedown. Ass up.

Josephine's body began to tremble from the inside out. "Oh, shit!"

"Whose pussy is this?" John growled.

"Yours! John! This is your pussy!"

Josephine squealed and then burst. Her body contracted and then pulsated.

Afterward, Josephine rolled over and slowly ran her fingertips along her cheeks and neck.

Oh, yeah. Now she remembered.

Twenty-six

"Josie, I wanna get together. I think we need to talk."

"Aren't we talking now?" Josephine asked.

There was an exasperated sigh on the other line. Josephine realized that she was being a bit unfair. A face-to-face meeting didn't seem like too much to ask. They were still married, after all.

And not only that, except for two surprise visits to the school—one shortly after she moved out and the other this morning—Darren had behaved like he truly understood and respected her need for room to think.

"And, Darren, I want your just showing up here at the school to stop," Josephine said.

"Why?"

"Because I work here," she said, mystified as to why he would ask that question. "I don't like to bring my private life here. Besides, I'm usually very busy—like I was this morning when I was running around trying to do a thousand things and didn't really have time to talk to you anyway. So, it was a wasted trip for you."

"Not really. At least I got to see you, Josie," Darren rationalized. "I hadn't seen you in almost a month. I guess I have to come up to that school if I want to actually see you."

No, that's definitely not necessary, Josephine thought, thinking of how uncomfortable Darren running into John would be. In her place of work? Lord.

"The only reason you're still walking upright to even be able to come to my job is because all my tests came back negative," Josephine said. She had received the good news from her doctor the previous Friday. The afternoon before the night at John's house. It had been a load off her mind.

Darren didn't say anything, so Josephine took the lead. "But you're right, Darren, I think we should get together," Josephine said. "When do you want to do it?"

"Tonight."

"Tonight?" Josephine repeated.

"Yeah, Friday's a good day to do it," Darren said. "That way neither of us has to worry about work tomorrow should the evening run long."

Josephine wanted to nip any preconceived notions Darren might be having right now. "You do know this is just gonna be a conversation."

"I know, Josie," he said. "I'm not brazen enough to think anything is going to happen. I just meant if our talk starts to run long, neither of has to worry about getting up the next morning."

"Oh." Josephine realized she had jumped to conclusions. "Where and when?"

"Why not at the house?"

Josephine thought about it for a moment—she did need to pick up some more clothes. She decided against it, though. She'd rather meet on more neutral turf.

"No, let's meet at Divino's instead," Josephine suggested. That was the name of their favorite restaurant in Morristown.

"Fine," Darren said. "I'll make the reservation. Seven o'clock okay?"

"Yes. I'll see you there."

" 'Bye."

Josephine hung up the phone and started rubbing her temples.

* * *

John and Jules, and two of John's employees, Don and Jeff, had come for a Boys to Men meeting. They were discussing a planned fishing trip they were going to take the kids on.

"Hopefully, this guy won't stand us up," John said, pointing to Jules.

"What are you talking about?" Jules said. "Why would I miss a chance to show you up again?" He looked at Don and Jeff. "When we used to go fishing when we were kids, the only fish John would come home with were the ones he took as bait."

Don and Jeff laughed.

"It's just that I'm wondering if Gloria is gonna let you go," John said. He looked at Jeff and Don. "I went by her apartment to see him—because that's where you gotta go if you want to see him—and I'm in the hallway about to knock on the door when I hear Gloria working him so thoroughly that this cat is singing hymns."

"Shut up, man," Jules said, laughing.

"Gloo-o-ori-a, in Excelsis Deo," John sang, off-key as usual, which only made it funnier.

Mrs. Derossa approached their group. She was dressed like she was leaving for the day. "Good afternoon, gentlemen," she said.

"Good afternoon."

"Mr. Sebastian, I was wondering if I might have a word with you."

"Okay," John said. "I'll catch up with you guys downstairs."

The three men left, leaving Mrs. Derossa and John alone in the hallway.

"What can I do for you?" he asked.

"Good heavens, John, you've already done more than enough for all of us here," she said with a chuckle. "Your generosity on Christmas morning was certainly noteworthy."

John picked up on the word "noteworthy." The local black publication, City News, had run a piece on what happened

Christmas morning, and John was certain that Mrs. Derossa didn't like being outshone by her vice-principal. John had warned Josephine not to underestimate Mrs. Derossa. After all, Josephine was inherited, and John was sure that Mrs. Derossa would love nothing more than to put in a person of her choosing as vice-principal.

"As a matter of fact, I was telling Mr. Prescott recently when he stopped by—it's a shame you missed him again, he was here earlier today—what a blessing you've been to the school," Mrs. Derossa said.

John was certain that she was trying to fuck with him. And it was working.

"Well, I just wanted to say that," Mrs. Derossa said, satisfied. "I know you want to get with the group downstairs."

"Yeah," John said, distracted.

"Have a nice weekend," she said cheerily.

She walked away, leaving John standing in the hallway. John was looking forward to meeting with the kids, but they would have to wait until he cleared up something.

He knocked on Josephine's door.

"Come in."

Josephine had a young blond woman sitting in her office.

"Hello, Mr. Sebastian," Josephine said. "Have you met Ms. Murphy? Ms. Murphy, this is Mr. Sebastian."

Ms. Murphy rose and extended her hand. "So this is the famous Mr. Sebastian," she said. "I've heard wonderful things about you."

"Thank you," John said. accepting her hand.

"In fact, I sometimes have to remind the boys that they're in class and not in the Boys to Men program," Ms. Murphy said. "They're always talking about the activities you all do."

John smiled. "Ms. Murphy, please feel free to let me know if any of the boys in the program ever give you a hard time."

She returned his smile. "I'll do that. Thank you."

Josephine rose from her chair and came around the desk. "Ms. Murphy is doing a great job for us here at the school. We're lucky to have her. She's part of the Teach for America program."

Ms. Murphy blushed. "Well, September was a little rough. . . ."

Josephine pooh-poohed her. "You were just finding your way. September is rough for all of us. As a first-year teacher I'd say you handled it very well."

"Thank you."

"Well, I won't keep you any longer, Ms. Murphy," Josephine said. "I know you want to get started on your weekend."

"Yes, that, and grading some papers." Ms. Murphy scooped up her purse and a large tote bag full of papers and books off the chair.

"Nice to meet you, Mr. Sebastian," Ms. Murphy said, smiling.

"The pleasure was mine," John replied. "And please don't hesitate to let me know of any disciplinary problems."

"Will do." She looked back at Josephine. "Have a nice weekend, Mrs. Prescott."

"You, too. See you Monday."

Once Ms. Murphy had shut the door behind her, Josephine poked John in the ribs.

"You trying to get me jealous?"

"What?" John asked.

"Where is your offer to me to send disciplinary problems to you?" she teased.

"I know you can handle them yourself."

"So can she," Josephine said. "She's a very effective teacher." She sidled close to John.

"Well, we can all use a hand sometime," John said.

"How about I use my hand right now," Josephine said as she began stroking John's penis through his clothes. It began to stiffen. "Umm," she whispered, "it makes my mouth water. Murphy can have the disciplinary assistance. I'll take this."

" 'This is disciplinary assistance, too."

"Ohhh," Josephine said. "I need the disciplinary assistance."

She turned around and placed her palms on her desk. "Spank me, Daddy."

John couldn't resist Josephine's sweet ass, especially in his semi-aroused state. He rubbed it. "Why? Have you been a bad girl?"

"Very bad."

I'll bet, John thought. John remembered what Mrs. Derossa had told him in the hallway. He still wanted to get to it before he went down to the Boys to Men meeting. He smacked her once on her behind and sat down in one of the chairs in front of the desk. Josephine turned around to face him.

"What's up?" she asked, looking at the clock on the wall. "Shouldn't you be downstairs?"

"Do you expect me to go down there like this?" John asked, pointing at his groin area.

"Maybe it's best that you wait." Josephine laughed. "You wouldn't want Jules to get the wrong idea. To think you like him a little too much."

"Shoot," John said, "Jules ain't likely to notice too much of anything that doesn't start with a *g* and end with an *a*."

"Jules has to take the eighth-grade GEPA test?" Josephine asked.

"Ha ha," John said.

"Well, it's good that he's so enthralled," Josephine said. "Because Gloria's *all* in. I've never seen her so happy."

"So, how was your day?" John asked. "Anything monumental happen?"

"Nope." Josephine walked around to the other side of her desk and sat down. She began straightening the top of her desk.

"Didn't have to put out any fires or anything?"

"Nothing out of the ordinary," Josephine said casually.

John didn't like her keeping Darren's visit a secret from him. Not one little bit.

"So what's on the agenda tonight?" John asked "You wanna catch a movie or something?"

"No. I can't tonight."

John waited for a reason why. When none was forthcoming, he stood up. "Okay, well, I'm going to the meeting."

"I'm meeting Darren," Josephine blurted out.

John relaxed a little bit. She wasn't keeping secrets from him. He sat back down. "What for?" he asked.

"He says he wants to talk." She went to the file cabinet and put the manila folder containing Ms. Murphy's teacher observations back in it.

"What do you have to talk about?" John asked

For a brief instant Josephine had a flashback to the controlling John of her past. She wasn't going there again.

She closed the drawer, rested her hands on her hips and eyed him sourly. "I guess I'll find out when I hear it, John."

He didn't like that answer at all, but could see that her mind was made up. He stood up. "I'm heading downstairs."

"I'll give you a call later tonight," Josephine said.

John nodded tightly and left.

Truth be told, she wouldn't have minded seeing John tonight. But she didn't know how long she was going to be with Darren, and she didn't want to be responsible for being somewhere else at a specific time.

And as far as John trying to dictate her comings and goings, she had already been down that road. That was a trip she wasn't taking again.

"How's your fettuccine?" Darren asked.

Josephine gestured to indicate that it was good. She looked at the fresco of a Venice waterway on the wall over Darren's shoulder. Josephine loved how the classic Old World buildings along the bank reflected off the shimmering water below. She wanted to visit Italy one day.

For now, Italian food would have to do. She and Darren were at a table in Divino's restaurant, digging into their entrees.

Throughout the appetizers Darren had just made small talk. Josephine wondered when he was finally going to get around to talking about something of consequence. She took a sip of her chianti.

"Josie," Darren said as he cut into his veal, "I know about John volunteering in your school."

Josephine set down her glass. She had to admit to being a little embarrassed, though she didn't want to show it. She picked up a piece of bread. "When did you find out?" she asked.

"Way back in September," Darren said, still without looking up.

As Josephine slowly chewed the bread and absorbed this bit of information, Darren went on. "When you thought I donated the computers," he explained. "I did some investigating. I called a friend of mine at your central office. He told me about John Sebastian donating the computers and about his working with the mentor program."

Josephine was certain the shame was staining her face now. "His donation was supposed to be anonymous," she said quietly as she fingered the rim of her glass.

"Nothing's truly anonymous anymore," Darren said, "not in this day and age."

"Why didn't you say something?"

"Why didn't you?" Darren asked as he lifted a forkful of food into his mouth.

"Darren, it wasn't out of a desire to conceal John from you," she said. "I didn't want to give you a reason to try to pressure me to quit my job. Lord knows you were always looking for a reason anyway. I imagined you blaming me for the school allowing John to be a mentor."

Darren set down his knife and fork and chewed.

Here it comes, she thought. Josephine readied herself. She was ready to defend her actions if need be.

Darren swallowed and said, "I can see why you would think that, Josie. I know I wasn't nearly as supportive and understanding of your job as I should have been."

Josephine couldn't believe she'd just heard that.

"However, at the time," Darren said, "I didn't see it that way. I just thought you wanted to keep him from me, and that messed with my mind something awful. It made me doubt myself." He paused and bit his bottom lip. "I think that was part of the reason for my indiscretion."

He'd had Josephine going up until then. "So let me get this straight," she said. "You're trying to say that me not telling you about John was the reason you were going to a nudie bar?"

"Yes."

Josephine laughed nastily. "Yeah, Darren. Okee-dokee."

"Josie, I just needed to feel special again."

"So to feel special you go to someone you have to pay?" she asked.

"It didn't have to be real," Darren said, "as long as it felt real." He put his elbows on the table and rubbed his knuckles. "She was telling me all the right things, boosting my self-esteem."

"That's her job, Darren."

"I know it sounds silly, but I wasn't in my right mind," Darren said. "I thought my wife was sleeping with her younger, much richer ex-boyfriend. I think you can pardon me for being a little nutty."

Josephine had to admit he made some sense.

"As a matter of fact," he continued, "that's why I think I chose to go to a club in Newark." Darren winced like he was having trouble putting his thoughts into words. "So that I could be closer to you, him, it . . . the scene of the crime, so to speak."

"I wasn't doing anything with John," Josephine said.

"But I didn't know that," Darren said. "I just knew you were keeping him a secret from me."

"So why not just come to the school?" Josephine began mimicking his voice. "Why not confront me, him, it . . . at the scene of the crime, so to speak."

"You can mock me, Josie," Darren said. "I guess I deserve it. But if you had told me about John, then I wouldn't have had reason to doubt."

True, Josephine admitted to herself. However . . .

"Are you trying to tell me that your affair didn't start until after you suspected I was having one with John?"

"Yes."

"And that you *never* cheated on me prior to this time?" Josephine asked.

"No, not once, never," Darren said emphatically.

Josephine tried to remember how far back those route sheets she had seen went. Was it September or earlier?

"And if you ever see fit to take me back," Darren said, "I can assure you it will never happen again." He wiped the corners of his mouth. "But I know even the thought of such a prospect is a long, long way off."

Josephine studied Darren. If he wasn't being sincere, then he was doing a good job of looking contrite.

Too good a job.

"Darren, since I've moved out, I've become intimate with another man," Josephine said.

Darren gripped his fork tightly and shut his eyes.

"How do you feel about that?" she asked.

Darren opened his eyes and exhaled. He looked sharply at her. "I've had more pleasant images in my head, if that's what you're asking me."

Josephine took a sip of her wine.

"I also recognize that there were a myriad of problems in our marriage, most of them my doing. My insensitivity, my callousness, my selfishness sexually, that pushed you away from me. Your fling with John is a symptom, not the problem."

"Who said it was with John?" Josephine asked.

"Come on, Josie," Darren said, chewing.

"Who said it was a fling?"

"I'm banking that it is," he said. "That because I haven't been doing a good enough job of being your husband, you searched for something better. What could be more ideal than renewing a relationship with an old boyfriend from your youth?"

"You just have all the answers, don't you?" Josephine said as she took another sip of wine.

"But while it's idealized, it's no more real than my silliness with that stripper," Darren said, jabbing the air with his fork for emphasis. "Right now all you're focusing on is the good times you had with John. You'll start to see his negatives again soon enough, believe me, and then you'll be reminded of all the reasons you broke up with him in the first place."

"Ooh, that does it," Josephine said sarcastically. "I'm definitely gonna start calling you the Answer Man."

"By the way, what caused you and Johnny boy to ever break up in the first place?" Darren asked.

"None of your business," Josephine replied brusquely.

Darren leaned back and smiled smugly as he took another sip of chianti.

Twenty-seven

The next day, Josephine and John were in her new apartment. She had rented one in Gloria's building. They hadn't said much to each other since John had come by. Mostly he watched TV while she unpacked some kitchen items she had bought from IKEA. She suspected he was still upset about her meeting Darren the night before.

There was a knock at the door. Josephine opened it and let Jules and Gloria in.

"Whadup," John said by way of greeting.

"Hey, John," Gloria said as she and Jules walked into the living room. Jules took a seat in Josephine's chair. Gloria sat on his lap.

"Did y'all enjoy the game?" Josephine asked as she sat down on the couch. She and John hadn't gone. John said he hadn't felt up to it.

"Yeah, they won," Jules said, looking at John. "Kenyon Martin acted a fool today. Dunking on everybody. Plus, we took Mr. Duke out for brunch this morning, so he went to the game with us," he added. "He asked about y'all."

John shifted uncomfortably. Even from the other end of the couch, Josephine could feel his aggravation.

Gloria looked at Josephine. "Nakira went with us."

Josephine raised her eyebrows. She knew how nervous Gloria was about hitting it off with Jules' daughter. "How'd it go?"

Gloria's smile told Josephine all she needed to know.

Jules answered for her. "I don't know what Gloria was so nervous about. She's a child, not an ogre."

"She's a child not used to having to share her daddy," Gloria said. "This morning when you picked her up and brought her back to your place, I was afraid she'd look at me and say, 'Who is this bitch and why is she in my house?'"

Josephine laughed.

"But it went pretty well," Gloria said.

Jules smiled and squeezed her hip.

"What did you introduce Gloria as?" John asked.

"As Daddy's friend," Jules said. "That's all she needs to know right now."

"Humph," Gloria said, "like she doesn't know better. Nakira is a woman of the world."

"What do you mean?" Josephine asked.

"On the way to the ladies' room at halftime," Gloria said, "she asked me, 'What's up with you and my daddy?'"

"Really?" Jules asked. "How come you didn't tell me?"

"Because it was girltalk," Gloria said, poking him in the ribs. "It was none of your business."

"What did you say?" Josephine asked.

"I repeated the company line," Gloria said. "I told her that I was her daddy's friend. That's when it got funny."

Jules wrinkled his brow. "What do you mean?"

Gloria stood up, placed a hand on her hip, then spoke in a tiny voice. "'Well, I think you should give my daddy a taste. He needs somebody in his life.'"

"What?" Jules popped out of his chair. Josephine and John did the opposite. They fell backward, collapsing with laughter.

"What did you say?" Jules asked.

Gloria shrugged her shoulders. "What else could I say? I told her that I'd think about it."

"Lord, Lord, *Lord*," Josephine said, wiping her eyes.

Jules was shaking his head, trying to figure out what the hell he was going to do with his daughter. "A *taste*?" he repeated.

"I can appreciate Nakira's bluntness," John said. "She's thinking of your long-term happiness. Why waste time if two people are right for each other?"

Josephine knew that remark was intended for her.

"John," Jules said, "my seven-year-old child said 'a taste,' and she wasn't talking about food. I can't appreciate anything except finding out where she's getting this from."

Gloria took Jules' hand. "Let's go up to my apartment. We're gonna take a nap, then catch a flick later." She looked at Josephine. "Y'all wanna come with us?"

Josephine cut her eyes at John and gestured as if to say, Ask him.

Gloria looked at John. "You wanna take your lady out to a movie later, Sebastian?"

"Ooh, I don't know, Glo," John said, his eyes widening with fear. "I don't know if Josephine and I are ready to take such a big step."

"What is he talking about?" Gloria asked.

"I don't know," Josephine said indifferently. "I just ignore him when he gets like this."

"All right, well, let us know," Gloria said. "We're gonna try and catch the eight o'clock show." She turned to Jules. He still was preoccupied by what his daughter had said earlier. "Come on, Dad," Gloria said, clutching his hand. "I think I feel like giving you 'a taste.'"

After they left, Josephine and John made eye contact.

"Josephine, why are we bullshittin'?"

"How do you figure that?"

"Why did you sign a lease for an apartment when I have a

beautiful home in Bernardsville just waiting for you to move in?" Not to mention the one in Charlotte, he thought.

"John, I need my own space. At least for a while. Can't you understand that?"

"I do, but"—John shifted uncomfortably—"it's just that I want our life together to begin. I've already lost the last eight years."

"And I was married for seven of those years, John. Can you understand that my life is in a helluva transition now?"

Josephine had her hands out, pleading for understanding, and John spied her wedding ring.

"Is that why you're still wearing that ring," he asked. "Because you're still undecided about the direction you're going?"

"I wear this ring for practical reasons only," Josephine said. "Taking it off exposes me to too much drama at my job, and I don't want to have a buncha people in my business."

"Josephine, I'm sure you wouldn't be the first employee in the history of Lyons Avenue School to ever break up with your husband."

"John, I'm an administrator, and I need to maintain a certain amount of distance from the staff if I'm going to be effective. I do not wish to become the prime target of gossip or conjecture. If they see me without this ring, they're gonna immediately make the leap that I'm sleeping with you and that is the cause of my marriage failing. I don't need all that in my face."

John granted that that made sense.

"So you still don't have feelings for your Darren."

Josephine mulled it over before answering. "I spent seven years of my life with the man, so it'd be natural for me to have some bond with him, right?"

John's shoulders lifted. "Yeah, I suppose," he said quietly.

Josephine continued. "It's not an easy thing to do—at least for me it isn't—to say I'm a failure at marriage. I thought I'd only be married once, and that it would last forever, like my parents. You know?"

John nodded and looked down at the carpet. He was about to tell her that she wouldn't be failing, but rather that her sham of a marriage wasn't meant to be in the first place. He decided to let her speak, and to just listen.

Josephine stroked her forearm. "But I know that I could never trust Darren again, so what would be the point of clinging to that dead vine? So I could fall further next time?"

John smiled uneasily. Though he would take Josephine any way he could get her, he'd prefer if it wasn't by default. He wanted Josephine to want him, not to just be with him because her husband is an asshole.

Though maybe there was some symmetry in that, John reasoned. After all, the only reason Darren got her in the first place was because John has been an asshole.

"You're not blaming yourself in any way, are you?" he asked.

Josephine hesitated. "Well, no, I wasn't the one sleeping with the stripper."

"Exactly."

Josephine exhaled. "But still, it isn't easy. I can't help but wonder about certain things."

John didn't like that at all. That Josephine was still examining the shards of her marriage.

"I can make it easier though, Josephine," John offered. "You're not striking off on your own, facing the prospect of being alone."

"I know, John," Josephine said. "But this is something, I have to go through. Nobody else can go through it for me."

"I know, I'm just saying that you don't have to go through it alone." He scratched the back of his neck.

Josephine smiled. She appreciated John not making her feel weak or stupid. The old John would have told her to take her bullshit somewhere else and laughed her out of the room.

Still, Josephine knew people can only change but so much. Somewhere under all this newfound maturity and perspective, there had to be a remnant of the old John who wanted to tell her to "stop with this bullshit and just be with me, girl." Josephine appreciated him suppressing it for her, she knew it couldn't be easy for him to do so. In fact, she loved him for it.

"Do you spend a lot of time wondering about your marriage?" John asked. "It doesn't preoccupy you all the time, does it?"

Josephine smiled. "Not when I'm with you."

She walked over and knelt down in front of him, resting her head on his knee. She peered up at him.

"John Sebastian, I'm falling in love with you. Against all odds, I'm falling in love with you, again. So can you please just give some space and time so that I can ready myself to love you properly? To learn myself a little better? To give ourselves the best chance for success?"

Space? She could've asked John for a limb at that point. He was on cloud nine hearing her say she loved him.

Twenty-eight

The following day, Sunday, John took Josephine out driving in his Porsche. She had no idea where they were going, other than for lunch, because John was keeping it as a surprise. She had a feeling that it was related to yesterday evening, when John had disappeared for a couple of hours.

She leaned back in her seat and looked at Newark as it passed by her window. The flurries from earlier had abated, but a layer of snow had stuck, leaving the city with a fresh coating.

When John made the turn onto Broad Street, Josephine knew they were heading downtown. Maybe he was taking her to his office.

When he made the turn into the Robert Treat Hotel, she cringed.

"John, what are we doing here?"

"For lunch," John said as he pulled in front of the hotel. "The restaurant here, Maize, serves excellent food."

Josephine looked down at her jeans and boots. She was dressed for comfort, not for eating in an upscale restaurant.

"Why didn't you tell me we were going somewhere so nice?"

"Trust me, you'll be fine," John assured her.

The valet opened the door for her. "Good afternoon, ma'am," he said.

"Good afternoon."

"Good afternoon, Mr. Sebastian," the valet said.

"Good afternoon." John handed him the keys.

The doorman tipped his cap and welcomed them to the Robert Treat Hotel. Josephine noticed that he was already familiar with John.

Josephine and John crossed the marble floor past the crackling fireplace with columned chimney and sitting area. As they approached the concierge desk, the employee manning it whispered something to a bellman and handed him a key. The bellman then disappeared into the back.

"Good afternoon, Mr. Sebastian. Ma'am."

"Good afternoon," Josephine and John replied in unison.

"Everything has been arranged, sir."

At that moment the bellman returned from the back. Josephine gasped when she saw what he had with him.

He was carrying, on a luggage cart, a resplendent assortment of tulips, roses and calla lilies, all of them in a variety of colors. Josephine was struck not only by the dazzling reds, yellows and lavenders and the fragrant aroma that seemed to fill the room, but also by the sheer size of the bouquet.

Josephine was also impressed that John remembered that calla lilies were her favorite flower.

"Shall I lead you to your suite, sir?" the bellman asked John.

"Yes." John extended his hand, and Josephine accepted it.

As the bellman closed the door behind him, Josephine looked around the suite. The neoclassical desks, tables, and chairs were a deep, rich mahogany. Rose-colored divans were set off by the deep blush-tinted carpet. The color of the drapes was a mixture of pinks, roses and crimsons. Further enhancing the room was the lustrous gold of the lamps, chandelier and mirror and picture frames.

On a cart next to the dining table was a marble ice bucket, and two champagne-filled flutes waited atop a silver tray. The bellman had poured two glasses before he left.

On top of the long dining table was the flower garden that the bellman had brought up. Josephine leaned over to enjoy their fragrance.

John went to the champagne and picked up the flutes.

"These are beyond lovely, John," Josephine said as she admired the enormous bouquet. "Thank you."

"You're welcome." He handed her one of the flutes.

She looked at him with playful suspicion as she took the slender glass.

"And you remembered how much I adore calla lilies," Josephine added.

"I remember all your passions," John said, winking. "It's my business to remember anything that pleases you."

Josephine's cheeks felt like the color of the carpet. She steadied herself, however. "What are we doing here?" she managed to ask.

"I'd thought you'd like to change before lunch."

You got that right, Josephine thought. Her jeans, turtleneck sweater and parka didn't exactly jibe with the opulent surroundings. "Change into what?"

John took her hand and led her into a bedroom. In the middle of a four-poster bed lay two white boxes. One was a dress box, the other was smaller.

John gave her a kiss on the cheek. "I'll leave you to get ready. Lunch in an hour, is that okay?"

Josephine nodded, like she was of a mind to say no to anything he asked at this point.

John studied her for a moment. He then took her champagne flute from her and along with his set it down on the desk near the window. John then gingerly cradled Josephine's face with both hands, stroking her cheekbones with his thumbs. Josephine felt her body go limp. Her arms dangled lifelessly by her sides.

John kissed her softly on the lips.

"Umm," he whispered.

Josephine agreed.

John picked up his flute and began to leave the room. He paused at the door and turned around. "I love you, Josephine." He shut the door behind him.

She decided to wait to see what John had for her to wear until she was ready to put it on. She walked into the rust-colored, marble-walled bathroom and smiled when she saw what awaited her. John wasn't lying about remembering what she liked.

Cucumber melon body cream, bath bubbles and body spray filled a big basket atop the vanity, along with her favorite lotions, hair oil, lipstick, nail polish, facial cream, even toothpaste. Beside the basket was a loofah, brush and a comb. And a thin crystal vase with two pale-green calla lilies.

On the other end of the vanity was a Bose compact disc player. Next to it was a neat stack of all five of Sade's CDs.

As Josephine luxuriated in the vast ceramic tub, sipping champagne and listening to Sade, she lost track of the time. Lord knows, it was easy to do. She could've stayed in there forever.

The phone rang. Perched on the wall between the shower and the sink, it couldn't be reached from the tub. Josephine turned down "Cherish the Day" with the credit card–size remote and stepped out to answer it.

"Hello?"

"Hi."

"Hi."

"How you making out in there?"

"Beautifully," Josephine replied, looking around at all the amenities.

"I'd thought we'd eat in the suite, if you don't mind," John said.

"That's fine."

"What time would you like to eat?"

"Will you give me another half hour?"

John paused. "I'd like to give you forever, if you'd let me."

Josephine smiled. "Let's start with the half hour, okay?"

"Okay."

Josephine hung up the phone, released the drain and toweled off. She slipped into the plush white terry-cloth robe hanging in the bathroom.

She picked up the creams and lotions she wanted and went into the bedroom, where she sat on the bed and began lotioning her legs. Josephine unfastened her robe and lay back on the bed and let the heated air of the room wash over her nude body.

As she lay there she noticed the boxes next to her head. She sat up and, studying them, decided to open the smaller of the two boxes first. She lifted the lid and unwrapped the tissue paper.

It contained a beautiful, heavy ebony picture frame. Inside was a picture of Josephine and John that had to be at least a decade old. They were dressed up, Josephine in a beaded black-and-copper evening gown and John in a black suit with a matching copper-and-black tie. Josephine remembered when the picture was taken. It was the night of the Luther Vandross concert at Caesars. They'd had a marvelous night. The only blemish had been when John's non-singing behind tried to sing "A House Is Not a Home" back in their hotel room afterward.

Josephine chuckled at the memory. She again looked at the photo. It was almost as if John hadn't been ready for the picture to be snapped, because while Josephine was looking directly at the camera, John was instead looking at her. For all posterity, the snapshot had captured the warmest, most tender, admiring gaze imaginable in John's eyes.

Josephine started to feel a lump in her throat, so she put the photo back in the tissue paper and closed the box lid.

John knocked on the door. "You okay in there?" Receiving no answer, he opened the door. The bedroom was empty, as was the dress box on the bed. John saw the light spilling from the bathroom.

"You okay, Josephine?" he asked.

"Yes," came the meek reply.

John furrowed his brow. "The food just arrived."

"Okay," she said in a voice even more timid than before.

Worried about the tone in Josephine's voice, John walked over to the bathroom and looked in.

Josephine was standing in front of the mirror with her bathrobe tightly wound. He saw an anxiousness on her face that matched her reticent tone.

"What's wrong?" John asked.

Josephine looked at him and tried to will a smile onto her face, but it was no use. "I have on the outfit you provided."

"You like mine?" John spread his arms and did a turn. "It matches yours." He was wearing African print pants with matching vest. The primary two colors of the ensemble were vivid azure and shimmering gold.

"Yes, I do," Josephine said. "It's just that I think my outfit is incomplete."

John grinned mischievously, and Josephine knew why. Back when they were a couple, John used to relish having Josephine nude from the waist up. Josephine, knowing what a thing he had for her breasts, would often accommodate him by going shirtless.

"I thought we'd eat African style," he said. When he saw her continued distress, the smile disappeared from his face.

"John, it's just that . . ." Josephine looked back at the bathroom mirror and self-consciously tugged at the lapels of her bathrobe.

Oh. Now John understood.

This was going to be the first time he had seen her nude in the light of day. Since he'd been back, all their lovemaking had occurred at night.

He walked into the bathroom and stood behind Josephine,

looking over her shoulder into the mirror. "Have you gone and forgotten what a beautiful woman you are?"

John wrapped his arms around her waist and undid her bathrobe. He slid his hands around her waist and pulled her close to him. "Now that I'm back, I won't ever let you forget it again."

Josephine smiled tightly as tears welled in her eyes.

His hands slowly rubbed across the fabric of the skirt where it tightly wrapped around her hips, thighs and stomach.

As John's hands deftly navigated Josephine's body, he closed his eyes, rested his chin on her shoulder and let out a soft groan of appreciation.

Josephine knew he meant it, too. Even through the thick terry-cloth robe, she could feel his erection poking her behind.

John smelled like an intoxicating blend of soap, cologne and incense. Josephine shut her eyes so she could concentrate on the scent.

She and John opened their eyes simultaneously and again made eye contact in the mirror. From the heated look on his face, Josephine thought he was going to bend her over the sink and take her right there.

Instead, John took a step back and coaxed the bathrobe off Josephine and let it fall to the floor.

"There, that's much better," he said, taking her hand. "Now let's go eat."

The dining table and chairs had been pushed to the wall, and in their place lay a green tablecloth on the carpet. On top of it rested three covered platters.

John handed Josephine another flute of champagne and sat at the edge of the tablecloth. Josephine knelt down alongside him.

"Okay, let's see what we have here, courtesy of the chef of Maize." John lifted the first serving lid. The aroma of the food competed with the scent of the flowers for dominance in the room.

"Here we have the hors d'oeuvres."

On the platter lay shrimp tempura with rice wine dipping sauce, roasted honey-soy chicken wings, and satays of chicken, beef, shrimp and duck with spicy peanut dipping sauce.

Josephine and John took turns feeding themselves and each other. Noticing she had a little excess sauce on her lip, John leaned over and licked it off. His tongue sent an electirc charge through her.

She felt her essence getting wet. This was made even more noticeable by the fact that she wasn't wearing any panties.

Because they were both starving, they quickly worked their way through the hors d'oeuvres. John decided to get the second platter. As he climbed up to his knees and picked it up, he felt Josephine's hands reach between his inner thighs to stroke his sac. John's penis hardened quickly. Josephine's hands moved to his butt and started tugging at his pants, trying to pull them down.

John put the second platter down and reached for the third. He decided to skip the main course and head straight for dessert.

To the yearning, ethereal sound of Sade's "No Ordinary Love," John lay Josephine on her back in the center of the bed. John, who was already nude, began slowly unwrapping her skirt.

Any concern Josephine might have had about her weight was melted away by the loving look in John's eyes.

After he finished his unwrapping, John placed his hands on Josephine's knees and gently spread them apart. John then climbed on her body, letting his nakedness rub against hers: thigh to thigh, nipple to nipple, cheek to cheek.

Josephine writhed with pleasure as she wrapped her arms around his back.

He licked her earlobe and whispered, "Baby, are you already wet for me?"

"Yes," Josephine huffed.

"Baby." John started gyrating slightly. The tip of his penis brushed against Josephine's thigh. "May I please suck your already wet pussy?"

Josephine placed her hands on John's shoulders and began pushing him down on her. "Umm, I think you better," she panted.

As Sade's "Paradise" filled the room, John gripped the back of Josephine's calves and held them aloft as he stood alongside the bed pumping her.

Josephine reached hysterically for pillows, covers, dress boxes (wrong room, she realized), anything she could hold on to because John's dick was taking her on an otherworldly journey.

John released her calves and guided her hips farther back on the bed. He then climbed on, spread Josephine's legs apart and re-entered her.

"You feel like velvet, Josephine," he said, as he thrusted.

Josephine's eyes rolled to the back of her head.

"I need you in my life, Josephine," John moaned. "I've been without you too long, ya hear me? Too long."

"I'm yours!" Josephine wheezed.

John got onto his knees, grabbed Josephine's hips and brought her to him. One of his hands stayed on her hip, the other pressed down on her stomach. He started pumping again, slowly at first, then more frenetically.

Josephine was done for. "Aaaaaaaooowwh!" she screamed as her legs started to quiver uncontrollably.

"The Sweetest Taboo."

"Yes, yes, oh God! That feels good!" John exclaimed.

Josephine was riding him and had her hands placed on his thighs for balance. John always enjoyed this position because he loved to watch Josephine's ass bounce.

"You like?" Josephine puffed.

"I like!" Overcome, John wet his fingertips and began licking the perspiration off Josephine's ass.

She resumed bouncing while John pleaded with her not to stop. Finally, John threw his forearms over his eyes and groaned, "Uhnnnnn!"

Josephine stood over him and wiggled her ass seductively. John did his imitation of a geyser. They both watched their fluids mix as they ran down the sides of his penis.

John reached up and gripped Josephine's ass.

"Damn, girl, I love you!"

Josephine laughed and lay down next to him, exhausted.

Exhausted and happy.

Twenty-nine

Josephine decided to take the day off Thursday. She headed over to the house to pick up some items, particularly a pair of Prada boots she had bought and never got to wear before she moved out. She knew Darren would be at work, so she wouldn't have to look at him.

Darren had not called her all week. Josephine couldn't help but wonder if the cause of this was apathy, but he had said that he was respecting her need for space and giving her all the time she needed to decide what was best for her. In fact, last Friday night he'd said all the right things:

"I miss you," "I want you back," "I know I need to work on myself first," "I now know what a jewel you are."

Why do men always get sense after you leave them? Josephine wondered. Only to lose it again once they think they have you where they want you. Darren used to be as sweet as cherry pie when they were dating and when they first got married, only to turn into a critical asshole the last few years. Now that she wasn't with him, he'd morphed into the most sensitive black man this side of Babyface.

She drove down the long, quiet lane on which their Tudor house was the last home on the left. She wondered if Darren had

had to explain her disappearance to any of the neighbors, and if so, what he had told them. Something along the lines of "Josie's mother is sick, she's tending to her, you know, helping out her family" sounded a whole lot better than "my wife caught me fucking and now she's out fucking."

Josephine pulled into the driveway and parked in front of the two-car garage.

Home sweet home.

She had laid out a couple of dresses, two purses and a pair of jeans that she hadn't been able to fit in for a while, but now hoped she could. Though she refused to weigh herself, her clothes had been fitting a little looser of late, so she knew she had dropped a couple of pounds. Good sex will do that for you.

She danced around the room. She was playing one of Darren's Maze CDs and was bopping along to "Before I Let Go."

Josephine grooved down the hall into the bathroom and looked into the closet. Paydirt. Two unopened bottles of cucumber melon. That was definitely coming with her. She had been running low of late and hadn't had time to get to the mall. Her gaze gravitated down to the cleaning supplies.

Speaking of late.

Josephine knew she should have gotten her period last week. Had put it out of her mind. With so much else going on in her life, it had been easy to do.

She knelt down, moved the bottles of Pine-Sol and Clorox out of the way, reached underneath the pile of cleaning rags and pulled out a hidden home pregnancy kit. Josephine put the rags back in place to hide the other three kits and stood up. She soon had the absorbent end of the stick wet. She had conducted these tests dozens of times over the course of her marriage, only to be inevitably disappointed by the results.

She had been late before, so Josephine wasn't too concerned. As she washed her hands, she looked in the bathroom mirror. Besides revealing her lack of sleep, her face told another story. She had definitely dropped a few pounds. Even her cheeks looked thinner.

Maybe she could get an infomercial hawking her "Josephine Prescott Weight Loss Program for Women." The Plan: Find a big buck Negro who humps you long, hard and often. Watch the pounds melt away, girls! And you'll find that the more time you spend fucking, the less time you have for eating. Throw in the added pressures of a crumbling marriage and a contentious relationship with your boss. Result? An ungodly amount of stress. Watch your appetite diminish, ladies. Voilà! You're a size six again!

Josephine chuckled. Size six. Yeah, right. That would be the day when she could wear Gloria's clothes.

From the countless tests she had done, she had a built-in internal clock that let her know when three minutes had passed. Josephine picked the test up off the paper towel she had laid it on and looked at the windows. The first of the two windows had a line in it. As usual, the second window was—

Josephine heaved and stumbled back into the towel rack. She covered her mouth as tears welled in her eyes.

Clear as day, in the second window, was a blue line.

Josephine slid down the wall onto the floor. Every emotion a woman could have was clamoring and clanging for space inside her heart. Dread. Elation. Trepidation. Guilt. Fulfillment. Wonder.

Not knowing how to best satisfy these competing emotions, or which one to deal with first, Josephine hugged herself and screamed as the tears rolled down her cheeks.

Josephine didn't know how long she sat on the bathroom floor. She just knew that it was time to get up and start to handle her business. After all, she didn't have just herself to consider anymore. She stood up and rubbed her stomach. She was comforted that the feeling she felt right then was warmth.

She put the testing stick back in the box and carried it into the bedroom with her. If she was indeed pregnant, she wanted to keep it as a memento.

Josephine walked into the bedroom and called her ob-gyn. They had just had a cancellation so there was an opening on the following day, which she immediately jumped on. Though she hated missing two days of work in a row, she knew she had to know for sure as soon as possible or she'd go crazy.

Josephine remembered to give the scheduling secretary the new phone number at her apartment. The last thing she wanted was someone from the office calling here telling Darren something.

As she hung up the phone, she could see that her hands were trembling. She tried to calm herself down by telling herself that it wasn't even confirmed medically yet, that she shouldn't be getting worked up. At least until she could get it confirmed, she wasn't going to breathe a word of this to anybody. Not to Gloria, John—nobody.

She scooped up her clothes and her positive pregnancy test and box. She walked into the bathroom and got her cucumber melon products. She did a study of the bathroom, making sure she had left nothing there incriminating before turning off the light.

As Josephine got to the bottom of the winding staircase, she realized she had never gotten the Prada boots that she had come there for. Not only that, she had left Darren's Bose on, because she could hear Frankie Beverly singing "Back in Stride" again.

Girl, how could you not notice the radio being on? She forgave herself. She was a little more preoccupied with more important things.

Josephine dumped the items she was carrying into the occasional chair in the entrance foyer. Then turned around and headed back upstairs.

Darren pulled his Expedition into the driveway next to Josephine's Avalon. He had just completed a round of golf at

Tamarack with the mayor, the police chief and a councilman. He turned the car off and looked at the house. Josephine was probably picking up some items, trying to do it at a time when she thought he wouldn't be home. He wondered if she was currently soaking in that huge anchored vessel that she called a tub taking one of her long, hot baths.

If so, maybe he could sneak in and join her. A little mid-afternoon pussy never hurt anybody.

Darren figured he more than deserved some. He had been on his best behavior since she moved out. How many men were willing to put up with what he was putting up with? Waiting for their wife to stop sleeping with another man and come back to him? And damn if Josephine hadn't looked good last Friday night.

Darren's member stiffened at the memory of Josephine in that long jean skirt. He definitely wanted some, but knew she might not be totally down with the idea. He decided being furtive was his best chance. He could by accident walk in on her, and before you know it they were into something before she had a chance or reason to object.

Hell, he *was* her husband.

Darren left his golf clubs in the car, lightly closed his door and made sure he didn't activate the alarm to his truck. He quietly opened the front door and peeked in. He heard music coming from upstairs. Good. Maybe she was listening to Maze as she soaked. Darren gently closed the door behind him.

He saw the mound of clothes on the chair. Looks like he had been right. She was picking up some items on the sneak tip.

Darren was heading for the winding staircase, deciding whether or not to take off his shoes and shirt, when he stopped dead in his tracks. He backpedaled.

He noticed that on the chair sticking out from underneath a pair of jeans was one of Josephine's pregnancy kits. He recognized it from the stash in the bathroom closet that she didn't think he knew about.

Darren looked back up the stairway and saw that the coast was clear. He then opened the box and pulled out the stick.

He stood there for five seconds, numb. But while his body was paralyzed, his mind was scheming. He set the stick back in the kit, the kit back under the jeans and quietly walked back out the door.

Josephine was tearing apart the closet looking for those boots. The chaotic state she was leaving the closet in was a metaphor for her life. She still hadn't found the boots, but she had found a purse that she had forgotten about.

Her ears perked up as she heard a car horn. She turned off the radio and went across the hall into the guest bedroom, which had a window that faced the front yard. She saw Darren pulling some golf clubs out of the back of his truck. He looked up at her and waved. "Josie!"

Oh, shit, Josephine thought. The pregnancy kit.

Clutching the purse she had just taken out of the closet, she flew back down the stairs into the foyer. She picked up the pregnancy kit, put it in the purse, zipped it up and waited for him.

She heard Darren slam two of his doors, engage his car alarm, and yell, "Josie!" one more time before he noisily clambered in dragging his golf clubs.

"Hey, wife," he said, smiling. "You coming back home?"

"You know better," Josephine said. "And why are you yelling my name like a fool?"

Darren beamed as he walked up to her and gave her a kiss on her cheek. "Because I'm happy to see you, that's why."

Josephine could tell by his clothes that he had been golfing. In February?

Darren anticipated her next question. "Tamarack's open year 'round."

"So is pneumonia," Josephine said. She adjusted her purse strap. "Have you seen a pair of my boots?"

Darren shrugged. "I've seen a lot of your boots. You have like a hundred pair."

"These are brand-new. Still in the box."

"Oh. I did put a bag in the closet here a while back," Darren said. He opened the closet, pulled out a bag and handed it to Josephine.

She looked in and smiled. She had forgotten that she had bought a belt, too.

"So," Darren said, looking at her items on the chair, "I guess you were on your way out the door, huh?"

"Yeah," she replied.

"I guess I have no chance of convincing you to join me for lunch."

"No, not today, Darren." She walked over to the chair. "I'm gonna head on back."

"To Newark?" he asked. "Or you going to your apartment?"

"I'm going home," Josephine answered. "You're not the only one who can take off from work, you know."

Josephine was struggling to pick up all the items.

"Here, let me help you," Darren said.

"Sure." Josephine stepped back and let Darren pick up her clothes.

A woman in your condition shouldn't be straining herself, he thought as he gathered them up.

She carried the bottles of cucumber melon and the boots. And the purse with the test kit in it. They walked out the front door to the driveway.

"Sorry about the condition of the closet, Darren," Josephine said. "I was tearing it up looking for these boots." She slid behind the steering wheel as he finished laying the clothes across the back-seat.

"That's okay," Darren said as he shut the rear door. "I miss your messiness. I can pretend you're home."

In reply, Josephine started her car. Darren leaned down.

"Though I know there's no chance of that happening anytime soon."

You got that right, Josephine thought. Because if she was indeed pregnant with John's child, Darren wasn't gonna be able to call his divorce lawyer fast enough. Or call her much worse.

"Right?" he repeated.

"Darren." Josephine rolled her eyes.

"Okay, okay," he said. "I just miss my wife." He gave her another kiss on the cheek.

" 'Bye."

"Drive safe," he said, closing the door.

After Josephine's car disappeared, Darren headed into the house, straight into the kitchen and picked up the phone. He pressed the redial button. When Josephine's doctor's office picked up, Darren hung up the phone. She was probably setting up an appointment to make sure, he reasoned.

His mind raced, trying to figure out the best way to use his fortuitous discovery. Okay, Darren, think. If she called the doctor's office to set up an appointment, there's a good chance that she wouldn't tell John until she knew for sure she was really pregnant.

A wicked grin spread across Darren's face.

Josephine might not be going to Newark today.

But he was.

John was sitting alone in the conference room, very satisfied. He and his staff had just finished a very upbeat meeting. Landing the Dorn account had proved to be just the start of positive things for his team. In the last month and a half, his salespeople had had a run of success extolling the virtues of Sebastian Safety Systems. This move up North was turning out to be quite profitable.

John was about to leave for the airport to catch a flight to Charlotte. He would be down there for a couple of days. That evening he was meeting some bigwigs from Doneto Chemicals for a business dinner. Landing Doneto would be huge. John needed to talk to some of his people in Charlotte beforehand to go over some things.

The next day were quarterly meetings. The following morning a golf outing with some stockholders, then he would catch a flight back Saturday afternoon.

A voice came over the speaker.

"Mr. Sebastian?"

"Yes, Judith."

"There's a Mr. Prescott down in the lobby to see you."

John straightened up. This was a surprise.

"Would you like for them to send him up?"

Sure, why the hell not? John thought. As long as his soft-as-tissue-paper ass wasn't trying to get brave. He remembered what Mr. Duke had said.

"Yes, Judith. But have security wand him first, please."

"Yes, sir. Would you like for me to bring him to your office?"

"No, bring him into the conference room," John said. His punk ass wasn't worthy of the office.

Three minutes later, John and Darren were facing each other.

"Thank you, Judith," John said.

She left, closing the door behind her.

"I don't believe introductions are needed," Darren said brusquely, "other than I'm the man whose wife you're fucking."

John smiled. "And you've come all the way up here to thank me for fucking her *right* for you?" He waved his hand. "Don't mention it. But don't hesitate to let me know if you have any other family members I can tighten up for you."

Darren sneered as he sat down in a seat at the opposite end of the long table. "You don't even know how irrelevant you are."

"When I was hitting your wife from the back last night, she found me very relevant." John shuddered. "Ooh-wee, she does have a sweet ass, though."

"Yeah, I know, I've been enjoying her for the past seven plus years," Darren said. "That's part of why I married her, gave her *my* last name."

John was pissed that his efforts to provoke Darren had failed so far. He wanted an excuse to whip his ass. "That's a situation that will soon be rectified."

Darren bit his bottom lip and looked at the ceiling.

"I'm glad you can find humor at the thought of another man having his way with your wife's body," John said.

"Uh-no, I don't find that prospect pleasurable at all, John." Darren rose from his chair and casually walked a quarter of the way around the table, taking in the view of downtown Newark. "But what can I say? I was out doing my thing."

"I know, you were doing your thing with that blond lollipop-head," John said, laughing. "If that's where your tastes lie, what the hell are you even doing with a voluptuous sista like Josephine?"

Darren looked at him. "How the hell do you know who I was with?"

John just laughed at him again.

"Of course!" Darren said, approaching him. "*You* were the one who told Josie."

"Nigga, you best back up," John warned, "before I back you up."

Darren sat down in a seat two chairs away. "Well, your schemes didn't work, Sebastian," he said coolly. "I admit, I was a little upset last week when Josephine first told me she was pregnant, but I am over that now."

Darren noticed John's eyes widen when he mentioned the word "pregnant."

John scoffed. "Man, you're lying. That's pathetic."

"Really?" Darren asked as he leaned onto the table. "Have you noticed a period, genius?"

John thought about it. He and Josephine had begun having sex over a month ago. He couldn't remember her having one during that time.

Darren snarled. "What's pathetic is that she told me instead of you."

He could tell by the look on John's face that he had him stumbling. He decided to take a chance and go for the knockout.

"Why did she tell me and not you—Mr. baby's daddy?" he asked, his palms lying flat on the table. "I don't know, maybe she was afraid you would want her to get rid of it."

"That's nonsense," John said quietly. "She knows I would never put her through that again."

Darren's suspicions were confirmed. He filed away his newfound knowledge for later use.

"John, you just don't get it," he said. "Josephine is just using you for revenge because I got caught cheating."

"Yeah, right," John snarled, "because you're such a fucking catch."

"I was catch enough for her to marry."

"Only because I fucked up, and she was half out of her mind," John said. "Certainly not because she loved you." He leaned toward him, sizing him up. "Tell me, dawg, why would you marry a woman who you know doesn't love you? Is it that hard for you out there?"

When John saw a flash of anger in Darren's eyes, he knew he had read him correctly.

"You talk a lot of shit for a man who's baby mama doesn't even want him to know she's pregnant." Darren leaned back in his seat smugly. "And make no mistake, that's all Josie is to you, your 'baby's mama,'" he added, making it sound as ghetto as possible. "She's *my* wife."

John tried in vain to think of a reason why Josephine would tell Darren and not him. He couldn't. But he also didn't trust Darren as far as he could throw him. Which, right about now, he was feeling a great urge to try out.

"Since you aren't even cognizant of the fact that Josie is pregnant, then I'm also sure you're unaware that me and her have been meeting for dinners—talking, you know, trying to iron out our problems," Darren said. He yawned to further show his complacency. "As a matter of fact, we were together earlier today."

John knew Darren might be telling the truth. Josephine hadn't gone in to work that morning. She had told John she was too tired.

"So, you see, pardner," Darren said, "she's already begun phasing you out."

"If that's the case," John asked, "then why are you here? If it's such a foregone conclusion that she's gonna come back to you?"

Darren leaned forward, elbows on the table. "Because I want her life to be as seamless as possible. Whether you like it or not, Josie is a married woman. I don't know how you justified it in your head, but the bottom line is that you've been sleeping with a married woman. And that makes you a piece of shit."

Normally, John would've put the fear of God in him for the insult, but his mind was still reeling with the news of Josephine's pregnancy.

"So what do you do now?" Darren asked rhetorically. "Hang around and be an even greater nuisance, fucking her life up even more than you already have? Haven't you done that enough, man?"

"As much as it kills you to hear it, hubby," John said, "that's my child."

"Then do what's best for the child," Darren said, pounding his fist into the table. "How is you stalking her, stressing her, when it's painfully clear that you were only intended to be a fling, helpful for the child? Now that you have fucked up her life—again—at least let her have her child in peace."

John eyed Darren with scorn. "And we both know that you only have Josephine's best interests at heart."

"I've already shown I'm willing to give her space. Are you? I'm willing to support my wife as she chooses to have another man's baby. Would you be willing to do that for her?" Darren snarled. "Hell no, you wouldn't. You're the nigger who once made her kill your *own* baby."

John snapped. Within a half-second he was across the conference table and on top of Darren.

Darren tried to defend himself, but John easily overpowered him. He put his forearm in his neck as he pinned him to the floor.

"Man, the girl don't want you," Darren gurgled.

"Shut the fuck up!" John said, exerting more pressure. "Let me tell you something—I know what you are, you sick, twisted fuck! You don't really love Josephine—you just don't want to be alone. That's the real reason you would endure another man fucking your wife and getting her pregnant."

Darren struggled to get up. John slapped him hard across the face as punishment for even trying.

"It has nothing to do with you loving her," John continued. "It's about your weak ass doing whatever it takes to ensure that you don't have to be alone!"

John drew his fist back and aimed for Darren's jaw, determined to break it. He stopped when he saw a look in Darren's eyes, one beyond fear. A look that almost seemed to be inviting John to hit him.

Sick fuck.

John yanked him up by the collar of his golf shirt instead and threw him onto the table. Grabbing hold of his belt and collar, he slid him down the length of the long conference table, letting him go at the edge. Darren fell in a heap near the door.

"Now get the fuck out!" John shouted.

Darren woozily stood up. He checked his lip for blood and gathered himself. Then he sneered at John. "It's not my fault that she doesn't want you."

Darren purposely overturned a chair and hurriedly ducked out the door.

John shook his head with disgust.

He then pulled his cell phone out and began dialing Josephine's apartment. No answer. John thought about leaving a message, but couldn't think of what to say over the phone, so he hung up.

John's next thought was to try her cell and find out where she was, so he could meet her somewhere.

"Mr. Sebastian."

Judith had come into the conference room instead of using the intercom. Probably to make sure he was okay. She had to have heard the commotion between Darren and him, as if asking security to wand him wasn't enough to already concern her.

"Yeah."

"Your car to the airport is here."

John exhaled. "Thanks, Judith."

John hesitated momentarily, folded his phone up, then briskly walked out of the room.

Thirty

"Take a load off, Mommy."

Josephine made her way over to the space Gloria had reserved for her on the bench. They were on the lower level, near Macy's at the Short Hills Mall, and were shopping for all the items that Josephine would need for her maternity stay. It had been Gloria's idea. Though Josephine was eager about the baby, Gloria was absurd in her level of excitement. On her list was a small radio, nightgown, diapers, change of clothes, overnight bag, baby clothes and a book.

Josephine checked her watch. "What time is Jules picking up John, again?"

"His plane lands at three, Jo," Gloria said. "I know you can't wait to see him. It's probably killing you that you haven't told him yet."

"It sure is," Josephine said. She had spoken to John briefly by phone last night but wanted to tell him the news face-to-face. She looked down at her shoes. "Though I have to admit, I'm a little nervous about his reaction."

"What do you mean?" Gloria asked. "John loves you."

"And I love him," Josephine said definitively. "But that doesn't mean he wants to be a father."

"Jo, you know he isn't going to ask you to not have it."

"Oh, I know he wouldn't do that again," Josephine said, remembering the conversation they had in her office, "and even if he did, I wouldn't."

"I know that's right," Gloria agreed.

"It's just that . . ." Josephine's voice turned soft. "I hope he's as excited as I am. You know?"

"I'm sure he will be, Jo," Gloria said assuringly. "John's ego will feed off the idea of having a 'mini-him' around."

Josephine laughed despite her nervousness. "You think so?"

"Yeah," Gloria affirmed. "John is probably itching for a child. Hell, he has everything else. That's the only thing left."

Josephine smiled. She motioned to the Mrs. Fields cookie stand. "Do you feel like some cookies?"

"No." Gloria peeked at her through the corner of her eye. She took the list out of her pocket and perused it.

"You do know you're being ridiculous with that list, right?" Josephine asked.

"You can never be too prepared," Gloria said. "Let's see." She crossed the radio off the list. "We got everything except the books. We'll have to wait on that one. Which book would you want? The new E. Lynn or the new Dickey?"

"Those guys are usually summer releases. I'd probably have already read them by the time I'm having the baby," Josephine replied. She inhaled deeply. "My, those cookies smell good."

"How about Zane?"

"Yeah, that's great, Glo," Josephine chided. "I'll get all worked up and hot in the maternity ward. What am I gonna do? Romance the new mother in the next room?"

Gloria laughed. "True."

"How about nonfiction?" Josephine asked.

"What did you have in mind?" Gloria asked. "A biography?"

"No," Josephine responded, "more like a real-life crime book. The title is *Hungry Woman Kills Skinny Friend for Denying Her Cookie.*"

"All right, all right," Gloria said, glancing at the cookie stand. "We'll get some in a minute, when the line goes down. But when you give birth to an eight-pound, seven-ounce white macadamia chunk cookie, don't say I didn't warn you." She reached into the Baby Gap bag and pulled out a pair of knitted blue booties. She pretended they were walking along the bench. "Aren't they cute?"

Josephine laughed. She reached into the bag and pulled out a multicolored pair. "I like these."

As she was playfully walking them, Josephine's elbow accidentally knocked over the box that the small radio was in, causing it to land on the floor.

"Let me get that for you," a voice said from behind the bench.

"Oh, thank you—" Josephine stopped short.

"Mrs. Prescott?" the man asked, his eyes focused on the booties in Josephine's hand like they were being compelled by a tractor beam.

"Dr. Harris," Josephine said, simultaneously faking her enthusiasm and hiding her shock. "How are you?"

"Um, I'm fine." Dr. Harris picked up the radio and set it on the bench next to her. "I'm fine," he repeated.

"Warren, I—" Mrs. Harris then caught sight of Josephine. "Hi, Josephine! How have you been?"

"Hi, Linda," Josephine said as she stood up and hugged her.

She noticed the booties. "Are those for you?"

"Yes," Josephine said, smiling.

"Isn't that just wonderful!" She hugged Josephine again.

Josephine beamed. She had forgotten how warm a person Linda Harris was and scolded herself for letting Darren put distance between them. Josephine also noticed that Dr. Harris apparently didn't think her being pregnant was a wonderful thing. When he found out the booties were hers, his face contorted noticeably.

"How's Darren?" he asked.

"Oh, he's fine, Dr. Harris." Josephine felt uneasy at the mention of her husband's name. She hoped the doctor didn't ask her why Darren had dumped him, because she honestly didn't know.

"So you're still married?" Mrs. Harris asked.

"Yes." Barely. Yet still, Josephine found the question odd. Who asks a person if they're still married?

"This is my friend, Gloria," Josephine said.

The Harrises and Gloria exchanged pleasantries.

"I'm gonna go now, Jo," Gloria said. "The line has gone down."

After she left, there was an uncomfortable silence. Josephine noticed Dr. and Mrs. Harris exchanging looks.

"So," Mrs. Harris asked, "did you and Darren go for artificial insemination?"

"Linda!" Dr. Harris exclaimed.

Josephine regarded Mrs. Harris with curiosity. Despite the question's inappropriateness, something in the motherly way she was looking at her made Josephine trust her.

"No, Linda, we didn't," Josephine said cautiously. "Why would we have to?"

"It was nice seeing you again, Josephine." Dr. Harris made a move to take his wife's arm. "Say hello to Darren for us."

His wife snatched her arm away.

"Linda."

Mrs. Harris took Josephine's hands in hers. "That child you're carrying isn't Darren's, is it?"

"Linda!"

Mrs. Harris shushed him and concentrated on Josephine.

Strangely enough, Josephine felt neither compelled to lie nor embarrassed by Mrs. Harris' question. This woman had always been in Josephine's corner. There was no reason to think she wasn't now.

"No, Linda, it isn't," Josephine said quietly. "Darren and I tried for seven years to get pregnant, and it just didn't work out for us."

Mrs. Harris released Josephine's hands and shot her husband a withering look. Dr. Harris dropped his eyes to the floor.

"I told you!" She slapped her knee. "Didn't I tell you I bet she still doesn't know? And that the reason he got rid of you is because he was tired of hearing you telling him to do the right thing?"

Josephine's eyes widened. She looked at Dr. Harris, then back at his wife. "Doesn't know what? What right thing?"

"And isn't Darren the reason why you avoid me?" Mrs. Harris said.

"Yes, Linda, and I feel awful about that," Josephine said. "I really miss your friendship."

They hugged again.

"Darling, I've been so worried about you." Mrs. Harris wiped her eyes. "I feel like I've let you down—listening to him." She pointed at her husband.

"Honey, it wasn't our affair," Dr. Harris protested.

"It's obvious you've never been a woman," she retorted.

"But the doctor-patient confidentiality privilege—"

"Doesn't supercede this woman's right to be a mother!" Mrs. Harris snapped back.

Dr. Harris was cowed, but still resistant.

Josephine felt like her heart was in her throat. What were these people talking about?

"Warren, you know right is right," Mrs. Harris said. "Tell this woman."

Dr. Harris deliberated for a moment, then leaned in close to Josephine. "Dear, look up a condition called azoospermia. A-zoo-spermia. Okay?"

Josephine nodded.

He smiled. "Congratulations on the baby."

"Thank you, Doctor," Josephine said, still distracted by what he had told her.

Dr. Harris looked at his wife. "Can we go now?"

"Yes. Now you"—she placed her hand on Josephine's forearm—"don't be a stranger. Call me if you ever need anything, you hear me? Or even if you don't need anything. I wanna see this baby!"

"I'll be in touch, I promise."

Mrs. Harris hugged Josephine again. She took the opportunity to whisper in her ear, "That word you're about to look up? Darren has known he's had it for almost twenty years."

Josephine felt her head steam up as she strode toward the Borders bookshop in the mall. Gloria didn't know what was going on, but she knew it was something important because Josephine was completely disinterested in her cookies.

Josephine had tried to explain to Gloria the conversation she had just had with the Harrises, but was so excitable that Gloria could only get bits and pieces.

"What is it called? This thing Darren has?"

"A-zoo-spermia," Josephine said, sounding it out like Dr. Harris had.

"And whatever that is, he's known about it for twenty years?"

"Right."

They entered the bookstore. Gloria struggled to keep up. She had the radio under her left arm and the bags under her right.

Josephine made a beeline for the Health and Fitness section. Once there, she began perusing the section on infertility. Gloria caught up to her.

"How do you know it has something to do with infertility?" Gloria asked.

"Because of the way they reacted when they found out I was pregnant."

"Oh," Gloria said, scanning the shelf. "Plus, wasn't the word 'sperm' in there somewhere?"

"Yes. A-zoo-sperm-ia," Josephine repeated. She found two books that focused on the diagnosis and treatments of male infertility and plucked them off the shelves. She then looked for a place to sit. Not seeing a chair, she settled for a step stool used for reaching higher shelves.

Gloria tiredly set the bags and radio on the floor beside Josephine and peered over her shoulder.

Josephine went to the index of the first book and looked up azoospermia, then flipped to the page on which it was defined. She ran her index finger along the page until she found the word.

"Here it is," Josephine said.

Azoospermia: the complete absence of sperm in the semen and as such, means the man will be completely infertile.

"What?" Josephine gasped.

"Oh, *hells* no," Gloria said. She pulled out her cell phone and began dialing.

While Gloria was in conversation with someone, Josephine kept reading. "Two percent of the men in the general population . . . rare that no sperm is produced at all . . . normal ejaculation . . ." but her mind kept returning to the words "completely infertile."

Darren. Twenty years.

Josephine rested the book on her lap. Then, unable to hold it anymore, she let it tumble to the carpet. Josephine was shaking like a leaf. She was so heated that she felt that her skin was blistering and peeling off her body. Tears streamed down her face. She limply leaned her head back and emitted one long guttural moan.

Gloria ended her call and tried to steady Josephine. She knelt down and wrapped her arms around Josephine's shoulders. "Don't strain yourself, Jo," she said, hugging and rocking her. "Think about your baby. Think about your baby."

Jules, Mr. Duke and John were in a car coming from the airport. John was happy that Mr. Duke had decided to tag along with him.

"Gloria and Jo are at the mall," Jules said. "I told them we would meet them back at my house for dinner."

"Okay." John nodded. "How did the Boys to Men meeting go yesterday?"

"Well," Jules replied, "we taught them how to balance checkbooks, among other things." He smiled. "And Antoine challenged me to a pop-lock competition, so you *know* I had to represent."

All at once John decided to come out with it:

"Josephine's pregnant."

Jules did a double-take. "Congratulations, man!" He turned and smiled warmly at Mr. Duke in the backseat. Then he noticed John's dour expression. "Why ain't you grinning?"

John breathed deeply. "Darren—"

"To *hell* with Darren," Jules interrupted. "That's nothing a quickie divorce can't rectify." He happily slapped the steering wheel. "This explains why Jo and Gloria were acting so strangely last night. Whispering around me and stuff, all secretive." He laughed. "They were probably afraid I'd tell y—"

Jules stopped short. His face turned serious. He eyed John.

"Wait a second," he said, "if you already know, then why are they trying to keep it a secret from me?"

"Because they don't know I know."

"How'd you find out?" Jules asked.

"Darren told me."

"*Darren?*" Jules had to concentrate to keep his car in the lane.

"That's right, her husband," John said, leaning forward. "Not only that, he tells me that he's been seeing her on the regular."

Jules shook his head. "You don't believe that, do you, John? You do believe the baby's yours, right?"

John didn't say anything.

Mr. Duke spoke up. "John, I don't think Josephine is the type of woman to sleep with two men at the same time."

"I know, I know," John said. "I believe the baby is mine. It's just that, well . . . how come he knows before I do?"

Jules stared at the road ahead, trying to come up with a reason. "That doesn't make sense. Gloria told me that Josephine was unhappy before he even got caught out there. She never gave me any hint that Josephine still even talks to Darren."

"They have to talk," Mr. Duke said. "Y'all have to remember that they had a life together. There are credit cards, joint accounts, insurance matters, a whole bunch of things to consider. That's probably the extent of their dealings right there. I bet Darren is trying to get inside your head to make it seem like more than that."

"Okay, I can buy that simple nigga doing that. But tell me something," John said, "why in the hell would Josephine tell Darren that she was pregnant before telling me?" He jabbed his thumb into his chest. "*I'm* the father. Why does she need to tell him shit?"

Jules hesitated as he tried to think of a reason. "None, unless . . ."

"Exactly," John concluded. "Unless she wanted to be with him."

"And that's too preposterous a thought to even consider."

"Exactly," John said. "I still don't know what she saw in that soft-ass nigga in the first place."

"Why would this Darren tell you?" Mr. Duke asked. "What did he want you to do with the information?"

"He asked me to leave Josephine alone," John said, "for her and the baby's good. So he and Josephine could rebuild their marriage."

Jules cackled. "Rebuild what? That is too funny."

Mr. Duke dropped his chin. "He's okay with raising another man's child that his wife conceived while she was married to him?"

"I can't figure it out," John said helplessly.

"Something doesn't smell right, and I'm not just talking about this swampland we're passing through," Mr. Duke said. "That man has an agenda, and I'd be willing to lay odds that it's rotten."

He leaned forward and placed his hand on John's shoulder. "Son, talk to Josephine. I'm sure she will clear things up."

* * *

Later, after Josephine was able to regain some semblance of composure, she and Gloria were driving along Route 24 on their way to see Darren.

Josephine wiped her eyes with a tissue. "You know, Glo, I just can't believe that a man could lie like that to his wife for all these years."

"I can," Gloria said, "especially Darren. He's a snake. Always has been."

Gloria checked her rearview mirror. A black Chevy Suburban was tailing them.

Josephine blew her nose. "To have me thinking something was wrong with me all those years. What kind of person is that, Glo?"

"A monster."

"I can't believe this," Josephine said, shaking her head. "I can't believe this. . . ."

"Jo, don't get yourself all worked up again." Gloria made the left onto the Sussex Turnpike. She looked in her rearview. The black Suburban was still following closely behind.

They pulled onto Darren and Josephine's long country lane. After they worked their way around the third bend, the house came into view. Darren's truck was in the driveway.

"He's home," Gloria said.

"Good," Josephine replied. Now she could confront him.

Once the car was stopped, Josephine stormed into the house, with Gloria right on her heels. She found Darren sitting in the den watching a Mets spring training game.

"You cold-hearted bastard! I hate you!"

"What?" Darren said, jumping out of his seat.

"You motherfucka!" Josephine continued, "You, you . . . azoospermic motherfucka!" She looked for something to throw at him.

"Easy, Jo," Gloria said.

"What? What?" Darren asked, his voice awash with panic and alarm.

"I'm talking about azoospermia, Darren!" Josephine said. "Tell me you don't know what it is."

Darren stammered, "I-I don't . . . what?"

"Darren, tell me the truth!"

"The 'truth' is a foreign concept to this man," Gloria said dryly.

Darren snapped at her, "Mind your own business, cunt!"

Gloria's mouth fell open. No, he didn't. She simply nodded and left the room.

"Don't you talk to her that way!"

"Then tell her to mind her own goddamned business," Darren said. He looked at Josephine and his face softened. "Josie, I—"

Josephine held up her palms. She went and sat down on the sofa. "Darren, don't tell me anything else except, *why*."

Darren studied her for a moment, then sank back into his chair. "So, who told you? That asshole Harris?"

"Don't worry about how I found out," Josephine said. "Just tell me why."

"I'm gonna sue that old cocksucker," Darren muttered, his eyes dancing wildly.

"Darren!"

"What?" he yelled angrily. "What do you wanna know?"

"Tell me *why*," Josephine repeated.

"Because, that's why," Darren said. "Because it's not my fault that I can't father a child. Because I didn't want to lose you for the same reason I lost my first wife. In my twenties, when I first found out that I was infertile," he said glumly, "she divorced me shortly thereafter."

"So you figure that next time, you just wouldn't tell the woman," Josephine said. "Right?"

Darren shut his eyes. "Josie, please understand, I didn't want to lose you. I love you and—"

"That ain't love, you selfish jackass," Josephine said, rising. "If you loved me you would've told me instead of making me think it was my fault for the last seven years." She started crying again.

"When I think of the years of lies, excuses, and innuendoes you directed at me regarding our inability to conceive. When all along you knew you couldn't. You miserable sonofabitch! Why?"

Darren looked at the floor. "Because . . ."

"Because I might leave you like your first wife did?" Josephine finished. "Are you so demented that you can't see what a fucked-up, totally selfish and evil thing that is to do to somebody you're about to marry, somebody who you know wants kids in the worst way?"

"And it's not fucked up to leave a man because he's incapable of producing a child?"

"No, motherfucker!" Josephine yelled. "All you had to do was just find a woman who didn't want to have any kids, you imbecile! I *hate* you! I'm filing the divorce papers first thing Monday morning, and"—she took her wedding ring off her finger and hurled it at him—"take your fucking ring back!"

As Darren watched the ring bounce off his chest and land on the carpet, he knew Josephine was too far gone to ever forgive him. "Josie, if you wanted kids so badly," he snarled, "you shouldn't have killed your first one."

"Fuck you, Darren." She was a little surprised that he knew but didn't care that he did. "What's that got to do with your lying ass?" she said. "And my name is *Josephine*."

"You coming, Jo?" Gloria called out from the foyer.

"In a minute," Josephine yelled back. The screen door opened and closed.

She looked at Darren with disgust. "You never loved me, and you didn't care that I never truly loved you. I know that now. You were just scared to be by your sorry self. Scared that nobody else would ever want you."

"Fuck you, Josie."

"And you've *never* been able to do that right," Josephine said. "I know azoospermia prevents you from being a father, but what's your excuse for not being able to fuck?"

Darren let out a snort.

"You know what?" Josephine decided, "you're not worth any more of my time—seven years is enough. My lawyer will do my speaking from here on." Josephine turned on her heel.

Darren followed her to the foyer. "I don't need you, bitch! Go have your little bastard child."

He knew she was pregnant. Again, Josephine wondered how he knew, but not enough to care. She walked out the front door, with Darren in hot pursuit.

"Get the fuck out of here!" he yelled, following her toward Gloria's car. "Take your fat black ass back to that cesspool of a city you came from and go have your bastard child! You whore!"

He eyed Gloria, who was waiting for Josephine with the car running. "And fuck your ghetto ass too, you slutcunt!"

Gloria just laughed and adjusted her sunglasses. As Josephine got into the car, she couldn't believe that Gloria was laughing.

Darren pointed at Josephine as the car backed away. "I was the best thing to ever happen to you, hoodrat!" He was practically foaming at the mouth.

"Would you look at that fool?" Josephine said.

Gloria laughed even louder. She was nearly hysterical.

Josephine looked over at her. "What's so funny?"

Gloria finally reached the end of the driveway. "That!" she said, pointing back up toward the house.

From the other side of Darren's Expedition stepped two squat, muscular black men. Both had their hair in cornrows and were wearing Timberland boots and baggy Phat Farm jeans. The one with the nasty disposition had on a replica Latrell Sprewell Knicks jersey. The other wore an even nastier disposition and a black DMX T-shirt.

Both were iced down.

Darren turned to face them. His jaw dropped.

"Oh, snap," Hakeem said. "Isn't this the cat from Adele's? The one that be falling all over the *one* white girl that dances there?"

"Yeah," Rashahn replied. He gave a quick nod at Darren. "This that nigga."

Hakeem shook his head vehemently. "Naw—*tell* me I just didn't hear this boozhee nigga disrespecting no sistas, calling them 'whore,' 'black bitches,' 'hoodrat,' and shit."

"Don't forget 'slutcunt,'" Rashahn reminded him. "Whatever the fuck that is. Probably some sick suburban shit that his sick suburban ass made up."

"W-what are you guys . . . what do you . . ."

Hakeem ignored Darren's stammering. "And *tell* me that this busta didn't just put down our beloved Brick City."

"I can't lie to you, dawg," Rashahn replied. "Dude called it a cesspool."

"Come here, pa'dner." Hakeem took a step toward Darren. "Let me talk to you a li'l bit."

Darren turned and dashed for the house. Hakeem and Rashahn took off after him. Hakeem caught him on the front stoop, grabbed him by the scruff of his neck and dragged him into the house.

"Noo!" Darren shrieked.

"Shut your punk ass up, *bitch!*" Hakeem said. Darren fell in a heap inside the foyer. Rashahn gave Gloria and Josephine the thumbs-up. Right before he closed the door, they could see Hakeem already putting the foot to Darren.

Gloria smiled contently as she began to drive away. As they passed by the black Suburban parked along the road, Josephine looked at her and waited for an explanation.

She shrugged. "I told you they owed me a favor."

Josephine and Gloria laughed their ghetto asses off all the way home.

Thirty-one

Mr. Duke took a pass on going back to Jules' house, and he was so secretive as to why, Jules and John suspected he had a date. Instead they dropped him off back at his condo.

When they got home, John took a seat in Jules' living room, awaiting the arrival of Gloria and Josephine. Jules went to the kitchen, and soon he was simultaneously grilling chops and talking to Nakira on the phone.

John peeked through the curtains. Still the same staid suburban scene as five minutes earlier, when he had last checked.

He wasn't sure why he was so apprehensive. Well, of course becoming a father was a life-altering experience. But he felt he was ready for that.

He wanted to find out why Darren knew about the pregnancy before he did. If Josephine was having any doubts about building a life with him.

Gloria's Volvo pulled up in front of the house. Finally.

John opened the door and waited for the ladies to come up the walk. He noticed they both seemed to be in a genial mood. When Josephine spotted him, she smiled. But John could tell it was a smile tinged with a little caution. She was probably as nervous as he was.

Gloria reached the house first. "Hey, Sebastian, where's my man?"

"He's in the kitchen, Glo."

She headed for the kitchen. Josephine stepped into the living room and gave John a hug and kiss. "How was your trip?" she asked, laying her head on his shoulder while he stroked her back.

"Same ol, same ol," he said. They separated.

"I wanna talk to you."

Josephine nodded. After hugging her again, he led her over to the couch.

Once they were sitting down, John picked up her hand and stroked it.

"Josephine, do you love me?"

"Yes."

He swallowed hard. "Are you happy to be carrying my child?"

Josephine gasped. "H-how did you know?"

That's not the answer John wanted. He let go of her hand.

Josephine saw his discomfort, and she hurriedly assured him, "Of course I'm happy to be carrying your child, John. I'm thrilled. Ecstatic. Overjoyed, and whatever other adjective you want to use."

She put her hand back in his. John smiled uneasily.

"What?" Josephine asked, girding herself for the worse.

"Look, I know Darren is still technically your husband and everything—"

"A situation that will soon be taken care of, trust me," Josephine said.

John furrowed his brow. "Then why did you feel the need to tell him about our baby before you told me?"

Josephine let go of his hand and drew back. "What are you talking about?"

"Darren came to my office Thursday afternoon and told me you were pregnant," John explained. "That y'all had been talking about getting back together. That I should get out of the way so that you and he could rebuild your lives."

"Wooo!" Josephine laughed loudly. "That's absurd!" She laughed again. The only thing that Negro would be rebuilding is his skeletal structure after the beatdown he got today, she thought. She fixed a look of incredulity on John.

"Don't tell me you believed him!"

"Not really," John said, "but why did you tell him first?"

"I didn't tell him anything. Why would I?" Josephine said. "Don't ask me how he found out." She thought it over. "Maybe someone from the doctor's office called the house by mistake. Or maybe he snooped around and saw my home pregnancy test. I was there picking up some clothes when I took it."

"With him there?" John asked.

"No, I was trying to be there when he wasn't, but he came home when I was finishing up," Josephine said, anxious to move on. "The point is, when it comes to deceit, Darren ain't just a snake, he's an anaconda."

Josephine placed her hand on John's knee. "How do *you* feel about me having your child?"

Now it was John's turn to look incredulous. He took her hand in his and gently squeezed it.

"Josephine," he said softly, "I believe we're granted one person in our lifetime that we have a true connection with. So if you find that person, you should consider yourself lucky. If you sustain the relationship with that person, then you're lucky *and* smart, because while you can always find another someone, you can never find *that* one again."

John exhaled. "As one of the few people to lose that special person and get a second chance . . . well, I know I'm very fortunate." He rubbed his thumb along her fingers, along the spot where the ring was now missing. The spot where he hoped his ring would soon be.

"I don't know what I did to deserve it, but I do know that I've been blessed to have you in my life again. And I'm doubly rewarded by having another opportunity to bring a child into the world with you." John paused as his emotions threatened to get the best of him. "That is almost more joy than I can bear. Josephine, I love you and I want to be with you, and our child, linked together. In love forever."

She and John embraced. Josephine softly wept on his shoulder.

Gloria had been right. Josephine had almost started to believe that she didn't deserve to be happy.

Or maybe she had never known what true happiness was.

But she knew one thing. The way she was feeling right now was the way she wanted to feel always.

So thank you, John Sebastian. For being man enough to admit those times when you weren't enough of a man before.

And for this time, helping me become the woman that I need to be. I love you.

Epilogue

Nakira gently cradled the baby's head as Mr. Duke supervised.

"Like this, Poppy?"

"That's it, Nakira," Mr. Duke said. "You're doing a great job." He smiled warmly at the sight. "What do you think of little Jeremiah?"

"He's cute," Nakira said, kissing him on his forehead.

"Thank goodness he don't take after his daddy."

"I heard that," Josephine said, walking back into the living room with a bottle of breast milk in her hand and a burping cloth across her shoulder.

"Can I feed him?" Nakira asked.

"Sure, baby." Josephine sat on the couch next to her. She helped Nakira position the bottle correctly to feed Jeremiah.

As Jeremiah sucked, Josephine looked at Mr. Duke. "I heard from a colleague of mine," she said. "Mrs. Derossa just resigned from Lyons."

"Your principal? Why?"

Josephine shrugged. "There was an opening in another district. Montclair."

Mr. Duke laughed. "She probably jumped at the chance. Old girl couldn't cope in Newark without her star vice-principal."

Josephine flipped her wrist. "Shucks, she was probably happy to be rid of me." She was taking a year's leave of absence to be with her son.

"That's probably what she thought at first, too," Mr. Duke countered. "Until she found exactly how much you really did there. Then reality set in."

Nakira was getting restless, so Josephine took Jeremiah from her. The child left the room and bounded toward the kitchen, followed by the sound of the back door opening and closing.

"Are you going back in September, Josephine?"

"I haven't decided yet," Josephine answered. Right now she couldn't fathom the idea of being away from Jeremiah.

She looked at her son, at her engagement ring and then back at Mr. Duke with a satisfied smile. "This'll do for now."

The back door opened again. "Poppy," Nakira exclaimed, "my daddy and Uncle John want you."

Mr. Duke got up and headed toward the kitchen. Josephine, cradling Jeremiah, followed behind.

Mr. Duke stepped outside. Josephine stayed in with Jeremiah and looked out the window.

On the asphalt basketball court in the backyard, John and Jules' one-on-one game was on hold as they argued a call. They had apparently gotten Mr. Duke to be the arbiter because each was trying to state their case to him.

Off to the side, in a hammock, and in her own world, Gloria gently swayed as she read a magazine. She had earphones on and was listening to a Discman.

She spotted Josephine in the window. Gloria took off her sunglasses and smiled.

Josephine returned it.

Gloria nodded in the direction of the basketball court.

"Mr. Duke, I told him that he can't be picking up his pivot foot like that—"

"I have to! This cat is knocking me off balance by pushing me in the back!"

"I'm allowed to place a forearm in the small of the back. . . ."

Gloria rolled her eyes. Josephine recognized the look. It said: "Would you look at these fools?"

Josephine rolled her eyes back in acknowledgment. They both laughed.

Gloria then held up her hand and wiggled her fingers. Her wedding ring sparkled in the sunlight.

Through the window, Josephine flashed her engagement ring.

Gloria nodded approvingly and put back on her sunglasses. Josephine recognized that look, too.

Glad they're *our* fools.

About the Author

Marcus Major is the bestselling author of two previous novels, *Good Peoples* and *Four Guys and Trouble,* and a novella in the anthology *Got to be Real.* He lives in Somerdale, New Jersey.